Praise for
A Form of Godliness

"*A Form of Godliness* is a breathtaking read, full of the dilemmas and triumphs of the age now upon us—nuclear blasts, world war, acts of terrorism, and acts of heroism. I read every page as quickly as my eyes could move. With this spellbinding tale, Shane Johnson retains his place as one of our finest Christian novelists."

—JEFFERSON SCOTT, author of *Operation: Firebrand—Crusade*

"Full of political intrigue, terrorist threats, and prophetic insight, *A Form of Godliness* calls out a warning that should not be ignored. Shane Johnson proves once again that he is a powder keg of ideas."

—ERIC WILSON, author of *Dark to Mortal Eyes*

"Shane Johnson's imagination takes him on unforgettable, thrilling journeys—thankfully, he invites us to go along. A Shane Johnson novel is more than a book; it's a ride to remember."

—ALTON GANSKY, author of *Beneath the Ice and Out of Time*

"Thought-provoking and chilling—*A Form of Godliness* will engross readers to the last page."

—LINDA WINDSOR, award-winning author of *Along Came Jones*

SHANE JOHNSON

a form of godliness

A NOVEL

WaterBrook
PRESS

A FORM OF GODLINESS
PUBLISHED BY WATERBROOK PRESS
2375 Telstar Drive, Suite 160
Colorado Springs, Colorado 80920
A division of Random House, Inc.

ISBN 1-57856-549-9

Library of Congress Cataloging-in-Publication Data
Johnson, Shane.
  A form of godliness / Shane Johnson.— 1st ed.
    p. cm.
  ISBN 1-57856-549-9
 1. Presidents—Fiction. 2. Secret service—Fiction. 3. Christian ethics—Fiction. I. Title.
  PS3560.O38638F67 2004
  813'.54—dc22

                                                            2004007078

Printed in the United States of America
2004—First Edition

10 9 8 7 6 5 4 3 2 1

This novel is dedicated to

George W. Bush

Forty-third president of the United States,
who has faced new and unrelenting challenges
in the protecting of his people.

Mr. President, may God continue to be with you
as you confront the forces, both foreign and domestic,
who seek to destroy this great nation.

Also dedicated, in loving memory, to

**Those who perished that warm September morning,
when out of clear skies came gleaming wings of evil.**

We are diminished by your loss and will remember you.
You did not die in vain.

Author's Note

The initial draft of this novel was written during the period from July 2002 through March 2003. At that time, the wounds of Nine-Eleven were still fresh, and with images of the fallen towers vivid in our minds, we had gone into Afghanistan, had routed the terrorist networks there, and were in final preparation for the necessary follow-up action to be taken in Iraq. As of this writing, no further attack has taken place on American soil, but by the time this book goes to press, that may change. I pray it does not.

The extreme events described in this novel were chosen and structured to create a plausible, fictitious portrayal of future struggles in the conflict forced upon us. No disrespect or insensitivity was intended toward anyone who has suffered through the horror of a terrorist attack, or toward their families or friends.

We cannot know what the future holds for the United States, or for any of its people. But rest in the assurance that whatever befalls this nation, our mighty God is, and always has been, in control of all things. Remember the words of Joseph, spoken to the brothers who had betrayed him: "As for you, you meant evil against me, but God meant it for good in order to bring about this present result.... So therefore, do not be afraid" (Genesis 50:20-21).

—SHANE JOHNSON
June 2004

Cast of Characters

OLLIE AL-RASHID	*Washington, D.C., police officer*
SAMIRA AL-RASHID	*Ollie's wife*
ARTHUR BRADFORD	*director, Homeland Security*
MATTHEW BRIDGER	*president, United States*
SUSAN BRIDGER	*first lady*
CYRUS BRIGGS	*Senate majority leader*
ROGER BROOKS	*special advisor to the president*
MILLIE CARSON	*secretary of Health and Human Services, United States*
JOHN CREEDEL	*secretary of state, United States*
VASILY DESDEROV	*Russian premier*
KAREN FOLEY	*vice president of PR, Sacred Child*
MEL HOFFMAN	*secretary of commerce, United States*
JACQUELINE KELSEY	*Richard's daughter*
RICHARD KELSEY	*retired pastor*
BRYSON LAWE	*Secret Service agent*

And they were bringing children to Him so that He might touch them; but the disciples rebuked them. But when Jesus saw this, He was indignant and said to them, "Permit the children to come to Me; do not hinder them; for the kingdom of God belongs to such as these."

—MARK 10:13-14

"Somehow [Tiny Tim] gets thoughtful, sitting by himself so much, and thinks the strangest things you ever heard. He told me, coming home, that he hoped the people saw him in the church, because he was a cripple, and it might be pleasant for them to remember upon Christmas Day who made lame beggars walk, and blind men see."

—BOB CRATCHIT
CHARLES DICKENS, *A Christmas Carol,* 1843

"A person's a person, no matter how small."

—HORTON THE ELEPHANT
DR. SEUSS, *Horton Hears a Who,* 1954

"To the extent that you did it to one of these [Jewish] brothers of Mine, even the least of them, you did it to Me."

—MATTHEW 25:40

Vengeance is Mine, and retribution,
In due time their foot will slip;
For the day of their calamity is near,
And the impending things are hastening upon them.

—DEUTERONOMY 32:35

Prologue

I t was a dark and stormy night.

At least, it had been. The moon finally shone upon Philadelphia, breaking through the wispy gray ghosts that crossed overhead, casting its signature against the black waters of the Delaware. Water in storm drains flowed along the glistening city streets, but the tempest itself had moved on, and bright flashes of violent light still ignited the starless horizon. The unexpected weather had been severe, and under normal circumstances any sane man would have sought shelter from its savagery.

But this was war.

The fury that had filled the skies had failed, at first, to stop the action. The combatants endured the winds and blinding rain, sustaining the conflict, and only the increasing proximity and magnitude of lightning had brought the battle to a momentary halt. Claps of thunder, given birth by strikes too near for even a moment's delay, rang sharply within scarred helmets as the men finally ran for cover.

More than half an hour had passed before calm descended. Now, with the storm's cessation, armored warriors once again advanced into enemy territory, driving onward against all odds, all obstacles, all adversaries. They would not quit, would not retreat, would not surrender.

It was no mere war. It was the National Football League.

The seventh game of the season was drawing to a close, its fourth quarter half gone. The Philadelphia Eagles had not fared well, drawing the vocal disapproval of the home-field crowd. The men in green had fallen two scores behind the archrival Washington Redskins, and the clock had become an enemy now, threatening to cut short their march to victory.

Almost a hundred thousand damp yet passionate spectators looked on from the safety of their much-coveted seats. Most had sought shelter during the downpour, finding it in the stadium's club lounges and enclosed concourses. Fortunately, their retreat had been brief and, with the on-field action renewed, was all but forgotten.

It was not too late, not yet. All was not lost. Like the heavy scent of wet concrete, victory hung in the unmoving air, tantalizingly near. With time running out, the Eagles once again were driving, moving yard by hard-earned yard into scoring range.

Then came the big play. And like those around him, Randall Sullivan rose from his seat in Section A, Lower Bowl West, cheering the deep pass and resulting touchdown that revitalized players and spectators alike. His voice was strained and hoarse, yet still he shouted encouragements that were swallowed up into those of the thousands around him. The triumphant music of Sam Spence, barely heard above the roar, blared from the speakers.

"Sit down, Daddy," Sullivan's teenage daughter implored, her voice lost in the noise. She had not risen and looked up at him with scolding eyes, sweeping her chestnut hair aside. "Your throat is bad enough already."

She tugged at his green windbreaker, and he took his seat sooner than the others. "What?" he asked, his words swept away. "What did you—?"

"I said you need to stop shouting," she said more loudly. "Your throat is going to be in bad shape tomorrow as it is. You know you're just getting over a cold."

"I raised a party pooper," he smiled. "Eat your pretzel, Janessa."

As the crowd quieted, she turned to the seat on her other side, to the friend who sat there. Dipping her soft pretzel in a small cup of mustard, she shook her head. "He won't take care of himself."

"I know," Marlene said, the wisdom of seventeen years heavy in her voice. "My brothers are the same way. You constantly have to look after guys… They're like children all their lives."

"Aren't they though?"

Janessa noted the small puddles that dotted the area, reflecting the glow of the floods above. The overhead lights, mounted within their shallow overhangs, eclipsed the dark sky beyond and lent a sense of daylight to the place.

"That was some storm, wasn't it?"

"Yeah," Marlene agreed, "and now, it's so still. Not even a little breeze. Kinda weird."

The girl looked up and around, her eyes lingering on the field before scanning the rest of the stadium around her.

"Too bad we couldn't get seats on the rail. But you know, these are good too."

Janessa nodded. "I guess. Daddy got them from a guy at work who couldn't go."

"Thanks for inviting me. I've never been to a football game before."

"Didn't you go to homecoming last year?"

"Well," she admitted, her face a picture of playful triumph, "technically I did. But I spent the whole time on a blanket, under the bleachers with Andy. Oh girl, he is one serious kisser."

"So you've told me," Janessa smiled. "Over and over and over."

"I don't know why you wouldn't double-date with us on the Fourth of July," Marlene went on, taking a bite of her own pretzel. "We had a great time, and his brother likes you."

Janessa winced, almost imperceptibly. "Yeah, well…I know, but he isn't my type."

"I'm starting to think you don't have a type. You've turned down every boy I've sent your way."

"I just don't think I'm ready to…"

The girl's tone became more serious. "Janessa, come on. Kerry broke up with you over four months ago."

"He didn't break up with me," she firmly corrected her. "He just needed some space."

"I'm sorry," Marlene said. "I didn't mean anything. It's just that I hate to see you so mopey all the time."

"I'm not mopey."

"Okay, okay. Forget I said anything." She took a long sip from her lipstick-stained soda straw and heard the wet, hollow echo of a drink devoid of all but ice. "I could use another one of these," she said, raining cold drops of condensation on her knees as she rattled the empty cup. "Wanna go with me?"

"I'll take care of it," Sullivan cut in. "I need to make a trip to the men's room, anyway. What do you girls want? Just soda?"

"Same as before," his daughter smiled. "Two Cokes, please."

"Two Cokes, it is."

"No, wait," she said, the words stopping him cold as he began to walk away. "Make mine a Frank's black cherry. And could you maybe get some of those chocolate raisin thingies?" Her dark, lovely eyes went soft as she looked into her father's, as they always did when she wanted something— as they always had since her fourth birthday, when she became convinced that "the look" had been responsible for the shiny new tricycle he had given her that day.

Sullivan chuckled. "Coming up. You two stay put."

"Thank you, Daddy," the girl said sweetly, watching as the man made his way along the row of seats.

"You're so lucky," Marlene said. "My father isn't nearly that nice."

"He's wonderful. We can talk about anything."

"Do you ever see your mom?"

"No. After she left, she didn't want much to do with us."

Marlene let the subject drop. They turned their attentions to the field and spent a few silent minutes watching the game, enjoying their pretzels and the ambiance. The Philadelphia kickoff was deep, carrying all the way into the end zone, and the crowd again stood as one as the ball was brought back into the field of play. Despite the protests of the fans, the return was a long one, finally ending at the Eagles' thirty-two yard line.

"How do you know Andy's brother likes me?" Janessa asked, trying not to show any real interest. "Did he say so, or…"

Her words trailed off as something in the black sky caught her attention, just above the stadium rim opposite, high and to the right. It glowed yellow, trailing fairy sparkles, a deep, brilliant gash cut into the darkness.

"Ooooh, look at that!" she pointed. As Marlene's eyes found the object, puzzlement crossed her pretty face. Whatever the thing was, it was moving, and quickly.

"A shooting star!" she concluded. "How pretty! Or fireworks over the river."

"I don't think so. It's coming closer…"

And then another one appeared.

In seconds a silvery blur trailing smoke and firelight arced downward, slamming into the southern end zone. The crack of its sonic boom was smothered by the impact, a blast that blew a thirty-yard-wide crater into the field and sent shrapnel of metal, concrete, and turf onto the players and into the stands. The concussion was still ringing as the second object struck midfield, its blow as severe as the first. A shock-twisted goalpost, thrown backward and into the end-zone seating, killed an unlucky few who had no chance of getting out of its way. Most of the players on the field, none of whom had seen the missiles coming, were killed instantly. Some were gone altogether. Others fell hard to the ground, their helmets and armored bodies pierced by flying debris.

But there was more.

As the crowd began to panic and flood toward the exits, a dense, blue white fog rose rapidly from the twin craters. Like ethereal hands clutching for prey, it filled the still air and spread into the surrounding seats, touching those who could not escape quickly enough. Screams filled the stadium, drowning out the exultant music that still played over its public address system. Thousands were trampled and crushed as far too many tried all at once for the only avenues of flight, their survival instincts overriding all else.

Janessa and Marlene crouched low as others rushed over and around them. Marlene took a knee hard in the shoulder as one man climbed past, and another man's boot caught Janessa in the temple. Too frightened to feel pain, the girl lifted her head and peered over the top of the seat in front of her.

Her view, though limited by the fleeing spectators, allowed glimpses of the part of their section nearer the field. A couple of dozen rows away, people were staggering and falling, their legs failing them as they were overtaken by the expanding cloud. To Janessa's horror, she saw its victims convulse before going horribly still. Disfiguring blisters arose from their flesh and tore at them, rendering them inhuman in moments. Turning away, her focus now on the exits, she thought she smelled something oddly sweet.

"You're bleeding," Marlene said, indicating the smeared, twin streams coursing down the side of her friend's face.

"Come on!" Janessa yelled, grabbing Marlene hard by the arm and leaping to her feet. "We have to get out of here! Now!"

Alone in the restroom, Sullivan rubbed his hands under the wall-mounted dryer, cursing the day the things had been invented.

"What's wrong with paper towels?" he muttered, barely able to hear his own raspy voice above the din. "Not a thing, that's what…"

There came a sudden, resounding thud from beyond the restroom walls, deep and alarming. Then another. The lights flickered for an instant. A shrill sound pierced the roar as a hairline crack traversed the wall mirror. Sullivan thought he felt the room shake.

"A *quake?*"

Another sound filled his ears, one he could not immediately place—indistinct, higher in pitch, growing louder.

"What in the world…?"

Wiping his still-damp hands on his jeans, he rushed back out onto the concourse, only to find it flooded with the echoing screams of thousands. Before he could take more than a few steps toward his section, a deep and strengthening rumble rose up through the soles of his feet.

A rushing sea of terrorized people bore down on him, faces masked with fear, eyes wide, throats filled with deafening cries.

He dove behind a pillar as the flood surged past. Small children, their tearful faces as twisted in alarm as those of their parents, were carried or dragged like rag dolls.

"What happened?" he yelled, but he was not heard. "What happened out there?!"

Near him, away from the sanctuary of any solid obstacle, an older gentleman lost his footing and was shoved to the cold, hard floor. The stampede found his body and moved over and beyond him, crushing his glasses, breaking bone, and bruising muscle. Sullivan crouched low and tried to pull the man to safety, but the impenetrable crowd knocked him back. The thunder of desperate footfalls roared in his ears, pressing in on him, thickening the air, making it hard to breathe.

Others fell. Some managed to crawl behind pillars or to roll against the walls. Most did not.

Again, the bewildered Sullivan shouted, his hoarse words drawn under and lost in the terrified flow.

"*What happened?!*"

His mind flashed on a precious face.

Janessa!

Knowing he risked his life, Sullivan moved from behind the pillar and struggled against the current. He had to reach his daughter. Panic-driven fists, elbows, and knees found his body, smashing him, bruising him, lacerating him. One savage blow caught his brow, and within seconds blood curtained his left eye. Caught and contorted, he fell to the hard, polished floor, and others trampled him. A rib gave way—he heard the crack. With clublike force, a knee found his lower back, fracturing a vertebra, hurling knives of pain through his body. Finally, in agony, he managed to reach his feet and battle forward, gaining but a few yards, perhaps half a dozen.

But no more.

"*Janessa!*"

The terrified, mindless mass swept him along, carrying him away from her.

Ten Years Later

Bryson Lawe checked his watch.
Eight twenty-two!

He was late. Too late. As the moon rose over Washington, fear filled him, driving his right foot harder against the accelerator. His position with the Secret Service was a demanding one—he was on the president's personal detail—and its burden was one he always had been willing to accept.

But now he had let time get away from him, and the consequences would be grave.

"Come on!" he cried out in frustration, wondering why every other car in the city had chosen that moment to pull into his path, crawl at a snail's pace, and keep him from his destination. "Let's go! Let's go!"

He tried to keep his focus on the road, but his deeper mind, seemingly at odds with his will, turned his gaze to one side, toward a pair of identical monoliths that rose high in the distance. He did not wish to look—he *never* did—yet the enemy within forced the sight on him time and again, stirring a pain that often slept but never died.

Outlined in blue neon, the forty-two-story Hartnell Center dominated the skyline, a triumph of architectural engineering. Only seven years old, it had become the center of Washington commerce, a modern landmark set amid the more historic wonders that lay nearby. Separated by an interconnecting complex of financial institutions and shops, its twin, soaring towers, when viewed from an acute angle, presented a haunting profile, one much like another that stood no more.

Even now, years later, the silhouette evoked within Lawe memories of a horrific day that had shaken a world—the day his father, along with almost three thousand others, had lived a nightmare and had died too young.

The man had been at work on the ninety-ninth floor of the World Trade Center's north tower when the first commandeered airliner had slammed into its vulnerable, latticed face. Trapped above the engulfing flames, he had no means of escape, no recourse, no hope. His young sons had learned of the attack while sitting in their elementary-school classrooms. That morning, still asleep when their father had left the house, they had not even said good-bye.

For what seemed an eternity, Lawe had struggled with the loss. It had changed him, his heart struggling to contain an anger it never before had known. That rage had threatened to turn him against all who shared the nationality of the terrorists, their blood, their faith. But his head finally had won out over his wounded heart, and he had managed to evade a descent into the darkness of racial hatred.

But only just.

He drove onward, agonizingly aware that every moment counted. The slow-moving, inconsiderate obstacles all around him gradually fell away, and he found clear sailing. The traffic lights changed allegiances and now seemed to be aiding him. He rounded first one curve, then another; one hard turn and then the next, and finally the colossal white edifice loomed before him.

His deep blue, government-issued sedan screeched up to the curb, coming to a sudden rest in a zone marked at the foot of the building. Barely pausing to shut off the engine, he sprang from his seat and fled the vehicle, trapping the seat belt in the driver's door as it slammed shut. Up the outer steps, through the door, up the stairs.

Maybe I made it in time. Please, let me be in time!

Finally. The door.

He slid a key into a waiting slot and gave it a twist, perhaps too hard. There was a click as the mechanism reacted and a latch pulled back.

He was in.

Lawe entered the room, gently closing the door behind him. At once, he knew.

He was too late.

"Well," came a voice. "Is it six o'clock already?"

"I'm *so* sorry," he begged, calling out. "Today was a killer. Speeches at three public schools in two different states, a photo op with the Israeli ambassador, and that thing at the museum..." He paused.

Silence.

"Honey?" he tried again, cutting a sideward look across the room, where white candles, silverware, and fine china for two rested accusingly on the dining table. On the wall directly behind the immaculate spread, a decorative mirror reflected the form of a determined, sandy-haired man of thirty-two clad in a dark suit, a loosened tie, and a concerned expression. Soft strains of classical music drifted on the air, as always.

Gathering his courage, he pushed his way through the swinging kitchen door and found a lovely creature beyond, dressed in evening attire, her long auburn hair styled becomingly, her makeup deliberate and perfect. Her elegant black dress complimented her attractive figure, and the high heels she wore, while not made for comfort, amplified the perfection of her legs. Around her neck hung a delicate platinum-and-diamond necklace, one Lawe had given her only weeks before for her birthday.

I guess the brownie points I earned for that expired—

She stared him down, her brow furrowed and threatening, daggers in her sparkling green eyes.

"I'm glad the president knows how to cook," the woman said sternly, never taking her gaze from him, her words punctuated by a backhanded slam of the oven door. "He's going to have to feed you tonight."

Lawe inhaled deeply, rushing through his options. The lingering scent of the spoiled meal scolded him. On the countertop, he noticed, a few serving bowls sat uncovered, filled with side dishes grown cold.

"I was beginning to wonder if you'd forgotten where I live," she added. "The roast I so carefully chose at the market yesterday was exquisite almost two hours ago. I hope you have shoes that need resoling, because now it won't be much good for anything else."

Karen Foley was a lot of things, but a natural chef was not one of them. She had worked hard to get everything right, planning this dinner for weeks, consulting friends and relatives and cookbooks, and borrowing treasured family recipes from her mother.

*Only to have this, this—*man—*go and spoil it all.*

Lawe came up behind her, put his arms around her waist, and kissed the side of her neck.

"I'm mad at you," she stated.

"I know." He kissed her again. "And I deserve it."

"Stop that. I *want* to be mad right now."

"I'm sorry, Karen. I tried to get here. The security meeting ran long."

"Our fourth anniversary comes only once."

"I know." He felt her annoyance begin to wane.

"Four years since our first date."

"I know."

"Four *long* years."

"How can I make it up to you?" he asked, softly kissing her neck once more, holding her close.

"Same as last time," she replied, trying unsuccessfully not to let him see her emerging smile. "When you weren't here for our *third* anniversary."

"Okay," he agreed. "Marcel's it is."

Karen whirled around and kissed him, then pulled back and wiped her lipstick from his mouth with her thumb. "You are one lucky man," she teased. "I've killed for less, but I *love* French food."

"Yes ma'am," he smiled.

Shaking her head, she picked up the serving platter and dumped the dried-out hunk of meat into the kitchen trash. It landed with a painful thud. "Too bad I don't have a dog."

"Or a wood chipper."

She spun to him, only to find the rugged, disarming smile with which she first had fallen in love. "You're in enough trouble," she said, wagging a long burgundy-polished nail. "Don't go making it worse."

"Yes ma'am."

"I'll need my coat," she said, playfully tapping the tip of his nose. "It's getting a bit nippy outside." Taking a few steps toward the door, she indicated the bowls of food on the counter. "Put those in the fridge for me, will you? We can have them tomorrow." She paused and looked back. "And you *will* have them."

Like silk on air, Lawe thought as he watched her, his eyes never leaving her as she crossed the kitchen. She vanished into the living room.

"I was afraid it would be a lot nippier *in here,*" he said to himself, thankful that the crisis had been averted. After cinching his tie, he took a deep breath and turned to the task at hand.

"Brussels sprouts," he moaned, peering into one of the bowls, "with… what is that? Gravy?"

The quiet times were precious and came too seldom.

A warm golden fire crackled in the Oval Office as President Matthew Bridger sat sorting out a few of the day's final demands. His staff had gone home for the night, and he too would be heading toward the mansion, his wife, and his waiting dinner as soon as one last appointment was kept.

He ran his fingertips along the dark, polished surface before him, awed by what it symbolized, thinking of all it had witnessed here in this room. It was the Resolute Desk, commissioned by Queen Victoria and carved from the timbers of the HMS *Resolute,* a British naval vessel. A gift to President Rutherford Hayes, the veteran fixture had been a witness to some of the most critical moments in the history of the presidency. It had been used by Roosevelt during World War II, by Kennedy during the Cuban missile crisis, and by George W. Bush during the multiple ordeals that followed the World Trade Center attack of Nine-Eleven.

So much history embodied within a single piece of furniture—

The old grandfather clock chimed nine as Bridger rose, stretched, and walked toward the fireplace. The flames there reminded him of the winter nights he had shared with his family as a boy so many years before. He missed his parents, their counsel, their love.

I wish you could be here, Mom and Dad. Who would have thought Mrs. Bridger's boy would be in this room, behind that desk? But then, maybe you are here, *watching, listening—I hope I do you proud.*

Two years earlier the man had been elected vice president, the running mate of a former governor whose popularity had risen to unprecedented levels in mere months. But only seven months after assuming office, the chosen president had suffered a massive coronary, and all attempts to revive him had failed. Before another hour had passed, Bridger had been sworn in, there before that fireplace, in that room.

He reached up and pulled a book from the mantel. It was an old tome and one of his favorites, a gift from his grandfather, received on his eighth birthday.

Hello, old friend.

Turning as he enjoyed the familiar sight and feel of its cover, he took a seat on one of two plush, facing sofas, upon which many a visiting head of state had rested. As he began to read, the words flowed from the pages as they had so many times—words written more than a century and a half earlier, words of gentle humor and often of great wisdom, words from which he had drawn enjoyment time and again.

The curtained glass door leading from the Rose Garden opened. Bridger looked up to see his anticipated guest enter, escorted by a lone Secret Service agent.

"Thank you, Jack," said the president, rising to his feet, the book still in his hands.

"You're welcome, sir," the agent said. "Just buzz when you're ready."

The man departed, closing the door behind him, leaving the blond woman in the company of the president.

"Rachel," Bridger said warmly, walking over to her. He shook her hand gently, then took her coat.

"Mr. President." She smiled a bit nervously. "Thank you for seeing me."

"You're welcome here, as always. Please…sit down."

He led her to the twin couches, and over the back of one he draped her coat. As he crossed to the other, she took a seat and laid her purse and a sealed manila envelope on the cushion beside her.

"Mark Twain?" she noticed.

"Yes," he said, setting the volume aside as he sat opposite. "This book's almost as old as I am. Holding up a little better, though."

The woman looked at him, hope in her eyes.

"There wasn't much I could do today," he said with reluctance, getting to the purpose of her visit. "They took the vote as scheduled, and the outcome was as we expected."

"I'm very sorry to hear that."

"You know I stand with you in this, Rachel. Unfortunately, the situation is one I inherited, and despite my best efforts, I've had little effect on it since taking office. Congress was responsible for putting this into motion, and convincing them to see the matter differently won't be easy. The two years remaining in my term may not be enough…in fact, I'm not sure another full term would make any difference. I have no illusions about that."

"Our only hope may lie with the public," Rachel said. "I know it's an uphill battle, but if we can sway the voters and change the makeup of Congress…"

"Uphill, to say the least. We're in the vast minority here."

"I know," the woman nodded. "But I've decided one thing."

"What's that?"

"I'm bringing in a PR director. I shouldn't be the face of the organization, not anymore. Too many out there have demonized me. It's time for someone new, someone they might listen to. My prime candidate's currently with Health and Human Services and has a sterling résumé. I haven't gotten a definite response from her yet, but she hasn't said no, either."

"Millie Carson isn't going to be happy about you mining her staff," the president said. "You know where she stands on all this."

"I know," Rachel sighed. "But the woman I've spoken with stands with us already…and from what she's told me, she's butted heads with Ms. Carson more than once. She's looking for a change. I just hope the current controversy doesn't keep her away."

"She doesn't sound like one who's easily shaken," the president offered.

"Her poise under pressure is remarkable. She'll make such a difference…and we need all the help we can get."

"You'll always have whatever support I can give you. But my hands are tied in so many ways."

"I know what you're up against," she said, glancing down at her clasped hands. "And I appreciate your help. We're doing what we can within the confines of the law, but it's David against Goliath."

He drew a breath. "If I could push a magic button, none of what led to this would ever have happened. One mistake in judgment piled on top of another and another over so many years. If you'd told folks fifty years ago that one day this would be the law of the land, they'd never have believed you. Problem now is that the system's so firmly entrenched we may *never* overcome it, short of a miracle."

Rachel stared into the fire. "I've been waiting and hoping…but so far, no sign of one. We have our little victories here and there, but they get swallowed up in the overall fight. We lose more than we win, and with every day that passes the beast gets bigger…" Her voice fell away, a weariness there.

She picked up the envelope and handed it to him.

"I wanted to deliver this personally. It's our internal semiannual report. It'll give you a better idea of where we are, warts and all."

"You know I'll continue to do what I can," he said, accepting it. "And know that every night, when I hit my knees, this cause is one of the first things I pray about."

"Me too," she nodded, sadness living in her eyes.

"You and your people may be David," Bridger said, "but there's a stone out there with this Goliath's name on it. I'm sure of that. All you have to do is find it."

It was a savage beast made harmless and caged for display, a violent thing subdued by time. For some, it would prove a catharsis—for others, a renewed call to arms.

It was a documentary reliving a night of great pain.

Police sergeant Jeffrey Lawe sat on a midtown Manhattan barstool, nursing a watery cola and nibbling from a bowl of Spanish peanuts as he watched a wall-mounted hi-def screen. It was a quiet night at Lou's Place, perhaps more so for an imposing man in a blue uniform whose presence seemed to have a calming effect on his surroundings. His transceiver rested on the bar, its full-color display cluttered with a flow of numerical codes from the dispatcher:

"Seven-oh-nine…"

"Seven-oh-nine, go ahead…"

"Ten-thirty at One-fifteen West Fifty-first…code three…"

"One-fifteen West Fifty-first…ten-four…"

Its volume was low, yet the exchange was clear to the trained listener. Jeffrey looked to his right, to the new partner he was helping to train, a blond man in his early twenties. The rookie stood with the tavern's owner at the end of the bar, discussing the events of the day.

He was a good one, born to be a cop. Jeffrey could always tell. And given a few years—

It was ten years ago tonight that the attack occurred, a terrorist assault that took the lives of so many before they knew what was happening to them…

His attention returned to the big screen. The haunting images there had grown all too familiar in the years since that fateful October 17. Again and again the same camera footage, the same anguished survivors, the same police and fire and government officials had appeared on all the major news channels, becoming an indelible part of the collective American psyche. Now, as he watched them anew, Jeffrey considered the innumerable lives that had changed in an instant on a night forever etched into the history books alongside December 7 and September 11.

"You sure you don't want something different?" the bartender asked, drying his hands on a blue towel. "It's on the house."

"On duty, thanks," Jeffrey said. He glanced at the man and smiled in appreciation. "Another soda would be fine, though."

"Coming up." The man looked over at the screen. "You want anything to eat? I got some wings in back."

"No, I'm good."

The narrator went on, his voice carrying a detached and almost eerie calm. *It was the seventh game of the season. The Philadelphia Eagles, hosting the division rival Washington Redskins, were mounting a comeback as the*

*game's final minutes ticked away. Then, with no warning, came chaos and
death, both on the field and in the stands."*

Jeffrey held his breath as that portion of the presentation began to
unfold, watching intently as part of the game's original network telecast
was replayed. At first, with commentators casually analyzing the play on
the field, it was much like any other night of football.

But then, suddenly, it was not.

A bright flash of light appeared, filling the stadium. The picture
began to swing wildly, switching from one unstable view to another. The
second impact was caught live by a rogue camera whose operator had
been killed by shrapnel from the first. Microphones caught the screams of
horrified thousands as they scrambled to flee. The shaken play-by-play
men, to their credit, remained on the air for all of thirty seconds before
dropping their headsets and running for their lives.

*"Those who carried out this attack, Saudi members of al-Qaeda, claimed
in a prerecorded message to have done so in retaliation for repeated American
incursions into Arab territories, which had occurred as a part of this nation's
ongoing war on terror."*

A clinking of ice cubes met Jeffrey's ears as a fresh glass appeared
before him.

"It was like the towers comin' down all over again," the bartender
said, "that night."

The sergeant barely nodded, a long-buried pain glowing like a
neglected coal.

"You always remember where you were. I was standing right here,
where I am now, talking to a cop like you as a matter of fact. The game
was on. Bunch of guys in here watching. We always get a full house on
game nights. Anyway, it looked like the Skins were gonna win one, and
then…" Air hissed between his teeth. "Friend of mine was there, in Philly.
Big Washington fan. Made a special trip to see the game. *He* made it out."

"He was lucky. A lot of folks didn't."

"Poor guy was never the same after that. Lost touch with him years ago."

"Amazing how fast things can change."

"What kind of people could do such a thing?" the bartender asked, his voice laced with resentment. "They don't deserve to live, I tell you, none of 'em. They're inhuman, plain and simple."

"There's a lot of evil out there."

"Worse than Nazis, these animals. Changed everything. You know how it's been since Nine-Eleven."

"That's been a while."

"Not for me. I lost my brother. I miss him every day."

"Right there with you," Jeffrey said. "I lost my dad."

"I'm so sorry." The man shook his head and groaned in disgust. "Took 'em long enough to forget all that PC garbage and start profiling, huh? Finally quit strip-searching grandmothers and started looking for actual terrorists. You gotta screen for the *man,* not the weapon. Israel learned that a long time ago."

"I suppose."

"Turban-wearing monsters," the bartender said, under his breath. "Nothing's beyond 'em. Random shootings, hacking into hospitals and power plants, poisoning food and water supplies…" His hand tensed into a fist. "They've blown up tanker trucks and brought down planes. And if the feds hadn't stopped those big attacks in Chicago and Vegas a few years ago, there'd be a *whole* lot more good folks dead right now."

"Well, you can thank Homeland Security that there aren't."

"Friend, I do. Every night. We took our lumps, but so did they, and then some. They attacked Uncle Sam and paid for it. If not for you fellows who put your lives on the line, day in and day out…" Emotion swelled within him. "God bless *all* you guys."

The man paused, wiped the bar for a moment, then walked away. As Jeffrey took a sip from the new glass, other file footage filled the screen, images of advanced weaponry being loaded and used in a combat setting. He wondered if the show would reveal anything he had not already seen or heard.

"It later was determined that a pair of American-made Sandviper missiles, such as those seen here, had been launched from a container ship on the Delaware River, mere miles from the stadium site..."

A new graphic appeared, an animated map of the Philadelphia area, showing positions and trajectories determined from the evidence, all in vivid color.

"Guided by the Global Positioning System, the missiles struck with terrifying accuracy, filling the stadium in seconds with what at the time was an unknown and highly corrosive nerve agent, Keragesin-D, since used to devastating effect by Iranian forces in the battles of Qasr-e Shirin and Dasht-e Kavir."

More footage, this time of the Iranian War, a short-lived conflict fought three years after Ten-Seventeen. It was intercut with stills of the carnage in Philadelphia.

"Twenty-nine thousand perished in mere moments. Fortunately, due to calm winds and the bowl-shaped nature of the stadium, the short-lived chemical weapon remained largely within its confines until the Keragesin's unstable molecular structure broke down. Otherwise, it is believed, the death toll would have risen dramatically as many in the surrounding city became exposed as well."

Jeffrey again saw the emergency rooms, the frantic city and federal offices, the grieving friends and relatives. He reflected on the day, thankful that the tragedy, as bad as it was, had been no worse.

"The National Football League, in an unprecedented move, cancelled the remainder of the season. The site of the attack was painstakingly decontaminated, and the stadium was razed. Within a year, a memorial park had been erected in its place."

"Went there with Bry, once," he whispered, recalling the towering marble obelisk with so many names engraved at its base.

Ten-Seventeen had been a turning point for Jeffrey. Paired with the childhood loss of his father, the incident had convinced him to dedicate his life to the *preservation* of life. The following day he had applied to serve with the New York City police department. The training had been rigorous, the rewards many. Like his older brother, he now lived for the service of others.

The rectangular screen flooded the room with glaring light, an image of a vessel afire and surrounded by fireboats. Their hoses were trained on the floating inferno, streaming plumes of vivid white.

"Those who launched the missiles perished minutes later aboard their own ship in an explosion believed to have been a final act of defiance and martyrdom. Ten-Seventeen, as Nine-Eleven, would not see the arrest of those who had perpetrated the attack."

Jeffrey scowled.

We couldn't get our hands on them—they robbed us even of that!

"Cowards," he muttered.

It would not happen again. If he had anything to say about it, it would not happen again.

"Why are you watching that?" Janessa asked. "You know how it upsets you."

Her father reclined on the living room sofa, its cushions worn with age and contoured by use. His eyes were trained upon the Ten-Seventeen documentary, the room dark save the glow of the screen. He stared for the moment without seeing, the images on the screen supplanted by his mind's eye, his mind's ear. He recalled clearly the sudden crack of the shock wave, the trembling of the ground beneath him, the screams, and the rumble of tens of thousands of panicked feet—

"I'm fine," Sullivan said, pausing to take a deep breath.

The narrator continued to speak, his polished voice overlaid on a montage of persons being taken into custody by law enforcement officials. *"Only four days after the attack, the president of the United States, by executive order, put into motion a dramatic and wide-ranging course of action that called for the rounding up and deportation of tens of thousands of illegally resident Arab nationals, and for the sealing of our national borders by military forces. All student visas were cancelled, along with those of all citizens of any Arab nation who had entered the country for any reason."*

Images of burning American flags and presidential effigies shone forth from the television, animalistic demonstrations that had filled the streets from Libya to Saudi Arabia to Iran. Many had died in those protests, Sullivan recalled.

"This action, branded as illegal, deplorable, and unconscionable by some, and applauded as long overdue by others, drew loud protests from the Arab world. The deep ideological divide created by the issue tore at the heart of Congress—"

"I don't get you," his daughter went on, from a spot near the room's wide bay window. The curtains were drawn and she stood to one side, partially silhouetted by the pale throw of a street lamp as it spilled gently through the sheers. "Anytime anybody brings up the subject, you won't talk about it. But whenever there's something about it on TV, you watch."

He raised the remote and shut off the set, then reached up and switched on the warm, gentle light of the table lamp next to him. "It was about over, anyway."

"I'm not picking on you, Daddy," she said. "I love you. I'm just concerned."

"I love you too, honey," he returned, looking upon her. "Have I ever told you how beautiful you are?"

"Only about a million times," she smiled. "Listen, did you eat? You have leftover fried chicken in the refrigerator..."

"I'm fine. I ate earlier, before you came." He swung his legs over, sat up, and ran a hand through his graying hair. "By the way, I saw Marlene today."

"So I heard."

Moving his shoulder in a circular fashion, a grimace arose. He rubbed the sore joint. "My tendonitis is acting up again."

"Did you take your pills?"

"Yes, a couple of hours ago."

"I'm sorry I was late," she said. "I know I told you I'd be here by seven."

"No problem, honey. I can't imagine what it's like for you."

"You need to take better care of yourself. Have I ever told you that?"

"Only about a million times." He smiled, watching with pride as she crossed the room and grew close, her motion fluid and feminine and graceful.

She looked around in the soft light, clearly noting every piece of furniture, every knickknack, every framed photograph.

"This house hasn't changed in twenty years," she observed. "Not one bit. Even the TV… You got it when I was little. I'm surprised it still works."

"I like the place this way. I have my memories for company."

"I'm here, too, you know."

"And I'm grateful for that," he said. "How long can you stay?"

"All night, if you'd like," Janessa smiled. "I know you hate to be alone."

"Yes, I'd like that…especially tonight."

Supporting his weight on a cane, Sullivan rose and went into the kitchen as Janessa followed. He drew a glass of cool water from the tap and, as he drank it down, stared at the refrigerator. Its doors were covered by magnet-pinned notes, photos, and dozens of expired lottery tickets, all of them years old. His former job as a beverage delivery driver had brought hundreds of stops at convenience stores and gas stations, and at each stop he had bought a single ticket. None had won him a thing.

You'd think at least once—

"You need to stop watching those shows, Daddy. What's done is done. No sense in dredging up the past."

He looked away. "But that was when it all began, sweetheart. It's as if my life before that night was a dream, or someone else's life, or a movie I once saw but can barely remember. Everything changed in a matter of minutes. Everything."

"I know, Daddy. I know."

"I'm not up to this Canada trip," the man moaned. "They want me there on Thursday, for three days."

"But you *have* to go," Janessa said. "It's important."

"I know, but it's too much. The crowds, the flight, everything. I never should have said anything to anyone…should have just kept it to myself and lived my life."

"And what would you have done for income? After you hurt your back, you ran through your savings. You barely got by. Until this."

He glanced again at the refrigerator door. "I don't know. Something would have worked out. Lottery, maybe."

She playfully scolded him. "I think we both know how unlikely that was."

Sullivan smiled, his thoughts bathed in irony.

Unlikely, she says, as opposed to impossible, *which is paying the bills right now*—

"They need you."

"And I'll be there," he said. "But I won't enjoy it."

The restaurant was far from crowded. Its main dining room, in fact, was as sparsely occupied as Lawe and Karen had ever seen it.

"Ah, Mr. Lawe," the tuxedoed maître d' smiled, greeting the couple as they entered. "And Miss Foley. Welcome to Marcel's. We received your call and are most happy to have you with us tonight. Your table is right this way."

"Thank you," the couple said, almost in unison.

They stepped forward, following the man's lead. Lawe brushed against a potted plant as he rounded a corner, drawing a giggle from a young girl who sat nearby, dining with her family.

"Slow night?" Lawe asked.

"It is the middle of the week," the man said. "And late. Most of our patrons dined earlier in the evening."

"I'm sorry about the hour. Wound up working a bit later than I'd planned."

"Please, do not make an apology. As I mentioned, we are glad you're here."

The man led them to a table near one corner, a cozy spot he recalled as being a favorite of Karen's. The place was elegant yet comfortable—its lighting was subtle and warm, the atmosphere pleasant and inviting. The tables were covered in white linen.

"Will this be satisfactory?"

"Quite," Lawe nodded.

"It's lovely," Karen smiled. "Thank you."

After the two were seated comfortably, the maître d' left them with a pair of menus and the name of their waiter. Lawe, as was his habit, watched the man walk away then scanned the room, his eyes jumping from doorway to window to wall hanging, from one wall sconce to the next. Karen knew exactly what was running through his mind and watched as he held his menu inconspicuously before him, quickly sizing up the few other patrons who sat enjoying their meals.

"No one's here to shoot us," Karen whispered, a playful smile on her lips as she glanced at him over her own raised menu. "Relax."

"I *am* relaxing," he smirked, caught red-handed. "I didn't knock you to the floor or dive in front of a bullet, did I?"

"Not yet." She thought back to an evening a few months earlier. "Last time we were here, when we sat out on the patio, I remember you watching the windows across the street. You just *knew* there was a terrorist up there."

"The lights were off," he said, gesturing. "But I thought I saw motion, like a flashlight behind the glass."

"And when that car backfired—"

"Could have happened to anybody," he grinned. "It was a reflex. And I explained everything to those people."

"Bry, you pulled a gun in front of the table next to us."

"I'm sure they had a good laugh over it," he reminded her, returning to his menu. "Gave them a story to tell their friends back in...what was it, Indiana?" A welcome quiet descended as he pretended to read his menu. "Hmm...I think I'll have a steak. The filet mignon, maybe..."

Karen, amused, let the subject rest and turned her attentions to her menu. "The roasted quail and frisee salad look good..."

She paused to let the silence settle again and stifled a laugh.

"Smarty," Lawe said, loving her.

The woman smiled widely, her face hidden from him.

"So, how's it going at HHS?" he asked.

"Same old, same old," Karen said. "I'll be glad when this whole CloneTech scandal is done with."

"Are you still thinking of taking that other job?"

"I don't know," she replied. "It doesn't pay as well, but it has so many other positives..."

"Positives?" he asked skeptically.

"Making a difference, for one. It would be nice to know I'm doing something important. Something to save lives."

"You're doing that now."

"Not really. Not the same way."

"Karen, I wish you wouldn't get mixed up in all that," he moaned. "It's trouble waiting to happen, and life has plenty of headaches as it is."

"I can't just sit back and do nothing."

"I'm not asking you to," he insisted. "I just don't think you want to get involved with a group like that."

"Why wouldn't I? All they're trying to do is—"

"*Whatever* they're trying to do, your life will be turned upside down. And I for one don't want to have to worry about you being attacked by some nutball…I get enough of that at work."

"Let's not discuss this, not right now," she asked. "I want to enjoy the evening. There'll be time for debate tomorrow."

"Okay," he conceded. "You're right. It's just that I love you, and I'm worried about you."

"I know."

They continued to scan their menus. Karen felt the lingering heaviness around them.

"I'm looking forward to coming here when you propose," she said, trying to lighten the moment.

"Did I miss a memo?" he smiled, a bit uncomfortably.

"No. Same one."

"When I move up," he said, as he always did. "When I'm off the detail."

"Just think. You and I on Christmas morning, watching our three children gathered around the tree, opening their gifts. Two girls and a boy. And a dog…something snuggly, like a cocker spaniel. With a fire in the fireplace and Christmas music playing…"

"Nice."

"Of course, this all hinges on our getting married before we reach retirement."

"How much before?"

His sense of humor had played a large part in her falling in love with him, but there were other things, too. His honesty, his bravery, his dedication. Not to mention—

"You have the most beautiful eyes," she said, enjoying the mischievous twinkle there. "Our kids will be gorgeous."

The man saw their waiter approaching from the open kitchen. "You know what you want?" he asked.

"Yes," she said. *You,* she thought.

And then she heard it—the subtle buzzing she had grown to dread.

The agent reached down, pulled his netphone from its waistband holster, flipped it open, and checked the incoming number. "Lawe," he crisply answered, forgoing the unit's video display for the more secure avenue of private audio.

For a few awful moments she looked upon the steel gray of his irises, watching as he listened intently to a voice she could not hear.

"On my way," he said, then snapped the phone shut again. "I'm so sorry, honey…"

"Go," Karen resignedly said.

He quickly rose, leaned over, and kissed her. "I'll call as soon as I can."

"I know." She smiled, trying to hide the bitter disappointment swelling within her.

"Why don't you get hold of Nancy?" he suggested. "She's off work by now. Have her come down here. I'll take care of the bill. I'm sure it'll beat having dinner with her cat."

"I might."

"Sir?" the waiter inquired, arriving at their table.

"I've got to go," Lawe said, straightening his suit coat. "The lady would like to…" He looked to her.

"I'll stay," she decided. "I'll eat here, then get a taxi if Nancy can't take me home."

"I need to go ahead and pay," Lawe said to the waiter, who reached into an apron pocket and withdrew a rectangular, leather-bound pad. Opening it, he revealed a small, luminous oval disk, against which Lawe pressed his thumb. Within seconds, a tiny adjacent indicator lit blue.

"Very good, sir," the waiter said. "A twenty percent gratuity is standard."

"That's fine."

Lawe again kissed Karen, contrition in the gesture. "I love you. Happy anniversary."

"You too."

He rushed for the exit, leaving her alone. Again.

"Do you wish to order, madam?" the waiter asked.

"Yes," she said, through a brave smile. "I suppose so."

2

Richard Kelsey sat on a park bench, savoring the rustling of leaves as he made a few notes in a leather-bound journal. Its cover, cracked here and there with age, hinted at the weight of the words it contained.

The autumn reds and golds danced before him, fluttering here and there to the ground below, dotting the jogging path that coursed by. Sleeping lampposts stood sentinel along the paved walk, their frosted globes dark, their black iron lattice showing only a hint of rust.

It was a cloudy day, and the temperature was cool but not uncomfortable—the beige fabric of his buttoned V-necked sweater provided comfort, even against the breeze. He peered upward, noting that the trees had changed little since he had started coming here so many years before. Squirrels played, darting from trunk to trunk, searching for acorns to store in anticipation of the snows that were not far behind. The food he had brought for them had lasted but a brief time, leaving an empty, carefully folded paper sack in his pocket.

Each day at the same hour he came to this bench, the bag of feed in hand. Today he was alone, allowing him a quiet time to jot down a few thoughts. During the warmer months, a friend would meet him, and together they would share each other's company, enjoy the outdoors, and exchange pleasantries with those who walked past. But as they did each September, Gus and his wife had left Washington for Florida, leaving Kelsey alone to uphold their daily ritual until the return of spring.

The air, crisp and refreshing, smelled of burning wood and carried on its invisible shoulders memories of past walks, past loves, and warm child-hood Thanksgivings.

If he tried hard enough, he could almost imagine that things were as they once had been. But much had changed during his seventy-three years.

Too much.

Louis, what became of the "wonderful world" of which you so beautifully sang?

He closed the journal, placing it and his pen on the bench beside him. Looking up, he found some distance away an unshaven indigent man who stood imploring a hot-dog vendor for food. His clothing was soiled and worn.

Hello, Robert, Kelsey thought. *How are you today? You managed a hair-cut, I see—*

The old man knew many of the homeless who inhabited the park. More lived here now than ever before, due in large part to the sweeping societal changes for which they had been unprepared. They seldom approached him anymore, having heard once too often of his faith, turn-ing their attentions instead to others who might simply and silently give them a measure of food or clothing or drink.

Kelsey looked with sympathy upon the man, who now was wolfing down the morsel he had been given. Even as he ate, he glanced around, seeking a further source of sustenance.

How fortunes can change.

The man once had been a microtech engineer, Kelsey remembered. But that had been before the advent of the Japanese liquid circuit and the quantum changes that had developed in its wake. Molecular-level elec-tronics had changed the world, and much of American technology had fallen by the wayside.

Profanities suddenly filled the air, voices seemingly too young to have uttered them. Kelsey looked aside and found a group of children playing nearby, their repeated, crude, and sexually laced words an embarrassment to him.

What have we done?

There was a time, Kelsey remembered, when there was such a thing as right and wrong, when decency and accomplishment were traits to be admired, when men strived to treat others as they themselves would be treated.

Those days were long gone.

Too many years of political correctness and misguided thinking had taken their toll. Like a poison, it had begun slowly and subtly, as first the little things were turned upside down. Personal achievement had been shoved aside in favor of self-esteem, even to the point of prohibiting the childhood game of tag in schools for fear of offending slower children. Classroom success lost all meaning when, rather than encouraging those with poorer grades to improve, those with higher levels of ambition or ability were held back in order that the more challenged children not feel left behind. Schools no longer chose valedictorians or salutatorians for fear of insulting those whose grade point averages rested farther down the scale, and many schools no longer used a grading system at all.

Rather than teaching the value of resilience, they had chosen instead to remove challenges in any way possible during the crucial formative years, resulting in a weak and morally disabled youth culture.

Fewer and fewer knew the satisfaction of rewards for a job well done. Instead, all were taught that anything they wished was owed them, that mere existence demanded recompense. Their own opinions of themselves, it was emphasized, were of prime import. Self reigned. That mind-set took on larger and more serious consequences as those who had been indoctrinated grew up and took positions of greater power and influence.

All the more amazing, Kelsey mused, *for no person ever born had a problem loving himself—it was selflessness that had been lacking all along.*

No guidelines were laid, no boundaries set, no moral framework put in place. Rather, children, with only a few years of life experience and utterly ill-equipped to make moral decisions, were left to sink or swim on their own. None of them were taught the most basic respect for their elders or for authority but instead were told that their own convictions and those of their parents had equal footing.

No students were given the strength of character to fully bear or deflect the tribulations of the coming teenage years, and some, who simply could not cope, chose to take up weapons and kill their fellow students for reasons of revenge or rebellion or simple cruelty. The suicide rate among teens skyrocketed, as did drug use and juvenile crime. Again and again, proposed solutions treated only the symptoms, leaving the cause intact.

The concept of personal responsibility had become archaic. There no longer existed black or white, right or wrong—instead, there were only shades of gray, with personal point of view and the wants of self the only remaining measure.

Truth, in effect, no longer existed.

Of course, not all children grew up so morally destitute, but those who did not were few. They had been blessed with parents whose strength of character was sufficient to overcome the assaults of the public schools, whose faith or intrinsic moral fiber had been strong enough to keep their children on the straight and narrow despite the unrelenting onslaught of society.

Driven by pride, needlessly trying to give its children a greater sense of self-worth, America instead, in a few short generations, had destroyed itself from within.

But then, Kelsey had expected that. He had expected it all.

"In the last days difficult times will come. For men will be lovers of self, lovers of money, boastful, arrogant, revilers, disobedient to parents, ungrateful, unholy, unloving, irreconcilable, malicious gossips, without self-control, brutal, haters of good, treacherous, reckless, conceited, lovers of pleasure rather than lovers of God."

He knew the words by heart. Recorded millennia earlier by the apostle Paul in a letter to the young Timothy, they could not have been more relevant had they been written yesterday.

Kelsey became aware that he no longer was alone and noticed a young woman sitting on the other end of his bench. A light blue diaper bag rested next to her. Barely in her twenties and dressed simply, she cradled an infant, rocking it in her arms as she held a bottle to its suckling lips. Her light coat had seen better days. She wore no makeup, and though she was young, her eyes bore dark circles as if too often she had gone without sleep. Her demeanor was one of worry and fatigue.

"Oh, hello," Kelsey said, offering a gentle welcome and a kind smile. "I'm sorry...I didn't see you sit down."

"Hi," the girl replied, her voice flat.

"Boy or girl?" he asked, indicating the baby.

"Boy," she said.

"He's a big one," the man went on, hoping to bring at least a measure of cheer to her morning. "A beautiful child."

"Thanks," she said, "but he's not well."

"No?"

"No, but it's complicated. I'd rather not go into it."

The elderly man nodded, choosing not to pry and keeping his distance at the far end of the long bench. He noted that she had chosen to sit on his bench rather than taking one just down the way. Assuming she was lonely, he continued to chitchat.

"My name's Kelsey," he smiled. "I live over there." He pointed, indicating a direction beyond and behind her. "I love this place. So peaceful, away from everything. I come here every day to sit and look at the trees and the birds and the squirrels. I bring food for them. I used to come here with my kids, before they grew up. I've always loved this time of year, when the leaves begin to turn. So much color."

"It's pretty," she agreed. "We come here a lot too...usually in the afternoon though." She gently rubbed the baby's nose. "This has always been our bench."

"Well, I'm happy to share."

"I'm Melissa," she said, smiling politely. "Nice to meet you."

"Hello, Melissa."

"This is Joseph."

He smiled anew at the baby. "Hello, Joseph."

After a short silence, the girl renewed the conversation. "So, are you retired?"

"Oh yes," Kelsey said. "For years now."

"What did you used to do?"

"I was pastor of a church. A little one not too far from here."

"Why did you quit?"

"Well, I was very sick and getting worse. I had to leave."

"Oh, I'm sorry."

"Don't be, Melissa. All things happen as they are meant to."

"Are you okay now?"

He slowly nodded, though his expression was not a positive one. "Yes…they were able to help me."

"I'm glad." She shifted the weight of the baby to her other arm and continued the feeding. "You have a family?"

"Well," he began, "my wife passed away some years ago. I still have a son and a daughter. She lives a few miles from here, and he's in South Carolina."

"Do you see them often?"

The man frowned. "No…no, I don't."

"Oh. I don't have anyone either. Except for Joseph."

They sat in the presence of the overhanging trees, united for that moment in their solitude, letting the world just—*be*.

After a time, the girl rose and, clutching the baby to her chest with one arm, hefted the diaper bag onto her other shoulder.

"Thanks," she said, a deep yet subtle sadness underlying the word.

"For what?" he asked.

"Just…thanks."

He gave her a gentle smile and watched as she walked away, down the path. As the troubled girl vanished into the distance, Kelsey closed his eyes, bowed his head, and prayed that the child would survive to see his first birthday.

An uneasy truce existed in the Middle East.

More than a decade earlier, following a prolonged and fiery debate within the Jewish government, the disputed lands of the Gaza Strip and the West Bank had been handed over to the Palestinians, granting them the sovereignty they long had demanded. And only a series of forced elections, giving them a new and supposedly stable political leadership, had made the move feasible.

Many Israelis had protested the withdrawal from the disputed lands, claiming it was suicide to give up so much territory and allow their enemies the freedom to act against them. Others, however, weary of the conflict, had prayed that the show of good faith would be enough.

The Palestinian people had seemed satisfied for some time afterward. They had celebrated the birth of their long-awaited state—its two territories declared East and West Palestine—sending ambassadors into neighboring lands. The bombings and assassination attempts ceased, and the people of the Jewish state breathed a bit easier. The world applauded the cessation of hostilities and the air of hope that appeared to have arisen in the region.

Ultimately, the concessions had not been enough. The lessons of 1939 had gone unheeded by a populace that had not lived through the ancient experience, for whom the names Chamberlain and Hitler were but dusty reminders of a time nearly forgotten.

☆

The tension in the room might have been unbearable for lesser men. Five of the most powerful and decisive people in the United States sat in the Oval Office, waiting for a phone call. The news from a land far from America's shores was not good and foreshadowed worse things to follow.

"If this is Rashoud's idea of independence," Defense Secretary Warren Sumner said, his fingers kneading his brow, "then all bets are off. It's the turn of the century all over again, and probably worse."

President Bridger, enveloped by his padded leather chair, shared their apprehension. "I think we can count on it, Warren. He hasn't exactly been a pillar of rational thought since he took office. And now he's killed some of our boys."

"And to do it right on the heels of the anniversary of Ten-Seventeen…" Sumner commented. "Unbelievable. Almost makes you long for the days of Arafat." Bridger raised an eyebrow. "I said almost."

"All these years, we've been able to keep a lid on the situation only because they were willing," added Secretary of State John Creedel. "But if they keep up this kind of aggression, things are going to escalate out of control, and fast. Israel's made no move against them… Why the attacks? Three homicide bombings in the last two months, with no explanation given and no response to demands for one. And now—"

"And now," the president finished, "we may be dealing with a full military offensive."

"It was bound to happen," said Roger Brooks, special advisor to the president. "Since well before any of us were born, the Palestinians have been dedicated to Israel's destruction."

"Some would say it's been a two-way street," said national security advisor Rhonda Varner.

"Some also said the United States was responsible for Nine-Eleven and Ten-Seventeen." He shook his head. "No, if they said that, they'd be wrong."

"How so?"

"Way back in '67, Israel somehow managed to take a deadly viper by the throat. For decades after that, through occupation and limited military action, they kept the threat at bay and survived. Whenever the world protested, the Jews tried to explain that to lessen their grip was to risk death. With the exception of the United States, no one heard them. And those times when they *did* bow to international pressure and relax their hold, even a little, the Palestinians used that additional freedom to mount attacks. It was never a question of *whether* the violence would come, but only how intensely and how often."

"Look, Roger," Varner said, "we all know the problems they've faced. But you can't oppress an entire people year after year, and Israel finally figured that out. Eventually, you have to learn to get along and—"

"No, no," Sumner jumped in. "There *is* no getting along. I was stationed in the region for six years. I saw the hatred there." He turned toward the president. "The Palestinians were *never* just seeking independence or anything else Israel could give them. Then and now, state or no state, their only goal has been the extinction of the Jewish nation, and the intensity with which they've pursued it has been building for decades. It's something no Westerner can fully comprehend."

"Pretty broad brush you're painting with there," Varner said.

"There's a lot to cover. Their kindergartens and elementary schools still teach that the Israelis are lower than animals and undeserving of life, demons to be killed at every opportunity. Almost from birth, it's pounded into their skulls, and I've seen the frenzy it stirs in them as young adults. It was years ago, but I'll never forget it. The way they'd kill, then mutilate the bodies and wave the internal organs in the air."

"I refuse to believe that. No one could do such a thing. It's *barbaric.*"

"Believe what you want. I saw it with my own eyes. And I'm telling you…today's Palestinian, same as ever, would gladly die and march into Hell so long as he could drag two Jews behind him."

The president watched the debate, allowing his top-flight team to blanket the matter as he examined all sides. "That doesn't leave a lot of room for diplomacy, Warren."

"No sir. I'm afraid it doesn't."

"We can't turn our backs on the diplomatic option," Creedel insisted. "The Palestinians were satisfied for a long time, but now…well, we have to step in and get to the root of whatever new disagreement has arisen."

"You haven't been listening," Sumner said. "We're not talking about a 'disagreement.' There are no issues in dispute. There never were, and nothing new has brought this on. It isn't that the Palestinians have been *satisfied* for all these years… They were laying low. And they won't rest until Israel ceases to exist."

"All the more reason we must work with them to reach a peaceful settlement."

"I wouldn't bet on them being too open to anything we have to say. They hate us, too, remember? We're nothing but Zionists in their eyes, and through the terror factions they supply with weapons, they've attacked us again and again. We've seen *our* share of homicide bombers and bio-terrorism…New York, Kansas City, Miami…and if you'll recall, there was dancing in the Palestinian streets on Nine-Eleven and Ten-Seventeen."

"They'll listen," Creedel insisted. "With diplomatic pressure, we can restore peace and—"

"And what? Enforce a peace they don't want? Even if we managed to bring an end to Arab aggression against Israel and the U.S., they'd still turn on *themselves*. While I was over there, I learned a very old and closely held Arab saying: 'Me against my brother, my brother and I against my cousin, and the three of us against the infidel.' They unite *only* in the cause of fighting an outside enemy, and absent that, they wage war against each other. Tribal warfare is rampant, even now. You know that, John. They'll never come together in the name of peace. History bears that out."

The president took a sustained breath, then spoke on the outflow. "If our left-leaning friends heard you saying that…"

"I know, I know," he said. "But I saw what I saw, political correctness notwithstanding. Look, don't misunderstand me… Most individual Arab folks, away from the hotbeds, are as good and decent as anyone you'll ever meet. But there are way too many governments over there dedicated to sustaining the hatred, and there are too many leaders whose reputations depend on it. The agenda at work here is *thousands* of years old, and it thrives because the people hear only what their self-appointed dictators want them to hear. Lifelong indoctrination can't be overcome. We can only hope these regimes one day fall of their own weight, or are toppled, so some future generation can be spared."

"I don't agree," Creedel said. "Nothing's set in stone. Change can happen. Beneath the cultural veneer, we're all the same."

"Hardly," Sumner countered. "The differences go deep, in thousands of ways we'll never fully fathom. Why do you think there are no Arab democracies? Even when they *do* hold elections, they're a joke. Their leaders won't give the people a say in their own lives because they see it as an abrogation of power. We try too hard to force other cultures into the Western mold, to convince ourselves that all nationalities think as we do. They *don't.* Our way of reasoning is as foreign to them as theirs is to us."

"Mr. President," came a voice from the intercom. "Prime Minister Levi is ready on line one."

"Thank you, Lucy." Bridger looked at his advisors. "Here we go…" He pressed a button, and the speakerphone came to life. "Mr. Prime Minister."

"Mr. President," came a weary voice, heavy with age and wisdom. Sirens and chaotic cries could be heard in the background. "The explosions were missile impacts. Our radar detected their approach, but there was no time to stop them."

"Missiles?" a surprised Sumner asked.

Bridger leaned into the phone. "One moment, Zelle...we have a slight technical problem on this end." He hit the mute button, rose to his feet, and targeted his defense secretary with a piercing gaze. "Warren, you told me that our peacekeeping troops stopped a *ground* attack."

"They did," Sumner insisted. "Our boys said nothing about missiles. The report we received an hour ago concerned a raid into West Jerusalem. They blew a hole in the electronic fence with a shoulder-launched rocket. A force of maybe a hundred men stormed in...rifles and other small arms, but that was it. All but a handful were killed, and the rest fled."

The president returned to the phone. "Zelle, where did the missiles come down?"

"Here in Rehovot, and within a few hundred feet of each other. I suspect the city was targeted because I am here dedicating a new school."

Sumner pulled an encrypted netphone from his pocket and dialed his staff, urgency and anger in his eyes.

"Was the raid a diversion?" Brooks wondered. "What would be the point?"

Bridger, his mind working the puzzle, spun and looked without seeing toward the sun-drenched curtains of a window. "When did the attack happen? Have you gotten a casualty estimate?"

"The missiles struck perhaps fifteen minutes ago. They were loaded with a chemical weapon that"—his voice was lost in the roar and wail of passing emergency equipment—"your own Philadelphia. We cannot yet know for certain, but with the winds, we believe at this time that thousands may have died."

"Keragesin-D," Sumner concluded. "Bad stuff."

"Oh no," Varner whispered, putting a hand to her mouth.

"We tried but could not shoot them down. From the moment of first warning to the time of impact, barely ten seconds had passed. We got Arrow-5 interceptors into the air, but too late."

"Ten seconds?"

"Yes. We estimate a launch point in East Palestine."

Sumner gestured for attention. "We have confirmation of that," he said, passing along information as he was receiving it. "Triangulation verifies a twin launch from the southwestern quadrant of Ramallah. More precisely, from the parking lot of a mosque."

"You've got to be kidding," Varner said.

"Must have used mobile launchers," the defense secretary surmised. "And by now they're sure to have been hidden again. Judging from the radar, the missiles were too large to have been Sandvipers…"

"All the Palestinians *have* are Sandvipers," the woman protested.

"Which they got from *us*," Brooks pointed out. "Three administrations ago and still it's haunting us. Goodwill gesture, my eye."

Sumner went on. "Radar tracking indicates size and velocity consistent with Chinese CSS-12s. Thermal signature matches too. Single stage, solid fueled…range about 240 miles."

"Our pals in the East," Creedel said sharply. "Terrific. So much for the weapons-ban treaty."

"How did they get them in there without our knowing about it?" Brooks asked in frustration.

Creedel shook his head. "Any number of ways. Eighteen-wheeler, boxcar, whatever. We have no hands-on inspectors on the Jordanian border."

"So, the viper strikes," Sumner said, nodding to Brooks as he closed his phone.

The prime minister went on, his filtered voice haunting, closer than the other side of the world. "Almost an hour ago, there was a raid into West Jerusalem, as I'm sure you have heard. Your forces stopped it, Matthew, but not without casualties of your own."

"Yes, we know," Bridger said, his countenance hard and determined. "We lost twenty-two men."

"I am sorry."

"Thank you, but we can't allow them to have died in vain. What can we do to help you now?"

"Pray, Matthew…and let us do what we must."

"I promise you, my friend. You have that."

"There is something else. We have just received a broadcast message from the Palestinian leadership. They mean to repeat the attacks if we do not give them what they want, and they warn us that we can expect no help from the United States."

"That's ridiculous," Creedel said. "We're not going anywhere."

"Why would they say that?" Varner wondered.

"What is it they want, Zelle?" the president asked, leaning over the phone, head down.

"They want Jerusalem," the prime minister replied. "They mean to take it as their capital. They have demanded that we abandon the city and pull back to a line two miles beyond its western limit." A pause. "We cannot do that."

"I know," Bridger scowled. "What are your immediate plans?"

"If we send fighters across the border to knock out any missile sites we detect, there can be no going back. It will be war. Palestine is a sovereign nation, and Israel cannot stop until it has made itself secure. As for the moment, we are in a heightened state of alert but will take no military action before we have assessed the situation fully. I am headed back to the Knesset… We are convening a special session."

"All right, Zelle. Please keep us posted. We're with you every step of the way."

"Thank you, Mr. President." The phone went silent. Bridger pointedly hit the disconnect switch, dropped back into his chair, and for a moment allowed an ominous silence to hang in the room.

"Be ready, Warren," he said. "If full-blown war breaks out, we'll have to move on a moment's notice." He drew a breath. "Good thing we've distanced ourselves a bit from the Arab states, at least where oil's concerned. If Russia hadn't offered to meet such a large part of our import needs…"

"Thank Heaven for that," Varner said. "We'd have considerably less freedom to act, otherwise."

"So, Warren," Bridger asked, "let's say it escalates. If worse comes to worse, what do we have in the area?"

"The carrier *Reagan* is in the Mediterranean, but she's wrapping up six months of duty. Might be a good idea to cut the hitch a few weeks short and get a fresh crew on station. We can have *Ike* there in three days. We also have another two dozen strike fighters on the ground in Israel, along with the two thousand or so peacekeeping troops we keep rotating in and out."

"I'm issuing an alert. Do whatever you have to do to get everyone ready and in position."

"Yes sir."

Varner shook her head. "This makes no sense. The Palestinians don't have one-twentieth the military that Israel has, if that. Why risk a retaliation they know will come?"

"Maybe they're wanting to draw Israel into a war with the whole Arab community," Creedel offered. "Iraq tried that back during the first Gulf War by lobbing Scuds into Tel Aviv."

"I don't think that's it," Sumner said. "Militarily, Israel's as powerful as all the Arab nations *combined*. They'd hold their own and then some. And if push comes to shove, Israel also has the nuclear option, which the Arabs don't, and Levi isn't afraid to use it."

"Are we *sure* they don't?" Creedel wondered. "After all these years?"

"Iraq was the only one close to the threshold, and we took care of that. Just in time, I might add. There's been no sign that anyone else tried to pick up where Saddam left off."

"Maybe they ordered a little Chinese takeout."

"We have to make sure this never leaves the conventional theater," Bridger said. "We'll be there, ready to back Israel on the ground and in the air, and if they don't need us, fine. We hang back and let them fight the war. But we can't let this thing reach a point where a nuclear strike, however limited, becomes Zelle's only option…and we better pray the Arabs are smart enough not to try a nuclear strike of their own. Should that happen, Israel's 'Samson' policy will take down the whole region before the dust clears."

"Did you mean what you said?" Varner asked of Sumner. "About Palestine marching into Hell?"

The defense secretary nodded grimly, his lips tight.

"They know Israel will never give up Jerusalem," the president said. "They intentionally made an impossible demand."

"Why?" Varner asked.

"They're up to something," Bridger said. "They're setting the stage. Now we have to figure out for what."

4

I t had risen from the earth in 1924, a jewel set near the heart of the growing Manhattan theater district. Towering to a height of twenty-four stories, the Beaumont Hotel became a favorite of the art, government, and industrial communities and welcomed, during its fifty-seven-year career, the cream of the American cultural elite. George M. Cohan, Dwight Frye, and George and Ira Gershwin all spent time enjoying its lavish accommodations and unmatched service—as did, during the hotel's winter years, a young musician named Elvis Presley.

Outshone by the newer, taller, and more impressive structures that emerged during the latter half of the century, the red-brick hotel struggled for patronage and eventually was forced to close its doors. A succession of businesses made a home within its walls, but as the new millennium approached, it was abandoned and left a darkened, lifeless shell.

Later came talk of demolition as property values skyrocketed, and the obsolete structure was seen as a hindrance to the proper development of a valuable parcel of land. A tenacious and privately funded "Save the Beaumont" campaign, spurred into action by the elite of the city, spared the former hotel from destruction and resulted in its being designated a historic landmark. After a series of extensive renovations brought it up to code, the resurrected structure served as an apartment building for more than a decade.

A failed real estate deal left the building gutted when a new and ambitious renovation project was halted, and the place sat empty for several more years, awaiting a purpose.

Then, finally, came new life.

Margaret McCarthy stepped out of an elevator and into the halls of the beautiful facility, having left her top-floor office moments before. Walking the building always filled her with pride, and she felt akin to the captain of a great ship out at sea. She had been enraptured by the center. It was the heart of a grand and powerful entity, the national headquarters of the cause to which she had dedicated so much of her life, and it was an edifice worthy of such an honor. The place embodied style, warmth, and elegance, as well as functionality. It owed its beauty to a dedicated army of contractors, who had finished their work some eight years earlier, right on time and on budget. Upon completion, the building became the heart of the young organization, the flagship of hundreds of similar centers located nationwide.

She herself had overseen the final refit, taking command the moment the interior walls had gone up. Day and night Margaret had labored, creating a place that would affect the lives of countless stricken families.

Life Quality. The very name spoke of its mission, its devotion, its cause.

It was a place born of need, the culmination of a wondrous chain of medical events that had led to the curing of several debilitating diseases. Those marvels had brought hope to the childless and life to the dying, and Margaret felt honored to have been a part of it all.

"Good morning, Susanne," she smiled, entering the ground floor reception area. "How are you this morning?"

"Oh, Ms. McCarthy," the dark-haired nurse said, looking up from her clipboard. "Good morning. I'm doing fine, thank you."

"How's that husband of yours? When will he be back?"

"Much better, thank you. He'll be off the crutches in a week or two."

"You tell him for me that we've missed him around here. Computer techs like him don't come along every day."

"I will, ma'am. Thank you."

A girl in her midtwenties approached, a clipboard in her hand. Her striking features and dark eyes displayed her Saudi heritage. The long black hair she wore contrasted with the pale baby blue of her fashionable smock, which bore the organization's logo embroidered on its left upper breast.

"Yes, Leila?" Margaret said, addressing her secretary less cordially.

"I'm sorry to bother you, but I need your signature on this acquisition form."

The woman swept the clipboard from her, signed in the appropriate place, and immediately handed it back.

"Why wasn't this taken care of *yesterday?*" she demanded. "It's dated *yesterday,* and I remember telling you to get this placed *yesterday…*"

"Yes ma'am," the girl said. "But by the time it came down you'd already left the office and—"

"So it's my fault?"

"No ma'am. I'm not saying—"

"In this business, a day will kill you," Margaret said sharply. "The sooner you learn that, the better."

"Yes ma'am," Leila said weakly. "I'm sorry."

She turned and hurried down the hallway. Margaret watched her go.

"I swear," she muttered. "The help these days."

The nurse, well within earshot at her station, looked away and said nothing.

It had been only a couple of hours since Life Quality had opened for the day, but already the usual crowd had gathered. The building's basic layout was much like that of any medical facility, with waiting areas, private examination rooms, and small lounges for personal consultation. But rather than utilizing a sterile, hospital-like décor, its general atmosphere mimicked life and cordiality. Its higher floors, which took a luxurious approach to interior design, held national corporate offices, an executive restaurant, a private fitness center, and even a day-care facility.

Margaret walked into the cavernous lobby and main waiting area and took a seat in an inconspicuous spot. She liked to sit back, in the shadows as it were, and observe the smooth operation of the most crucial aspect of their services, the final interaction with the beneficiaries.

This room once had been the lobby of the Beaumont, and several of the hotel's old Art Deco touches, many of which had been accommodated by the new design, had been expertly restored to their original splendor. Soft, deep green carpeting covered the floors. There were no hi-def displays or scrolling news screens, nothing to tie the room to the outside world. Lush plant life lined the walls, with flowing waterfalls, fish ponds, and living murals lending an open, outdoor feel. An expansive domed ceiling held a simulated sky, with gentle moving images of windswept clouds and birds in flight. Gentle music and delicate floral scents filled the air.

"Barbara Norbert?" a counselor asked tenderly, walking into the waiting area. She scanned the seated dozens. A young woman, well-dressed and clearly of means, looked up from the baby carrier at her feet and lifted a hand in acknowledgment. The counselor smiled, walked over, and picked up the carrier for her. "Come with me."

As others watched, the women walked from the room and disappeared into the concourse beyond. A short time later the young mother emerged, tucked something into her purse, and headed toward the door. Her heels clicked on the tile flooring of the foyer, and she was gone.

Without her child.

Melissa Torrance entered her modest apartment, dropped the blue diaper bag next to the door, and let her keys fall to the floor. With its dark tan walls, worn carpeting, and northern exposure, the place had a certain gloom to it. But it kept the rain off and the cold away, and she could afford nothing better.

After sliding the deadbolt home, she switched on a table lamp, kicked off her shoes, and laid her son on a blanket on the sofa.

"Home again," she said softly, leaning over to kiss him on the forehead. "Safe and sound."

As she began to check Joseph's diaper, a blinking light across the room caught the corner of her eye.

Not again—

She had few friends and no family and had grown to dread that little red light. It always meant bad news.

"Now what?"

She pressed a button on the phone's cradle.

"Melissa Torrance, this is Hart Financial. Please give us a call at—"

She pushed it again and cut off the message, skipping ahead.

"Melissa, this is Dr. Kerr's office. I'm calling in regard to the payment we were promised—"

And again.

"Hello Melissa, this is Carolyne Melita. I'm going to be over your way tomorrow afternoon and was wondering if you'd like to get together for lunch. I'm ready to help…just let me know. You can reach me at extension 612. Bye-bye."

The messages ended.

"We were gone at most an hour," she muttered to Joseph, "and they just won't leave us alone. Maybe I should have let them turn the phone off last week. At least then we'd have some peace."

Melissa hung her coat on a rack next to the door and walked toward the kitchen, the call from Carolyne weighing heavily on her mind.

"Help me, she says," Melissa mumbled. "She wants to help me…"

The girl had tried to be a good mother, despite her limitations, despite the poor choices she had made. She was determined not to be like so many parents who took little or no part in the raising of their children. The majority, too busy and self-absorbed to become involved, relegated the rearing of their children to the self-christened "village" of local authorities, educators, and experts. But Melissa had been determined to do as her own mother had done and raise the child herself.

She recalled a newspaper article she had read the day before. Many parents, despite their tight schedules, managed to find time to generate and sell sexually provocative images of their children via the Internet. It was an activity that almost half of all Americans found not only "harmless" but beneficial—after all, sexual confidence was an important part of self-esteem, it was argued, and to be worthy of being looked upon in such fashion could only increase the child's sense of worth.

"I could never do that," she whispered, pulling a can of diet soda from the refrigerator.

Returning to the living room, she set the drink on a table and lifted Joseph from the blanket. Carrying him toward his nursery, she could feel him breathing and heard the odd little sound he always made in doing so. Joseph was not a healthy child. He never had been and never would be.

The whimsical mobile she had bought for him during his first weeks in the hospital hung over the crib, its black and white cows jumping colorful fences and moons. She laid him down, covered him up, and as he closed his eyes to sleep she stood looking down at him. The peace she saw there belied the serious conditions within, congenital conditions she had dealt with since his birth. So much was wrong—the child struggled in so many ways. His body was unusually large for his age, well above the curve. His enlarged heart was weak, his breathing irregular. His eyes were dull, lacking that brightness that should have shone from within. His brain activity was well below average for his age, indicating the neural deficiencies with which he had been born. He might never recognize her, they had told her. He likely would not live past the age of five, they had said.

He did not cry. He never cried.

What money she had saved before his birth was gone, spent on medical treatments that could only prolong Joseph's life, not cure him. She wondered where the boy's father was, a college student who had vanished as soon as she had told him she was pregnant. They had met in a coffee shop near the campus, and she had fallen hard for him, but her devotion, despite his words of assurance, had not been returned. She had fallen in love with him, but he had seen her from the start only as someone with whom to share a purely physical act.

Melissa had not aborted the child, choosing instead to raise him alone. She wanted the baby—*needed him*—needed someone to love who would love her back, someone who always would be there for her.

Her prenatal medical care had been almost nonexistent. She read a few books and did the things she thought she should do to ensure a healthy child. She did not drink during the pregnancy, was not a smoker, was careful with medications, tried to eat right, and got as much sleep as she could. When her condition reduced her ability to work the long hours required of her, she had been forced to leave her job as a waitress, as low-paying as it was.

After the baby was born, Melissa was told of his condition. The boy spent weeks in the hospital, his survival tied to one machine or another. Finally, when he had been stabilized, his mother had taken him home.

The weeks of treatment had wiped her out financially. Using her car as collateral, she had managed to secure a small loan to help with the expenses, but it was not enough and only slowed the monetary bleeding. She could not keep up with the payments, lost her car, and without its mobility was severely limited in finding a job. Without work, she could not afford childcare, and without childcare she could not work. Only the pantry of a local church had allowed her to keep her baby fed, and the kindness and patience of an elderly landlord had allowed her to stay off the streets.

A few months had passed. Joseph's condition worsened, and Melissa had become desperate.

Then, as if on cue, Carolyne Melita had contacted her.

The woman was with Life Quality. She spent time getting to know Melissa and worked hard to befriend her. The first call had come only three months after Joseph's birth, mere days after the girl first had brought him home, and a knock had come at her door each month since. It was always Carolyne who visited, and each time she treated Melissa to a meal, helped her get caught up on a few vital bills, and took her shopping at the supermarket, using her expense account.

Life Quality offered itself to the public—and more specifically, to the vulnerable and suffering—as a merciful, caring group, a fount of salvation when seemingly there was no other.

Melissa remained there beside the crib, watching her sleeping child. She gripped the rail hard, running her thumbs against its plastic sheath. She looked into his tiny face, her eyes wet, her heart torn by an ache she never had known before his birth. A part of her worried that he would stop breathing. Another part, one she hated and feared, hoped he would.

At least then she wouldn't have to choose.

Tears streamed down her cheeks, and she leaned on the railing for support, her vision curtained, trying not to cry.

Nor could Melissa see that she was being watched.

Cold, compassionless eyes scrutinized the girl's every move, as they had for almost two decades. Every word the girl had uttered, every action she had undertaken, every event she had experienced had been witnessed. The onlooker knew who she knew and remembered what she remembered, had accompanied her during her first day of school, had been there for her first visit to the zoo, had chaperoned her first date, and had been close at hand throughout the painful and sudden trial of losing her parents, gunned down during a robbery of their home. Melissa's undetected companion had watched as her baby was conceived, had stayed nearby throughout her pregnancy, and from a short distance had witnessed her seven grueling hours of labor.

And soon, the knowledge so patiently gained would come into play.

Two men sat silently in a quiet midtown Manhattan coffee shop, their minds on a shared goal, a common cause. They met there each day, their duty clear, their focus set.

They ate their lunch, watching the passersby flow along the sidewalks of the great city. Both scowled as their dark eyes tracked the oblivious masses. The overstuffed shopping bags they saw, the revealing feminine clothing, the decadent language of the citizenry disgusted them deeply. This was a hedonistic Hell on earth, a place deserving of divine judgment.

The men had dedicated themselves to that end, offering themselves up as vessels of destruction.

And soon, by their hands, the judgment would fall.

The plaque outside said *Sacred Child.*

Karen passed through a pair of bronze glass doors and into the national offices of the organization. The place was as modest as she had expected, clean and functional. As she crossed the lobby, the receptionist greeted her with a warm smile.

"Hello," said a dark-haired young woman barely out of her teens. "May I help you?"

"Yes. I'm Karen Foley. I'm here to see Ms. Webster."

"Oh yes. One moment." The girl pressed a key on her datapad and after a moment spoke into the microphone of the headset she wore. "Ms. Foley is here." She smiled, then closed the link.

"She'll be right with you. Please make yourself comfortable."

"Thank you." Karen moved toward a sofa that stood against one wall, walking slowly as she fingered the strap of her purse and looked at the painting that hung there. Its pastoral image was soothing and poignant— cloudless blue skies over a field of yellow and white flowers, among which a cluster of young children in white shirts, shorts, floppy sun hats, and summer dresses played.

In moments, before Karen could take a seat, a woman dressed in pale blue workout sweats and white sneakers emerged from the corridor. She appeared younger than her age of fifty-three and more fit than average. A matching blue terrycloth headband held back her mane of blond hair. As she drew near and their eyes met, Karen noted that she and the woman were of equal height.

She was Rachel Webster, the national president of the organization and a woman of vision.

"Karen," she smiled, approaching and extending a hand. "Please forgive my appearance… I just got back from a short jog around the park. Thank you for coming. I'm so glad you're here."

"Me too," she answered. "I'm sorry I took so long to get back to you."

"There aren't enough hours in the day, are there? Come, let me show you to my office." As she turned, she took note of a tall potted plant that stood in the corner, its leaves drooping and color poor. Pausing, she took a step toward the ailing flora and extended a hand.

"Can't we do anything?" she asked the receptionist, gently running her fingertips along one leaf. "It looks worse today than last week."

"I don't know," the girl replied. "I've been watering it and using the plant food. It doesn't seem to want to get better."

"Okay, call Herbert at the nursery. They're in the database. Maybe he knows something that will help."

"Yes ma'am."

Rachel led Karen down the hall and into a corner office. One wall was entirely hidden by a tightly packed bookshelf while another was dotted with framed family photos, diplomas, and personal awards. Sunlight streamed through one tall, narrow window in the corner, while its twin in the adjoining wall was half covered by a piece of corrugated cardboard, held in place by duct tape.

"It was a brick," Rachel said, noting the question playing subtly on Karen's face. "Or rather, half of one. Just yesterday. I came in and glass was everywhere. I suppose I should be used to it by now."

"A Halloween prank?"

"I wish it were."

"It happens a lot?"

Rachel shook her head. "Let's just say we're on a first-name basis with Ed's Glass and Storm Door Company. I think we more or less bought him a new truck these last few months. I don't know how to break it to him that we're considering going to Lexan." She gestured toward an inviting upholstered chair and, as Karen sat down, took a seat behind her desk, pulled off her headband, and fluffed her hair.

"Our group is young," she said. "Only three years, come December. We have offices now in New York, Miami, Atlanta, Charlotte, Dallas, Kansas City…more than a dozen others, with new ones springing up each month. Our people are dedicated and make sacrifices for our cause. And they're mobile. Anyplace we're needed, we're there." She paused, hope brightening her eyes. "I gather from your phone call that you've made a decision."

Karen nodded. "Ms. Webster, I've—"

"Rachel, please."

"Rachel…I've prayed about this a lot, and I feel led to help in this cause. I'd like to accept your offer."

Rachel smiled widely. "Wonderful! Oh, Karen, we're so happy to have you with us. Is there anything you want to know? Do you have any further questions?"

"No. I've researched the group quite thoroughly and learned what I needed to know. And your letters covered the matters of salary and hours and laid out the general job description."

"Then let me ask…what can I do for *you?*"

Karen was taken aback, and no answer came to mind. "For me?"

"Yes," Rachel said. "This is not going to be an easy job. As VP of public relations, you'll be the face we show the world. You'll *be* Sacred Child. When there are debates or interviews or personal tours, it will be *you* they see and your voice they hear. The position carries a great deal of responsibility. That's why I chose you."

"I meant to ask," Karen said. "How was it you came to think of me?"

"I saw you during an HHS briefing, fielding reporters' questions in the midst of the CloneTech scandal, and was impressed with your poise, your focus. You're a woman of strength and conviction. You displayed a determined yet sympathetic quality that's rare and precious, and it's something Sacred Child desperately needs. Most important, I came to know that you believe as we do…not only where the activities of Life Quality are concerned, but as regards higher, spiritual issues."

"Yes, absolutely."

"Excellent. That's crucial. Whoever speaks for this organization must share its heart and believe not only in what we are doing but in who we are."

"I do, but I don't recall ever having said anything publicly that would have expressed that."

Rachel smiled. "We know our own."

Karen nodded, understanding.

"As you know, we've taken a beating in the press. Life Quality has deep pockets and government backing, and their recent campaign has greatly damaged our image."

"Yes, I've seen their public service spots. Seems they run a hundred times a day."

"You'll speak for the rest of us with a voice of compassion and reason, and you'll carry our minds and hearts within your own. You'll help to open people's eyes, to make them realize the horror they've come to accept as beneficence. So I ask again…what can I do for you?"

Karen thought for a moment. "Let me make a *real* difference. My father… *He* made a difference. He was a doctor, a family practitioner in a little rural town, the place where I grew up. Barely a wide spot in the road. He was just about the only doctor the people in that part of the county ever knew. He saved lives and delivered babies, and the world is better for his having been here."

"You never considered going into practice yourself?"

"When I was a girl, I wanted to follow in his footsteps. I used to spend afternoons with him in his office, visiting with the patients in his waiting room and playing with the children if they weren't the ones who were sick. He used to call me his 'special little nurse.'" She smiled, then sighed. "But as I got older I realized that acting like a nurse or doctor and being one are two different things. Takes a special kind of person, I guess. I knew medicine wasn't my calling, and I didn't feel it would be right to pursue it for the wrong reasons. I thought government service might allow me to contribute something, so I came to Washington and worked my way up from intern. But even that never quite seemed to be what I needed. I know that may sound silly…"

"No," Rachel said. "Not at all."

"I've never really mattered, not like my father did. But now, with this…" She paused. "I *can* help. I want to do whatever it takes to make us heard…to convince as many as possible that life is precious and is *not* a commodity."

Rachel looked into the woman's eyes and smiled gently. It was exactly the answer for which she had hoped, for Sacred Child's struggle quickly was swelling into full-blown combat—and she knew the coming conflict would be a major battle in a war they could not afford to lose. The odds were poor—they were outmanned, outgunned, outbudgeted, and out of time.

And if they failed, millions would pay the price.

"Daddy!"

Jeffrey Lawe bent down as the child ran up to him and lifted his young daughter, Melody, into the air. She wore pink pajamas with teddy bears on them. "How's my little angel?"

"I'm fine, Daddy." She laughed, stretching her arms toward him before wrapping them around his neck in a loving hug. "Did you get the bad guys today?"

"Yes, sweetheart, we got the bad guys."

He locked the front door and moved into the den, the girl still clinging to him.

"Did you bring me anything?" she asked, giggling as her hands began to explore the inner pockets of his duty jacket.

He laughed, looking into her radiant little face. Her curly brown hair, brushed and held back by a blue satin scrunchie, shone in the lamplight. Her hazel eyes sparkled.

Jeffrey quietly reached into his back pocket, knowing the girl expected her trinket to be elsewhere. She frowned when her fingers found nothing, and he knew he must wait no longer.

"Like this?" he smiled, presenting her with a toy bracelet of silver plastic.

"Oh, Daddy, you tricked me!" she laughed, taking it from him and slipping it onto her wrist. "You're silly…"

"Where's my kiss?"

She puckered and gave him a peck on the lips, sugar as sweet as any. "Thank you, Daddy."

"You're welcome, honey," he said, lowering her gently to the floor. "Where's Mommy?"

"She's washing clothes," the girl said, running toward her room, totally preoccupied with her shiny new plaything.

Jeffrey walked through his New Rochelle house, stripping off his duty jacket along the way. After raiding the refrigerator for a cold drink, he found his wife, Brenda, folding laundry in the utility room.

"Hi, honey," she smiled. A brief kiss, and his welcome home was complete. "You're home a bit early," she said, looking at her watch. "It isn't even seven yet."

"The traffic was great," he said, setting his drink to one side so he could help with the last few towels. "It was amazing. I can't remember ever seeing it like that, not on a regular weekday."

Leaving the fresh laundry to be put away later, they walked back into the living room. It was comfortably decorated and furnished, with a rustic, almost western feel. Rich wood accents gave the room a warm, organic ambiance. A gas fire crackled in the fireplace, the false logs casting their orange glow. The high raftered ceiling increased the room's spaciousness. Photos on the mantel spoke of a closeknit and loving family.

As Jeffrey plopped into his favorite recliner and kicked off his shoes, Brenda took her usual spot at the near end of the sofa and rested her iced tea on a coaster on the lamp table.

"Supper smells good," he said.

"It'll be ready in half an hour. Nothing fancy."

"How was Melody today?"

"Fine. As soon as she got home from preschool, she cleaned up her room...but only after I threatened her with no TV for a week. She was good about taking her bath, though."

"Anything else happen?" the tired sergeant asked, wiggling his stockinged toes as he began to sort through the mail.

"Not too much," she answered. "Oh, I did hear from Samira this afternoon. She said they want to have us over for a barbeque party week-end after next. It's Ollie's birthday. They've invited Bry and Karen, too. And they have a snazzy new grill they're dying to try out."

"Sounds good. On the weekend you said?"

"First Sunday of November," she smiled. "At two o'clock. Don't worry…you won't have to miss the football game. I'm sure the guys will all be watching it."

"Good thing it isn't this coming weekend. I'm pulling the night shift again."

"But you did that *last* week," Brenda said. "Jeff, you were supposed to be on days for a while."

"Phil Conner's gone into the hospital for bypass surgery. He was on stakeout a couple of days ago when a heart attack hit. It was a mild one, but they need to take care of it, pronto. David and I are filling in. Should be a light weekend. Easy duty, simple surveillance. A cakewalk."

"It's been a while since you did that."

"It's like riding a bicycle," he smiled. "Without moving. And with coffee."

"I'll dig out the thermos."

He thumbed through a sporting-goods circular. "So…what will we need to bring?"

"What?"

"The barbeque…"

"Oh." She shook her head. "I asked, but she said they already had everything they needed, sides and all. They're fixing brisket, steaks, and bratwurst."

"Ollie knows me too well."

"I think I'll bring something, anyway. How about that three-bean salad you like?"

"I love you," he smiled.

"Well, I'm glad to hear that…because tonight, it's frozen lasagna."

5

L istening intently to his earpiece, Bryson Lawe ran along the pillared colonnade connecting the White House mansion to the West Wing.

"Iron Chef has arrived at Brady," came a voice. "We're ready for the go-ahead."

"Roger," Lawe responded.

A pair of guards at the south entrance waved him through as he flashed his identification and entered the double doors of the James S. Brady Press Briefing Room. Anxious voices buzzed in his ear as he made his way along, scanning the crowd of reporters before finally taking his position along one wall, opposite a row of windows that overlooked the north lawn. An agent near the rostrum discreetly nodded to him, verifying that all other security checks had been completed.

"We're clear," Lawe said into a tiny microphone. "The room is secure."

In moments, the president, clad in a dark gray suit and a red tie and carrying a single sheet of paper, emerged from the entrance at the front of the room, and the members of the press rose to their feet. He took his place at the podium, the familiar blue curtain and impressive oval seal behind him, framing the moment.

"Please be seated," the president quietly asked.

The reporters complied, their silence laced with anticipation.

"At nine-fourteen this morning, Eastern time, Palestinian army forces made a surprise raid on the western Jewish-held section of Jerusalem. Fifty-six civilians were killed, most of whom had been shopping in an outdoor produce market, and seventy-two others were injured in the attack.

Fourteen American peacekeeping troops also lost their lives. Fifty-three minutes later, a pair of ballistic missiles launched from within Palestine, struck the Israeli city of Rehovot. The warheads contained Keragesin-D, the same nerve agent used against the United States on Ten-Seventeen. At this time, Israeli estimates place the number of dead between six and nine thousand.

"I have ordered our forces in the area on alert. The aircraft carrier *Ronald Reagan* has been ordered to take station off the Israeli coast, and three thousand ground troop reinforcements are being sent in.

"The United States will stand with Israel. It is our hope that these preparations will be sufficient to deter any further attacks on the Jewish homeland, and that no war will erupt in the region, where a relative peace has endured for so long."

He turned abruptly and stepped from the dais as aides deflected questions hurled by dozens of reporters at once. The press secretary took the podium and tried to calm the gathered press.

Lawe made his way through the throng, joined his fellows, and followed the president out of the room. As they passed through the staff viewing room and into the West Wing, the shouts of the press faded behind them.

"Boys," Bridger began as they walked, "there's an old Chinese curse: 'May you live in interesting times.'"

Lawe smiled. "I just hope things don't get *too* interesting."

"Bry, how's that lady friend of yours doing?"

"She's well, sir, thank you."

"A lovely woman. Reminds me a lot of Mrs. Bridger at her age. My apologies for the interruption the other night."

"No apology necessary, sir, but thank you."

"Ed, how are we looking for the Camp David trip?"

The agent spoke up. "Fine, sir. Everything you requested is in place. Aspen is ready."

Everything meant big, healthy rainbow trout, which hopefully had survived the stocking of the pond outside Aspen, the presidential cabin.

"Very good...and I'll be wanting you fellows to grab some poles, too. I don't like to fish alone. What's the forecast for the weekend?"

"Sunny and cool. Cold at night, but still above freezing."

"Great. The fish will love it."

They reached a hallway junction and split off. The president, joined now by his special advisor, returned to the Oval Office while the bulk of the Secret Service men took a side corridor and headed toward their own office on the basement level.

Lawe paused to sip from a water fountain, then rose and wiped his lips with his thumb. A motion attracted his eyes, and as he peered through the open door of the press secretary's office he saw a woman in gray, the lines of her tailored suit emphasizing her curvaceous form. Her honey-blond hair hung to her shoulders and perfectly framed her oval face. Surprise swept Lawe as he realized that hair, those shoulders belonged to someone he had known for a long, long time.

Jacqueline Kelsey, his first real crush, his first love.

"Jackie?" As the woman looked up from her filing, her glossy burgundy lips widened into a joyful smile.

"Bry?" She ran up and hugged him, holding him tightly as if he were a dream that might vanish at any moment.

"I'd heard you were working here," she said, almost in a whisper. "Presidential detail, right?"

He smiled. "What about you? When did you start here? Last I heard from your dad, you were in the Ford Building—"

"Right...Representative Massey's office," she confirmed. "But then there was an opening here, so I tried for it, and here I am. Started just a few days ago."

"Here you are." He smiled at her, feeling fifteen again.

"I've always wanted to work in the White House," she said, as he looked into the depths of her ocean blue eyes. "But then, I guess you knew that."

"You only said so a thousand times," Lawe chuckled. He leaned lightly against the doorframe, struggling to keep focused. "Wow… How long has it been?"

"Almost fifteen years."

"Where does the time go?"

"I know."

"You haven't changed a bit," Lawe said. "You look great."

"Thank you," she smiled. "You do too."

An awkwardness filled the space between them.

"So," she asked, "how are things? Family? Picket fence? Dog?"

"No, no. I'm not married. I am seeing someone, though… She's a PR rep with Health and Human Services. Karen Foley. I don't think you'd know her."

"Oh," she said, disguising her disappointment. "No, I don't."

"What about you?" It occurred to him too late to steal a fleeting glance at her ring finger. Jacqueline, her mind replaying images of a certain date they had shared, was caught off guard. She and Lawe, throughout the high-school years, had been an item, but her career designs had superceded all else, and shortly after graduation they had gone their separate ways.

"Oh, me? No. I'm not," she said, visibly nervous. "Not at all."

"I find that hard to believe."

"Well, you know me," she smiled anew. "Miss Honor Roll, president of the Careers Club. Once I get where I want to be, maybe then."

"You're not there yet?"

"Not even close."

"So, where is *there?* The big chair in the Oval?" he smiled.

"We'll see." She laughed.

"How's your dad?" he asked. "I haven't seen him in a while." Her levity drained away, and the sudden change of demeanor surprised him.

"Fine," she said. "As far as I know." The woman went silent for a moment. "It's been a while for me, too. We don't much speak anymore."

Bry had crossed a line, and though the lapse had been inadvertent, he felt no less an idiot. "I'm sorry."

"Hey, it's okay," she brightened. "I'm sure he'd like to see you again, though. You should give him a call."

Lawe paused. "I will."

"Well, I really should get back to work. We've got a conference in New York tomorrow, and I have a ton of things to do." She looked upon him, memorizing him anew. "It's great seeing you, Bry."

"You too," he grinned.

"Hey," Jacqueline suggested, "maybe sometime we can go for coffee or lunch or something?"

"Sure."

She hugged him again, then turned away. Lawe continued down the hall, toward the stairs to the Secret Service office.

The woman resumed her work but was slowed by a lingering distraction. The office felt more quiet, more lonely, more isolated than it had only minutes earlier. She found herself turning her attention toward the open doorway.

Somehow it, too, seemed much emptier than before.

Melissa poked at her food, her mind cluttered with conflict.

It was lunchtime, and the restaurant was busy. It was a favorite place of the girl's, an informal family restaurant, one she could not afford despite its reasonable prices. Black and orange streamers crossed the ceiling and outlined the doors and windows. Tissue-paper ghosts, pumpkins, bats, and witches hung from strings, dancing as they caught the currents of the air conditioning. Here and there, children sat dressed in Halloween costumes, enjoying a holiday promotion.

"You've barely eaten a thing," her charming lunch companion observed with a voice rich in compassion. "Aren't you hungry, dear?"

"It isn't that, Carolyne."

The girl looked at her infant child, asleep in his carrier on the chair beside her. The baby's raspy breathing was audible to them both.

"Honey," the lithe blond woman began, "you have to look at what's best for all concerned. Please, let us help you."

"I don't want to lose Joseph."

"I know," she said, taking her hand across the table. "But if you and I can make a difference in someone else's life…well, that's what you have to consider. You can't support the two of you. You have no one to turn to, no way to get a job, and no chance for a future if things stay as they are. You know I've done all I can to help, but my hands are tied by a budget, and the baby will need more medical attention than you can hope to provide."

"I know." Wetness darkened her lashes. The girl had heard it all before, each visit more persuasive than the last.

"And the money will allow you to make a new start. Your life can mean something again. No one will be hounding you day and night, demanding one thing or another. You'll finally have some peace and be able to move on."

"I don't care about that."

"You should. It matters…your well-being, your happiness. You have the choice. It's your life, your future. We've fought hard to secure and defend your right to *make* this choice, you and all who are in your position. You deserve to be happy, Melissa. Don't throw away the fulfilling life you *could* have.

"I do so wish this wasn't something you had to deal with. I wish the baby was healthy and strong, but it isn't. Every specialist you've seen has told you the same thing. Five years at most…"

"I know!" the girl almost shouted, drawing looks from nearby tables. Realizing, she pulled her napkin up and dabbed at her eyes, composing herself.

Carolyne went back to her meal, allowing Melissa a few moments to think. In the months since Joseph had left the hospital, she had felt the girl's stance weaken with each discussion.

She just has to get past her feelings. Once she does that, she'll come to us—

"Are you sure?" Melissa quietly asked, almost in resignation, without looking up from her plate. "Are you sure it will make a difference?"

"Oh, honey," Carolyne smiled. "All the difference in the world. You're such a special and loving person…you can look beyond yourself and see that there are so many others out there who are hurting, who need the help that only you can give them."

Finally, she's starting to believe—

The girl looked upon the tiny face next to her. "I…don't know. I want to do what's right, but…" Her tears returned, and the woman handed her some tissues.

"Melissa, I know you're torn. Yours is a very difficult position. I can understand you not wanting to give up the child. I know what you're feeling. Trust me."

"What do you mean?"

"Well, I never told you this…" She paused, taking a cleansing breath as if preparing herself. "When I was about your age, just out of high school and still unmarried, I had a baby too. She was born, well, incomplete. I tried to help her, tried to get her the treatment she needed, but it was too much of a burden for me to bear. I didn't have the resources or the ability to help her the way she needed to be helped. I was all alone, and I knew the only way I could have a future was to turn to Life Quality for help. So one day I finally worked up the courage and gave them a call, and I left my baby with them."

"You really did that?"

"Yes, Melissa."

"How long did it…" Her voice became small. "How long did it hurt?"

"Just for a little while. Soon, I realized that I had done the right thing. My baby no longer was suffering, and I'd made a real difference in someone else's life. Everything turned around for me, and before long, the sense of loss had turned to joy."

Melissa looked away, wavering.

"Don't be afraid, honey," Carolyne said. "If you decide to do this, to take this bold step, I'll be right there with you. You won't be alone."

The girl looked away, choking back tears as the conflict raged within her.

"Did you…do you…ever regret it?"

"No, Melissa. Never."

Carolyne watched her, the gentle smile she wore belying the thoughts residing behind her beneficent facade.

It's only a matter of time, now—

Melissa began to eat her salad, her mind clearly still in turmoil. New doors had been opened within her, Carolyne knew, pathways she never before would have considered.

She had reached the girl. She recognized the signs. She had seen them time and again reflected in the eyes of those who could not find it within themselves to see beyond repeated, eloquent influences or to discern right from wrong.

She resumed her meal, letting Melissa come to a conclusion she would never have reached on her own. Carolyne's well-practiced and oft-spoken words—learned during her training as a Life Quality counselor—had planted seeds that not only had taken root but were beginning to thrive.

Carolyne Melita never had given birth to a child.

6

September Mall was a busy place and, as the holidays drew near, was becoming even more so. Built near the old World Trade Center plaza, its hustle and bustle had helped bring life and much needed normalcy to lower Manhattan. With time, wounds had healed. But scars remained.

Shoppers crowded the floors, driven by obligation as much as by love, moving from store to store as they searched for the bargains they were sure lurked just out of view. One customer after another jockeyed for position, rushing in their competition for the best deals.

No longer did the holiday shopping season officially begin on the day after Thanksgiving, a delay that cost weeks of valuable sales. It was the first Friday of November, and already Christmas music filled the air, piped in through speakers hidden in molded fiberglass boulders and sparkling plastic ice formations. Strings of twinkling lights made even the most mundane structural elements festive, throwing small pools of color against columns, walls, and railings. Joyful animatronic penguins and polar bears skated on artificial ponds at the center of each of the mall's five atria, surrounded by hills and bare trees encrusted with snow that would never melt. Glistening houses of popular legend rose nearby, busy workshop displays peopled by toy-laden elves and levitating reindeer. It was an indoor winter wonderland, the North Pole on steroids, a place easily torn from Santa's most intense fatigue-induced hallucinations.

Jacqueline, in town and on a lunch break, sipped a nutrition shake from a straw as she browsed the shelves of Page Me, a crowded, high-volume bookseller. The mall adjoined the hotel where the conference was being held, affording her the brief opportunity to visit a shopping venue she had long heard of but never experienced.

She scanned thousands of printed spines as she walked the aisles. About half the stock on hand consisted of microbooks—palm-sized, self-contained electronic texts featuring full-color illustrations and optional music and sound effects—while the remaining tomes were fairly split between audio books and conventional bound volumes.

The woman picked up first one item then another as she considered a gift for a friend, avoiding the newer technologies in favor of the bound editions that, for her, were more familiar. She once had loved the smell of bookstores, but that long cherished scent had changed over the years and, judging by her nose, the place might have been an electronics store.

"Well, Susan likes lighthouses," she whispered, thinking aloud, "but I gave her a book on those *last* year…"

A commotion drew her attention to the front of the store. Stepping into the aisle, she saw a pair of uniformed police officers pinning a young, handsome, well-dressed man hard against the side of the entry portal, while another knelt next to a young boy of perhaps five years of age. The man struggled while issuing loud and censorable protests. Curious, Jacqueline moved closer, weaving around customers who blocked her path. Other voices rose.

"…anything you say may be used against you in a court of law…"

"…told you not to move! Hands down…*hands down!*"

As the two lawmen struggled with the man, another did his best to comfort the crying, frightened boy, who had been removed to a point some fifteen feet away. His words carried a much different tone than did those of the other officers.

"We're not going to hurt you, Son…"

Jeff?

Jacqueline immediately recognized the officer. Dating his brother had brought with it many a visit to their home. A smile burst forth.

Small world!

She also recognized the object in his hand. It was a seeker, a localized tracking device sensitive enough to home in on the identichip of a given person at a range of some two hundred yards.

Identichips—subcutaneous implants, tiny and undetectable to the human eye, inserted using a specialized hypodermic injector. Tracked by the system's orbital sensor web, they allowed authorities to pinpoint the locations of abducted children, escaped criminals, and lost Alzheimer patients, among others.

Each chip, smaller than a grain of rice, also held medical records and sometimes more. Almost all children now carried one. The chips even had become part of the Social Security program, implanted along with each new number assigned to a minor. Successful child kidnappings had become a rarity.

So had personal privacy.

Jacqueline stepped forward, trying to see past the knot of shoppers. She and dozens of others watched the unfolding drama as the dapper man was taken into custody, his hands now bound behind his back.

"All right, folks," Jeffrey said to the crowd. "Go on about your business. Everything's fine here."

The lawmen did their work swiftly. Before Jacqueline could get Jeffrey's attention and say hello, the officers had escorted both father and son from the scene and were gone. All was as it had been, Christmas music and all.

"…here comes Santa Claus, here comes Santa Claus, right down Santa Claus Lane…"

The crowd dispersed with a few murmurs. As Jacqueline rounded an aisle, she noticed a large, half-empty floor display. Bright colors, clever graphics, and snappy text splashed its header:

THE BEST-SELLING VERSION

OF THE BEST-SELLING BOOK OF ALL TIME!

READ THE BOOK THE BIBLE WAS MEANT TO BE

THE LOVING BIBLE

IN MICROBOOK AND LEATHER-BOUND HARD COPY FORMATS

FINALLY, A FAITH YOU CAN LIVE WITH

She read the words, then reached out and picked up a copy.

"I remember when this came out…"

"Oh, you should get that!" a loud middle-aged woman said, stepping up beside her. "It's marvelous!" Her styled blond hair and provocative blue dress seemed better suited for a designer's runway than a bookstore. "I got a copy for Christmas last year, and you know, I actually read a good bit of it! I never knew how much God loved me until that hit the shelves."

"Is that so?"

"Oh," she replied, waving her long-nailed, precisely manicured hands in small, brief circles, "where to start? For one thing, it reveals the truth that, since there's no such thing as sin, God loves us just as we are. She's fully accepting of us, right from birth."

"*She?*"

"Well, when you read that, you come to understand that you have to visualize God in whatever form is most comfortable for you. Since she isn't a physical being, you have to give her a body so you can relate to her, one on one. Female or male, it makes no difference, though I think female works best. The Mother Nature thing, you know."

"Really?"

"Sure, it's all in there. Took years to write, and it shows. That book is *such* a blessing."

"What about all that controversy, back when it first came out? There were protests…"

"Oh, sure," the woman said, dismissing the thought, "but any time you try to drag the Bible out of the Stone Age, some people are going to react that way. Thank heaven there aren't as many of those nuts as there used to be."

Jacqueline bit her lip. *My father was one of those "nuts."*

The woman picked up a copy and tapped its cover. "This Bible got rid of all the dusty, outdated stuff. It makes so much more sense now."

She opened the book, flipped to John 3:16, and read aloud.

"For our creator so loved us that we were sent one of its most beloved children; and whoever follows his example in love and tolerance will know eternal joy."

"Well," Jacqueline said, "it's different."

"It even supports reincarnation, which, if you ask me, *has* to be true. My sister loves it. She's into everything spiritual...stuff like ghost hunters and Tarot cards and that man who talks with the dead. In fact, all of the more enlightened churches now teach from this version. Just about all of Europe does. I saw a thing about it on TV."

"Is that so?"

"I go to the Unitarian Universalist church on Brady Street, and it's the only one they use."

Jacqueline smiled politely. "I'll think about it. Thanks."

"Hey, anything I can do to get the word out," said the energetic woman, walking away. "That book made a huge difference in my life. You have a nice holiday, honey."

Jacqueline shook her head and took a breath as the woman disappeared. It was as if the oxygen had been sucked from the place.

Making no purchase, she left the store.

Randall Sullivan pressed the accelerator, rushing forward through the yellow traffic light.

"You barely made it," Janessa said from the passenger's seat. "If I had done that, you would have thrown a fit."

"You were learning then," he smiled. "You have to drive more carefully when you're starting out, pay more attention to the rules. Later, when it's second nature, you can develop your own…style."

"Style?" she laughed. "Is that what you call it?"

He watched the passing store fronts as they drove along. So much had changed—few of the places he once had frequented remained, and those that still stood had been remodeled within an inch of their lives.

"I used to go to movies there," he said, indicating an old facade that now fronted a market. "The Cherokee theater. Now *that* was a showcase. None of the digital stuff they have today, the glorified television that passes for movies. Good old film stock, with good old projectors shining on a silver screen… She was the last single-screen theater in the state."

"I know, Daddy," she intoned. "You've told me that story a hundred times."

"And I'll tell it a hundred more," he said, smiling softly.

"You do and I'll leave," she teased.

"I look around, and the world seems like such a crowded place now. Everywhere, even in the alleys and the out-of-the-way places. So many people."

"Stands to reason."

The light ahead turned red, and Sullivan stopped. As he sat, his fingers drumming the steering wheel in time to a song playing silently in his mind, he spotted a figure crossing the street a couple of car lengths ahead.

"Well, look at that," he said, pointing. "That's Jerry Calloway. Used to work with me at the distributorship before his accident. Drove a truck like mine…completely totaled it."

"I've seen him around."

"Well, I haven't. Wow… Good to see his face again."

"You want to follow and say hello?"

Sullivan shook his head. "Naw. Don't know what I'd say to him. Nice to see him again, that's all."

The light changed. As they moved on, Sullivan casually glanced into his side mirror and tried to catch a last glance of his former coworker, but he could not find him there.

"Good old Jerry," he smiled.

"When do you have to go on the road again?" Janessa asked, changing the subject.

"Not until the end of the month. It'll be a long tour, though. More than a dozen cities. Detroit, Portland, Kansas City, even Washington."

"Mind if I come along?"

"As if I could stop you," he laughed.

Clouds swept past overhead. Flocks of birds danced against the sky, the music of their calls small and distant. The steady whisper of a cool waterfall filled the air. Melissa, weary and cold, sat in the Washington, D.C., Life Quality facility. The zipper of her coat had broken, providing her little protection on the way there. Unable to reach Carolyne for a ride that morning, she had managed to scrape up enough money for bus fare, at least for most of the nine-mile journey.

The combination lobby and waiting area looked much like the one at the national headquarters, or like that of any of the organization's centers, for that matter. It was a grand oasis, a synthetic Eden, a place of natural beauty and tranquility that seemed disconnected from the world outside, crowded though it was.

Melissa took no notice of the splendor around her. Her eyes never left the baby in her arms. The infant's gaze, likewise, was unaffected by the things around him, locked in place as if fixed on some unmoving thing.

Do you even know I'm here? Does my face mean anything to you?

Even now she was unsure, working hard to convince herself that she had made the right decision. Carolyne's repeated words to her still echoed, carrying their compassionate authority, the weight of which finally had convinced her to make the call:

"There are so many others out there who are hurting, who need help that only you can give them—your life can mean something again—you'll finally have some peace and be able to move on—"

Melissa's thoughts were a fragmented jumble of conflicting emotions, with nagging, genuine vestiges of right and wrong still lingering in the shadows.

I love you, she thought, looking at Joseph, *but I can't be selfish about this—I have to do the right thing—*

"Melissa Torrance?" a voice asked tenderly, wedging itself into her awareness.

Cradling Joseph, she turned her head and saw a dark-haired woman in white standing a few feet away, datapad in hand. With a final look upon the serenity in her arms, Melissa slowly rose and followed the counselor, who first stooped to pick up the light blue diaper bag on the floor.

"Come with me."

The girl accompanied the woman through a frosted door of sculpted glass. Beyond was a wide circular foyer that served as the hub of a cluster of numbered consultation lounges. What looked like a nurse's station stood at the center of the concourse, behind which a corridor led to a bank of elevators.

The lounges were almost as extravagantly decorated as the main waiting area. Renaissance-style murals covered the walls, and healthy plants brought life to the décor. Each room featured a luxurious sofa, before which stood a low table of handcrafted walnut. A white file folder, resting there, contrasted with the dark, polished wood.

The counselor entered Lounge Six. Melissa followed and was directed to take a seat on the sofa. As she did so, the woman dropped the diaper bag onto the floor next to the couch.

"Hello, Melissa," she began, moving to sit beside the girl. Her voice was bright and loving. "I'm Lauren. Carolyne told me about your decision, and I have your file right here. She's so sorry she couldn't be here today. She did so want to be." The woman leaned forward and opened the white folder, revealing a stack of case reports much thicker than Melissa had expected. "I'm so happy you've chosen to let us help you to help others. After your call last week, we contacted a family in Iowa and told them of your decision, and they now have hope again."

The synthesized murmur of wind among tree branches sounded low in the background. The girl remained quiet, holding her baby tightly as she looked down at the folder. She made out her name there among the many documents, but little else.

"All of the arrangements have been made. In fact, the waiting family called this morning to tell us of the joy you've brought into their lives."

Melissa fought tears, but they began to stream anyway. She held Joseph tightly, subconsciously rocking him. She looked down into his dark eyes.

Please—see me!

Her voice broke slightly. "Where will he… I mean, who exactly is it who'll wind up with—"

"We can't release information pertaining to our destination protocols," Lauren said. "I'm sure you understand. Such things must remain confidential for your protection, as well as that of our benefactors. Rest assured that the child will make a crucial difference in the lives of others."

"He won't…hurt, right? That's what Carolyne said."

The woman shook her head and spoke softly. "No, Melissa. Not at all."

The tears came harder, running in warm rivulets, but still the girl resisted. No sound of sorrow escaped her lips. She looked up at the woman. "Are you sure that—"

"This is your voucher," Lauren said, abruptly changing the subject. "We've already placed a credit for ten thousand dollars in your account, which will be activated the moment you sign the datapad and relinquish custody. And now, if you would." She gestured toward the small, waiting screen.

"I'm not sure," Melissa said.

"Please, Melissa," the counselor said, her voice kind. "If you refuse, you'll doom a family to the grief of losing a child needlessly. Their time is running out. Your baby will die soon, you know that, and once that happens, it will be too late."

"He'll hurt."

"The child will feel nothing. I told you that. And it will help so many, in so many ways. It's a wonderful thing to be able to make that kind of a difference, and we're offering you that chance."

"But I'll miss him so much…" Her voice quivered.

"You mustn't be selfish about this, Melissa."

The girl said nothing and continued to rock her baby.

"You made a verbal pledge, Melissa."

No response.

"Listen," the woman said, gently but firmly. "Ten years from now, when you look back on this day, will you do so knowing that you could have prevented the death of a viable child but didn't? Or will you do the right thing, and one day look back joyfully, knowing that you saved a life? How many of us get the opportunity to do that?"

Melissa shuddered slightly, then leaned forward and picked up the datapad stylus. She could barely see. Slowly, with a shaky hand, she signed her name at the bottom of the screen.

"Excellent," the woman smiled, patting the girl warmly on her knee. "You've made the right choice, Melissa." She punched a code into the pad and entered a few other brief number sequences, then shut it off.

"As I mentioned," she said, reaching down to the file folder and handing the girl a half-sheet of paper, "this is for your records. I've entered the release code, so the payment is available to you as we speak. These funds are tax exempt, so don't worry about that. Just focus on getting things in order and moving forward. If you need any further counseling, we have a Web site that will allow you six months' access. It's all explained in the paperwork we'll be sending you."

Melissa did not hear her. Part of her mind, that which governed her maternal drives, was mortally sundered. Mired in denial, it sought refuge within itself, shutting down altogether. She became numb.

A woman in a nurse's uniform, having been summoned by Lauren's final datapad entry, entered the room and walked up to the girl.

"You are so brave to give so much of yourself to save another," the nurse said with practiced compassion. "Our tomorrow will be brighter because of you and others like you."

Bending low, she took the baby from his mother, slowly turned, and carried the child away. Melissa watched them go, feeling the emptiness, the weight now missing from her cradling arms. She had gotten so used to Joseph, to feeling him there, to bearing the tranquil, precious burden of his presence.

"Let me see you out," Lauren said, checking her watch.

Hugging her purse, Melissa rose and silently followed the woman back to the glass door, where a man in a black suit stood waiting.

"A happy life," the counselor said, taking the girl's hand for a moment. Melissa noticed the soft iciness. "As happy a life as you've chosen to give to others."

Lauren gave a final, smiling nod, then turned and walked away. The man in the suit, without a word, firmly led Melissa back through the wondrous lobby toward the exit.

"Jennifer Wylie," a voice sounded behind her, as another young mother was called beyond the door.

The man stopped and watched as Melissa walked past the inner door of the security foyer, through the final exit, and onto the sidewalk beyond. Once she had left the property and the doors had closed behind her, he returned to his station.

A biting wind arose on the streets, coursing through the wooded avenues of Washington. It had grown colder, the sun hidden by dark clouds. Melissa crossed her arms, pulling her coat closed. Dozens walked past, the fog of their breath at once carried away, their minds on their own lives, their own affairs.

For the first time in more than a year and a half, Melissa was not with child in any manner. She felt hollow and alone, suffering a gaping emptiness. She glanced down and found at the curbside a fire hydrant of gleaming silver, recalling that, when last she had seen it, Joseph had been hers and in her arms.

Cradling her purse as she had her child, she began to walk. Unseeing. Deadened. The doors and windows passed unnoticed. In a span of moments, the world had become a bleak place of loneliness, despair, and indifference.

The choice had been hers, and she had chosen.

Lauren Savage returned to Lounge Six, one final piece of business on her mind. Moving around to the side of the couch, she retrieved Melissa's diaper bag. It was a personal game she played, a way to break up the day.

With a hopeful smile she picked up the bag, opened it, and checked its inner compartments for anything worth salvaging.

Baby wipes, diapers, a bottle—all the usual things. Just once I'd like to find something of some value.

She carried the bag from the room, zipping it shut as she walked. Pausing at the nurse's station, she plopped the bag onto the counter and smiled at the woman on duty.

"Good afternoon, Judy," she said to the head nurse, an older woman nearing retirement. "How are you today?"

"Tired," she admitted. "I didn't get much sleep last night."

"What's the problem?"

"I don't know. I've just had trouble sleeping lately."

"Oh, not me. I can sleep anytime, anywhere."

"I wish *I* could."

"Check something for me, would you, dear?" Lauren asked in a sweet tone. "I need the dissemination schedule for the Torrance case. The mother completed the transaction a few minutes ago. It should be in the system by now."

The nurse pulled up a file and read from her screen. "Yes, there it is. Central has designated four recipients…bone marrow to Toledo, liver and kidneys to Seattle, neural samples to Berkeley, and eyes to Phoenix Medical. The rest goes to the national tissue bank." She paused. "My… looks like it was a big one. The body mass merits a level five subsidy."

"Not bad," Lauren nodded. "A nice, sizable return on our investment. Better than ten-to-one. Print up a hard copy and send it to my office, will you?" She leaned over the counter and dropped the diaper bag into a trash chute. "Here's another one. You'd think for once these empty-headed girls could manage to leave behind a datapad or a netlink or something, but *everything* they bring in here is worthless."

She returned to her office, where the next file sat waiting on her desk. Unlike the Torrance case, this one was a cloning aberration. Such had paved the way for the birth of the organization and now it thrived, supported by a citizenry that found valor in the act of putting its children to death.

7

B ry, how do you want yours?"

"Say what?" Lawe asked, his attention fixed on the unfolding drama. "Sorry, Ollie…what did you say?"

"Your steak. How do you want it?"

"Medium, thanks."

The game was getting intense. Late fourth quarter, with one team holding a slim two-point lead and the other driving for a score. Lawe glanced over as his friend took a pair of tongs and flipped the steaks on the grill, still holding the basting brush he had used on the brisket in the smoker.

They called him "Ollie," a casual take on his given name, Alija Al-Rashid. He was a Washington, D.C., police officer, one of the best. His record was spotless, his career filled with commendations and special awards. He once had taken a bullet for his partner—the fully healed shoulder wound bothered him still when the weather changed—but fortunately, as he was fond of saying, he had not been struck in his donut-dunking arm.

Ollie had been born in Lebanon, but at the age of three had moved to the United States with his parents. His family was Muslim and he had been raised as such, experiencing the difficulties that came with each new terrorist attack on the United States. He always felt it, the judgmental way the eyes of others alighted upon him whenever new visions of destruction filled the airwaves, but none of the accusatory looks ever had translated into action against his family, and for that he was grateful. His father and mother had died while he was still a minor, and he had spent his late teens living with an uncle. Life as an American was all he had known, yet still he had lived much of that life under a microscope. His voice, unlike his face, carried no trace of foreign origin.

"On the phone, I'm as good as Irish," he often teased.

Lawe and Jeffrey had met Ollie in college. Both considered him one of the finest men they had known, and his friendship was one they treasured, even on graduation day—when he had stolen their shirts, pants, and underwear at the last moment, forcing them to attend the ceremony in nothing but their caps and gowns.

"Medium coming up," Ollie said. "Man, that is one fine cut of meat."

"Make it well for me," Jeffrey said. "Burned, if you've got it."

"One chunk of carbon for Jeff," he smiled. "No problem."

"Touchdown!" Lawe called out. The others swung their attentions to the portable screen, which stood to one side on the large, covered patio. "Take that, Brockenfelt."

"No flags?" Jeffrey asked.

"Nope, not a one. And the kick…" A cheer went up from the three men. "It's good! Yes! Up by five with four minutes to play."

"You know," Jeffrey said, "if you'd brought the football we could've thrown it around a bit, like old times."

"I thought about it last night," Lawe said. "Then before we left, I forgot."

"Ah, well. No harm done. Bring it next year, though."

"Will do."

Meat sizzled and smoke rose, and with renewed hope on the gridiron and the promise of the feast to come, things were going well.

"Look at them out there," Brenda smiled. "Three kids and a football game."

The wives sat at the kitchen table, watching through a window as their men handled the time-honored masculine art of outdoor cooking. The rest of the food already had been prepared and sat waiting, covered in foil or plastic, on the kitchen counter.

"Your potato salad looks great, Karen," Samira said. "What are those dark things?"

"Raisins," she smiled. "I thought it might add a nice twist."

Samira, reserving judgment, replied simply, "Ah."

The sound of laughter and hurried feet echoed from the next room. "No running!" Samira called out, directing the warning toward the pack of children at play. "If you want to run, go outside."

The front door slammed.

"I guess they heard me."

"We can only hope."

"Melody is getting so big," Karen said. "It's hard to believe."

"Tell me about it," Brenda agreed. "She starts school next year. Only yesterday she was pulling up and learning to walk."

"Well," Samira smiled, "try raising a couple of boys. Under this expensive hair color is more gray than I want to think about."

They laughed and sipped from their tall glasses of iced tea, pausing as the conversation flowed around the corner and into the next subject.

"So, Karen," Brenda began, "does Bry know yet?"

"No," she admitted. "I took the job two days ago, and I haven't figured out the best way to tell him. He wasn't thrilled with the idea, and I didn't want to mess up the weekend if he objected."

"Would he be that upset about it?"

"No," she said. "I'm sure he wouldn't, but I thought it best to wait."

The table presented a bountiful spread, the bowls and serving plates largely concealing the checkered tablecloth beneath. As the children sat separately a few feet away, eating little of what had been dished out for them, their elders enjoyed good food, good company, and good conversation.

"Lousy gift touchdown," Jeffrey muttered, taking seconds on the brisket. "Who fumbles with three seconds left? Nobody, that's who."

"Well, it isn't the first time," Lawe said, "but usually you take a knee and that's that. Those bad snaps'll kill you."

"It did today," Ollie agreed. "So much for a two-game lead."

"It's early yet."

"Must we talk about football?" Samira pleaded. "Isn't there anything else? Something that lets us *all* join in?"

"Sure, hon," Ollie said, his tone apologetic. "What do you want to talk about?"

Jeffrey made a quiet whip-cracking sound with his mouth, and Brenda playfully slapped him. Lawe laughed, and Ollie tried hard not to.

"Well," Samira went on, ignoring them, "I don't know. Maybe..." She glanced over at the kids' table and noticed her son was only staring at his plate. "Eat, Milon. It's good."

"This potato salad tastes funny."

"Just eat it."

She returned her attention to her husband. "I'm sorry. Anyway, how did things go on the job last week?"

"Same old, same old," Ollie said. "You know what they say. Police work consists of long stretches of boredom and paperwork punctuated by moments of terror. Haven't had too many moments lately, though."

"Had a little run-in at the mall the other day," Jeffrey offered. "Some guy who had kidnapped his own son. Little boy, about Milon's age. Got an identichip lock on the kid and found them in a bookstore at the mall. Three of us went in. Went down pretty easy...the guy made noise, but that was about it."

"I wish that was as terrifying as it ever got," Brenda said.

"Now, it hasn't been too bad," Jeffrey said. "All these years on the force, and I've had only a couple if real incidents."

"A couple?" his wife came back. "Try thirty-seven."

"You keep count?"

"Only of the ones I know about."

The men exchanged amused looks.

"I hate those things," said Karen.

"What things?" Samira asked, glancing down at the woman's plate. "Deviled eggs?"

"No," Karen said. "Identichips."

"Why?" Brenda wondered.

Karen was silent for a moment. "It's like branding cattle, and anyone can know anything about someone who has one of those just by waving a reader at them. There's no privacy…no human dignity."

Lawe watched quietly, chewing his steak. He did not always agree with her, and this was one area in which they differed.

"They help find lost kids," Jeffrey said. "And old folks, when they wander off. I can't tell you how many times—"

"For now, maybe," Karen said. "Malevolence usually starts out that way. Something's meant to be beneficial, then someone twists it into a weapon."

"So what is it you expect to happen?" Ollie asked.

"What happens when we get to the point where *everybody* has one of these, and every one of us can be found at any time by anyone? When there's no place left to hide…"

"You planning on hacking a bank?" Jeffrey asked, casting an amused glance at those around the table.

"No," Karen said, quite seriously. "But things change. Governments, laws, the kind of rights people have…"

"You're worried about that Christian end-times stuff again," Lawe said. "You expect some monstrous world dictator to hunt down all the decent folks someday."

Karen glared at him. "It could happen, and things seem to be pointing to it."

"I believe in Jesus and all that," Jeffrey said, "but who knows what will happen down the road? It's all so unclear. I say we trust God to sort it all out."

"I never understood that, Jeff," Lawe said. "Why you became Christian. Ever since you dated that girl from Baltimore..."

"What can I say?" Jeffrey said. "She opened my eyes."

"Can we change the subject?" Brenda jumped in.

"All I'm saying," Lawe added, "is that it makes no sense for any one faith to claim exclusivity. Ollie and Samira here are Muslim, and so's a quarter of the world. Makes a lot more sense for *any* sincere faith to find God, assuming He exists in the first place."

"He does," Jeffrey and Ollie said in unison.

"Whatever."

"In any case," Jeffrey said, returning to the prior subject, "I think we can trust God with the future. Whatever is supposed to happen will happen."

"But look at the kind of world we've made," Karen said. "An abomination like Life Quality thrives while Sacred Child is scorned. There's such a thing as right and wrong, *serious* wrong, and we can't sit by while this kind of thing goes on."

"Well there's nothing you can do about it," Lawe said.

"I already have," she said, looking down at her plate.

"Have what?" Lawe asked.

"I accepted Sacred Child's offer."

Karen heard Lawe's fork clatter onto his plate. Dead silence filled the room. She looked up and found on his face an expression she seldom saw.

As if the move had been choreographed, the others rose and quickly carried their plates to the kitchen. Lawe and Karen continued their silent, visual debate for a few moments. Finally, he rose and left the room, headed outside.

Karen slipped on her sweater and followed, intentionally lagging behind.

Nice job, Karen, she scolded herself. *You could at least have waited for the drive home.*

She found him in the backyard, standing under a spreading maple. Leaves of brilliant red and purple surrounded him above and below, as many on the ground as still clung to their branches. A chilly breeze gently billowed her skirt as she slowly approached, her steps sounding in the cool grass.

"Why did you take that job?" he asked without looking at her, the question calm and deliberate. "I thought we discussed this. I thought you understood that it wasn't a good idea."

"How could I not, Bry? You know what Life Quality is. They deal in children as if they were—"

"I know what they do. But now you're going to get embroiled in the middle of this whole thing, and our lives are going to change. Day in and day out, you're going to get dragged into every single fight that crops up, and the stress and the mudslinging are going to change who you are."

"They will not."

"How can they *not?*" he asked, turning toward her. "I've seen it happen before, to guys I work with. Either they or their wives get dragged into this kind of thing, and before long it tears them apart. Breakups, divorces, whatever. It turns things upside down and eats away at everything else in their lives."

"It's only a problem because you...well, you don't..."

"What?" he asked, more loudly. "Believe in God?"

"Yes."

"We've been over this a thousand times. I'm glad you believe, and I'm glad it makes you happy. But I'm not you, and I've learned that the only things worth having faith in are the things you *know,* the things you can touch, the things that are solid and sure. I've never seen God, and He's never once bothered to introduce Himself, and I'm not going to waste my life waiting by the phone for a heavenly call."

"This isn't only a Christian issue," Karen said. "What that organization does is morally abhorrent. I *have* to try to stop it." She leaned close and took him by the arms. "Bry, all my life I've wanted to make a real difference, to make the world better for my having been here. With Sacred Child, I can do that."

"HHS helps people," he insisted. "And they pay better. *Lots* better."

"Is that what this is all about? Money?"

"No, of course not." He pulled away from her and walked to the trunk of the tree, then struck it hard with an open hand and leaned there. "Karen, I can't stand by and smile while you run off on some idealistic religious crusade. If that happens, I'm the odd man out, and you and I wind up going our separate ways."

"I'm not leaving," she insisted. "Are *you?*"

"You say that now. But what happens down the road when you have to devote all your time and effort to this cause? The deeper you get into this whole righteous-duty thing, the wider the gap between us grows and—"

"I'm not going anywhere," she reiterated, more firmly. "How do you think it's been for *me* these last four years? How many times have you had to cancel a date or leave in the middle of one because that phone of yours rang? How many times have I been the one on the outside looking in while you and your suit-and-tie buddies tended to business?" Tears filled her eyes. "I'm not going anywhere, Bry. I need you to believe me. If I can stay with you this long, through all that, at least you can do the same."

He softened. She saw it. His shoulders fell slightly, a motion that would have gone unnoticed by anyone but the woman who loved him and knew him better than anyone else.

He had made a decision. He turned toward her.

"I don't want to lose you," he said.

"You won't," she said again. "There *is* one sure way to keep that from happening, you know."

A subtle smile cracked his stern face. "Oh, sure. Throw that at me. Hit a guy when he's down."

Karen moved close and wrapped her arms around him. "When something's inevitable, you may as well sit back and enjoy it," she smiled.

"Yeah, well," he muttered. "I'm allergic to rice."

"They have shots for that."

"Wouldn't surprise me a bit."

They kissed and stood in the soft autumn air for a moment.

"By the way," Lawe said, softly caressing her auburn tresses. "I like your hair like that. Just down to your shoulders and turned under..."

"I was beginning to wonder if you'd even noticed," she said. "I haven't worn it this short since high school, and the highlights are new."

"I noticed."

They walked toward the patio, his arm around her. As they neared, they noticed Jeffrey crouching low, partly concealed by the grill and pretending to tinker with it.

"So, you on stakeout?" Lawe asked.

"Yup," his brother confessed in a flat, official tone.

He nodded in the general direction of the kitchen. "They send you out here?"

"Yup."

"You hear much?"

"Enough."

"Dangerous assignment. They paying you well?"

"I get ice cream when I give them my report."

"What are you going to tell them?"

"The yard needs raking."

"Might be worth a couple of scoops."

"Yup."

8

The wind howled as it usually did. The sound pierced the soul, freezing the spirit.

Yuri Druzhinin, clad in parka and snowsuit, peered through the multipane window, straining to discern a moving shape amid the swirling whiteness. It *had* to be there—the only alternative was unthinkable.

"Dmitri," he called into his handset radio. "Do you hear me?"

No reply came, only empty static. He pulled away from the frost-edged window and walked over to the fire, which roared angrily within its stony prison. Survey maps and geological charts covered the walls, their most vital elements noted in red by a hand that to most would have been illegible.

The station was remote, well north of Noril'sk, above the Arctic Circle. The outpost operated a single towering oil well, tapping into a reservoir small but deep and rich in output. The source consistently had provided up to twenty-two thousand barrels per day, feeding into a buried pipeline that carried its dark bounty south for refining.

The storm had moved in from the Kara Sea with amazing speed, trapping a dozen men at the drilling site a quarter of a mile away. Their last words had indicated some kind of trouble, but the specifics had been lost in transmission.

The fireplace splashed golden light across the supervisor's office and threw precious warmth into the room. The heating system was on maximum, yet the temperatures inside had fallen almost to freezing.

I hope the toilets don't freeze up again.

Temperatures beyond the insulated walls of the small building, a structure no larger than an American fast-food restaurant, had plummeted more than sixty degrees in a single hour, and Yuri cursed the weather office that had failed him and his men.

His second in command, Dmitri Sublova, had risked the wintry maelstrom in an attempt to reach those who were stranded. The Snowcat should have had little trouble navigating the winds and rising snows, assuming its instrumentation had guided it straight and true to its target. If Dmitri had strayed too far off course, if he had missed the drilling site altogether and plunged into a crevasse, he might never be found.

And if death had taken him, it also would befall the others.

Yuri returned to the long-range radio on the communications desk. Keying in a security code, he donned a headset and began to speak in his native Russian.

"Nozsterov Oil, this is Station Seventeen. Do you read me?" His voice carried a tone of buried panic. The response came after a moment's delay, an interval lengthened by fear.

"Go ahead, Seventeen," a voice said, filtered by distance and interference.

"Sublova has not returned. Should have been here more than twenty minutes ago. He is not answering my radio calls, nor have I been able to reestablish contact with the drilling site. There must be equipment damage."

"What are the conditions there?"

"Level four and growing worse. Down to minus sixty-three now. Winds sustained at eighty-four kilometers per hour…visibility zero."

"Understood. We estimate the storm's duration at another seven hours."

A reverberation swelled into Yuri's ears, cutting through the harsh whistle of the brutal wind, a deep mechanical rumble as sweet as any music. White light spilled through the window, casting his shadow on the map-cluttered wall. He dropped the headset and ran to the door.

The mechanical roar went silent. The headlights went dark.

He eased the door open, fighting the battering gale. Snow rammed its way through the narrow opening and struck him, spotting his heavy-rimmed glasses with opaque white. He felt the cold, even through the many layers of his thermal suit.

And then, voices.

Yuri backed away from the door in time for several dark, hulking figures to rush inside, their boots heavy against the hard, cold floor, snow falling from their hurried forms.

"Come in, Seventeen," pleaded a tiny voice at the communications desk, unheard within the cacophony of wind and hearty greetings that suddenly had filled the room. "Respond…"

Yuri embraced his fellow oilmen as they piled through the door and out of the perilous storm. Their faces, deeply reddened and almost frozen, were revealed as they stripped away the heavy woolen masks they wore beneath their fur-lined hoods.

Dmitri was the last one to enter. Putting his weight into the effort, he sealed the door against the icy air and found Yuri's outstretched arms. They laughed and patted each other on the back, celebrating the safe return. The room suddenly seemed wonderfully, gloriously crowded. Gloves were tossed aside. The blazing fireplace became the heart of the world.

"Something happened to our radio," Dmitri said. "I tried to contact you, but there was no answer."

"No matter," Yuri grinned, his weathered cheeks aglow. "You are here!"

As the men broke out bottles of vodka and gathered around the fire, Yuri rushed back to the transceiver. "Nozsterov…they are alive and well! All personnel have returned to base."

Dmitri pulled his gloves from his hands and huddled over the seated Yuri. "We managed a few final readings. It is true," he said, his voice suddenly grim as he confirmed a dread suspicion. "I don't know how, but it is true. There is no doubt of it."

"Did you get that, Nozsterov? Sublova says that—"

"We hear you," the radio voice said abruptly. "That confirms our findings. It is as we feared. Every site east of the Urals has been affected, and the others are showing early signs."

"Nothing," one of the men uttered, his voice shaken by shivers, his cold-numbed hands raised to the fire. "There is nothing down there. How can it be?"

The chill of night had descended, bringing a late November freeze that frosted windows sealed against the biting cold.

Lawe sat in his robe in the living room of his sparsely decorated apartment, sipping from a mug of hot spiced cider as news alerts played on his sixty-inch hi-def screen. Its light alone illuminated the room, casting jumping, flickering shadows as the images quickly shifted from one scene, one angle to the next. Coverage of an intensifying India-Pakistani conflict filled the airwaves—he flipped channels, checking the broadcasts of the various networks, hoping for something fresher than the hour-old information he had been hearing.

He expected his phone to ring at any moment but hoped it would not. It had been a long and trying day, and he was weary.

How could you go and take that job, Karen? Do you know what that's going to do to us?

As he flipped his way through the channel lineup, a familiar face suddenly filled the screen.

Karen's.

Not again—

She was pushing her way through a crowd of reporters, a cluster of microphones surrounding her. Lawe had become used to seeing that.

However, he was not used to hearing the words that now flowed so passionately from her lips.

"…and this organization is dedicated to saving the lives of all infant children, born or unborn, natural or cloned, healthy or unhealthy."

"Ms. Foley," one reporter shouted, "how can you associate yourself with a group as radical as Sacred Child?"

"Radical? I'll tell you what 'radical' is. 'Radical' is murdering millions of children a year and selling the body parts for profit. *That's* radical."

"But the government has stated repeatedly that—"

"The government is wrong," Karen insisted. "These are children with inalienable rights as valid as yours or mine, rights given them by God."

God—right.

Night after night he had seen her, but not in person. It had been only weeks, but already the job was taking her from him, making their time together virtually nonexistent. And when they *were* alone together, she was obsessed with this crusade, dedicated to a cause he did not share. A wedge was being driven between them in almost every facet of their lives—philosophically, spiritually, and socially.

I told you, Karen—I told you!

The news clip fell away, replaced by a shot of war protesters a world away. Lawe leaned back, shut off the screen, and tossed the remote onto the sofa beside him. He heard it bounce once and drop to the hardwood floor.

He sat there in the dark, staring into blackness.

"How bad is it?"

"Bad."

It was nearly midnight at the White House, but on the other side of the globe, it was midday and things were happening fast. Sumner and Creedel rushed through multiple security stations and into the situation room, a place few not directly involved at the uppermost levels of government ever saw. Located in the basement of the West Wing, its multi-paneled display provided a constant real-time flow of data from intelligence networks and government sources around the world. The president, his special advisor, and the vice president already were there, sitting at the conference table, their eyes trained on the largest screen. Images of war, all too familiar, played repeatedly, heralding an escalation all had feared.

"India just moved across the Pakistani border," Sumner said, having come directly from the Pentagon. "They've gone to nuclear alert, both of them. One mistake, one little spark, and the whole thing blows."

"Not three weeks ago, at the summit conference," Bridger said, "both countries assured the world at they'd reached a settlement and had avoided going to war. So what happened?"

"Someone looked at someone the wrong way," Brooks said.

The vice president, Harper Lund, shook his head. Only that night he had returned from the funeral of the Brazilian president and still was feeling the effect of so many hours in the air. "Doesn't take much," he observed, "not with the history they have."

Bridger scowled. "Both sides know that once the nuclear genie's freed from the bottle, there's no going back. Unless cooler heads prevail…"

"Unfortunately," Creedel said, "in that part of the world, cool heads are hard to come by."

The president pounded a fist against the table. "I'm tired of being the world's policeman, stepping in to break up every major fight that comes along. I don't want to drag this country into a war ten thousand miles from our shores, but I can't let a nuclear strike, or a series of strikes, destabilize an entire hemisphere. The fallout would carry who knows how far, and…" He looked to Lund. "Harper, get the House and Senate leaders to my office. Now. I want you there too." Then, to Sumner, "Get ready, Warren…looks like our DEFCON status is about to change."

As Lund rose and headed for the door, a red phone rang. Its shrill tone commanded the attention of all in the room, for it was a direct line linking the White House to but a few other world leaders, used only in cases of emergency. Lund paused in the doorway.

Bridger took a deep breath.

"This can't be good," he said, moving toward the phone. "Must be Nuhasa, warning us to stay out of it."

"His finger's on the button," Sumner agreed, referring to the Indian prime minister. "And I don't doubt for a second that he'll push it."

Varner, nearest the phone, picked it up as Bridger approached. After listening for a moment, she looked into the man's steel gaze.

"It's the Kremlin," she said with some surprise. "Premier Desderov."

He scowled and took the receiver from her hand.

"*Ivan* must be nervous," Sumner quietly commented.

"He's not the only one," Creedel said.

"Bridger," the president stated flatly into the secure phone. "Yes, Vasily, we're watching too." He listened, and with each passing moment his expression grew more grave. "No, we've made no moves as yet."

He closed his eyes and rubbed them. As his hand slowly fell away, he stared at nothing.

"How is that possible?" Anxiety soaked the room. "Even the fields you leased in northern Iraq?" As he listened intently, every eye was on him. Moments passed, their weight increasing by the second. "What are your options? Is there anything *we* can do?" He shook his head, then nodded after a moment. "I understand. When does it go into effect?" His shoulders fell slightly as he exhaled sharply. "All right, Vasily. We'll do what we can on this end. Thank you for letting me know."

Bridger dropped the phone into its cradle and turned to address the others. His expression had grown more grave, less certain.

"Russia and the allied states have halted all oil exports," he said. "Effective immediately. Their supply has become critical… It's dropped seventy percent in the last eleven days, and *still* it's decreasing. They no longer have enough to meet their own needs, let alone those of other countries."

"What?" Creedel asked. "I'm no expert, but a nation's entire oil supply just doesn't dry up that fast. And Russia's a big place. They drill at so many sites that are so spread out, they're tapping thousands of isolated reservoirs. They *can't* all be depleted at once. It's impossible."

"Be that as it may," Bridger said, "it's happening. Their national reserve will sustain them for less than a year. Our imports, like those of every other country they've been selling to, have been cut off indefinitely."

"Japan's going to scream bloody murder," Sumner said.

Bridger returned to the table, stood alongside, and watched the screens, his thoughts torn in multiple directions.

"Terrific," Creedel said. "You can bet the Saudis will know about this within the hour. And when that happens, we'll be getting a call from them, informing us that the rules of the game have changed."

"What about Israel?" Varner asked. "We'd better give them some kind of assurance that—"

"First things first," Bridger said. "We have to stop financial panic in this country before it starts. Unless one of you has a better idea, I'm going to open the strategic reserve. That should keep both Wall Street and gas prices stable until we've had a chance to get a solution into place. Things are going to be hairy enough with the news out of Pakistan. Second, we've got to find another source of oil." He looked to Creedel. "John, find me *someone* who'll deal. Anyone but the devil. Those Russian imports represented almost forty percent of our crude supply."

"That's a tall order, Mr. President, if by the devil you mean OPEC."

"I know the odds aren't good, but do your best. If you have any overseas favors hanging out there, call them in." He paused for a moment. "And third, get Nuhasa on the phone."

They departed the situation room. Sumner and Creedel headed for their own offices to gather the materials they would need for the assembly. The vice president returned to his office and summoned the congressional representatives Bridger had asked for. In the moments following the president's issuance of the order, however, much had changed and there now were not one but several critical reasons for the meeting.

Varner followed Bridger into the Oval Office and took a seat close beside his desk. As the president took his own chair, he glanced at his watch and sighed. The woman glanced up from her datapad and noted his discomfort.

"Sir?" she asked.

"Oh," Bridger said, "I missed dinner and my stomach is reminding me." Taking his chair, he reached for the phone and pressed a button. "Lucy, would you please have a chicken-salad sandwich and a root beer sent in here?" He looked to Varner. "Rhonda, you want anything? Midnight snack?"

"Oh no, thank you, sir. I grabbed a bite a short while ago."

"Just the sandwich and root beer, Lucy. As quickly as they can manage it... No, make it wheat this time. Thank you."

Bridger ended the call, and with a deep breath returned the handset to its cradle. "It's going to be a late one, Rhonda..."

No sooner had he leaned back in his chair than the phone rang. Varner, closer to it now than he, reached over and lifted the receiver. Her expression immediately went sour.

"Mr. President," she said, "it's the Saudis. Prince Alarubi."

"I could've set my watch by that."

9

I t was quiet, and within that quiet lived pain. No music played, no television, no radio.

Such was not proper during a time of mourning.

Melissa stood on tiptoe in her kitchen, reaching up to place the last of her groceries into the cabinet. Food was no longer a problem, at least for the moment, and she had fallen on it as a source of comfort. Her weight was up a few pounds, but not so many that it was obvious. Thanksgiving was only days away, and she had bought just enough to provide herself with the trimmings she had missed since being on her own. A small turkey roast, instant stuffing, a can of jellied cranberry sauce, a deli container of green bean casserole, and a pumpkin pie would make a sumptuous feast for one, and she tried to look forward to it, hoping it might invoke pleasant memories.

A glance toward the back of the high shelf revealed a partially hidden can of baby formula, one she never had brought herself to throw away. Seeing it was unpleasant, but abandoning it, in her mind, was worse.

She closed the cabinet door, wadded the plastic grocery bag and dropped it into the trash. Reaching for a cup of hot tea she had prepared, she walked into the living room—but not without taking a glance down the hallway, toward the closed bedroom door that haunted her. She had not entered Joseph's nursery in weeks, not since her visit to Life Quality, and still could not bring herself to do so.

How long—when will the pain go away?

She was not sleeping well, at most a few hours a night, and the lack of rest was taking its toll. Physically and mentally she was exhausted, and even the simplest tasks tested her. The inner turmoil she fought to suppress kept her drained, taking such effort that she had little mental energy for anything else. Life seemed to have lost its flavor, its color, its purpose.

I had to do it—it was the right thing—

As before, the attention of another was on her—watching, learning, preparing. She was unaware of the eyes that saw, the ears that heard. Nor did she suspect the fact that a plan had been set in motion, an ancient and proven strategy, a subterfuge of imposing scale of which she, unwittingly, was a part.

The silence of the room was broken as the central heat came on, its airflow quietly rattling the ducts. Melissa took a seat on the sofa, sipped her tea, and stared absently through the glass of the patio window. The sky was clear, the wind cold. The sun hung above as if adrift in the crisp air, carrying little warmth but sharing its light with a world well along the path toward winter.

Her mind drifted back, as it always did.

Joseph—

She saw his unresponsive face, felt his weight in her arms, and missed him more than she had thought possible.

But I had to do the right thing—

A sudden noise snapped her back into the moment. She listened. Something coming from the patio. Motion, uneven and repeating, a cause for concern.

What is that?

She set her tea on the table and rose from the couch. Cautiously moving to stand beside the window, she leaned out as far as she dared, trying for a better angle on the doorstep.

The sound came again. She moved to the door, placed her hand against it, listened, then peered through the peephole. She saw no one.

"Who is it?" she quietly called out. No answer came.

Melissa reached for the doorknob, unlocked the trio of deadbolts, and

slowly pulled. The door creaked as inch by inch she peered outside, seeing no one still.

Again, the odd little noise.

She opened the door wider, felt the cold against her cheeks and heard
wind-driven leaves skittering across the lawns and driveways of the complex. Leaning out, she peered in the direction of the sidewalk but saw no
one there, either.

"Hello?" she called, her hair tickling her nose in the sideward breeze.

The sound repeated, startling her, drawing her attention down and to
the side.

A juvenile bird, a blue jay, sat huddled near the wall beneath the
window and largely concealed by a hand-painted, ceramic flower pot.
Hatched unusually late in the year, it was still young but old enough to
have gained its crest. Melissa leaned down and the bird looked up at her
in naive silence, its glistening eyes black and innocent and unafraid.

It moved again, an awkward flutter that threw it against the wall.
Melissa crouched low and saw that the fledgling's left wing was deformed
and incomplete, incapable of flight.

"Oh, you poor thing," she said, her voice soft and heavy with compassion. "Can't you fly?"

She knelt next to the bird, ignoring the cold that fogged her breath
and watching the helpless creature. It shivered slightly.

"Aw, are you cold?" she asked, not knowing what to do to help. She
began to consider her options. "I can't just leave you here. If you stay on
the ground, Mrs. Dauber's cat will get you for sure. Maybe if I get a
shoebox—"

She was interrupted and startled by a series of shrill squawks. Looking up, she saw another blue jay just a few feet away, atop the wooden
patio fence. It glared at her, crying out again and again, fluttering its wings
and raising its feathers in an attempt to look as large and menacing as
possible.

The mother.

She carried on, confronting Melissa, unafraid, fighting to protect her fallen baby—despite its physical flaws, despite the great size of the apparent, looming enemy, despite the insurmountable odds.

And then, for the girl, it all came crashing down.

She began to weep, filled by the enormity of what she had done, the horror of the choice she had made.

The doorbell rang, something it did not often do, and the chime was followed quickly by four raps of knuckle on wood.

Richard Kelsey set his book aside, rose from an old, comfortable chair, and made his way to the front door. Upon opening it, he was met by a smile he had not seen in years, a welcome one.

"Bryson Lawe," he smiled, pushing the screen door open. "As I live and breathe. It's good to see you. Come in."

"Hello, Uncle Rick," Lawe smiled, stepping over the threshold. "I'm sorry to drop in, but I was in the area…"

Kelsey extended a hand in greeting, placing his other on Lawe's shoulder.

"It's been much too long, Son," he said as they shook hands. "What, five years or better?"

"About that."

They passed through the entry foyer and into the living room. Kelsey gestured toward a couch half covered with books and old newspapers. "Please forgive the housekeeping of an old man. Helen used to do the tidying up around here. If it doesn't jump up and bite me, I tend to let things lie."

"No, it's fine," Lawe said, looking around as he took a seat. He spotted a shadow box on one wall, framing a display of American coinage and paper currency. "Cash money," he pointed. "You know, after my years in counterfeit investigation, I don't miss that stuff one bit. One less thing to worry about."

"I *do* miss it," Kelsey said. "There was something about feeling that jingle in your pocket and having those bills in your wallet. Those"—he indicated the display—"were from the last minting of each denomination. Two of each, front and back. Dimes, nickels, tens, twenties... I miss them all."

"Well, I don't miss having to deal with ATM's and long lines. Hated that when I was a kid. Thumbplates are so much easier."

"And sterile," Kelsey noted. "Impersonal. Nothing tangible, nothing you can stick under a mattress. Now, it's all just...*electrons.*"

Lawe nodded silently. "The house hasn't changed much. Nice to see a familiar place."

"I never was one to tamper with perfection," the old man smiled. "Can I get you something to drink? Tea, coffee...?"

"No, I'm fine for now. Thanks."

"Just let me know."

"You have plans for Thanksgiving?"

"Not sure yet. I'll probably just watch the parades on TV, then the game. Might grab a bite somewhere."

"Why don't you come to my place?" Lawe asked. "We'll have more than enough, and we'd love to have you."

Kelsey smiled. "I'll think about it."

"You look good," Lawe said. "Working out? Keeping fit?"

The man held up his thumb, turning it from side to side. "Look at that...a hundred reps a day with the remote. A more muscular thumb you'll never see."

Lawe laughed. "I've missed that sense of humor."

"How's Jeff? You guys still the terror of the Chesapeake?"

"Not so much," Lawe smiled. "We haven't been fishing in a good while… I don't think we've taken the boat out all year. He's doing great, though. Has a little girl now. Melody."

"That's wonderful." The elderly gentleman lowered himself into his chair. "So, what brings you around?"

"Well," Lawe began, "I've missed talking to you. You were always…" He paused, searching for words. "Lately, I've had a few things happen in my life, and I need to talk to somebody."

"I'm right here."

"Thank you. I know I used to come to you a lot, back when my family was going to your church, right after we lost my dad. Got so I felt closer to you than to either of my *real* uncles. Seems I was always welcome here, no matter what. It was pretty rough back then, and having you to talk to really helped."

"I miss your father," Kelsey said. "He was a good friend…knew him for almost half my life. And your mom… What a special lady she was."

"I know," Lawe smiled, recalling their faces as he often did. "I just want you to know what it meant to me to have you there. You always listened."

"Doesn't take much to do that."

"Oh, yes it does. And you made a real difference in my life."

Kelsey smiled softly. "Well, Son, thank you for that." He took a sip of his iced tea.

"I ran into Jackie a few weeks ago."

The man looked down and away, his expression one of quiet regret. "How is she? Doing well?"

"Yes, she looks good. I'm sorry, I don't mean to dredge anything up. I know you two have had your differences."

"No, no. I'm glad to know she's all right."

"Actually, it was she who suggested I come to see you…and as I thought about it, I came to realize how much I'd missed your counsel."

Kelsey smiled. "Well, tell me. How can I help?"

"I'm having a problem. Involves someone I've been seeing. Her name's Karen, and I've known her for about four years now. She's done a few things that, well, it's like there's a wall going up between us. I'm afraid she's going to drive us apart, and I don't want to lose her."

"What kind of things?"

"Well," Lawe went on with a sigh, "at first, it was great. She was so much fun to be around. I could always count on her to brighten my day, no matter how rough it had been. But then, about three years ago, little by little…" He paused, gathering his thoughts. "Things started to change. She met this woman who got her involved in a church she was going to. Next thing I knew, every other word was about Jesus."

Kelsey had heard this before, many times. "New Christians usually are pretty vocal about it, but they tend to settle down in time."

"She has."

"And you don't share her faith."

"No, I don't."

"Do you love her?"

"More than I can say. And that's what scares me…there's this chasm between us that wasn't there before, and it's getting wider. Her interests have changed, and we don't do the things we used to. And now, on top of everything else, she's gotten mixed up in that Sacred Child group."

"How so?"

"She's their new vice president in charge of PR."

"Indeed." The man paused a moment, considering. "You haven't supported her in this or otherwise tried to share the things that are important to her?"

"It isn't that easy," Lawe said. "I'm not Christian, and I don't see the problem with Life Quality. And before she discovered religion, she really didn't either. For me to pretend to, even for her sake, would be a lie. I don't want a relationship based on lies."

"If she went so far as to join Sacred Child, Bry, her convictions must run pretty deep. I'd imagine she's *always* had a problem with Life Quality's activities."

"If she did, she never said so."

"Son," Kelsey said after a pause, "when two people find themselves growing apart, it's often because one has moved forward and the other hasn't. Or one chooses a path that the other refuses to follow. I know you've always blazed your own trail. If there was so much as one wheel rut on a road, you wouldn't go that way because someone else already had. You're quite proud."

"I guess," Lawe admitted. "I do okay on my own. Call it self-reliance."

"No, no," Kelsey said. "*Pride* is something very different. It places a man on the throne of his own life, and—"

"Nothing wrong with that. I like being in control. I'm doing fine."

"Sounds to me like you're about to let a good woman get away." Kelsey removed his glasses and tapped them against his knee. "What Karen is undertaking is valuable and necessary. Life Quality is an atrocity, plain and simple."

"Plenty of people disagree. A lot of great things have been accomplished due to their efforts."

"As soon as they opened that Pandora's box and allowed cloning for medical research, they started down a road no one had the wisdom to leave. One thing leads to another, and before long, you end up where we are now."

"Where we are now," Lawe repeated. "It helped *you,* didn't it?"

"Yes," Kelsey admitted, his expression grim. He spoke more slowly, more deliberately. "That was one of the justifications they gave, at the outset…the curing of Parkinson's. They did their research and found the key they were looking for, and I was healed. But the price was too high, Son." He rose from his chair and went to the window.

"I wake up each day, and I see the sunrise. I watch the birds and the clouds and the children playing…and I realize that the only reason I'm

still here, and not in a pine box under a hillside, is because so many innocent lives were taken on my behalf."

Lawe furrowed his brow. This was something new.

"I knew where that cure had come from," he went on. "I sat back and
watched on the news each night as each new medical breakthrough was
announced, and I buried in the back of my mind the actions behind each
advance…all because I wanted *the cure*. I knew they were killing children
in the name of research, but despite everything I believed, everything I
held dear, I let them wheel me in there and heal me. I was so sick. I'd left
my church because it had gotten so I couldn't even serve at the pulpit on
Sunday.

"When they finally got approval for the treatment, I was one of the
first in line. I convinced myself I needed the cure so I could get back to
my ministry, back to my *good work*. I convinced myself I needed to relieve
my wife of the burden of caring for me. But above all else, overriding
everything I was, everything I stood for, I wanted to be whole again and
free of the pain. And ever since…" The words died away.

"I never knew," Lawe said. "I'm sorry."

Kelsey shook his head. "Don't be, Bry. I walked into it with my eyes
wide open. I knew what I was doing. But once the disease was gone, I came
to realize I could never dare to speak for God again. Not after that. I bene-
fited from the blood sacrifice of innocent children. I even *embraced* it."

"What other choice did you have? You would have died."

"Only physically, Bry." He turned from the window. "Ironic thing is,
since that day, I've died thousands of times over. Every time the sun comes
up in the morning or a bird sings or a cloud passes overhead or a child
laughs."

"Do you still believe?"

"In God, you mean?" Kelsey asked.

Lawe nodded.

"Yes, Bry, as much as I ever did. That's never been in question."

"Then why do you still feel that way? Don't you think He's forgiven you?"

Kelsey drew a deep breath and crossed back to his chair. "He forgave me *once,* Bry, for *everything,* knowing full well every moment of my life, from birth to death. It isn't something that has to be repeated or something that applies only so long as I do what I'm told. *His* forgiveness isn't in question here."

"But then…"

"His isn't, but mine *is.* For as long as I live, I'll know the kind of man I was when the time of trial came. Whether I can ever forgive *myself…*I don't know."

Lawe had no response for that, seeing for the first time the depth of sorrow within the elderly man. He allowed silence an uninterrupted moment. "I want you to know I'm sorry I never shared your religious convictions. But that never changed how much I valued your words. Jeff and I both… You've always meant so much to us."

"Seems he'd come to a faith in God, if I remember right."

"Yeah, he did. And I'd imagine you were partly responsible for that."

"No," Kelsey said. "I was just a messenger. One of many, I'm sure."

"I know you tried to convince me, too. But Uncle Rick, I can't see it. Even if there were some kind of life after death, in whatever form, it couldn't depend on us, on what we believe. How can opinion be a basis for destiny? If there is a God, or some kind of cosmic intelligence or whatever, then it has to be something *all* men attain whenever the time comes. I mean, surely the billions who never believed in Jesus weren't lost because of that."

"Why not?"

"Well, because it would make no sense. If they're decent, loving people, why make them suffer forever just because they believed differently? Even the pope once said that Hell's only a state of mind…that sincere believers of all faiths will find God."

"I remember that," Kelsey almost whispered. "He was wrong."

Lawe smiled wryly. *What other response could you have given?*

"It all comes down to one thing, Bry," the old man said. "And I want you to remember this always. If it were a matter of man reaching up to God, of finding our own way, then yes…all faiths would be equal, with many paths laid by many men. But it isn't. The barrier separating us from God is one we cannot broach; it is a gulf we cannot cross, not on our own. He had to reach down to us, by a method of His choosing, and because of that, we're given only *one* path to Him. One way, one truth, one life." He smiled. "*One,* Bry."

Lawe listened politely. "In any case," he said, "I guess we'll know for sure some day."

"I guarantee it," Kelsey agreed. He walked over to the fireplace and paused to wind an antique clock on the mantel. It was a beautiful object of wood and brass, with intricate, reverse-painted glass panels depicting towering mountains and proud sailing ships. It was a fragile piece that once had crossed the American prairie by covered wagon, yet had survived.

"But back to your problem," he continued. "For Karen, this isn't just another cause or a means to an end. The reason you love her, the reason you cherish the compassion you find within her, is the reason she had to get involved. For her, and for all who are involved in Sacred Child, there is no difference between stopping Life Quality and stopping a man from gunning down kids in the streets. It's a matter of life and death, with helpless children the victims. That's why it's such a heartfelt issue."

"But it isn't a matter of killing kids," he insisted. "No one would stand for that. If it were, I'd be behind Karen one hundred percent. This is different. Those who are taken to Life Quality aren't viable. Cloning mistakes, most of them. Genetically defective. They're going to die anyway."

"We're *all* going to die anyway."

"You know what I mean."

"And you know what *I* mean. You can't subdivide people with carefully contrived labels like 'viable' and 'nonviable.' Truth isn't determined that way."

"They aren't just labels. These children have things seriously wrong with them. They won't live anyway. We might as well use them to heal those who can be healed."

Use them?

Kelsey dropped his head.

How many times have I had this conversation—?

"Bry," he said, "that kind of thinking led to the original abortion debate, back when. People stopped believing that all human life is precious. Too many people began to value life using the criteria of real estate...*location, location, location.* While the baby was still inside the mother, he was only so much tissue and subject to her desires, a part of her body with no intrinsic humanity of his own. But move that tissue two feet to the left at birth, and suddenly he's a person."

"That's not the same thing."

"Sure it is. We all have a right to survival, whether we're unborn or genetically imperfect or a hundred years old. Lots of old folks aren't 'viable' and can't get by without a respirator or constant dialysis, but they have the right to live."

"They're adults. They've lived full lives."

"So, you're saying that having the right to live is determined by the length of one's résumé?"

A subtle smile crossed Lawe's face, and he waggled a finger at the man. "Now I remember why I stopped coming to see you."

"Just holding up a mirror, Son." The old man shook his head. "You know, it's amazing. After decades of devaluing life and ethical responsibility, we have the nerve to wonder why we live in a society where, every day, kids are stalked and killed on playgrounds. People are gunned down in schools and in churches and on street corners. The ailing elderly are encouraged to end their lives at state-run termination clinics…"

"It's *merciful*. They're allowed to choose not to endure the pain anymore."

"And sometimes the choice is made *for* them. In either case, it's the same horrifying mind-set put into play at the other end of the life cycle."

Lawe saw a sadness in those ancient blue eyes.

"You know, I barely recognize this old world anymore. And it all happened so fast. Didn't even wait for the handbasket." The sadness became tinged with resentment. "We've dug our own grave, and now we have to lie in it."

Lawe remained silent, words failing him. Kelsey took a deep breath and held it for a moment. He exhaled sharply, his expression softening into a smile.

"Well, Bry, sounds to me like you have a fine lady there. One worth fighting for."

"She is."

"Then I'd say you have a decision to make." The former pastor rose to his feet and placed a warm hand, softened by age, firmly on the man's shoulder. "You came here for guidance. Here it is. Give her all the support you can and be there for her. But also give her room to do the things she has to do and thank God He saw fit to give you someone with such clarity of vision. Her kind are few, and you are blessed."

"Mustard and pickle on mine, please."

Rachel took the first hamburger from the café window and passed it to Karen.

"My treat," she smiled, touching the glowing thumbplate atop the register.

"Well, thank you," Karen said, taking the sandwich. "But tomorrow, lunch is on me."

"Deal."

After choosing a couple bottles of water, the women took a seat on the covered patio.

"The food here is great," Rachel said, setting a small shopping bag aside. "I don't eat here a lot, though. It's a guilty pleasure of mine."

"There's a pizza place I feel that way about."

"What are you and Bry doing on Thursday?"

"For Thanksgiving? Staying in, at his place. His brother's family is coming down from New Rochelle, and Brenda and I get to do the honors. She's bringing the turkey and I'm doing the sides."

"What's his brother do?"

"Police sergeant in New York City. Almost ten years on the force."

"Sounds like it runs in their family."

"I guess it kind of turned out that way. His father was an engineer, though."

They watched the passing pedestrians and traffic and enjoyed their food and the cool autumn breeze. Across the street a stand of trees rustled gold and red, dropping leaves on the manicured lawns.

"What about you?" Karen asked. "Any family?"

"A little brother. He still lives back home in Minneapolis." She patted the plastic bag. "This microbook's for him, actually. Birthday present. An adaptation of *Treasure Island*—he loves that story."

"What does he do?"

Rachel paused. "Nothing. He's had cerebral palsy all his life and lives in a care center. I try to get back there every chance I get, but the opportunity doesn't come up as much as it used to. Which, at the same time, is a good thing. Means we're getting something accomplished here."

"I'm sorry."

"Don't be. I'll be seeing him right after Christmas. His birthday's New Year's Eve. We'll have a nice visit."

After sipping from her bottle and glancing around, Karen inhaled deeply.

"I adore this time of year," she said. "It's lovely. Even more than spring, I think. The smell of burning fireplaces, the cool air, the colors… everything."

Rachel nodded, her expression betraying distant thoughts.

"What is it?" Karen asked.

"You mentioned New York, and it brought to mind, well…" She paused, glancing around to make sure she would not be overheard. "I need to tell you about something, but for right now it's just between us, okay?"

"Sure."

"Next spring, in April, Life Quality will be celebrating its tenth anniversary. I got wind of a big celebration they're planning, tied into an advertising campaign. Tremendous coverage. A media blitz, nationwide. Could undo all the good we've done."

"What can we do?"

"I've been thinking about that. It's only preliminary right now, but I'm planning a mass protest on their anniversary. We bring in representatives from every one of our offices in every state and gather in front of the Life Quality headquarters in New York."

Karen smiled. "That way, we can use their own publicity against them…get more coverage than we ever could have managed otherwise."

"Exactly. Protest signs, the works. We set up some information booths and print up a lot of handout literature. Even if we bring in only a few hundred people, we might make a difference."

"Wow," Karen mused, "Margaret McCarthy will have a royal cow."

"I promise you, it will be a day that woman will never forget."

10

P atience."

"All these years we have waited," said the dark bearded man, watching the street beyond the coffee shop window. "Now is the time."

His compatriot, seated across the table, spoke in a low but urgent tone.

"Recklessness is their undoing," Khalid pressed. "Allah's time is his own... We act as he directs us."

"Yes, but—"

"He has provided the means and the opportunity, Ahmed. Soon the time for action also will be given us...and here, in the heart of the city of corruption, his wrath will be felt."

They studied the scene outside. Glittering stores and restaurants lined the bustling avenue, amid which, just across the street, the Life Quality headquarters was nestled.

"There," Khalid said, pointing. "The finger of Allah will touch their world just there...and they will know his power."

The crowd was huge, much larger than she had expected.

Melissa squeezed her way through the open double doors, past those who stood milling about, and into the grand ballroom of the Washington Imperial Hotel. Scanning the crowd, she located an empty seat only a handful of rows from the podium and took it. The hall was abuzz with

the voices of the faithful, those who believed and had come in the hope
of receiving evidence in support of that faith.

She peered around. The thousands surrounding her wore excitement
on their faces, anticipation in their eyes. They came from all walks of life,
all financial stations, all religions and races and cultures. In their diversity,
however, one common thread linked them all.

The death of a loved one.

Melissa looked up at the wide domed ceiling, at the glittering crystal
chandeliers, at the draped golden fabric that lined the walls. At the front
of the room was a raised platform, some three feet high, on which rested
a luxuriously upholstered chair. Next to it stood a side table, and on it a
pitcher of ice water and a single drinking glass.

The room was cold. She pulled her coat closed.

The lights in the room dimmed. The murmur of the crowd diminished, and in moments a large man in a dark gray suit ascended a trio of
steps and took the stage. As he reached the center of the platform, a lone
spotlight flared to life, gently bathing him in its warm glow.

"Welcome," the man said. "We hope you all had a good Thanksgiving holiday, and we're happy you could join us." He raised his hands
in a dramatic gesture. "We're here today to unlock the greatest of all mys-
teries through the blessed revelations of a man like no other. You've seen
him on the news, you've heard his words, you know his story. Beyond
your initial applause, I would like to remind you to refrain from speaking
as he begins. As was mentioned outside, no photography or other forms
of documentation will be allowed during the session. Please remain in
your seats, and should our esteemed guest call your name, please stand.
He will not take questions, but he will pass along every message he
receives, so please be patient.

"And now, ladies and gentlemen, I'm honored to present a man
whose extraordinary abilities have blessed us all—"

Applause filled the room, a standing ovation, cutting off the introduction. A security man opened a side door, and after a dramatic pause a lone figure emerged. Dark but graying hair, early fifties, the lines of trauma etched into his visage. Slowly, and using a cane, he made his way up onto the stage, eased himself into the chair, leaned his walking stick against the table, and took a deep breath as if in preparation.

He looked out over the crowd, waiting for their thunderous praise to die away.

"Thank you," he said quite simply.

His talent was unprecedented. His following was vast.

His name was Randall Sullivan.

The man looked to one side and found his daughter there as always, standing in the shadows near the stage, smiling silent words of encouragement. He nodded at her, ready to begin.

The gathered faithful took their seats, and silence returned to the room. Sullivan scanned the audience, watching and waiting.

And then, as always, it happened.

Scores of people rose from the crowd, seemingly out of nowhere, their eyes fixed upon him. They moved closer, leaving no empty seats behind them. In orderly fashion the men and women approached the stage, gathering in the shadowy area beside it. Several mounted the platform, as many as space would allow, and filled the dais to Sullivan's right. Their demeanor was one of great patience.

It began. One man broke from the silent group, stepped alongside Sullivan's chair, leaned down, and whispered in his ear.

"Rebecca Carter," Sullivan called out. A woman a dozen rows from the stage slowly stood, her quivering hands over her mouth.

"There is a box on the shelf of the guest bedroom closet," he said. "A blue shoebox with white lettering. Inside, along with several old letters and postcards, is an insurance policy of which you were not aware, in the amount of $750,000."

The woman began to cry.

The figure leaned down and spoke again. "Oliver loves you very much," Sullivan relayed, "and wants you to move on without him…wants you to be happy." She smiled, wiping her cheeks. "Thank you for coming, Rebecca."

Trembling, she sat down. Those nearby looked at her with reverence, as if she had been set apart. Blessed.

On stage, the first figure silently receded into the shadowed group. At once, another approached.

"Marie Johanssen," Sullivan called, as further words were whispered to him. Another woman rose to her feet. "When you and Jonathan drove up to Maine last year, you stayed at a bed and breakfast. Your husband, even then, knew his time was short. He taped the key to a safe-deposit box to the underside of a dresser drawer in your room, hoping to keep it hidden from his business partner, who was trying to seize control of the company. That box contains information and documents that will give legal ownership to you." She smiled tearfully, clearly overwhelmed that her beloved was contacting her. "Thank you for coming to see me today, Marie."

Another figure, another message.

"Bruce Wilmet." A tall balding man near the back of the room rose to his feet. "Your brother, James, is not happy that you sold his house. He had wanted it to go to his son once the boy had grown old enough. You must make it right. Thank you for coming, Bruce."

The man, both elated and embarrassed, sat back down.

Again and again the mysterious figures walked up to Sullivan and imparted words to be shared with one of those present and eager to hear them.

Sullivan had not always possessed this extraordinary ability. Some called it a blessing. He considered it a burden.

It had begun on Ten-Seventeen.

Swept away and trampled by the panicked mass, he had lain there on the floor of the stadium concourse, pain wracking his body, calling out weakly for his daughter. For almost an hour he had remained there, unable to move, drifting in and out of consciousness as blackness threatened to engulf him.

Finally, he had been taken by ambulance to a hospital, his back almost broken, his leg fractured, his head swimming in the throes of a concussion. As he recovered, he became aware of the masses who crowded the emergency and recovery rooms of the hospital, spilling out into the hallways, filling the nooks, the crannies. Oddly, they never seemed to be in the way—none of the hospital staff ever asked them to step aside or to leave the critical treatment areas.

And soon, noting Sullivan's eyes upon them, the strange visitors surrounded him, intent upon being heard, all insistent, all frantic.

All dead.

He could see them, could hear them, could converse with them as easily as one might chat with a friend. He saw them everywhere, lurking amid the living, unseen and unheard by all.

With one exception.

He doubted his sanity but chose to rely upon his senses, his mind, his will. He did not *feel* insane. He quickly decided he was not.

As the days and weeks slowly ticked by, the recovering Sullivan carried on conversations with persons the doctors and nurses could not perceive. His gentle insistence on their presence prompted great concern in the medical staff, who submitted him to brain scans and a battery of tests but found nothing unusual.

He came to realize his senses had been opened to a new level of reality. As the days passed, he learned to keep his mouth shut about it, denied it, and told the doctors he no longer was suffering the delusions they feared.

He did not want to end up in an asylum, after all.

His convalescence was slow and painful. Physical therapy and heavy medication made him miserable. Finally, he was allowed to return home. No longer could he manage his truck route or handle even moderate physical labor.

His options were few, and he had to eat.

Carefully, he began to share the fact of his newfound gift with others, those he trusted not to think him mad. Word of mouth carried the news beyond his small circle of friends and relatives, and soon the curious and the grieving were traveling great distances to speak with him. Others had claimed the ability to communicate with the dead, and some even had made a living of it, but most possessed a talent not for the paranormal but for cold reading and sleight of mind. Never before had anyone transcended the spiritual boundaries with such precision, such clarity, such certainty.

He willingly gave of his "gift," but only for a modest fee. Initially, though his bank account did not rise appreciably above the levels it had known during his years as a route driver, it kept the bills paid and the wolves at bay. But as his popularity grew, so did his income and the demands upon him.

He coined a new label, dubbing himself a "transmortalist," and local news coverage and Internet exposure further widened his circle of influence. More scoffed than believed, but his uncanny specifics persuaded many.

The world suddenly seemed much more crowded to him, for he saw the dead everywhere—in supermarkets, at gas stations, on city streets, and in movie theaters. They walked the neighborhoods, rode the buses, browsed the shops, and did all the things they had done in life—at least, those things their noncorporeal forms still would allow.

And now they spoke through Sullivan, passing along words no one else could hear. He had become their conduit, their link with the natural realm.

The session drew to a close. While the man would not take questions, he shared a few things, speaking on behalf of himself.

"Lots of people ask me about the afterlife," he said to his audience.

"They want to know what awaits them. What does God look like? Light…brilliant, comforting light. Is there a Hell? Well, I can tell you one thing… I've spoken with thousands of folks who've passed on, and not one of them was on fire."

The crowd laughed with a measure of relief.

"No, my friends, when we die, we *all* cross over into a wondrous place of peace and contentment. Trust me…I have it on good authority." More laughs. "There is no judgment, no condemnation, no pain. We become one with the essence of the Great Designer and are sustained by that divine light for all eternity." He stood, his weight on his cane. "Our time has drawn to a close. Thank you for coming."

The applause was loud and loving. The awestruck audience rose to its feet, and the thunderous praise continued until well after the man had departed.

Outside, the dark overcast skies had burst, and it had begun to rain. Icy drops splashed against Sullivan's shoes and pants legs as he crossed the parking lot and approached his leased luxury car. It was difficult managing both an umbrella and his cane while also fumbling with his keys—they slipped from his grasp and with a sharp sound hit the wet pavement.

"Here," he heard as he began to stoop to retrieve them. "Let me help you." Out of nowhere a young blond woman in a red coat appeared, bent down, and picked up the key ring.

"Thank you," Sullivan said.

"Mr. Sullivan," she began, handing him the keys, "you don't know me, but please…I need your help. I have to know if someone—"

"I'm sorry, Miss, it doesn't work that way."

"I lost my baby," she went on. "My son…"

Sullivan paused and looked at her. The rain fell against her face, her hair. He handed her the umbrella.

"You lost a child?" he asked, sympathy in his voice. "I'm sorry."

"Yes. My *only* child."

"Listen, I'd like to help you, but I'm not sure that—" He stopped abruptly as a figure appeared a few feet away, seemingly coalescing out of the rain. A young man in his early twenties. His hair was dark, his build full and strong.

He spoke to Sullivan.

"You're Melissa," the transmortalist said. "Melissa Torrance."

"Yes," she replied, her eyes widening.

The ethereal figure spoke again, whispers she could not hear.

"The boy's name is Joseph," Sullivan said. "A mobile of cows jumping fences hung over his crib."

Melissa gasped, her hand shooting to her mouth.

"He's here, Melissa."

She began to cry. "He's telling you this? But how? He was just a baby."

Sullivan smiled. "His spiritual form is not that of a baby, but of the strapping young man he was meant to be."

"But he was sick...so sick..."

"Not anymore. Not on the other side."

"What does he look like?"

"Dark hair, brown eyes. Good-looking boy."

She felt a faint glow of maternal pride. "Does he have a message for me?"

"He wants you to know he misses you and your life together."

Melissa glanced around, seeing no one. "He *knew* me? He never seemed to—"

"Of course."

She choked back tears. "I have to know...please...does he *forgive* me?"

"Forgive you?"

"He knows what I mean."

Sullivan looked to the figure, whose gaze fell away. No words came forth, no reassuring gesture. Then, to Sullivan's surprise, the figure shook his head.

"I'm sure he does," Sullivan lied.

"What did Joseph say?"

"Well," Sullivan began, wanting to spare her feelings, "he said…"

He paused as the figure's expression became menacing. Sullivan had seen that look before. He had learned to be careful in passing along the words of the dead, for casual visits could quickly become enraged hauntings were he to speak words other than those he had been given.

"I wish I could help you," Sullivan said. "I need to go." He unlocked the car door and pulled it open.

"Please," Melissa implored him. "Tell me. I *have* to know. Does he forgive me?" She turned, speaking to a son she could not see. "Joseph, please? I love you! Can you forgive me?"

Again the figure scowled and silently shook his head.

"I'm sorry," Sullivan told her. "I don't think so."

Melissa's countenance fell, overtaken by new pain. She handed Sullivan his umbrella and walked away, taking no apparent notice of the rain soaking her nor of the cold.

"Would it have killed you?" Sullivan asked Joseph with some contempt. The figure of Joseph remained silent and vanished before his eyes, like dust swept away on the wind.

"I'm sorry, Melissa," the transmortalist called after her, above the rain. "Are you all right?"

Giving no sign that she had heard him, the girl continued on and disappeared around the corner of the hotel building.

With some difficulty the man climbed into his car and placed his cane and dripping umbrella in the backseat. Janessa sat in front, on the passenger's side.

"You had to tell her," she said. "There was nothing else you could do."

"I know," he scowled, water dripping from his hair. "But I hated it. You'd think that once a person was dead and beyond caring, all could be forgiven. What's done is done."

"Anger is powerful," she said. "Even in death, it takes time to heal."

Sullivan glanced over at her.

"When I lost you," he said, "I couldn't have gone on had you been angry at me for taking you to that cursed ball game. I felt so guilty already. Blamed myself for years."

"What happened wasn't your fault," Janessa said. "I've told you that a hundred times. I know Marlene was mad for a while, but she got over it."

Sullivan nodded slightly. "I love you, baby. How I wish I could hug you."

"I love you too, Daddy."

He started the car.

Joseph, no longer visible even to Sullivan, watched as the man drove away. The creature reassumed its true form and laughed uproariously. Its kind had used Sullivan, appearing to the man through no talent or ability of his own. He saw them only because *they* wished it, in assumed forms they wore solely for his benefit.

Those who were willing to believe would embrace any message conveyed from the other side and delivered by such a man. They always had and always would.

Provided they were told what they wished to hear.

This is too *easy—*

Janessa and the thing that had posed as Joseph briefly made eye contact as Sullivan's car pulled away. She shared in its delight, a momentary half-smile on her lips. Unlike its job, hers was not yet done. While she continued on, it now would depart, briefly leaving the physical realm before assuming its next assigned duty in the great spiritual war.

It had watched Melissa for most of her life, from the time they first had sensed a hand upon her, one dedicated to bringing her into the fold and granting her the life and peace she sought. The thing that so briefly and effectively had impersonated her son had studied her, had watched her, had seen what she had seen, and had learned what she had learned.

All in preparation for that single moment, there in the parking lot, when finally the burden of her guilt would engulf her.

If all went well, Melissa Torrance would be dead before the enemy made His move.

A small, private meeting in President Bridger's office had laid a strategic groundwork, and now, a week later, a much larger one was underway. Not only were the House and Senate leaders present, but every cabinet member, the Joint Chiefs of Staff, and a group of carefully chosen advisors all were present and ready to chart a new course.

It had been a hard week. Most had spent the holiday in their offices, working to remedy the crisis. As of yet, no clear solution had made itself known.

None likely would, Bridger knew. It was going to be a tough call, and in the eyes of many, an unpopular one.

A tough call. *His* call.

The Cabinet Room was filled to capacity. A few additional chairs had been brought in and placed along the walls. Bridger sat in his place at the center of the table's east side and flipped through a report that hastily had been prepared for those in attendance. No press was present—much had yet to be decided, and until that time Bridger and his fellow servants needed the freedom to think aloud.

Already meetings had been held to discuss the India-Pakistan situation. The last eight days had brought some relief, as representatives of both nations again had met at a neutral site. The kettle was boiling, but not yet boiling over, and the attentions of the men and women at the top were focused now on the more immediate problem.

"So," the president said, "you've all read the report by now. Comments?"

"They're crazy," said Senate majority leader Cyrus Briggs. "These terms are ridiculous."

"You gotta give them points for originality," Defense Secretary Sumner said.

"Well, we knew they'd try something," Bridger said. "But surely they don't think we'll agree to this."

"Can this be what they meant when they said we wouldn't be there for Israel?" Varner asked. "Did they know about Russia's oil crisis before we did?"

The offer had been both ridiculous and amazing. The Arab states would pick up the ball and meet *all* of the oil needs of the United States at a per-barrel price barely a *third* of what Russia had been asking—on the sole condition that the United States would end its political and military backing of the Jewish state.

"Sure didn't take them long to get on the phone," Creedel commented. "Their intelligence has improved. Less than an hour, wasn't it?"

"Yup," Bridger nodded. "The phone line to the Kremlin wasn't even cold. The Arab world must be ecstatic."

"So we say no," Varner said. "What happens then? We need oil… What other options are there?"

"Finding a backup exporter is out," the vice president said, "as we figured. We've tried everywhere. There's not a barrel out there to be bought, dealt, or stolen."

"Not even from Canada?" Creedel asked.

"They can't afford to send us any more than they already are. Japan, Central America, and Greenland are putting a huge drain on their production as it is, and they aren't pulling as much out of the ground as they used to. Same goes for Venezuela. They're at capacity."

"What about Europe?" Briggs asked.

"Are you serious?" Sumner asked. "They're probably laughing their Euros off."

"You could declare a national emergency," Varner said to the president. "Sign a presidential order and resume drilling in the Arctic National Wildlife Refuge. Thank Heaven the equipment's already in place…"

"And don't think *that* wasn't a struggle," Creedel said. "I was with President Hannity's administration when they pushed that through. Hardest-fought piece of legislation I ever saw, on both sides. Roughest two years of my political life."

"And NPRA," the House majority leader offered, reminding them that the National Petroleum Reserve, Alaska, located west of ANWR, remained yet untapped. "It would take a bit longer to be up and running, but it could be vital."

"Hold on now," Briggs said, a threat inherent in his tone. "My people won't stand for that, and you know it. We tried that once and wound up with millions of gallons of oil on the ground."

"May I remind you it was an environmental fanatic who planted that explosive on the pipeline?" retorted Sumner. "The guy was determined to make Hannity look bad, whatever the cost."

"We now have safeguards in place," Creedel added. "Nothing like that can happen again."

The senator was unshaken. "If you use this emergency to reopen those wells, we'll seek impeachment."

"On what grounds?" the vice president asked. "Meeting a national need? Seventy percent of our oil comes from imports. Half of that came from Russia."

Bridger shook his head. "Cyrus, what kind of public support do you think a motion to impeach will get if ANWR's the only thing keeping gas prices from hitting five dollars a gallon?"

The senator muttered under his breath, loathe to give up a stand his party had taken for so long.

"You just can't do that," he insisted. "No bill advocating drilling up there will succeed. We'll never pass it."

"You're going to force my hand here?" Bridger asked, incredulous. "Make me do this alone? Fine."

The energy secretary, Kyle Morton, spoke up. "A lot of the equipment was dismantled, and what's still up there hasn't been maintained too well. Getting those drills up and running again will take the better part of six months."

"Not so bad," Creedel said.

"I didn't finish," Morton continued. "Factoring in the time it'll take to get the oil flowing through the pipelines and into the national system, we're looking at nine."

"Terrific," Sumner moaned.

"Hey, it's better than the seven years we'd be looking at if we hadn't already done so much of the foundational work way back when."

"How long will the strategic reserve hold out?" Bridger asked.

"Five, maybe six months," Morton said. "With conservation."

"Leaving us in a hole for an entire quarter."

"Yes, Mr. President."

Bridger covered his mouth with spread fingers and tapped the bridge of his nose.

"You can't reopen ANWR," the majority leader repeated. "We'll have to find another source. There has to be *someone* to buy from."

"Weren't you listening, Cyrus?" Creedel asked impatiently. "There are only so many oil-producing entities on the planet. Russia was the biggest, but they're out of commission. OPEC wants Israel's head on a platter. China's industrial buildup increased their petroleum demands tenfold in the last few decades, because the millions who used to ride bicycles are now driving gas guzzlers. They've soaked up most of the remaining available oil, and when you throw India's needs into the mix, forget it."

"Perhaps if we spoke to the Chinese," the senator suggested. "Explained the situation and paid the right price. They might find a way to divert a supply to us in the short term."

"Are you kidding?" Sumner said. "They're still irate over our interference when they tried to take Panama. Nothing would make them happier than to see us reduced to a smoking crater."

"We don't know that. Things have cooled down. We've had a cordial relationship with Ling Tsau for more than a year now."

"And for more than *thirty* years they've conducted both live and computer-simulated war games with America as the enemy."

"All right," Bridger cut in. "Let's stay focused here."

"Well," Creedel said, "whatever happens, we *can't* let OPEC dictate our foreign policy."

"Don't worry," Bridger said. "I'm not considering that soul donut for a second."

"So what happens when we tell them to go jump in the lake?" asked Varner.

"What do you mean?"

"We buy from them already. They don't comprise the majority of our imports, but a substantial amount. What's to keep them from stopping their sales to us altogether?"

"They can't afford to do that," the energy secretary stated. "They've never recovered from Russia's taking over so much of the world market. They need every dime they can get."

"But Russia isn't in the picture anymore," Varner observed. "Those who needed that oil are already looking to fill the void, and I'm sure OPEC will be more than happy to oblige."

"So," Bridger asked Morton, "how long until they *can* afford to cut us off?"

He thought hard, every eye on him. "Ballpark? Four months, maybe… at the outside."

A grim collective sigh, punctuated by a few choice expletives, filled the room.

"If that happens," Creedel said, "American industry has had it. Can you say 'standstill'?"

Bridger's voice rang with determination. "I want every well we have, opened up and producing. On-shore, off-shore, deep or shallow. Texas, Oklahoma, wherever. I don't care if the hole's been capped for a hundred years or if the last thing it spewed was dust. I want every well giving whatever it can, and I want it yesterday. And I don't want any flak from the oil companies on this. To blazes with profit margins. I'll sign an executive order if I have to. Speaking of which…" He looked to his press secretary, who stood near the door. "Bill, you better get me television time tonight. I'm going to reopen Alaska."

11

The studio lights were hot, as was the barrage of questions being hurled by one woman against another, questions carved both of ideology and sensationalism.

Karen sat in a plush red chair before the cameras of a local Washington talk show and defended Sacred Child against the program's host, a woman who clearly supported Life Quality.

The set, lined with touches of tinsel and decorative garland, seemed to promise a gentler, more joyful experience than the interviewer had any intention of delivering. She clutched a datapad filled with notes both on Sacred Child's brief history and Karen's personal life, all of which, once twisted, might provide ammunition.

Gail Winfield was a controversial figure, to say the least. Her show was hated in many circles, her on-air tactics often brutal. Politicians avoided her. Celebrities feared her.

Her viewers, however, thrilled by confrontation, loved her.

"Ms. Foley, how can your organization possibly justify its actions against Life Quality? You've used legal harassment, slanderous advertising, and netmail and phone campaigns. You've employed on-site protests that have terrified young, weary mothers who already were facing more hardship than they could deal with. You've—"

"Everything we've done is within our legal rights to stop the killing of millions of babies. Senseless deaths that—"

"Senseless? Hundreds of thousands of desperately ill people have been healed, and almost as many lives have been saved. Many more have been relieved of oppressive, painful burdens that threatened to destroy their futures."

"Every child who died had as much a right to live as you or I. Life Quality claims that ending a child's life is a matter of choice, that the mother must have the right to choose whether to endure the 'burden,' as you put it, of raising an imperfect child. But that child has no say in the matter, no choice, and Sacred Child is here to speak for him."

"But the 'children' in question are not viable, and a solid argument can be made against their being human in the first place."

"How intelligent or healthy or 'viable' does one have to be to be considered human? People have used that same argument for centuries to justify slavery, genocide, racism, and abortion on demand. In the case of the latter, all they've done now is push the line back from birth to the child's first birthday."

"Exactly where would *you* draw that line, Ms. Foley?"

"There *is* no line. There never has been. From the instant of conception through the moment of death, the human body experiences a constant, flowing continuation of physical processes—"

"So your answer is *at conception?*" the woman asked with amusement.

"Show me any other valid point of commencement. You can't. From the very beginning, that tiny cluster of cells has a unique genetic code. It's a new human being, not just part of the mother's body."

"*Of course* it's part of her," the host mocked. "And she has a right to dictate what happens with it, the same way she has a right to decide whether to get her ears pierced."

"If you offer to drive my child to school, and you sell your car on the way there, will you sell my child, too? Location does not determine essence of being."

"That's not a valid comparison."

"Why not?"

"We're not talking about cars, we're talking about a woman's right to do with her body as she sees fit."

"*Her* body, absolutely. If she wants to tattoo herself from head to toe or have cosmetic surgery or color her hair bright pink and grow it five feet long, more power to her. But her baby has inalienable rights over *his* body, just as she has over her own."

"It isn't a baby, not until it's born. And even then, if—"

"And here we are again."

The interviewer shifted uncomfortably in her seat, then reassumed her usual superior tone. "The point I was making earlier was that these genetically nonviable offspring should never have been born in the first place. Thanks to modern medical science, though, if something good can come of these births through medical research or organ transplants—"

"Do you even remember where this whole issue came from?" Karen snapped. "These children were born because of bad decisions made years ago by some of those who embrace Life Quality so fiercely now. When they allowed the full cloning of human fetal tissue for medical research, rather than limiting their work to methods involving unfertilized genetic implantation, they opened a door—"

"Which led to the cloning of children for childless couples who could not conceive," the woman interrupted. "Are you saying they shouldn't have tried to help bring a little happiness into so many lives?"

"Ideally, a lovely idea. But the world doesn't work that way. This wasn't mere fertility they were dealing with, it was the very substance of what makes us human. The concept wasn't thought through, and too many things went wrong."

"They couldn't have known—"

"Known what? That greed and moral laxity would warp the process? I remember all those TV commercials, running day and night. Cloning facilities practically begged people to use their services. There was no beneficence involved. It was a money-making machine from the start."

"*All* medical facilities charge for their services," the host pointed out. "Research takes funding. Should they have done their work for free?"

"I'm saying their actions weren't solely for the betterment of mankind, as so many have suggested."

"They brought hope to those who had none."

"Perhaps that was the intent of some, but not of most. Suddenly, there was a 'genetic creativity clinic' on practically every corner, cranking out cloned embryos. The places were run like fast-food franchises—"

"Hence, the 'McMurder's' label coined by your organization."

"—and were used too often for too many wrong reasons. Everyone, even those who weren't childless, began to go there because they were promised control over everything from gender to hair color.

"And then, political correctness stepped in. In order to prevent future acts of discrimination from cropping up, the government pushed through new legislation…the infamous 'Humanity Law.' It became a federal offense to draw a distinction between clones and 'naturals' in any way."

"Nothing wrong with that," Gail said. "It was the fair thing to do."

"Until the bottom fell out," Karen said. "Soon, safeguards at the clinics were dropped in the name of profit margins. Problems set in. *Serious* problems. Genetic instability became epidemic…we still don't fully understand why…and millions were aborted. Millions more, whose conditions had gone undetected, were born with severe or even lethal birth defects. Lawsuits were rampant. Ob-gyns were sued on the grounds of 'wrongful life' or 'wrongful birth,' because they'd brought children into the world who then suffered and brought hardship upon their parents. So to relieve the malpractice pressure that threatened to destroy the insurance industry, the first Life Quality laws went into effect, allowing parents to give up their ill-conceived children easily and without question, based on their level of hardship."

"Right…to relieve suffering."

"Suffering? What about simple responsibility? So few today have the moral wherewithal to take on the task of caring for a handicapped child."

"So they put them up for adoption," Gail recalled, "or turned them over to state agencies. Both honorable actions, right? Or did you object to that as well?"

"So many children were dumped by their parents that the national healthcare system was overwhelmed. And that was when Congress *expanded* the Life Quality laws, allowing any terminal, 'genetically compromised' child to be euthanized during the first year of life.

"And overnight, as with the clinics that had created the problem, facilities sprang up all over the country where parents could take their infant children without stigma or strings, places where their brief lives were ended 'mercifully.' Places where parents were *paid* for the surrendered child."

"What else could have been done?" the host asked. "The economy would've been devastated. The healthcare system would've been destroyed."

"They could have been smart enough not to have opened that Pandora's box to begin with," Karen insisted, "as so many tried to warn them."

"Maybe so, but once it had happened, there was no going back. They dealt with the situation at hand and did the best they could, given the circumstances."

"The best they could? These babies are *harvested* for whatever healthy tissues and organs they possess. It's an *industry*. And today it's even become a civic duty…killing a child for the good of others."

"And lives have been saved," Gail reiterated.

"So killing ten in order to save one is a legitimate act?"

"It is, if those ten are going to die anyway."

"How pragmatic," Karen said. "You and Mary Fullerton would have gotten along splendidly."

"Now, listen, Ms. Foley," the woman said, a warning tone in her voice. "I won't allow you to make this into a personal issue. That isn't a valid—"

"Why not? *She* was pragmatic. An attorney. She used the Humanity Law against itself, twisting it to get what she wanted. When she gave birth to a *natural* child with extreme birth defects…which likely were due to her own drug use, by the way…she decided she didn't want to deal with the burdens of raising the baby. So she demanded that if the lives of abnormal cloned children could be ended, then so could those of all children. 'There must be no distinction,' the law stated. 'All persons are equal, cloned or natural.' She took it all the way to the Supreme Court and *won*. And since then, every so-called imperfect child is lucky to see his first birthday."

The interviewer paused, agitated and lacking a response. Glancing at the stage manager, she was relieved to find the hand signal denoting the end of the broadcast.

"I'm afraid our time is up," Gail said with false cordiality. "Our guest has been Karen Foley of Sacred Child." The host smiled into the camera and spoke to the home audience, her tone strictly professional. "We'll see you again tomorrow. Be sure to join us."

"And…we're clear," the director announced.

Gail rose from her chair, threw her datapad onto the seat cushion, and stormed from the set, her high heels clicking sharply against the polished flooring.

"Wow," an amazed cameraman commented as she moved past. "What happened? You were lunchmeat out there."

"That woman is *never* to come back on this show," she hissed. "And you're fired."

What's wrong with this thing?

Kelsey clamped down harder. His hand trembled under the strain. He tried again, turning the wide blades of the key, but to no avail.

"Come on," he said, struggling anew. "Will you?"

Still, no success.

"Too worn out," he conceded. "Time for a new can opener." He set the can of beef stew sharply on the countertop and rummaged through a drawer, shoving utensils aside in search of a replacement. He found none.

Must be a church key here someplace—

His mind flashed on the power drill in the garage.

"Overkill," he muttered, abandoning the idea.

A sound came from the front room. Kelsey held his breath, listened, and heard it again.

Someone was jiggling the knob of the front door.

I locked it, didn't I?

Then it sounded like it was turning.

Slowly, he crept over to the utility-room door. There, leaning upright against the molding, rested the old baseball bat he kept for such an eventuality.

As he reached for his weapon he heard another sound, the familiar creak of the door swinging open.

Hoisting the bat, Kelsey silently moved across the kitchen and into the living room. Cautiously, his heart pounding, he leaned out, peering into the entry foyer.

Someone was there. He was startled, but only for an instant.

"Hello, Daddy," the blond woman said, turning as she hung her coat on the rack.

Kelsey drew a deep breath and lowered the bat. His hands still shook.

"Jackie," he said, surprised.

"I'm sorry," she said. "Did I scare you?"

"Oh no, no, honey. I was just practicing my stance."

She drew closer. "I *did* scare you. I'm sorry. I should have called. I was over this way and, well…" She paused. "I still have my key."

"You're always welcome," he said, then he smiled. "It's great that you're here."

He extended his arms, unsure that she would approach. After a moment, she did.

"Are you hungry?" he asked, hugging her. "I have stew, if you happened to bring a can opener."

"Daddy," she began, "I want to talk to you."

"Well, come in," he said, leading her into the living room. They sat together on the couch.

Jacqueline glanced around the room. "Everything's just as I remember it."

"Bry mentioned that, too."

"He was here?"

"Last week," the man said. "Dropped in to say hi."

"I saw him too," the woman began. "A month or so ago. We talked, and I started thinking about things. These last few weeks..." She struggled, unable to find exactly the right words. "It made me think that maybe..."

Kelsey saw his daughter's unease. He remained silent, giving her time.

"A lot of different things drove me away from here," she said after a deep breath. "Seems one piled on top of the last, until..." She swallowed hard. "I know you were always disappointed that I didn't believe in God. Must have looked bad to the congregation that you couldn't convince your own daughter."

"I never cared what anyone thought, but you."

"I didn't mean—"

"I can't force you to believe," he said. "And I was wrong to pressure you. I tried too hard, I know that. But I couldn't bear the thought of..." He stopped, letting the statement fade away. "I've always prayed that one day you'd see things differently."

"I know, and I'm sorry." She paused. "I just...can't."

He sat, loving her, but said nothing.

"And then, when Mom got sick and passed away," she continued, "I used it as a weapon against you. I attacked you for your faith…tried to make you justify the kind of God who would let her die like that. I hated the thought of Him, and I hated you because you loved Him, even stood up for Him. Mom had been in so much pain…" She fought the swell of emotion that rose within her, tears building. "I lashed out. Ridiculed you. I was so angry…"

"You had to direct it somewhere," he said. "I understand. I miss her too."

"I'm so sorry." She put her arms around him, and he closed his eyes in thankful prayer, feeling her heart beat in rhythm with his. "I let so many years go by. Wasted so much time that I could have…could have spent…"

He smiled, holding her. "You're here now."

A father tenderly kissed his daughter's forehead, as he once had done each night, each day, many years earlier.

"Mr. President, Millie Carson's here to see you."

Bridger hit the intercom button. "Send her right in, Lucy."

The door leading from the secretary's office opened, and a smartly dressed woman was shown inside. In her late thirties, her average features and form were enhanced by the fashionable hat and tailored suit she wore. Bridger rose from his chair and extended a hand in greeting.

"Millie," he smiled. "Come in."

The door was closed behind her as she stepped into the room. Pausing for a moment, she studied the Oval Office.

"I've always loved it here," she said. "Ever since I came here as a girl."

"Being the daughter of the vice president would have its perks," the man said.

"The place has changed," she noted. "But in a way, it hasn't. New paint, new carpet, new drapes…yet still it's as it always was. The heart of the free world."

She crossed the room and took a seat before his desk.

"Forgive me," he said, lowering himself gingerly into his chair. "I only have a few minutes."

"Thank you for seeing me. When I made the appointment, things weren't quite so hectic. This really could have waited…"

"No, please," he smiled. "I know you've been through the wringer yourself these last few months…"

"The scandal has brought one resignation after another. CloneTech has just about become a four-letter word, and HHS is dangerously close to being dragged down with it. Add to that the fact that I just lost my PR director—"

"I heard about that."

"It's been tough without her. Now, of all times, we need to present ourselves well to the public."

"From your phone call, I gather you have a favor to ask."

"I do," she confessed. "I'd like you to consider making an appearance at Life Quality's anniversary in New York this coming April."

"Millie, why would I want to do that?" he asked. "You know my stance on Life Quality. You and I differ strongly where they're concerned. I've never understood the 180-degree turn you took in your position and never demanded an explanation from you. But why would you think I'd even *consider* something like this?"

"Your poll numbers have dropped substantially among those who support the organization, even in your own party. Especially there. With all the potential negatives looming, I thought you might want to take advantage of such an opportunity. Let us spend the time between now and then promoting your—"

"You're not asking for *my* benefit," he interrupted, knowing better. "Just be honest with me."

Millie looked down, then met his eyes again. "The department's taken a beating. Fortunately, in the public mind we're already linked with Life Quality, and the organization's positives are very high. If you could show a measure of party solidarity by attending their anniversary gala, it could buoy not only HHS but the entire administration."

"What CloneTech did to its investors was inexcusable," the president said.

"They got in over their heads," Millie said. "To listen to their CEO, you'd think they were doing their stockholders a favor by faking results."

"They knowingly broke laws from here to Tuesday and financially ruined a lot of folks, and they're beginning to pay for that. But to suggest that we should try to use the event in April…"

"It's more than that. In one fell swoop we can undo a lot of perceived damage."

Bridger drew a breath. "Millie, your father was a good man and a dear friend. I watched you grow up and go through college and take the world by the horns. Your family was so proud of you. We all were. And when the time came to fill the seat at HHS, I knew you were the right person for the job. You know I'd do almost anything for you, despite your position on Life Quality…"

Millie drew a breath.

"…but I won't compromise in this. In no way will I give the impression that I support those people. I just won't. I hope you can respect that."

The woman looked away and nodded.

"That was the answer I expected," she said. "But I had to try."

"You'll weather this," Bridger assured her. "You and your department both. It won't be easy and may take a while. But stick to your guns and do the right thing, and you'll come through all right."

The woman winced.

"You sound like my dad."

"Thank you," he said. "He was a wise man."

After a beat, she rose from her chair, running a nervous finger along the edge of her purse. "Well…I appreciate you seeing me."

"Any time. You know where my door is… Feel free to knock."

She shook his hand, sensing that a hug would be less than appropriate. Together, they walked to the door.

"How's your mother?" he gently asked.

"It's been so hard for her," she said after a moment, seemingly distracted. "But the chemo seems to be helping. We're hopeful."

"Keep me informed, will you?"

He opened the door for her and allowed her to pass ahead of him. In moments, after a brief good-bye, he vanished, swept away by a sea of dark suits.

Millie slowly made her way through the corridors of the West Wing, haunted by his words.

Do the right thing—

Once, she always had. Or had tried to.

But that had changed.

Karen drove along the highway, headed home, her pace slowed by congested traffic. The radio, its volume low, was set to an easy-listening station, but she paid the music no attention—in her mind she was replaying the interview, thinking of dozens of things she should have said, better and snappier answers to Gail Winfield's assault.

Oh, I forgot to mention the Web site!

Disappointed in herself, she reached into her purse and groped for her netphone.

I wonder if Bry saw the show. I've seen him so little lately. Maybe a nice dinner tonight—

Having no luck, with one hand she turned the purse over and dumped its contents onto the seat. Her wallet, makeup, various scraps of paper and tissues, and other varied items covered the upholstery. Still, no phone.

There's that lipstick—I thought I'd lost that.

Then she remembered. The phone had been in its charging cradle in her office. She had intended to put it in her purse before leaving for the studio, but a last-minute discussion with Rachel had driven it from her mind.

"Oh, well," she whispered, "I'll call him from home."

The traffic, heavy for midweek, crawled slowly along. Finally, thankfully, she reached her exit. More traffic greeted her on the service road and stretched ahead, covering the thoroughfare with the unwelcome glow of brake lights.

"I am *not* in the mood," she said more loudly. Making her way into the right lane with some difficulty, she turned onto a side street and left the throng behind her.

Much better. It's a longer route, but at least I'm moving.

The farther Karen traveled from the highway, the lighter the traffic became. She wove down residential streets, enjoying the quiet. Smoke rose from chimneys. Warm lights shone from the windows of warm living rooms. Christmas lights twinkled on eaves and along walkways. The daylight quickly was fading, with night's approach hastened by the heavy cloud cover. Her car's headlights, sensing the dusk, snapped on.

Again she turned the wheel, left the neighborhood roads, and entered a street lined heavily with towering trees. Stripped largely of their foliage by winter's hand, their branches reached over her, obscuring the darkening gray sky. Five, then ten minutes passed, and she found herself virtually alone. The forest to either side grew thicker. Darker.

Bry should be home by seven, she thought. *Perhaps I can pick up something along the way. He likes Chinese—sesame chicken would be lovely—*

Her train of thought was broken by an acrid scent that grew stronger by the moment. A burning smell, one that could mean only trouble.

What is that?

The headlights flickered. The illuminated dash darkened. The radio went silent.

Then, suddenly, the engine went still.

It did not sputter, did not shake. It simply—*died.*

Gray white smoke began to pour from beneath the hood. Karen, fighting now without power steering, put all her weight into the wheel and managed to pull alongside the curb after briefly and inadvertently mounting it. She pressed her foot hard against the unassisted brake. The car slowly came to a stop.

Wary of a fire, she opened the door and emerged from the polished blue hulk. The smoke continued to rise from the engine compartment, carried away on the cold breeze. Walking around to the other side of the car, she opened the door, leaned in, and pressed a button, trying to use the on-board roadside assistance system.

Nothing.

There was no power at all.

She stood and peered down the street, looking in both directions. No other cars, no other persons were present. "Hello?" she cried out, but as she expected, no answer came.

She was alone.

"Terrific," she muttered, gathering her things and stuffing them back into the purse. She pulled her coat from the backseat and slipped it on, surveying her surroundings.

"Okay, there has to be a phone around here *somewhere…*"

A water tower rose above the trees nearby, almost silhouetted against the sky. Its simple lines and rare, antiquated design struck her as familiar.

Wait a minute—I know this place—

"I'm on the edge of that park." She smiled. "The one I used to walk in…"

Karen once had spent her lunches there, during a stint as a mortgage company temp. She had been in high school then, and the job had been her first.

There's a jogging path somewhere beyond those trees—at least, there should be—and there's a phone not too far along the way! I remember!

She grabbed her purse and closed up the car, but its power locks would not function. With little choice, she left it and headed out across the dry grass into the woods.

Night was falling too quickly. The ground was hard and cold. The wind picked up, cutting through her coat. Her hands in her pockets, she hurried, praying that help lay just ahead.

The farther she walked, the more dense the trees became. A thick carpet of dead leaves crunched beneath her feet, and she became wary of holes in which she might turn an ankle. Hills and gullies made the going difficult, and her high-heeled footwear was ill-suited for this woodland terrain. More than once her hose became snagged on the thin, snarled branches of dead undergrowth. She almost fell a few times but managed to catch herself on a helpful limb or tree trunk. Twice she dropped her purse, but the meager light would not allow her to see if anything had spilled.

Grasping the twisted, low-hanging branch of a tree for balance, she mounted a final rise. There, at its crest, the pedestrian path stretched from side to side before her, its edges covered in brown, fallen leaves.

Thank you!

She stepped out onto the paved strip, then paused.

Which way?

After considering a moment, a whisper sounded deep within her, and she chose to go to the right. She began down the walk, still uncertain, her feet aching.

Please let me be remembering correctly—this is such a long path.

The fog of her breath was caught in the gentle glow of each ornamental lamppost. They stood widely spaced along the way, just bright enough to allow her to continue safely.

Ahead, bathed in the soft throw of a lamp, someone was sitting on a wooden slat-backed bench. A woman, it appeared, her purse resting beside her. Karen, happy to see another person, quickened her pace.

"Hello?" she called out. "Can you help me? Do you have a phone I might…"

Her words fell away as she drew closer and saw that the young woman was asleep.

"I'm sorry to bother you," she began again, before realizing. "Hello?"

Something was wrong. Seriously wrong. She rushed forward.

Oh no!

The girl's head was slumped to one side, her face partly hidden behind her blond hair. Her cold lips were blue. In one of her hands was an empty soda can. In the other, glistening amber in the light, was a prescription bottle.

It too was empty.

"No!" Karen cried out, her limbs charged with adrenaline. She pushed the young woman to one side, laid her down along the bench, then sat on its edge. Breathlessly, quickly, she reached inside the sleeve of the girl's coat and pressed a fingertip against the small of her wrist.

There was a pulse. Ever so faint, but it was there.

Thank You, God.

She shook the insensate girl then gently slapped her, trying to awaken her, trying to get any reaction at all. None came.

Looking around in desperation, Karen cried out.

"Help! Someone?! Anyone?!"

There was no response save the whistle of the wind in the branches.

Reluctant to leave the girl's side, Karen nonetheless leaped to her feet and ran down the path, toward the public phone she prayed would still be there.

★

No stars shone in the dark gray sky.

Lawe pulled into a designated parking space near the West Wing and shut off the engine. It had been another long day, one now stretching into night—a three-city presidential-appearance tour was in the works, and there were protective strategies to be planned. The weary agent had not been assigned to the most recent similar trip, but it appeared this one had his name on it.

"Hey, buddy," a voice called out. "You have a permit to park there?"

Turning as he rose, he found a police car stopped behind him. A smiling Ollie was at the wheel, his head tilted out the open window.

"Hey," Lawe grinned. "Aren't you out kind of late?"

"Paperwork," Ollie said, rolling his eyes. "I swear, that's all this job *is* anymore. Give me the good old days… At least when I was a rookie I was too green to be bored."

"You still look pretty green to me."

"Big words for a guy who wants a ticket to the game on Sunday."

"Did you get them?"

"Two choice seats on the fifty. Doesn't get much better."

"You're the man," Lawe smiled.

"I'll pick you up at ten," the officer said. "That'll give us plenty of time to get settled in before kickoff."

"Sounds good. Thanks, Ollie."

"No problem. Later."

The patrol car pulled away. Lawe made his way along the walk and into the building, nodding to the guard at the door. "Hey, Charlie, how's that book coming?"

"Not so good," said the wannabe author. "Haven't worked on it much lately."

"Remember, I'll want you to sign my copy."

He passed through the security foyer and into the lobby, then proceeded down a hallway.

"Evening, Julie," he said, waving as he passed the photographer's office. The woman nodded and waved, her attentions on a phone call.

He continued along the hallway. The barbershop was dark, having closed hours earlier. Lawe ran a hand through his hair, mindful that he needed a trim.

The Secret Service office opened before him. Half a dozen other agents already were there, going over their notes and procedures manuals.

"*There* he is," said Kurt Morris, a tall, blocky sort who sat on the edge of a desk. He laughed, kidding his fellow agent. "How'd the girlfriend do?"

"I missed it," Lawe responded. "The president's speech at the Smithsonian ran long."

"Missed what?" asked another agent.

"Karen was on TV this afternoon. Gail Winfield."

"Tough gig."

"I'm sure she did fine. I can't remember the last time *I* won an argument." A chuckle swept the room. "So how are *we* doing, guys?"

"Looks good," said agent Jack Lundy, tossing a file folder onto a desk. "We had a few initial concerns, but the layout of the hotel in Boston won't present any problems. We've been going over the background checks on the staff. Only found a few who might pose a threat—three Iranian nationals with a history of activism. The advance team's in place…we'll be secure long before Iron Chef touches down at Hanscom."

Lawe took a seat at his desk and sighed at the new clutter there. Files and papers rested haphazardly in piles, covering almost the whole desktop.

"Hey, one neat stack, will you?" Lawe laughed. "I was only gone for five hours, guys, what happened?"

"That'll teach you."

He pulled the day's newspaper from beneath the pile. A bold headline declared:

BRIDGER OPENS ALASKAN OIL FIELDS

DEMS OPPOSED, VOW REPRISAL

Get a clue, Lawe mused, *will you, people?*

"When's wheels up at Andrews?" he asked.

"Oh-six hundred, Saturday morning. The speech is scheduled for ten-thirty."

Lawe nodded. "Okay, when do we land at—"

His phone rang.

"Lawe," he answered.

"Bry, it's me…"

"Karen?" He heard a muffled loudspeaker announcement in the background, apparently a doctor being paged. "Where are you?"

"At Victoria-Thorson Hospital," she said. "I tried to call you at home…"

"Are you okay?"

"Yes, I'm fine," she answered. "I rode here with the ambulance and—"

"Ambulance?"

The other agents paid closer attention, pretending not to eavesdrop.

"Bry, let me finish," Karen insisted. "On my way home from the studio, my car died. I was walking through a park, looking for a phone, when I found a girl who'd overdosed on pills. Cylirazine… She must have been terribly depressed. I called 911, but…"

"How is she?"

"Barely alive. They said she's serious but stable, but they didn't sound too confident."

He rubbed his forehead. "Do you need help getting home? Or are you going to stay there with her?"

"No," she said. "I'm about to leave. The doctors told me she might sleep for a day or two, so I gave them my net number and they promised to call when she's awake."

"Where's your car?"

"Nowhere near the highway. The traffic was awful, so I was taking a back way home. I'm going to call Triple-A and have it towed to that repair place that did my brakes."

You and cars, he thought.

"All right. I'll call tomorrow and see what they found wrong. You're sure you're okay?"

"I'm fine, Bry."

"Do I need to send someone to pick you up?"

"No, I already called a taxi." The woman was silent for a moment, and concern for their relationship guided her next words. "You know, I was wondering...how much later do you have to be up there?" Hope tinged her voice. "I thought we might get together for a late dinner. Chinese maybe?"

"Another couple of hours, looks like."

"It'll take me that long to get home and get ready, anyway. Royal Palace should still be open then. I'll call you as soon as I get to the apartment."

"Okay," Lawe said. "I'll be here."

"I love you."

"Love you too."

Morris, seated across the way, puckered like a fish and made kissing noises. Lawe threw the newspaper at him as he hung up the phone.

"Everything okay?" Lundy asked.

"Yeah," Lawe replied. "She's at Victoria-Thorsen. Some girl OD'd at a park, and Karen found her and called 911. Rode with the ambulance. They're not sure if the girl's going to make it."

"Well, at least she has a chance, now," Morris said. "Sounds like your lady friend was her guardian angel."

"Yeah," Lawe quietly agreed. "Maybe so."

He glanced up at the clock. *Seven thirty-four.*

"Come on, guys," he said. "Let's get this wrapped up. I've got a date with that angel."

12

Morning, Chief," Jeffrey said, passing the open door of his superior's office on the way to his own.

"Jeff, you got a minute?" the man called, stopping the sergeant in his tracks. Jeffrey spun and returned to the doorway.

"Sure. What's up?"

"Come in and close the door, sergeant."

Jeffrey entered, shut the door behind him, and approached the desk. *This is never good.*

"We got an alert from the feds," the man began. "The level of terrorist chatter is way up. Could mean trouble."

Jeffrey scowled. "What have they heard?"

"They think Islamic Sword's planning another attack, most likely on New York."

"When?"

"Sometime between a minute ago and a year from now. They've got nothing specific on the time or location yet, but we're to watch for anything unusual."

"Unusual? That could be half the city," Jeffrey commented. "Chief, this makes three times in the last six months that we've been put on alert, and so far, nothing."

"I know," the man said. "Let's hope it stays that way."

"It's been so long since we were hit. It was what, six years ago we had that homicide bomber at Rockefeller Center? Why would they attack us *now?*"

"Probably has something to do with Israel. Might even be tied into that missile attack in October."

"So what does that mean?"

"It means you keep your eyes and ears open for anybody of the fanatical Muslim persuasion who has so much as a funny glint in his eye. Grade-three protocol. You see anyone suspicious who matches the profile, you bring him in and we run a verification scan."

"We're on it."

"And keep a lid on this. Tell your partner but not your wife. The feds don't want to cause a panic, so the national advisory stays where it is for now. The stock market's been touchy enough already, what with this oil crisis, and they don't want to push things over the edge any sooner than they have to. I'll tell you one thing...when they catch these guys, it'll be because someone spotted or overheard something. And I want that 'someone' to work in this department."

"Gotcha."

Jeffrey left the man's office, his mind filled with images of Ten-Seventeen.

"Not in *my* city, pal," he uttered under his breath.

She felt starched, clean linen beneath her fingertips.

Melissa slowly became aware of the room around her, though still disoriented and with a fuzzy memory. Her blurry gaze was met by an expanse of white that stretched wide above her. She realized she was lying down, that a bed was beneath her. Lifting a hand to her waist, she again felt the cool fabric there, the sheet that covered her.

"Well," a woman's voice said. "Good morning, sunshine. You gave us quite a scare."

The girl turned her head and found a nurse rising from a nearby chair. She approached, checked Melissa's pulse and temperature readings, and smiled widely.

"Welcome back," the dark-haired woman said.

"Back? Where was I?" Melissa asked.

"Honey, we lost you twice right after you were brought in. If you hadn't been found when you were..."

Found?

She fought to remember. Her disorientation faded.

The pills—I tried to—

The nurse pressed a button on the girl's bedside monitor. "You just rest, Melissa. The doctor will be here directly." She smiled. "I'm Amy. I've been keeping you company."

"Hi." The girl swallowed hard. "I'm thirsty...so dry."

"I bet you are," the nurse smiled. "I'll get you some water."

"Where's my stuff?" Melissa asked, noticing the hospital gown she wore.

"In the closet there," the nurse said, bringing a cup of water from the bathroom. "Nice and safe."

The girl drank it quickly, then smiled and handed back the cup.

"What happened?" she finally asked. "How did I get *here?*"

"You were found in the park, and just in time, too. You're one very lucky young lady."

Melissa recalled Joseph's tiny, sleeping face. "I guess." She noticed the sunlight against the window curtains. "How long have I been here?"

"It's Friday, just past four in the afternoon," the nurse replied, checking her silver-tone watch. "They brought you in early last night."

The door opened and a smiling, youthful doctor entered.

"Well," he asked, approaching the bedside, "how are you feeling?"

"Okay, I guess," she replied as he looked into her pupils with a penlight. "I have a headache..."

"That's to be expected. You had a rough night." He looked at her chart. "I'm Dr. Wells. It looks like you're past the worst of it. Your signs are good. After a bit of precautionary observation, we'll look at sending you home."

"When can I leave?"

"I think we'd better keep you here for a day or two," he said, checking her vital signs on the bedside monitor. "To make sure you're completely out of the woods."

The nurse inwardly cringed at his choice of words but continued to smile reassuringly.

"Nurse Leighton will be sitting with you for a while," the doctor added, indicating the woman. "She'll attend to your needs and give you someone to visit with. I'll be in now and again to check on you." He smiled gently, his eyes twinkling. "You just get better, and let us do the rest."

"Thank you, Doctor," the nurse said as the man left the room. The door closed behind him with a soft thud.

"In other words," Melissa said to her, "you're here to make sure I don't try to kill myself again."

"Something like that."

Melissa paused. "Amy…thanks."

"For what?"

"For being honest."

The woman smiled and patted Melissa on the knee. "If you need anything at all, you let me know. Would you like me to dim the lights?"

"Please. And I'm kind of hungry."

"Coming right up. The food here is really pretty good."

The place was a smooth-running machine, its myriad intricate parts oiled by the blood of millions.

It had been a busy day for Life Quality Manhattan, even more than usual. Margaret McCarthy sat in her office, angered still by Karen's appearance on Gail Winfield's show, but glad that the woman's words apparently had done little to slow the flow through the doors.

If only there were something we could do to shut up those ridiculous baby's-rights fanatics.

After the broadcast, the press had become a nuisance. Fueled always by conflict and hoping to fan the flames, they had swooped in, seeking rebuttals from Life Quality's officers and staff.

"That horrid Foley woman," she muttered, hanging up, having given a brief phone interview. "As if all I have to do all day is answer that kind of rant." She hit a button on her datapad, and a voice sounded in response.

"Yes, Ms. McCarthy?"

"Leila, come in here, will you please?"

In moments, the girl walked into the room.

"Yes ma'am?"

"How long have you been my secretary, Miss Saban?"

"Two months, ma'am," the girl replied, her voice small.

"And in that time, have I not told you more than once that *all* press contact is to be directed to the PR office?"

"Yes ma'am…but they said it was urgent and didn't identify themselves as—"

The woman tapped her datapad. "Leila," she said firmly in a demeaning tone, "I have a two-gig file of résumés in here, all submitted by people who would love to have your job. One more brainless slip like that, and they'll get their chance. Do you understand me?"

"Yes, Ms. McCarthy."

"That's all," she said firmly, dismissing the girl with a wave of her hand. "You may go back to work."

"Yes ma'am."

Leila left the room and closed the door behind her. It had not been the first time she had been disciplined by her boss, and certainly would not be the last. Every day, it seemed, McCarthy dressed her down for one thing or another, usually in front of others.

Such a stupid girl, she thought. *But she's adequate and she's cheap, and I've got a budget to meet.*

McCarthy, shaking her head, returned her attention to the papers on her desk and the more pressing demands of her day.

Leila stormed back to her desk. She slammed a drawer shut, then glanced up at the smiling painted portrait of McCarthy that hung on the wall.

You'll get yours, witch, she thought, a fire in her eyes, *and I'll be here to see it.*

Wow, that wasn't too bad.

Melissa took the last bite of her country-fried steak and washed it down with a sip of cola. A late-afternoon newscast played on the room's television screen.

"That was good," she smiled.

"Told you," Amy said, thumbing through a magazine. "I've worked in three area hospitals, and the food here by far is the best."

As the girl began to push the bed table away, the door to her room opened and a striking woman entered. Her shoulder-length hair was auburn, her clothing professional and well tailored.

"Oh, Karen…hi," Amy said, rising from her chair. Their brief embrace spoke of more than a passing familiarity.

"Melissa," she went on, "this is Karen Foley…the woman who found you."

"Hi," said the girl, unsure and suspicious. She muted the television as Karen approached. As they shook hands, Karen smiled, enjoying the life she now saw in the girl.

"I guess I should thank you," Melissa said, not completely sure she was happy to have been found.

"I'm just glad they got to you in time."

"I've seen you somewhere," the girl observed, studying the woman. "I'm pretty sure... I have a good eye for faces."

"That's quite possible," Karen laughed. "I've been a poorly kept secret of late."

"Ms. Foley works for Sacred Child," Amy said. "She's been on TV quite a bit."

Oh no—she must know what I did!

"I guess that was it," Melissa nodded, suddenly and visibly uncomfortable.

Karen placed her coat and purse on a chair and returned to the girl's bedside. "May we have a few minutes?" she asked the nurse.

"Certainly," Amy said, happy to accommodate them. "I'll be at the nurse's station, just down the way. Buzz when you're ready for me."

Then she was gone, leaving them alone. Karen pulled a chair alongside the bed and sat down.

"Honey," she softly began, "is there anything I can do to help you?"

There was an uncomfortable silence. The girl would not look at her. Karen waited.

Melissa finally shrugged. "Like what?"

"Well, let's begin with the basics. Why are you unhappy?"

"Who said I'm unhappy?"

Karen paused, letting the question sink of its own weight.

"I don't know," the girl continued, "maybe some people just..."

The woman listened, but no other words were forthcoming.

"Just what?"

Melissa shrugged again, still looking away.

"Just don't get to be happy, I guess." The words were barely audible. "Things pile up on you, until..." Again, silence.

"What was it that made you feel the need to take your life?"

"It's a long story."

"I have all night."

Don't make me do this, the girl silently pleaded.

She allowed herself a lingering gaze into Karen's sparkling eyes and found there a compassion she had not known since her mother's death. It was not the type of kindness she always had gotten from Carolyne, which never had been real, she now knew. Something within her, to her surprise, wanted to trust this woman. Slowly, reluctantly, she began to open up.

"I'm just a horrible person," she began. "I hate the things that have happened in my life...the things I've done."

"What things?"

"You don't know?"

"No... How could I?"

"You *really* don't?"

"No, Melissa." The woman's puzzled expression was genuine.

"You'll hate me when I tell you," the girl said, her voice low. "Something I did was...unforgivable."

"I promise I won't hate you," Karen said gently. "And nothing is unforgivable."

"Yes. Something is."

The woman waited silently, patiently.

"I had a baby," the girl said, her voice small. "But not anymore."

Karen bristled. She had heard those words before, those exact words. A new and intense compassion for the girl swelled within her, accompanied by a spark of rage directed not at Melissa but toward others.

"What was your baby's name?" she asked.

"Joseph," the girl replied. "I have a picture in my purse."

"Where is it?"

"The closet."

"May I?"

"Sure."

Karen retrieved the handbag and gave it to the girl. Finding and opening her wallet, Melissa flipped to the photo taken only a couple of months after the baby's birth.

"He was ten months when I…" Her voice dropped away. "But in this picture he was only sixteen weeks." She handed the wallet to Karen, who now fully understood what had happened.

"He's beautiful," she said, saddened. She returned the wallet and watched as Melissa looked at the tiny portrait with deep sorrow.

"I know that now."

"What happened?" the woman asked, knowing the answer.

Melissa gently kissed the photo, then slipped the wallet back into her purse. "They told me it was the right thing to do," she almost whispered. "That I shouldn't be selfish. And then, *after*…" She struggled, the words choking her. "I could still smell him on me…on my clothes…in the apartment…" She faltered and began to break down, the pain flooding her. "And at night…I could…I could hear him *breathing*…"

The anguish flowed from her like water through a weakened dam. She began to weep, her hands rising slightly as if seeking a mother's embrace.

Sadness and rage filled Karen. She stepped forward and cradled Melissa, who loudly sobbed and trembled in her arms. A tear ran down Karen's cheek as she held the girl, sharing her pain, letting her release a measure of the intolerable grief she bore.

Amy napped in the lounge each afternoon and stayed awake through the night, sharing shifts with another nurse during the wee hours. Often she stood at the window of the sixth-floor room, looking out upon bare trees, quiet streets, and city lights that twinkled sharply in the cold, crisp air. Melissa did not sleep well, tossing and softly crying out from time to time.

Karen stayed with the beleaguered girl throughout the weekend, sleeping on a cot brought in for her.

The sun rose on Sunday morning, and life returned to the slumbering city. Melissa awoke early, still tired, her neck stiff. Karen soon followed suit.

Just before noon, Dr. Wells entered and found the three ladies chatting. "Well, good morning," he smiled. He noted the girl's brightened expression. "I see we're doing much better today."

"Mostly," Melissa said. "I didn't sleep very well."

"Hello again, Ms. Foley," he said. "Have you two been getting acquainted?"

"Yes," she said, looking to the girl. "We've had a nice visit."

Karen had spoken with Dr. Wells upon Melissa's arrival. He had promised her that she would be notified as soon as the girl had awakened, and true to his word, he had placed the call. And later, upon Karen's return to the hospital, they had shared further words.

"Well," the doctor said, "I would say that you're about ready to check out, Melissa. There are two conditions, however…"

"What?" she asked, not knowing what to expect.

"First, I want you to visit with another doctor, a colleague of mine. His name is Dr. Pearce, and he'll be talking with you over the next few weeks to make sure you—"

"Don't hurt myself?" she asked.

"Yes."

"He a psychologist?"

"Yes. Clearly, you were driven to attempt a desperate act, and we want to help make sure you don't feel the need to do it again."

"I know." She paused, considering. "I don't have insurance… I can't afford a counselor. I don't even know how I'm going to pay for *this*."

"Don't worry about that right now," Amy said.

"As for the second condition," Wells began, his eyes on Karen, lead-ing her.

"Melissa, you live by yourself," she said. "You told me yesterday that you have no family, no one to be there for you. It's the holidays, and no one should be alone at Christmas. So I'd like you to come home with me."

The girl looked at Karen with a bit of surprise. "Oh no…you don't have to do that. You must have enough to worry about. I'll be okay, really…"

"I'll manage."

"I'm afraid I'll have to insist, Melissa," Dr. Wells said. "Ms. Foley and I already discussed the matter, and Nurse Leighton will be there to lend a hand. She's trained in such care. We need to make sure you have someone to look out for you, at least for a little while."

She looked at the doctor, then to Karen again, and knew she had little choice.

"Okay," she agreed. "I'll need to stop and get a few things from home, though."

"That's fine," Karen smiled. "I'll take you."

"Nurse," the doctor said, "if you'll attend to the final details, we'll see if we can't have the young lady on her way in an hour or so."

With a nod and a smile she followed him from the room, leaving Melissa to get ready and Karen to help her. The girl rose from the bed with a little help, then spent a short time cleaning herself up and getting dressed.

"Thank you," she said, brushing her hair.

"Not at all," Karen answered. "I'm happy to have you. I have plenty of room."

"No…I mean, *thank you*."

Karen walked up and hugged her. The girl let herself accept the embrace, and for a moment—a fleeting moment—it was almost as if she were in her mother's arms, the one place where the world, and fear and guilt could never touch her.

13

No, I had the one with the onions."

The sky was clear and blue. The wind was cold. More than seventy thousand fans were gathered, watching the final division home game of the season.

"Oh, sorry." Ollie handed Lawe his hot dog. "They were out of sweet relish, so I got dill."

"That's fine."

They began to eat, juggling their food, drinks, and binoculars.

"Decent day for the Skins," Lawe said, taking a generous bite. "Better one for Dallas."

"We'll get 'em next year," Ollie said, his words muffled.

"Yup," Lawe agreed.

A familiar trill filled the air. Lawe tried to free himself of his concessions and reach into the inside pocket of his coat, where his phone insistently rang.

"Here," he said, shoving his soda off on Ollie. "Take it."

"Hey!"

Finally, after four rings, he managed to answer. "Lawe."

"Hi, it's me."

"Karen?"

He could barely hear her above the noise of the crowd. Dropping his half-eaten frankfurter into the crook of his friend's arm, he put a finger in his ear and tried again. "Karen? Louder... I can barely hear you."

"Yes, it's me," she said. "I just wanted to let you know..."

"What?" he strained. "Can you say that again?"

"I said," she repeated, almost shouting, "I'm back home now. I brought Melissa with me... She's going to stay through New Year's."

"She's there now?"

"Yes."

"Is she okay?"

"Mostly."

"Good. Well, let me call you back after the game."

"Okay," she replied. "Have fun. I'll talk to you later."

He clicked the button and the display window closed.

"That was Karen," he told Ollie. "She's at home."

"Terrific," the man said with feigned annoyance, shoving the drink and dog back where they came from. "Maybe later we can stop by and she can get the mustard out of my coat."

Karen hung up the phone and turned to find the girl admiring a painting in her living room.

"It's lovely," she said.

"That's a mountain lake in Switzerland," Karen explained, walking up to her. "A friend of mine painted it. She lives there now."

"She's good."

"Yes, she is."

"You have such a nice place," Melissa went on, scanning the room as she took a seat on the sofa. She found the apartment inviting and feminine. Stylish, comfortable furnishings of soft fabric and dark wood blended with objects of crystal and gold. Photos and personal mementos on the shelves and walls spoke of family and friends. A subtle scent of potpourri filled the air. A piano concerto played softly in the background.

"Thank you. I've lived here a couple of years. I used to have a cozy little place in Georgetown, but they sold the building and converted it to offices."

"Do you mind it?" the girl asked. "Being alone?"

"Oh, it's not like that," Karen said, knowing she must answer cautiously. "I'm not here enough to get lonely. I spend so much time down at the office or out in the field. Or with Bry... That was him on the phone."

The girl sat back, allowing the sofa to swallow her up a little.

"That music is pretty," she commented.

"It's Rachmaninoff. I like the classics... I find them very soothing."

"Where's the sound coming from?"

"Bry installed a hidden dimensional speaker system for me last year. They're small, but the effect is wonderful."

"Is he your fiancé? Bry?"

Karen smiled. "Yes. He just doesn't know it yet."

A corner of Melissa's mouth turned up. "How long have you been seeing him?"

"About four years now."

"You love him?"

"Yes."

"That's nice." Melissa absently stared at the sculptured carpeting beneath her feet. "It's important to have someone. There was a guy I loved once. Joseph's father. But he didn't love me. I don't even know where he is now."

"I'm sorry. That must have been hard."

She gave a subtle nod. "After that, Joseph was all the family I had... and I..."

Melissa's grief, clearly visible, tore at Karen's heart. Guilt clawed at the girl's soul, and Karen was reluctant to allow the added suffering that discussing it would bring. Yet she must, she knew. *Any time Melissa begins to talk about her ordeal, you have to let her,* the doctors had said. *Be there for*

*her, listen to her, offer what you can. She's got to release the pain that's inside
her—if she keeps it bottled up, she's sure to try to end her life again.*

"Melissa," Karen began, sitting down next to her, "It must be hard for
you to believe this right now, but with every day that passes, you'll hurt a
little less. One day, sometime soon, you'll be able to think of Joseph and
remember him with joy instead of sorrow."

"No," she insisted. "I'll always know he hates me for what I did."

"He doesn't hate you. Honey, he's in a place now that—"

"He does. He told me so."

Karen was surprised by that. "What do you mean, 'told you'?"

"Well…" She faltered, as if embarrassed. "I went to see Randall Sullivan last week, and Joseph told him he'd never forgive me for what I did."

"Sullivan? That man who says he sees the dead?"

"Yes. At that seminar at the Imperial Hotel. When I asked him about
Joseph—"

"Sweetheart," Karen said, "he can't possibly. People have been doing
this for a long time. They have a talent for pulling information out of
people with only a few questions, and then making it look like the words
are coming from friends or relatives who—"

"He never *asks* anybody anything," she corrected her. "He just sits up
there and *tells* them things. It's amazing. If you saw him, you'd believe it."

Karen chose not to argue the point and put an arm around her.
"Melissa, I *promise* you…Joseph doesn't hate you." She looked into the
girl's eyes. Pain lived there.

"I was supposed to protect him, and I didn't…"

"You turned to Life Quality because they put you under *extreme* pressure to do so. They knew you weren't equipped to handle those kinds of
stresses. That's what these people do, and that's one reason we're working
so hard to stop them. They seek out those who are most vulnerable and
convince them to make the wrong decision by making it look like the
right one."

"How could I have been so stupid?"

"It's a business, and they are very good at it. They don't care about you or about anyone who walks through their door. All they want is the funding the government gives them, and they use young mothers to get it. I'll bet they never even followed up with you, did they?"

"No. And the stupid automated phone number they gave me would never go anywhere. It was always 'press one…press four…press three…' and then back to the main menu again. Never a real person."

Karen's anger was rising. "How is it we live in a world where something like Life Quality is allowed to exist?" She held the girl tightly. "It wasn't your fault. You have to believe that."

"You don't understand," Melissa insisted. "It *was* my fault. I was tired of the doctors and the…" She began to cry. "Every night…hearing him in there…and not being able to sleep…and I couldn't get a job…and every minute of every day I had to…I had no time to…anything else… and I just…just couldn't…"

Karen held her.

"I killed my baby—"

"Listen to me," Karen said with firm tenderness. "You did what they had convinced you was the right thing. Think, honey… They pursued you, didn't they?"

"Yes…" she said, the word muffled by sobs.

"Almost from the moment Joseph was born, they worked to persuade you that you needed to bring him to them."

"Yes."

"Would you *ever* have given up Joseph if they hadn't?"

The girl drew an erratic breath. "I don't…know…"

Karen held her tight. "Honey, we all have to learn to forgive ourselves."

"How can I?"

"I know one thing for sure… *God* is ready to forgive you. Nothing you can do is so bad that He won't."

"You can't know that."

"Yes, I can, and I do. He's forgiven people who have done far worse."

"What could be worse?"

"Sending a man to his death so that you can take his wife for your own. Or persecuting and killing thousands before ultimately realizing your error and joining the ranks of their brethren. Or brutally murdering an innocent man after ridiculing and torturing Him. Or abandoning that man utterly in the hour of His greatest need, after claiming undying loyalty to Him...when you believed in your heart that He was the Son of God."

Melissa wiped the tears from her cheeks, her breathing settling a bit.

"I don't know," she said.

"Well, you think about it," Karen said, her voice warm and loving. "What a blessing it was, finding you that night."

"A blessing?" the girl asked, wiping her eyes and nose with a tissue. "I've been nothing but a pain to you."

"No, honey," the woman smiled. "I was blessed. God Himself must have led me to that spot in the park at that moment. I'd say He has something special in mind for you yet."

As night fell, the duty shift of two weary men drew to a close.

Jeffrey and his rookie partner, Officer Clay Breckenridge, pulled onto Eighth Avenue. It had been two weeks since the terror warning was issued, and both men scanned the sidewalks as they moved slowly along, straining to spot any who might fit the profile they had been given. Small gatherings of Arab men were particularly suspect, and a few had been dispersed earlier in the day after a series of field interviews.

"It's like a needle in a haystack," Clay said. "Almost three million people out there..."

"And we cover our part," Jeffrey said. "No more, no less. We stick to the grid and trust the foot patrols to see where we can't."

Jeffrey, driving, slowed as he neared an intersection and came to a halt at the stoplight. Traffic was sparse—rush hour had passed, and the bustling city had begun to settle in for the night.

"So you got any plans for Christmas?" the rookie asked.

"Yup. Bry and his girlfriend will be coming for dinner. We do it every year, and he and I trade off turns in the Santa suit."

"Who's got the duty this year?"

"Not I, my friend, not I."

"Melody still believes in Santa?"

"Oh, sure. She's only five. But they grow up so fast… Seems like yesterday she was learning to walk. Now she's in preschool."

"Where the kids who *don't* believe usually try to spoil it for the ones who do."

"Yeah, but what are you gonna do?"

"Beautiful wife, great kid. You're a lucky man, Sarge."

Jeffrey smiled. He knew.

"What about you?" Jeffrey asked. "Doing anything special?"

"Yeah…heading up to my parents' place. We're all getting together. My sister's coming up from—"

An instantaneous, blinding flash blazed hot against their faces, filling the street, and both men ducked and threw their arms up, shielding themselves. The deafening boom rang their ears as a shock wave blew out windows in dozens of surrounding buildings and hurled flaming chunks of metal against the patrol car. The windshield and the driver's side windows, struck by both the concussion and solid matter, went blue-white as glass showered the interior of the car.

Instinctively, Jeffrey dropped low, threw the transmission into park, and both men dove from the vehicle, taking cover behind the doors of the car, their weapons drawn. Both then slowly stood, stunned and awed by the devastation.

A double bus, parked at the curb on the adjoining street, had been obliterated, its sides and top shredded and completely laid open. A huge fireball still rose, high above what remained of the charred and burning vehicle, mirrored in the few surviving windows of the surrounding buildings.

A shower of flaming matter suddenly rained on the two men, small, jagged shards launched by the blast. Metal and plastic and glass and rubber.

And flesh.

Dodging the falling debris, Jeffrey lunged into the car and called frantically into the radio.

"Seven-twelve…" He waited. "Come on, come on…!"

Finally, after a pause, came the reply.

"Seven-twelve, go ahead."

"Ten-thirteen, ten-thirteen!" he cried, his voice strained and breaking. "Ten-seventy at Eighth and West Forty-seventh, bomb explosion, city bus…huge blast…maybe a missile…"

"Seven-twelve," the dispatcher's voice came back. "Confirm ten-seventy…"

"Ten-four on that… I need ten-fifty-four, *lots* of ten-fifty-four," he called, requesting EMS units, "and multiple ten-fifty-nines… We need help out here…civilians down, maybe a hundred… We need medics and a coroner…"

"Ten-four," the call came back. The intolerable silence of almost ten seconds seemed an eternity. "Units dispatched…"

He threw down the mike and ran toward the inferno, leaping over the piles of burning debris that littered the streets and sidewalks. The storefront directly adjacent the blast was all but gone, smoke rising from twisted steel and charred stone, the building afire. Pedestrians lay everywhere, badly burned and pierced by shrapnel. Shopping bags, torn and burning and filled with holiday gifts, lay scattered on the pavement. The red, green, silver, and gold of mangled foil-wrapped packages sparkled in the nightmarish firelight.

Clay already was at the wreckage, drawing as near as the intense flames would allow, pulling clear as many of the injured as he could. Those nearest the bus had died instantly and lay in awkward tangles on the pavement. The scores of passengers aboard the huge vehicle had suffered the full impact of the blast, shattering all, incinerating most.

Both officers, rushing to assist, had forgone the use of the rubber gloves they carried, and their hands and uniforms quickly became stained with blood. Sickened by the carnage, the rookie violently so, they fought to help but were overwhelmed by the scale of the devastation.

Jeffrey, the heat stinging him, helped one hobbled victim to get clear, an older man who had disembarked the bus and was walking away at the instant of the explosion. He was in shock—the clothing on his charred back and legs had been burned away, but he still possessed all of his limbs. In horror, the officer looked upon the man's bleeding arms, legs, and back.

They were covered in embedded nails, screws, and other more irregular metal objects, driven into his seared flesh and held fast. Dozens of other puncture wounds betrayed the entry of fragments buried deeper.

A bomb?

The explosive had been encased in a thick layer of such hardware, Jeffrey immediately knew, meant to cause the maximum number of human casualties.

That kind of shrapnel could mean only one thing.

A homicide bomber? But the blast was too big for that!

Sirens, air horns, and screams filled the air. Emergency personnel dressed in biohazard gear descended on the site. Some hurried to cordon off the area with crime-scene tape while others treated and evacuated those they could save. Others, dead at the scene, were covered with yellow plastic sheets.

The attack we've been waiting for—

Jeffrey, his face, chest, and arms covered in blood, slowly backed away from the blackened, smoldering hulk of the bus. Fire and rescue teams rushed grimly past him, their shouts almost lost in the wail of sirens.

His flesh cried out to him as he neared the damaged patrol car, the pain finally breaking through the adrenaline that had infused his body.

The blood on him was his own.

14

They've got C-9," Arthur Bradford said. "The equation has changed."

The man was director of Homeland Security, and for the first time in a long time his department had taken a severe blow.

"You're sure about that, Art?" Bridger asked, worry edging the question.

"Yes, Mr. President. The chemical analysis was conclusive, and the blast radius was too great to have been caused by anything else. If it was a homicide bomber, and we believe it was, he could never have caused a blast that big with conventional explosives…at least not that would have fit into a backpack."

"Has anyone yet taken responsibility for the bombing?"

"No sir," Bradford said with mild disbelief. "Not a peep, and that's never happened before. We're almost sure, though, that Islamic Sword was responsible."

"This isn't a scenario we'd planned on," Sumner said. "C-9 is the lightest weight plastic explosive we have, and the most powerful. More bang per ounce than any other." He held up a hand and pulled it into a tight fist. "A chunk of that stuff only this big will level a decent-sized house."

"Your tax dollars at work," Bradford commented.

"We missing any, Warren?" Bridger asked.

"No sir. I'd stake my life on it."

"So where did Islamic Sword get it?"

"We developed it in concert with the Israelis two years ago," Sumner answered. "There may have been a security breach somewhere over there…"

"Or over *here*," Bradford insisted.

"Well, wherever they got it," Bridger went on, "it looks like someone else has the recipe."

"Very bad," Sumner said.

"How many people died?" the president asked.

"They estimate around 280…about 90 on the bus itself, plus 191 bystanders. Christmas shoppers, most of them. We can't be sure of the number of on-board victims, though, because the blast was so intense."

"How many injured?"

"Another couple of hundred, including two police officers. They were the first on the scene. Saved a few lives."

"I'd like to meet those men," Bridger said. "Art?"

"Yes sir. I'll make the call myself."

"So," Sumner asked, "was this the attack we got wind of a couple of weeks ago?"

"I think we can make that assumption," Bradford replied. "And if they keep to their usual pattern, *and* if we're lucky, it'll be a good while before they hit us again."

"I don't think we should count on them to follow a timetable," Bridger said. "They have C-9 now… I doubt they'll wait so long to use it again. We could be looking at the same kind of ordeal as Israel went through before the Palestinians got their state. Every week, every day, a constant assault."

"If so, what do we do?" Sumner asked.

"Whatever we *have* to," Bridger replied. The burden of his office pressed him hard into his chair. "We have little choice. *Everything* is back on the table now."

The knock was expected, four taps in a familiar rhythm.

Brenda opened the door. "Bry…come in." They hugged, and she kissed his cheek.

"How's he doing?" Lawe asked as she closed the door. "The surgery went well, you said?"

"Yes," she smiled. "They got it all out. The stitches aren't too comfortable, though… He has to sleep on his back, and he hates that."

As they entered the main living area, Jeffrey emerged from the hallway. "Hey, little brother." He wore loose-fitting pajamas, his unbuttoned top revealing a number of white gauze bandages. They also dotted his neck, arms, and face.

Lawe walked up and they exchanged a careful hug. "Easy there, tiger," Jeffrey kidded.

"So what did they find in there?"

"The usual," Jeffrey said as they took a seat in the den. "Screws, nails, picture hangers… I'm going to open a hardware store."

"Sounds like it."

"And there was glass. Came from the windshield of the unit."

"You know, you're lucky you didn't lose an eye."

"Tell me about it."

"How long until you go back on duty?"

"Now, now," Brenda smiled, standing behind her husband's chair. "Let's not rush it. I'm happy to have him home for as long as possible."

"You just like having someone else here to do the laundry," Jeffrey grinned.

She leaned over and kissed him on the top of the head. "You saw right through me."

"Looks like I'm going to be down in your neck of the woods before long," Jeffrey smiled. "Got a call from the White House. The president wants to meet Clay and me. Seems we're *heroes.*"

"Well, Clay I can understand," Lawe smirked. "By the way, how is he?"

"Fine. Took less of a hit. Something to do with the blast angle."

"Wow. The *president…*"

"Jealous?" winked his brother.

"Last week, when I heard about the bomb, I thought, 'Nawww, Jeff couldn't be anywhere near there...it's a big city.' But sure enough..."

"You know me. I'm a magnet for this stuff. When that credit union shootout broke out last year—"

"You and Karen still coming for Christmas, Bry?" Brenda interrupted, changing the subject.

"Wouldn't miss it," he said. "Barring a crisis, I'll have the whole day."

"How's she doing? I saw her on Gail Winfield... The new job seems to have lit a fire inside her."

"Tell me about it."

"Problems?" Brenda asked, concerned.

"No, no. We're just having to deal with a bunch of new scheduling conflicts. We'll get it worked out."

A momentary lull settled in, and Jeffrey shifted in his chair. A slight wince appeared, then vanished.

"Oh, I heard from Ollie that you guys went to the game last week," he said. "Lucky dogs. I haven't been since the Jets playoff last year."

"Yeah, had a good time. I wish the score would have been the other way around, but other than that..."

"Karen didn't go?" Brenda asked.

"Nawww," Lawe replied. "She's spent the last couple of weeks with Melissa. She and a nurse are splitting time watching her."

"The girl's still staying at the apartment?"

"Yeah. Will be for a bit longer, too. It's almost like they're sisters now. They've really struck up a friendship. I'm told she's opened up a lot since being there. Seems to listen to Karen. She doesn't have any family or friends, as far as I know. Lives alone... I guess she needed someone to be around."

"Well, she's certainly welcome to come at Christmas, too. I'd like to meet her. We all would."

"I'm sure you will. They're connected at the hip."

"Ms. Foley, Melissa Torrance is here to see you."

Karen, sitting in her Sacred Child office, smiled. The girl's outlook had brightened more each day in the two weeks since leaving the hospital—the continual companionship of Karen, Amy, or both seemed to have helped considerably in diminishing her loneliness and despair.

"Please send her in, Annette," Karen said into the intercom.

In moments, Melissa walked through the door, her heavy coat rustling as she moved. A pink-and-white knitted cap covered the top of her head, and her nose and cheeks were rosy from the cold. Karen walked over and embraced her.

"Such a lovely surprise," the PR director said, sweeping the girl's windblown hair out of her face. "How are you feeling?"

"I'm okay," Melissa smiled. "At times I'm still kind of spacey, but not like before."

"How did you get here?"

"Amy brought me over…she's sitting out front. I wanted to see where you work. Thought we might all have lunch together."

"Well, I'm glad you're here," Karen said. "As it happens, I want to ask you about something. Have a seat."

"How long has she worked for you? Amy, I mean."

"She's been a part-time volunteer here for more than a year now. She doesn't advertise the fact… Most of her peers don't approve of our efforts, and there's no sense inviting needless scorn."

She indicated the chair opposite. The girl sat down, set her purse on the woman's desk, and smiled sweetly.

"I'll get right to it," Karen began. "I need an assistant. Rachel has okayed the position, and, well, I'd like you to come and work with me."

"Really? Me?" Melissa smiled, looking around the room. "Work here?"

"You're a bright young woman with a good heart and an honest attitude, and I sure could use your help."

"Wow." She then frowned. "But I don't have a car, and the buses don't run near here."

"No problem. We can carpool."

"Oh, Karen..." Melissa was overcome, and her smile was a wondrous sight for the woman who had never seen her so happy.

"And, by the way," Karen added, "as an employee of Sacred Child, you're hereby invited to our Christmas Eve party. Tomorrow night at seven. I'll be home a bit early, and we'll come back up here together. You, me, and Bry."

"That sounds wonderful." She brightened. "Wow."

The woman chuckled, delighted at the girl's enthusiasm.

"Everything that's happened these last couple of weeks...you've been like my own angel. I can never thank you enough for all you've done for me."

"No need, honey. All I did was what any decent Christian would have done, and I was happy to do it."

"Okay," the girl smiled, before her expression became serious. "I *want* this. I mean, after what those people did to me...*anything* I can do to fight them, I want to do. No one should have to...to go through that."

"Okay," Karen said, her voice soft. Melissa looked down at her hands, folded in her lap and fidgeting.

"You said you had something you wanted to talk about?"

"Well, yes," Melissa nodded. "These last couple of weeks you've told me a lot of things I'd never heard before. I started reading through that Bible you gave me and found the parts you were telling me about, the parts about forgiveness."

"I'm so glad to hear that."

"I'm not completely over that hurdle yet, but I want you to know I'm trying. And I also want you to know that I'm honestly considering it…the whole Christian thing. I went to church as a kid, but after my mom and dad died I went into foster care with a couple who didn't believe. I wasn't sure *I* did either, after losing my family…so I let it slide. I would have said something sooner, but I wasn't real comfortable talking about it."

"You are now?"

She brightened. "Well, sure. It's different now. You're not like anyone else I've ever known, Karen. You aren't all talk. Lots of people *say* things, you know, but you *live* them. You say more by your actions than anyone ever could through words. The things you've done…paying my rent so I wouldn't lose my place, taking me in, watching over me…not to mention saving my life. And your dedication to *this* place, all the work you do to save the children. I think I could tell you anything. I trust you like I've never trusted anyone."

"I feel the same way, Melissa." Locked on each other's eyes, they shared a special moment and a bond was sealed.

"Well…" Karen rose, walked around the edge of her desk and handed the girl's purse to her. She hugged the girl and softly kissed her on the forehead.

"My mother used to do that," Melissa beamed.

Karen fussed over her for a moment, sweeping her hair aside once more. "I tell you what. How about I introduce you to the staff and give you the nickel tour. We can wait and fill out your paperwork after lunch."

"Sounds great."

"And later this afternoon I'll take you to my salon. My treat. You'll love Janelle… That woman is fabulous."

So are you, Melissa thought.

For the first time in a long time, she belonged.

★

Zelle Levi peered through his office window, watching the traffic as it passed below, the people as they walked from place to place. Living in the land of their ancestors, they were headed home after a busy workday, shopping for the holidays, or gathering for dinner.

The prime minister scanned the crowds, the forests, the hills.

You are out there, somewhere, lying in wait—

"Almost two months," he said to an aide. "Two months since the missile attack, and all has been quiet since."

"Perhaps our strategy worked, sir."

"Or perhaps we should have defied the wishes of those who insisted on restraint, and retaliated at once. More than three thousand died that day…"

"So many of our people long for peace, sir," the man said. "Almost at *any* cost."

"Peace is a wonderful dream, my friend…but one cannot live his life in a dream."

"It was an isolated attack. The warning we issued may have had an effect. Their ground attack in Jerusalem, after all, was turned back decisively…and they know well our military capability if pushed too far."

"No," Levi said. "We turned down their sole demand, yet they never responded, never even said a word. They are waiting for *something,* biding their time, reserving their arsenal for…" He rubbed his forehead. "For what?"

An ominous silence filled the room.

"If true, sir," the aide then asked, "why attack when they did? Why launch missiles against us and not follow up?"

"To let us know there is a sword over our heads, perhaps. Strategy, Aaron…move and countermove…"

"They *must* know they can never win a war with us," the aide said. "With American air support, our conventional forces alone would devastate them."

"That is what puzzles me," the white-headed man confessed. "What is it they know that we do not? All of their actions must hinge on a single strategic element... They spoke with certainty that the United States would not stand with us when our time of trial comes."

"A bluff," the aide said. "We have seen it before. Many times."

"Perhaps," the elderly Levi said.

Perhaps not.

The aide closed his briefcase and locked it. "Will there be anything else, sir?"

"No, Aaron," Levi said with a kind smile. "Give my best to your family, and may the blessings of Chanukah be yours."

"I will, sir. The same to you. *Shalom.*"

"*Shalom,* my friend."

The man departed the room and closed the door behind him, leaving the prime minister alone at the window.

"A lion is circling," he whispered. "And if we are not very, very careful..."

The sun dropped below the horizon, and darkness descended.

In that darkness the eyes of a great beast glowed, watching and waiting.

15

A tree glistened in the corner, its branches decked out with garland and tinsel of silver and gold. Mirrored glass ornaments caught the light, red glistening amid the green, and tiny white twinkle lights slowly blinked on and off, counting the heartbeats of the Christmas season. Beneath the joyful boughs, a bounty of brightly wrapped gifts awaited their coming moment.

A tardy trio walked into the festive lobby, stripping out of their coats as they paused near the entrance. No one sat at the receptionist's desk, but music of the season and sounds of merriment wafted from the adjoining hallway.

"I smell gingerbread," Melissa smiled.

"We're late," Karen moaned. "They've already started. I shouldn't have spent that time at the mall."

"It doesn't matter," Lawe assured her. "It's just a party."

"Rachel's never late for *anything*," Karen pointed out. "She's the most punctual woman I ever met."

"I noticed that," Melissa said. "I don't know how she manages it."

"It's just a party," Lawe repeated. "And this isn't a competition. Try to relax."

Karen walked into the crowded conference room of Sacred Child, Bry and Melissa close behind. Almost at once, a woman stepped up, greeted them, and took their coats, which still carried the chill of the air outside.

"Karen," Rachel called out, drawing near in a festive red holiday dress. "I'm so glad you're here. Wouldn't be the same without you."

"Hi, Rachel," she replied, sharing a brief hug with the woman. "We wouldn't have missed it."

"Well, introduce me," the woman smiled, extending a hand. "You must be Bry."

"Yes." He reached out and shook her hand.

"How's your brother doing? Karen told me he was almost caught in the bombing. Coming away from such a terrible thing with only minor injuries is *such* a blessing."

"He's fine, thank you. I went to see him last week… He's coming right along. He'll be as good as new and back on the job in no time."

"I'm so glad of that." She looked to the girl who wore a green dress with sheer sleeves that she had borrowed from Karen. "And I know Melissa already. Welcome aboard. Look at you… Don't you look wonderful."

"Thanks," Melissa smiled, enjoying the compliment. Her hair, much shorter and styled now, framed her angelic face and gave her a new confidence.

"Why don't you come in and make yourselves at home."

The trio entered and began to mill about. Karen shared relaxed greetings with those around her while Bry and Melissa, not quite as comfortable, smiled and exchanged brief pleasantries.

The evening passed, a warm current of holiday wishes and varying conversation. Lawe spent most of the time near the buffet table, enjoying a selection of finger sandwiches and other treats, while Melissa was introduced to coworkers she had not yet met.

"Okay, people," announced a dark-haired woman in a red-sequined jacket. "Don't anyone run off. We'll be opening the gifts in about ten minutes."

"I didn't bring one," Melissa whispered to Karen. "I shouldn't participate."

"No one brought one, honey," she said. "Those were bought by Rachel, as a thank you to the staff. We can't afford to give bonuses here, but she wanted to do something for them."

"That's so sweet." The girl smiled.

Karen glanced over and found Lawe downing hors d'oeuvres and smiling politely. "The poor dear," she said. "He didn't have time to eat anything earlier. I suppose after we leave we should—"

"Rachel? Karen?"

Both women turned to find Gordie Wilson, Sacred Child's chief financial officer and one of the organization's founders, standing in the doorway, beckoning them.

"Yes, Gordie," Rachel began, nearing the door. "What is it?"

"I think you'd better come look at this."

Karen signaled to Bry, and he followed, his mouth full. Melissa brought up the rear as the group was led into Gordie's cluttered office. A television screen glowed on the wall.

"*…and this new evidence suggests that the recent bombing in midtown Manhattan was the work of extremist forces within Sacred Child, the Washington-based, anti-harvest group.*"

"What?!" Rachel cried out.

"*The site of the explosion was only a block from Life Quality's national headquarters, and it is believed that the bomb was meant to have detonated less than a minute earlier, as the bus passed the headquarters building…*"

"They can't be serious!" Karen echoed.

"Extremist?!" Melissa said.

"*…the anonymous letter, discovered less than an hour ago at the entrance to the Homeland Security building, took responsibility for the blast and demanded that all Life Quality facilities nationwide shut their doors immediately. We spoke with Life Quality national president Margaret McCarthy.*"

The image of the woman filled the screen, her mask one of oppression, a microphone before her.

"*We are shocked but not surprised, I must say. They've been escalating their attacks over the last couple of years, especially recently. I never would have thought they'd go this far, though. I'm truly frightened for the young women of America who need our services so badly."*

"This is insane," Karen said. "We had nothing to do with what happened."

"No," Rachel said, "but *someone* wants everyone to think we did." She looked to Karen. "Two guesses."

The woman nodded. "Has to be."

"What?" Melissa asked. "Who?"

"You just saw her...Margaret McCarthy."

"*She* blew up the bus?"

"No, no," Rachel said. "At least I hope not. I think she just seized upon the opportunity to utterly discredit us."

"This is a lie, and they know it," Gordie said. "They can't *possibly* have any evidence against us, outside of that 'letter' they mentioned, and it's a fake. The accusation won't stand up."

"It won't have to. The public perception may be enough."

"This is so *burn*," Melissa scowled, anger filling her. "It isn't fair! I *hate* those people."

"No, but that's how Life Quality works." Rachel groaned, shaking her head. "Our donations are way down as it is. We may never recover from this."

"Oh, yes we will," Karen insisted. She looked to Bry. "Give me a ride to the TV station?"

"You bet," he replied.

"You're not going without me," Melissa said, going for her coat.

CIA director George Wood ran down the corridors of the West Wing, a tiny red datastick in his hand. The Cabinet and Roosevelt Rooms were

dark and quiet, their contributions ended for the day. It was almost ten
o'clock Christmas Eve, and most all who labored within the venerated
walls of the old building had called it a silent night.

But the midnight oil, as usual, was burning in the Oval Office.

Wood knew Bridger well, having been a college associate and later, an
air force buddy. He had fought alongside the man, had celebrated birthdays and holidays and military victories with him. But there would be no
celebrations tonight.

He rushed past a hallway guard, who sharply saluted and waved him
through.

"Matt," he said, bursting in on the president, who sat at the desk.

"George?" Bridger asked, looking up from his work. "I thought you
headed home."

"I did," he said, waving the datastick. "Almost made it. But then the
download alert on my netphone went off." Approaching the desk, he
inserted the stick into the president's datapad and pressed the play button.

"Just got this from an agent in Riyadh," he continued. An image filled
the small screen, wavy at first but rapidly clearing. A small date and time
counter ticked away in one corner. "A bug relayed it less than an hour ago."

"Relayed *what?*"

"It's happened, Matt."

A large U-shaped table stretched wide, at which sat dozens of men in
formal Arab garb. They spoke, the exchange anxious, even excited. Their
words, in Arabic, were unintelligible to Bridger.

"Looks like an OPEC meeting," he observed, recognizing some of
the faces.

"Exactly."

The president checked his watch. "An hour ago? Must have been the
break of dawn."

Wood pressed another button in the datapad, and the unit's translator circuit kicked in.

"They will bow, or they will perish," the incongruous female voice of the device stated. *"We must be utterly unified in this… No one must yield. The Chinese have allowed us to make this move much sooner than we had hoped. Blessed is the name of Allah."* A chorus of muttered agreements sounded. *"The infidel to the north has fallen, and the feast is ours…"*

"They're pulling the plug," Bridger realized.

"Yes sir, they are. All exports to the United States are being halted, and OPEC-owned tankers in transit have been rerouted to other countries or recalled to their home ports. Even our own ships won't be allowed to leave for home until they've been emptied of oil."

Bridger glanced at the clock. "Who knows about this?"

"No one, not yet. Not even the oil companies. But that'll change any minute. Our man over there said the Saudis would be contacting Aljazeera before seven a.m. local time, with a simultaneous flood of net-mails going to the American press. They want to create a panic over here."

"At least the stock market's closed tomorrow. We'll have a little extra time to put out the new fires."

"This could be bad. Wall Street is still reeling from the bombing."

The president rose from his chair, picked up the phone, and pushed the button for his press secretary. "Bill, thank heaven you're still there. Meet me in the press room immediately. Call the networks, the papers, everyone. I've got to go on the air." He listened as the man replied, then shook his head. "No, there's no time for that. If I'm not speaking to the American people in ten minutes it may be too late. I'll explain when I see you."

He slammed the phone into its cradle, allowing his frustration to the surface. "Better they hear it from me," he said. "Who knows what OPEC will say."

"Yes sir," the CIA man said.

The president picked up his suit coat and they started toward the door. "Bill wanted to cobble together a speech, but we don't have the luxury of eloquence right now. I'm going to have to wing it."

"You'll do fine, Matt. Just tell 'em what *you'd* want to hear from a president."

"I always do that," he said, the words a prolonged exhalation. "You know, I think I need to go with something different."

"Like what?"

"As a boy, I never drew more comfort in the rough times than when my father would assure us in a relaxed, informal way that things were going to be okay."

"So what are you thinking? 'Mark Twain Tonight'?"

"Maybe a little," the president said. "Mostly Russell Bridger."

"You're not wearing a tie," Wood pointed out.

"All the better."

Karen settled into a chair on a standby set, seated before an array of display monitors and other equipment. A technician hovered over her, wiring her for sound, and a hairdresser quickly reversed the damage the wind outside had done.

"Are you ready, Ms. Foley?" a voice called. "We can begin at any time. This will air at eleven, so we have a bit of a cushion. Take a breath and…"

"I'm ready," she said.

"Good luck," Melissa said, waving from nearby.

The interview began, conducted by the lead news anchor, a man with silver hair who was a mainstay of the station.

"We are joined by a person familiar to many, Karen Foley of Sacred Child. Ms. Foley, allegations have been made linking your organization to the bomb attack in New York earlier this month…"

"That charge is absolutely false," she stated firmly. "The first we heard of it was this evening, during our Christmas Eve party, as a matter of fact. We do not take lives, nor endanger them… We never have and never will."

"The letter received by Homeland Security was printed on Sacred Child's stationery, was it not?"

"I hadn't heard that, but it makes no difference. Anyone can easily forge a thing like that. Once Homeland Security's finished an analysis of the letter, I'm sure they'll find no link whatsoever to Sacred Child. We've never carried out a violent act of protest against Life Quality, or anyone else, for that matter. Everything we've ever done to counter their deceptive tactics has been vocal or written. No one's ever raised a hand to anyone associated with the organization, let alone a busload of innocent citizens."

"Some might say there's always a first time."

"That would be a foolish change of strategy, don't you think? Everyone in our organization has undergone a rigorous background check, and none of our people has *any* history of criminal activity. We simply have no one working with us who is capable of such a thing."

"So where did the letter come from?"

"I don't know. As I said, until tonight I didn't even know there *was* a letter. Obviously, since *we* didn't write it, someone else did…and the only reason they would have done so was to harm us in the public eye. We have to ask ourselves who would stand to gain from that. And until we know more, that's the only answer I can offer."

"So you're saying Life Quality sent the letter themselves?"

"I didn't say that. At this time, we don't know *who* sent that letter."

"But it stands to reason that—"

The man abruptly broke off, listening to something in his earpiece. "Ms. Foley, I'm sorry. We have to end the interview… There's breaking news."

The camera on her went off, and she spun in her chair toward the screens behind her. Each one suddenly filled with graphics declaring a special report, as all broadcasters, almost as one, cut away from their regular programming.

And then, as if through an insect's eye, she saw the president's face everywhere, filling every screen, large and small. His shirt collar was slightly open.

Lawe, standing with Melissa, walked closer. "Turn that up," he called out to a technician.

"Buddy, we don't just—"

"Secret Service," Lawe almost shouted, raising his identification. "I want to hear him, and right now."

"Yes sir," the video tech said, crossing to the audio panel. Bridger's voice boomed from the speakers, calmly and smoothly.

"...apologize for interrupting your Christmas Eve festivities, but I need to speak to you. We've just been informed by our contacts in Saudi Arabia that OPEC, in protest of our continued support of the Jewish nation, has halted all oil sales to the United States."

"You're kidding me," Lawe said.

"Now, the effects of this won't be immediate, so don't worry about that. The strategic reserve will keep the flow of oil going. The price freezes initiated earlier will keep things where they are, so you won't have to pay any more at the pump tomorrow than you did last week. We're looking at our options, and the good men and women you elected have taken several preventive moves already, such as opening Alaska to drilling, that will ensure that we keep living with as little inconvenience as possible. Some conservation measures will be necessary, but it is our hope that they will be minimal. There's absolutely no reason to panic, no reason we shouldn't all enjoy our holiday dinners and our football games tomorrow, so please...put your minds at ease. We'll be rolling up our sleeves and working right through the holidays. Take care, and thank you for your time. Merry Christmas, Happy Chanukah, and God bless."

The president walked away from the podium, ignoring a flurry of questions. As he disappeared through the side door, the press corps gave up and turned to each other, unsure how to react. The networks then cut away to their waiting newscasters who, having received no advance notice of the content of the speech, were equally nonplussed as they began their analyses.

"Even *more* oil trouble?" Karen worried. "How much can we take?"

"Like he said," Lawe reassured her, "the reserve will keep us afloat until Alaska kicks in. I wouldn't worry."

"Sounds a little like famous last words."

"I'll tell you one thing," Lawe said, smiling, trying to lighten the moment. "Chuck must have been scraping the barrel. Not exactly the Gettysburg Address."

"Chuck?" Melissa asked.

"The president's speechwriter. He's usually a lot more eloquent than that."

"I liked it," the girl said. "He sounded like…well, like regular people."

"It was different," Karen said. "I'm not used to hearing such casual language from a politician." She stood and picked up her purse. "So much for Christmas at Jeffrey's tomorrow, I suppose."

"Not necessarily," Lawe said. "I think I'd have heard something by now if they were going to—"

His phone rang.

16

The sun shone in a cold blue sky, warming the interior of Karen's car as she drove the boulevard, Melissa with her.

"The whole thing?" the girl asked.

"The entire electrical system." She indicated the hood. "They had to replace all of the wiring and most of the gizmos under there. Took two weeks."

"Wow." Melissa absently fingered her seat belt. "If that hadn't happened...if your car hadn't...I'd be..."

"Well, let's not think about that," Karen smiled. "It's Christmas, and it's a beautiful day, and you're here with me."

The girl leaned her forehead against the cool glass of the passenger window, watching the frost-kissed barren trees and the smoking chimneys. A light snow had fallen overnight, whitening roofs, dusting lawns, and adding to the magic of the day.

"I love Christmas," she said, her tone like that of a child. "The world seems like such a friendly place. I wish it could always be like this."

"Me too," Karen said. "I can still smell the apple-date bread my mother used to bake every year. It was wonderful. Just melted in your mouth. And the whole house was so warm, and having the family together..."

Melissa sat upright and stretched her legs. Her left hand found the book that rested on the set next to her, and she picked it up.

"*The Loving Bible*," she read, the words inscribed in gold on the dark leatherette cover. "I've heard about this. They say it's really good."

"Oh no, no," Karen said. "It's something that should never have been written."

"What do you mean?"

"It's a politically correct rewrite, and the changes run so deep that it's altered the substance of the Scriptures. First, they made it completely gender neutral, even in some places where it refers to actual people. Then they omitted any references to man's sinful state and his need for a savior. According to this, no one needs Jesus."

"Why would they do that?"

"Because people would rather believe that God accepts them no matter what they believe or do. There's no longer any mention of Christ's statement that no one sees God other than through Him. According to this, everybody goes to Heaven no matter what, and no one is held accountable."

"I can see how people would want to believe that. It would make things a lot easier."

"Unfortunately for those who *do* believe it, it isn't true. Our relationship with God isn't based on what *we* want, it's based on *His* will." She shook her head. "They changed the text to embrace the gay lifestyle, omitted the book of Revelation altogether as 'irrelevant,' took out any reference to Israel holding a special claim to the land it occupies..." She paused to think. "Let's see, what else? They removed all accounts of God's wrath being poured out on the wicked, attributed the fall of Jericho to an earthquake, changed the book of Genesis to affirm evolutionary theory, and rewrote the story of Noah's flood so it's nothing but a fictional morality tale. Stuff like that. I could go on and on."

"I've seen so many ads for it on TV, and they only say how much God loves you, and how this is the first version of the Bible to really point that out."

"All this version does is rob God of His power and sovereignty. It turns Him into a cuddly old thing who's made a few mistakes along the way, craves our love and attention, and wants only to give everyone a great big hug."

Melissa looked confused. "So why do you have a copy?"

"Actually, it was a gift from a well-meaning aunt…but it's been valuable. Reading it has helped me warn people about it more intelligently. If you want to build an effective defense, it always helps to understand the enemy."

"I suppose so."

"A whole lot of churches out there have gone to this Bible exclusively. One has to wonder about the clergy who would use it. I mean, they create shining cathedrals and fill the airwaves, supposedly in the name of God, and then teach heresy from the pulpit."

The ladies continued along slush-lined residential streets, momentary wisps of white rising from the rear of the car. Another turn, another neighborhood, and soon they reached their first destination.

"There it is," Karen said, pointing. "The house with the blue mailbox."

They pulled into the empty driveway.

"They don't do Christmas, you said?" She noted the lack of outdoor decorations.

"No, they're Muslim. But they're good friends, and we share this time of year with them."

They approached the front door, each carrying a couple of glittering wrapped presents. Karen rang the bell, and Samira quickly answered.

"Merry Christmas," Karen said cheerfully. "Special delivery from the North Pole."

"Oh, you didn't have to do that," Samira said, looking at the gifts. "You sneak. Come in out of the cold."

They walked into the living room, Karen in the lead and Samira bringing up the rear. As the visitors gently placed their gifts on the coffee table, Melissa noted the perfume of fresh flowers that hung in the air, though none were visible.

"One each for the boys," Karen said, "and a couple for you and Ollie."

"Well, thank you…" They hugged, holding the embrace for a long moment. "That was sweet of you."

"You guys mean a lot to us."

"Yours are in the other room," she confessed with a grin. "I'm not done wrapping them yet. I was going to bring them by later this afternoon."

"Now who's sneaky?"

"Melissa," Samira said brightly, turning to the girl. "I'm so happy to meet you. I've heard so much from Karen… She's gone on and on."

"Nice to meet you too," she replied. "You have a lovely home."

"Thank you."

"How was the drive? I heard on the radio there was a huge backup on the Beltway. A big truck overturned and spilled lumber all over the place."

"We heard that too and took another route," Karen said. "Bypassed it completely. Longer way to go, but it gave us time for a nice chat."

Samira took a few steps toward the kitchen. "How long can you two stay? I've got some tea on the stove."

"Not too long," Karen said with a measure of reluctance. "We're supposed to be at Jeff and Brenda's by three o'clock for dinner, and it's almost eleven now."

"I'm sorry Bry can't go with you."

"He might come out tonight, depending. Melissa and I are going to stay the night." She glanced around. "I noticed Ollie's Jeep isn't in the driveway… Did he take the kids somewhere?"

"No," the woman answered. "The boys are down the street at a friend's house. Ollie went down to the precinct… He always works on Christmas so someone else can have the day off."

"That's so nice of him," Melissa said.

"That's my Ollie," the woman smiled.

Karen's netphone rang, and she reached into her purse.

"One second…" She flipped it open. "Hello?"

Her expression fell as she listened.

"No, I haven't talked to her this morning…" A long pause. "Who…? What time was this? Well, is she down there now? No, we're still at…okay, I'll…okay. We'll be right there."

"What is it?" Melissa feared, seeing her face.

"Someone broke into the office last night. I didn't get any details, but it sounds pretty bad. I'm sorry, Samira…we have to go right now."

"Is anyone hurt?" the girl asked.

"I don't know."

"No problem," Samira said. "When you get the chance, call and let me know if things are okay."

"I will."

As Samira watched and waved, they rushed back to the car, and in moments the driveway was empty once more.

Matthew Bridger sat at his desk, nibbling from a plate of ham, eggs, and toast as he worked to find ways to minimize the oil crisis.

The reserve isn't going to last long enough, he realized. *Not at this consumption rate—*

"We're going to have to ration before the end of January," he whispered to himself. "Gas lines…"

An hour passed. He sorted through the documents that littered his desk, dealing with one concern after another, all of which required his immediate attention.

"Never lets up," he whispered. "But then, I knew the job was dangerous when I took it."

Steadily, the files and printouts moved from one stack to another, gaining some semblance of order. Finally, he came to a report on Life Quality's subsidy funding.

He paused and prayed.

Please—there has to be a way to end this.

"We're no better than they are," he muttered, scanning the figures before tossing the file aside. "We actually *pay* for it, the wholesale slaughter of—"

"Are we going to get to see you at all today?" a voice asked from across the room. He looked up to see his wife, wearing her holiday finest, entering from the secretary's office. "You're supposed to come for a photo session by the tree…"

"I'm sorry, dear," he said. "I'm a bit preoccupied."

Susan Bridger walked up and leaned over him, rubbing his shoulder. "You work too hard, Matt. I couldn't even get you to spend any time at the breakfast table." She looked at the food on his half-empty plate. "Is that all you're going to eat?"

"No, I'll get to it. I'm just…"

"I know. The weight of the world. Well, the world can wait." She smiled. "You were in here until four in the morning. An hour won't make any difference, not on Christmas. Jody's brought the grandkids, and they're up in the Blue Room playing with their new toys. Please come spend a little time with them."

"I suppose an hour won't hurt," he conceded, rising from his chair. "You know, you should run for office. You can be very persuasive."

"Only where *you're* concerned," she teased.

They took their coats, left his office, and headed outside. "Snow," the president said with some surprise. "I had no idea."

"See there, you need to poke your head out a bit more often. Maybe if you see your shadow, the problems will go away."

"If only."

They walked along the colonnade, past the Rose Garden, and into the mansion, where family waited. Upstairs, the White House Christmas tree stood at the center of the Blue Room, towering eighteen feet, almost reaching the ceiling. Its lush branches, covered with crystal snowflakes, glass icicles, silver and gold glass balls, and white glass pine cones, sparkled in the room's warm light. At its base, the floor was littered with a few opened packages and discarded wrapping paper, amid which three small children played, oblivious of the room's historical significance. The mantel and lower shelves, well within range of a tossed ball, already had been cleared of breakables by the ever-cautious first lady.

"Well, there you are," said Jody Bridger Heaton, walking up to her father. "We were afraid you wouldn't make it at all. We went ahead and started."

"I wouldn't have missed this for the world," he grinned, winking at his wife.

"Me now," a young girl cried gleefully, searching the presents under the tree for a tag sporting her name. "Oh, this one," she said, selecting a box covered in gold foil. "It's so pretty."

The children continued to open their gifts. The two boys, ages four and seven, ran around the circular room with toy cars, spacecraft, and hoverballs, while the six-year-old girl hugged a plush doll she had received at home that morning and continued to rummage through the packages.

"Look, Grandpa," the older boy said, falling into Bridger's lap and waving a toy in the air. "Santa brought me a Mars lander."

"I see that," the man said. "Just like the real thing."

The man welcomed the respite, wishing it could go on. As he hugged his grandson, he noticed a figure standing in the doorway. A sheet of paper in his hand.

"Merry Christmas, John," Bridger said.

"May I see you for a moment, sir?" Creedel asked in a subdued tone.

"Grandpa will be right back," the president said, lowering the boy to the floor. The children continued to play behind him as he walked over to the door, his heels hard against the polished floor. His wife and daughter watched, knowing the secretary of state's presence likely did not mean good news.

"What do you have?" Bridger asked.

"This, Mr. President," the man replied, handing him the printout. Bridger took the sheet in hand and began to read. After a moment, he sighed in disgust, crumpled the paper, and handed it back.

"There's your reply," he said firmly. "You may pass that along."

"Yes sir," Creedel said. He turned and left.

Bridger walked back into the room. His wife, seeing his expression, approached and spoke quietly.

"Matt?" she asked.

"OPEC made an offer," he spoke in low tones. "They'll restore the flow of oil if we allow the Arab nationals we deported back into the country...*and* if we pull out of Israel and agree to no longer assist them militarily or financially."

"Which we've already said we can't do," she knew.

"Not on *my* watch."

She stepped close and embraced him, wishing she could relieve, or failing that, share the burden he carried.

"I love you," she said, her head against his chest.

It was a scene she had hoped never to see.

Karen, coming as near as the police would allow, pulled to the curb. As she and Melissa emerged from the car, the flashing lights before them cast surreal, moving pools of color against the brick face of the building. A dozen men, some uniformed, some not, stood in clumps around almost as many patrol cars and ambulances.

Up ahead, she saw a solid white vehicle pulling away. On its rear door, emblazoned boldly and in red, was a single word: *Coroner.*

A tangle of reporters quickly surrounded her, but she pressed forward, pulling Melissa behind her. Finally, amid a barrage of questions, she reached the yellow crime scene tape strung as a barrier. Climbing under, she was stopped by an officer who rushed forward.

"Hold on, there," he said. "You can't—"

"I work here," Karen insisted.

"I'm sorry, ma'am, but—"

"It's all right," a familiar voice called out. "They're with me."

The officer turned, saw Rachel hurriedly approaching from the other side, then allowed Karen and Melissa to pass. To Karen's relief, the press was held at bay.

"What happened?" Karen asked, dreading answers. She embraced the woman, whose reddened eyes betrayed that she had been crying.

"We can't go in, not yet."

"Why was the coroner here?"

"It's Gordie," Rachel said, clearly unable to believe the words herself. "They killed him."

"What?" Karen uttered, shocked. "Who? Why?"

Melissa gasped and covered her mouth with her hands.

"He stayed late last night…everyone else had left. About two a.m., someone broke in. They began to vandalize the place, and the police think Gordie surprised them. The door was locked, but the alarm was off because he was still here."

"Oh no…" Karen fought the tears. "Does Dana know?"

"Yes," Rachel replied. "I sent Julie and Annette over. I had to stay here."

This can't be, Karen thought. *Why, Lord—why did You let this happen?*

"To lose her husband," Melissa whispered, "and on Christmas Day…"

"Who found him?"

"I did," Rachel said. "Dana called me a few hours ago. She got worried when he didn't come home last night and wasn't there for Christmas morning. Said she tried to reach him up here but couldn't get through. I came up to check on him…"

"That must have been horrible."

"He was in the hallway... The police say it was a blunt-object injury."

After another hour, the police finished their work and the staff was allowed back into the building. At Rachel's request, an officer guarded the door so no member of the press could force his way inside.

The place was in shambles—the furniture shattered and hurled across the room, the computers destroyed—and scrawled in spray paint, hastily covering the walls, were the words ONE DOWN and MURDERERS.

"One down," Karen read, shaken. "Does that mean Gordie or this office?"

"I don't know," Rachel said. "Either way..."

"Murderers? Us?"

"The bombing on the bus, I guess. Whoever did this...and it had to be more than one person...maybe they lost loved ones."

"Maybe we're supposed to *think* that."

"Those monsters," Melissa muttered, stepping over the broken debris that littered the floor. "They smashed everything."

"Not everything," Rachel said. "My datapad and Gordie's... They're missing."

"You kept backup files, didn't you?" Melissa asked. "At the other offices?"

"Yes, but that's not the problem," Karen said. "Someone else has our files now."

"But if they were locked..."

"I think we can count on Life Quality getting around the security keys," Rachel said.

"You're sure it was them?" Melissa asked. "Not someone who thinks we bombed the—"

"It was," the woman fumed. "Karen, this could be bad. Every sensitive record we had...business, personal, financial...they got it all."

"Was there anything there they can use against us?"

"That depends. Our finances are clean, so there's nothing there. But they now know the name and address of every donor we've had, every political supporter, every employee. There may be something there they can twist into a weapon. At the very least, they'll probably try to pressure them all into jumping ship. We'd better be ready for that."

The two men met again, their rendezvous, of necessity, more private now. The long-awaited time almost was upon them.

"Why do we not claim the victory for Allah?" Ahmed asked as they drove the ornamented streets of Manhattan. "Our brother Rahman gave his life. His name should echo across the homeland."

"The people here fear what they do not know," replied Khalid, his eyes on the road before him. "To make the claim will lessen that fear. Our silence is a cold blade."

The man pulled to the curb directly across from the headquarters of Life Quality and stopped. He and his cohort watched as several young women departed. The women here were always alone.

"They are devils," he said, "these Americans."

"All is in place, and our people are ready. Why do we still delay?"

"They were expecting an attack, and now that they have received one, they will not be looking for another. We can move in safety, for the sleep of arrogance quickly overtakes them...and the deeper their sleep, the greater will be their pain when the sword of Allah truly falls. We will be told when to act... Until then, we wait."

Khalid's gaze rose along the side of the building, climbing halfway before coming to rest on a row of mirrored windows.

"Praise be to Allah," Ahmed said. "But others have claimed the glory that is ours—"

"Let them. The infidels have turned upon one another. Their confusion is our ally."

17

The snows of late January fell heavy on the White House, the white blanket unable to hide the turmoil underneath. The windows of the Oval Office glowed yellow, their light cast upon the sterile whiteness beyond.

The president sat on one of the twin sofas, facing his secretary of energy, Kyle Morton, and the commerce secretary, Mel Hoffman.

"Bad and getting worse," said Morton, going over a series of figures on his datapad. The bitter winds howled, pressing in on the walls and windows, fighting them. "The rationing we put into place last month has driven the economy into the ground, and the public is screaming. And now, this weather…the entire Northeast is shutting down. Hardest winter we've seen in over a decade."

"More than an inch of ice," Hoffman added, "and record snowfall on top of that. Power lines are down all over. Millions without power, and with the shortage of heating oil—"

"Most homes still have enough," Bridger pointed out. "The blizzard can't keep this up forever."

"I'm beginning to wonder."

"Almost four dollars a gallon now, for regular," Hoffman said. "Anger's building. We could have a revolt on our hands."

"I know that, Mel," Bridger said with a measure of irritation. "We had no choice but to ration. ANWR's still six months away from easing the shortage, and at the rate we were going, the reserve will be wiped out by April. The other domestic fields are helping, but not enough. At least now we have a fighting chance."

"When the major oil companies defied the price freeze, consumer confidence plummeted, and so did the polls. The administration's approval ratings have fallen from nearly seventy percent a year ago to below thirty percent. The damage may be irreversible."

"I'm not worried about reelection," Bridger said. "I don't get up each morning and check to see which way the wind is blowing. My job right now is to get this country back on its feet and keep it safe from its enemies, and to make that happen I'll do whatever I have to. Everything else, including any personal career goals I may have, is secondary."

"Yes sir," Hoffman nodded.

"There are whispers of impeachment on the Hill," Morton mentioned. "They're pulling together a committee to prove you exceeded your authority in reopening ANWR."

"So then, it's a race," Bridger said impatiently, "as if this won't be hard enough." His voice dropped nearly to a whisper. "If only they'd kept those fields open years ago, none of this would be happening now. We could have told OPEC to go jump in the lake and not have been any worse off for it. But no...we didn't want to offend a caribou."

"I've never seen anything like it," Morton sighed. "Gas lines around the block and stretching for miles sometimes. A lot of small businesses, couriers and local shipping companies and the like, have been devastated. Despite our efforts over the last couple of decades, more than three-fourths of the cars on the road still are fully dependent on gasoline...and if not for the hydrogen burners and electric hybrids that *are* out there, things would be a lot worse."

Bridger's face became hard and determined. "Okay, guys, we've got a week at Camp David coming up, and we're going to use it to get this sorted out. I want a workable strategy here. Scour the petroleum and financial industries, find me the best and the brightest, and get them on a plane. Enough heads put together might come up with a way to stop the bleeding and keep us going until our production levels pull us out of this."

"Sir," Hoffman pointed out, "there *is* an option already on the table. With the protests in Atlanta and Detroit, the rallies in Kansas and the conferences in California…not to mention all the polls and netmails… the public's been pretty adamant that we should—"

"*No,*" Bridger stated firmly, emphasizing each word, "that is *not* an option. Not now, not *ever.* Is that understood?"

"Yes sir," both men said.

"All right, then. The best and the brightest, and by Saturday. And gentlemen, if we fail…"

He did not have to finish the thought. They knew.

Like a woman following a difficult labor and delivery, Sacred Child was on its feet once more—a bit wobbly and not yet fully back in form, but up and around.

The recovery had taken weeks. The Washington office still showed signs of trauma, but Rachel considered them battle scars, proof that they were having a true effect on the daily operation of Life Quality. Public opinion of Sacred Child had been shaken following the false accusations that surrounded the New York City bus bombing, but the letter received by Homeland Security quickly had been proven false and no further "evidence" had been presented. Things were beginning to look up.

Rachel, alone at the office, sat at her desk, going over her schedule. It was a hectic time. Karen had been on the road for more than a week, making stops at several national offices and granting local interviews. The snows were making it difficult to continue gaining lost ground—the remainder of the staff, unable to brave the elements, were working from home via datalink and doing what they could. Rachel alone lived near enough to the building to allow her to walk that icy distance, and even *that* had been much easier said than done. With the storm, the office was not open to the public, the front door was locked, and the security alarm was active.

Mindful of her solitude, she glanced down at the top drawer of her desk. It now held a handgun, one loaned to her by Lawe as a special favor to Karen. Possessing such a weapon in the nation's capital was illegal for all but law-enforcement personnel, she knew, but in her mind the possible consequences of *not* carrying, on the heels of the Christmas Day break-in, were far worse than any legal penalty she might confront. Her hurried training in its use, while minimal, would prove sufficient.

She hoped.

A soft beep called Rachel's attention to her new datapad, which sat to one side on her desk. Picking it up, she found the netmail symbol flashing.

Maybe it's Karen.

She pressed the key, and a message filled the screen.

It was not from her friend and PR officer.

It was from *no one.*

There was no return path, no signature, nothing to identify the sender. Rachel scowled at the missing header, then began to read the message:

This is a warning… Your life is in danger. They will not stop until both you and your organization have been eliminated. I want to help you and will contact you again when it is safe. So that you know I am legitimate, I offer the following: $197,457.87, Treasure Island, and 256 Cherrywood Court.

Her heart pounded.

The message listed the September balance of Sacred Child's operating account, the book Rachel had bought for her brother, and the street address of the facility in which he lived.

Staring at the screen, she ran a hand through her blond hair and reached for the phone.

A fire crackled in the wide natural-stone fireplace of Aspen, the presidential cabin of Camp David. Heavy white linen curtains were drawn over the chilly night-darkened windows, sealing off the snowy world outside. The dancing flames cast an orange warmth on the rustic walls and décor of the comfortable lounge, a room that had enjoyed the presence of some of the most important men the world ever had known.

Lawe walked in, ready to begin his solitary, overnight watch, having relieved another agent, who had wasted no time in heading for bed. He found the lounge unoccupied, and was beginning a check of the adjoining sun porch when he was drawn in another direction by the sound of clattering metal. Nearing its source, a pleasant aroma met his nostrils, one he had experienced more than once, in more than one Italian restaurant.

Soft light spilled from the kitchen doorway.

The president was at it again.

"Sir?" he asked, finding the man at a stove-side counter.

"Bry," Bridger said, his attentions on the dish he was preparing.

"Just checking on you, sir. I thought you might want to call it a night." He moved closer and discovered the man rolling thin slices of what looked like beef around a blend of raisins, cheese, and a variety of spices and herbs.

"Your hands washed?" Bridger asked.

"Uh, no sir."

"Would you?" Lawe stepped to the sink and did so, then dried his hands on a small embroidered towel.

"Here," the man said, inviting the agent closer with a sideward nod. "Put your finger here while I tie this…"

"Yes sir." Lawe dutifully placed a fingertip in the appropriate place as Bridger securely tied a length of kitchen string around the roll, then repeated the procedure.

"Braciole," the president smiled. "It was my mother's favorite. She passed the secret along to me. Finest you ever tasted."

"Sure smells good," Lawe noted.

"That's the sauce," Bridger said, indicating a stainless steel pot on the stove. "All fresh. Nothing canned."

"Isn't it a bit late, sir?"

"I'm not sleeping much lately, Son. Thought I might as well make myself useful." He cracked a smile. "Besides, it gets my mind off things, if only for a little while."

A third meat roll was tied, then another.

"Sir," Lawe began, "I was wondering if I might ask you about something."

"You know you can ask me anything, Bry," the man gently smiled. "I've always enjoyed our talks. Shoot."

"Well, I know you've come down hard on the side of Israel through all this…that pulling back as the Arabs are asking is out of the question."

"Yes?"

"I was wondering *why*. I mean, we're taking a beating, sir. That oil would relieve a lot of suffering and hardship overnight."

"Why? You mean other than the fact that it would be wrong to abandon an ally?"

"Yes sir. It's almost as if…well, as if you're putting Israel ahead of your own country and your own people. I know that, back when it came time either to help defend Taiwan or let it fall to the Chinese, President McMillen had little trouble citing American national interest as justification for letting the island be taken."

The president continued to tie the meat rolls. "Here," he asked, redirecting Lawe's helpful digit.

"People are talking," Lawe continued. "Some are saying the Jews have you in their pocket, and the other party's started digging for evidence of some kind of payoff or quid pro quo…anything impeachable."

"First ANWR and now this. They're determined to find *something.*"

Bridger quickly browned the rolls in a skillet, then dropped each in turn into the simmering marinara sauce, covered the saucepan, and turned down the heat. After setting a timer, he washed his hands and dried them as Lawe stood by, hoping he had not gone too far.

"Tell me, Son," Bridger said. "Have you ever met a Philistine?"

Puzzled at the odd question, Lawe furrowed his brow.

"I don't think so, sir."

"Or a Babylonian? Or an Assyrian? Or a Roman emperor or a Nazi or a Stalinist?"

"No sir."

"There's a reason for that."

He wiped down the cutting board, then led Lawe back into the den. They sat near the fire, the room's sole light at this hour. The agent glanced up, momentarily taken with the geometry of the polished wooden rafters overhead, then returned to the flickering blaze.

"Bry," Bridger went on, "throughout recorded history, civilizations have risen and fallen based upon their treatment of Israel. That's a fact. It's also a fact that the Bible tells *why.* God promised Abraham that he would be the father of a great nation, which was and is Israel. He also promised, 'I will bless those who bless you, and curse those who curse you.' And sure enough, history has borne that out."

"But the Arabs, sir…*they're* still here."

"Their time is coming. I don't know how it'll happen, or when, but it's coming."

Lawe shook his head. "I'm not much for biblical things, sir. Scripture isn't something I put any credence in. It's an old book…can't be relevant, not anymore."

"Not relevant? Simply as history, it's invaluable."

"Well, maybe, but looking at the here and now, all I can see is that helping the Arabs would solve an awful lot of problems. I wonder if we shouldn't do something to talk Israel into giving up Jerusalem…to do what the Arab world wants in order to bring peace."

"It won't bring peace, Bry. It never has. This isn't an issue of land. It never was. These people want the total elimination of the Jews. Anything less *still* will result in bloodshed and war." He paused, watching the fire. "They're the only true democracy in the region. We have to do whatever we can to keep them afloat. And on a basic moral level, the United States cannot allow any other government to dictate our foreign policy. If we were to let OPEC or anyone else tell us who our allies could be, we'd be showing ourselves as weak and unreliable. No country would ever trust us again, and we'd lose every ally we have.

"No, we have to stand with Israel, despite the odds. We'll weather this storm, Bry. I'm not saying we won't take a few lumps, but we'll get through it. To abandon *any* ally would be wrong, but to turn our backs on Israel would mean…" He drew a deep breath. "I'm not willing to take that chance."

"But, sir…to say that God Himself is holding that country as special above any other—"

"When Israel was reborn in May of '48…which in itself was nothing short of miraculous, by the way…they were attacked on all sides, *the next day,* by five Arab nations who joined forces to destroy them with a single blow. The Jews faced impossible odds but still were victorious. And since then, for all these years, they've remained there in the land of their forefathers, pinned against the sea with enemies on three sides. Yet still they survive."

"I would tend to think that has something to do with their nukes, sir."

"In part, yes. Today. But they had none back then, and they still won. Decisively. God's fingerprints are all over that country, and I for one am going to respect that."

"So we should go along with *everything* Israel does? Every policy decision, every military move? Back in '67, they opened fire on the USS

Liberty and killed dozens of our men. Wounded many more. Some say it was because they knew the ship had detected their surprise invasion of the Golan Heights."

"We have to share responsibility in that. We failed to tell them the ship was ours."

"I know the official story. They claimed it was an accident. But there was evidence they *knew* it was an American vessel and attacked anyway."

"I'm not saying we should turn a blind eye, not by any means. They'll commit questionable acts and make poor decisions, just as we will. Show me a country that doesn't. But we have to help protect them and not leave them to the wolves."

"I never knew you were such a Zionist."

"Call it what you will." He gazed at the licking flames, his mind drifting back. "Years ago, when I was a much younger man, I spent a year over there as assistant to an envoy. During that time, I met a woman who had been the victim of a homicide bombing. She'd been standing about a hundred feet away and the concussion barely scathed her, but she caught shrapnel they'd built into the bomb. Small finishing nails…you know the type. An inch long, maybe. Her body was *filled* with them, and most were beyond the reach of surgery. She had to live like that, having all of that inside her. Every movement she made was agonizing, all day, every day." He paused, old and fervent emotions rising within him. "What kind of mind would conceive and implement a method like that, especially against civilians? To deliberately inflict a *lifetime* of torture…"

"Desperate measures, perhaps," Lawe said. "I mean, I'm not justifying their tactics, but there's been a great deal of suffering on both sides."

"True enough. But when one side is so filled with hatred that it won't rest until the other is completely destroyed, there can be no peace."

The Secret Service man looked upon his president, whose lined face and graying hair, even in the flickering light of the fire, reflected the pressure of his office.

"In any case," the president went on, "I believe with all my heart that the single best way we can keep this country safe and strong is to stand with Israel. As it is, I'd say that's the only remaining source of divine blessing we have going for us. Given our predilection for killing off our young and unborn, along with the way we've blasphemed God, kicked Him out of public life and even most of our churches, I'm surprised He's still with us at all. You want a definition of grace, Bry? That's it."

"But, the Constitution…I mean, separation of church and—"

"No such thing."

"Sir?"

"Down through the years, they've shoved the Lord out of sight and used that cry of 'separation of church and state' to justify it every time. But no such idea *ever* existed in the Constitution. *Nowhere* did our Founding Fathers state that faith in God…which they shared, by the way…was to have no bearing on the governing of the land. Quite the contrary. All they said was that the federal government wasn't to interfere in the states' rights to exercise their faith as they saw fit, nor was it to pass any law that established an official national religion."

"Then, why—"

"Did you know that the reading and spelling primers used in American public schools during this nation's first century of existence consisted of *Bible verses?* No, this wasn't a 'constitutional' matter. We finally banished God because we didn't want to answer to Him anymore. Didn't want to hear His words, didn't want any sign of Him. We hid ourselves. Then we even took His name off our money…and mind you, they did that less than a year before they planned to stop using physical currency altogether. What a slap in the face *that* was."

Lawe found himself looking on Bridger with new eyes. While he shared neither the man's Christian faith nor his stand on Israel, the agent could not help but be impressed by such principles. For two years Lawe had been ready to take a bullet for him, but never had he realized the extent of the president's strength of character. The majority of those serving in Washington based their decisions on factors of political expediency or party support or poll numbers.

But Matthew Bridger, Lawe now knew, was not such as these.

He's a good man—how in the world did he ever get elected?

"You would have made an inspiring preacher, sir. Not that you haven't been a good president…"

"You know, I did consider that. But I felt a calling to go into government, and things kept falling into place that way. I ran for one office, then another…and here I am."

For almost an hour, the men sat before the crackling fire, leaving the demands and tensions of their jobs behind. There in the winter calm, they discussed football, fishing, movies, and other nonpolitical subjects, getting to know each other better, all walls down.

The timer dinged. Bridger rose from his chair and headed toward the kitchen, patting Lawe on the shoulder as he passed him.

"Well, I suppose I'd best turn in," he said, "as soon as I get the braciole into the fridge. Morning's going to come early, and we've got a country to save."

"Good luck on that, sir."

"Would you like some of this, Bry? Trust me…my mom knew how to cook."

"Yes sir. I would."

"I'll fix you a plate."

The first lady's voice sounded gently from the hallway. "Matt? It's getting late…"

"Be right there," he replied. "Just cleaning up."

Lawe watched as the barefoot chief executive shut off the kitchen light, walked over, and handed him a generous plate.

"Bon appétit."

"It looks good, sir."

"I'll pass the compliment along someday," Bridger smiled, turning toward the hall. "There's more in there if you want it. Help yourself."

"I will. Thank you. Good night, Mr. President."

"'Night, Bry."

Lawe took a bite. He had not eaten since late afternoon, and the midnight meal was just what he needed.

Man, if we could can this stuff we'd make a fortune—

Alone, the agent enjoyed his food and began his watch. In the morning he would be relieved, freed to get some sleep as the fate of a great nation was decided.

God, if You're up there, be with that man tomorrow—he's going to need it.

Randall Sullivan sat in his living room and listened to a young man who wore a dark suit and blue tie. The two faced each other, Sullivan on the sofa and his visitor in a chair.

"This would open so many doors for you," the producer was saying. "Your name would be a household word. You'd touch millions more than you ever could through personal appearances."

"What would I have to do?" Sullivan asked, unsure he wanted to commit to such a project.

"Anything you want," the man said. "We'd structure the show anyway you want. The name, the format, the set design, everything...your call."

Sullivan raised an eyebrow. "Everything?"

"Everything."

The transmortalist watched as Janessa walked up behind the man and stood behind his chair. Smiling mischievously, she ran her ethereal fingers through his hair without disturbing it, then moved them along his shoulders. The man squirmed uncomfortably.

"Just got a chill," he explained. "Wow, that was weird."

Sullivan suppressed a chuckle. "When would it begin? The show, I mean."

"We'd start shooting in August. First airings would be in early September. If it's successful, we may even go live."

"Where would they do it?"

"Chicago. We have a brand-new studio and production facility just waiting for you. Four other shows are recorded there now, but yours would be the jewel in the crown."

"Long commute."

"We'll put you in a house in one of the nicer neighborhoods. Fully furnished to your liking, with all expenses covered."

"What about *this* house?" Sullivan asked. "I don't want to lose it. Too many memories."

"Mr. Sullivan," the man smiled, "you agree to this deal, and I'm sure we can see to it that the mortgage on this home is taken care of. They did as much for Garland Lucelli when they brought him in from Seattle."

"Who?"

"The Italian Scallion. He hosts one of the most popular cooking shows ever."

"Oh," Sullivan said. "Don't know about him... I don't cook much."

He looked to his daughter, who was smiling and nodding an enthusiastic yes.

"Do it, Daddy," she said. "It'll be so much fun."

He slowly nodded as if considering the question alone—the producer, of course, had not seen or heard Janessa.

"What sort of money are we talking about?"

"I'm not yet in a position to give you a specific number," he answered as if rehearsed, "but I can promise you you'll be quite pleased."

"Do it, Daddy," his daughter repeated.

"All right," Sullivan agreed. "I'll call my attorney, and we'll see if we can get it nailed down."

The young man rose to his feet, then extended a hand and shook Sullivan's.

"Excellent. This will be a landmark moment," the producer said, barely able to hide his excitement. "History in the making."

"Well, we'll see."

Sullivan escorted his guest to the foyer and saw him out. Closing the door, he turned to Janessa, who stood nearby, her smile almost victorious.

"Millions," she gleefully said. "Just think."

"This could be interesting, I suppose," he said. "I've never been to Chicago."

The girl indicated her father's well-read copy of *The Loving Bible*, which rested on an end table. "Maybe you could open each show by reading a passage or two from that. What a wonderful platform this will be for sharing the spiritual truths that have been revealed to you. Just think of it."

18

The best and the brightest, Bridger had demanded.

Their meetings on the enclosed sun porch of Aspen had gone on for six days, yet no one had found a workable solution. Geological science had devised no method for drawing petroleum from the ground any faster than was being done already, and the hard fact that any new drilling would take months to yield results presented an insurmountable obstacle.

Time, now the most devastating of enemies, would not be overcome.

Suggestions as extreme as the military seizure of Saudi oil fields had been tossed on the table, if only to get them uttered and out of the way. But ultimately, even the greatest minds the administration could find had not been up to the task. Asked to perform the impossible, they had failed.

They returned to Washington without fanfare. The president and his cabinet went back to work, fighting the crisis by whatever conventional means they could, while their critics grew louder and more brazen.

Bridger and his vice president sat in the presidential dining room, a private facility connected by a short hallway to the Oval Office, taking their lunch after a prolonged meeting with the FBI. Civil unrest was building as economic pressure increased, and rioting was becoming widespread. A hi-def display on the wall, tuned to one of the news channels, silently played images of the outbreaks interspersed with commentary by social experts and political figures.

"Good meat loaf, Harper," Bridger observed. "You should have tried it."

"I've never been a big fan," Lund smiled, enjoying the steak and baked potato he had ordered. "My mom never quite got a handle on it."

"A pity," the president smiled. "A well-made meat loaf is a wonder to behold."

A few silent moments passed.

"Matt," Lund began, his tone sullen, "we're losing support in almost every arena. Public approval is down to twenty-three percent. The House and Senate both are making noises that the time has come for—"

"I know," Bridger said. "So we hold them off as long as we can, and maybe by then things will show an upswing. As bad as this situation is, we can't let it dictate our foreign policy, especially where Israel is concerned."

"I know this goes way beyond hanging onto the Jewish vote…but Matt, there comes a time…"

"Have our finger in the air, do we?"

"We're here to do the will of the people… We can't just ignore them."

Bridger took another bite of his meal, letting the words die away. As he glanced at the screen, the face of the opposition leader appeared, the import of his words conveyed by a graphic splashed across the bottom of the screen. Bridger hit a button on a remote, bringing the sound up, and with it the familiar voice of Senator Briggs.

"…is long overdue, and we can only hope that the damage is not irreversible. This administration's irrational and dangerous refusal to reconsider its foreign policy stand has brought incredible hardship upon the people of America, and enough is enough."

"Senator," a reporter asked, "you've been opposed to Mr. Bridger on almost every issue… Do you truly feel that he is incapable of handling the position?"

"He's a fine man, I'm sure," Briggs replied, "but he simply is not suited for the job. When President Dreyer died so early in his first term, the responsibility was thrust upon Mr. Bridger…and let's face it, it's more than he can handle. This last-ditch effort at Camp David proved fruitless, as I think we all knew it would, and the time has come for serious action."

"Are you saying Congress is prepared to force an abandonment of Israel?"

"We're taking measures that will make that possible. We hope the presi-dent will come to his senses, but we are preparing for the eventuality that he does not."

Bridger hit the mute button as the scene shifted to another locale.

"Good ol' Cyrus," he sarcastically commented.

"This will be rough, Mr. President."

"I know, Harper," the man grimly said. "All we can do is circle the wagons and be ready."

"I have to go alone."

Karen watched Rachel gather a few things from her desk and stick them in her purse. It was a Sunday afternoon, the last in February, and the two women alone occupied the office. Snow and gray slush still spotted the city and the streets, though days had passed since the blizzard that had plagued the Northeast had moved out to sea.

"For now," Rachel went on, "I'm going to have to do things his way."

"You don't even know who 'he' is. You got an anonymous message, what…almost a month ago? You've heard nothing else in all that time, then suddenly—"

"I don't know what's going on. But today's message was explicit… He wants me to meet him at three, and that's what I'm going to do."

"Why?" Karen asked, as Rachel slipped into her coat. "They've already killed Gordie. The police may have no leads, but we both know who did it. Who knows what else they're capable of."

"If *this* person wanted me dead, he could have done it at any time. I'm sure they know when I come and go up here. Nothing I can do about that. This person, this contact, said he can give us information that could bring Life Quality to its knees. I don't know what that could be, but we need it, and he wants me to meet him alone. I have to do this on his terms."

"Rachel, you know he's involved with them up to his chin. How else could he have had access to the files they stole? How can you trust him enough to—"

"All the more reason to go."

"Then let me go with you. You have four hours… Maybe Bry can even—"

"No," Rachel insisted. "Listen. I understand and appreciate your concern, honey, but I have to do this his way. If he even suspects that I'm not there alone, he'll call it off."

"This is too risky."

"This could be the break we've prayed for. By this time next week, there may *be* no Life Quality. Think of the lives that will be saved! That far outweighs the personal risk."

Karen followed the woman down the hallway, headed toward the lobby.

"There has to be another way. Why can't you do this by netmail?"

"He said it had to be face to face. He's been paranoid about leaving a trail of any kind. Apparently, his life is at serious risk for contacting me."

"I really, *really* don't like this, Rachel."

"I don't either," the woman admitted, "but I have no choice. Besides" —she patted her purse—"I have Mama's little helper in here, and I know how to use it, thanks to Bry."

Karen reached out and hugged her.

"Be careful," she pleaded.

"I will. Try not to worry."

A weapons detector had been installed at the lobby entrance and everyone was screened, without exception. Not wanting to sound the alarm, Rachel reached over and shut the system off.

"Turn it back on after I leave," she said.

"I will."

Uneasy, Karen watched from near the receptionist's desk as the woman departed, locking the door behind her.

Please, Lord, she prayed, *keep her safe—*

Several sharp cracks filled the air, and a piercing screech sounded as the reinforced window in the front door whitened and shattered. Startled, Karen fell back against the wall, then cried out and rushed the entrance. She fumbled with the lock and pulled the door open.

No—please, no!

Rachel lay crumpled on the steps just outside, bright blood staining the pavement beneath her. A cluster of bullet hits marred the brick facade of the building.

Cold wind knifing through the light fabric of her dress, Karen dropped to the injured woman's side and cradled her head. Looking up and around, she saw no shooter. Pedestrians had turned and were looking in her direction, and a few slowly approached.

"Rachel!" she cried, gently rubbing the woman's cheek. Unfocused eyes fluttered open, searched, and found the face of a friend.

"Go," came words weakly. "The meeting...you have to..."

"Don't talk," Karen said, fighting not to break down. "I'll get help."

"You *have* to...important..."

"I will...just hold on."

A small crowd gathered. One man pulled a netphone from his pocket and summoned an ambulance.

"Did you see anything?" Karen cried out. "Did you see who did this?" There was no response, just the muttering of curious people jockeying for the best view.

"Stay with me, Rachel," she implored, stroking her mentor's forehead, her voice broken by tears. She watched helplessly as precious life seeped away and onto the sidewalk. "Please...we need you..."

As the wail of an ambulance grew louder, Karen held her friend tightly, praying for a miracle. Only when the paramedics arrived did she release her, and as she watched them fight to stabilize Rachel, she trembled.

"I've got a pulse," one EMT said as they placed the woman on a stretcher, "but it's weak. Pressure's low... She's losing a lot of blood..."

Please, Rachel—you can't die!

The ride to the hospital was a blur. For the second time in less than three months, Karen rode along in an ambulance, its siren blaring as it tore through the streets. She held Rachel's hand, praying that life would awaken her lovely features.

At the emergency room, Karen paced in the waiting area, still praying for the woman's life. She held Rachel's purse, having left her own inside the office, clutching it as if for comfort. As the shock eased and she became more aware of her surroundings, she came to realize her dress was stained with her friend's blood.

Badly shaken but still functioning, she used a pay phone to call Lawe and a few of Sacred Child's staff, told them what had happened, and promised to keep them all informed.

First the minutes, then an hour ticked by. Finally, a doctor appeared at the door, his green scrubs marked with dark blood, his expression dour.

"How is she?" Karen asked, her voice tinged both with fear and hope.

"Ms. Foley," he began, "I'm Dr. Gerard." She stood before him, wringing her hands. "I'm sorry, but the news isn't good."

"They shot her," Karen said. "I didn't see them, but..."

"Rachel was struck four times. We did what we could, but there's too much damage. If you want to see her, I'll take you, but I would suggest you not wait. Does she have family?"

"A brother in Minneapolis, but he's in a nursing home. I don't know which one."

In silence she followed him into the intensive care unit. *This can't be happening—this is a nightmare—it has to be!*

Rachel lay on a bed, wired to a complex of monitors. A quiet electronic beep counted the waning beats of her heart. As the doctor and a nurse remained near the door, Karen walked up to the bedside and took the woman's hand.

"Rachel," she said softly. "It's Karen. I'm here."

The woman's eyes remained closed, but whispered words escaped her lips. "Karen…"

She leaned low, clasping Rachel's left hand in both of her own.

"Yes. I'm here."

"Sacred Child…yours now. Only one who can…stop them…"

Tears clouded Karen's vision, and she drew still closer, leaning down, straining to hear. "Listen to me. You're not going anywhere. In no time, you'll be back on your feet and—"

"All in…datapad…"

"Rachel, stay here. We need you. Please…"

"Ramah…"

"What?"

"Yours now…can't let them…" Her words grew more faint. "You have to…meet him…only way…crucial. Promise me…"

"I promise," Karen said, gripping her hand tightly, her tears flowing freely. "We'll stop them. The children will live."

One corner of Rachel's closed lips turned almost imperceptibly upward. "Knew you…were the one…hired you. Hand of God…upon you…"

Karen kissed Rachel lightly on the forehead, then grieved as the gentle smile faded.

"Rachel…*no…*"

A constant tone sounded. Karen's gaze rose to a monitor above the bed. It had flat-lined.

Karen's hands began to tremble. Slowly, reluctantly, she released

Rachel's hand, letting it settle onto the bed. She backed away, one step, then two.

The doctor moved forward, leaned over the bed, and flipped a few switches. The electronics went dark and silent.

"Eleven-fourteen," he gently whispered to the nurse. Karen walked around the foot of the bed, her disbelieving eyes still on Rachel.

"I'm so sorry," the doctor said, but Karen did not hear him, her focus emerging from the pain, trained elsewhere.

"Lawe," he answered into the phone.

"Bry...she...didn't make it."

He took a deep breath. "I'm so sorry."

"They gunned her down like an animal. The doctors tried, but..."

"I'll be right there."

"No," Karen said, her voice betraying the fact that she had been crying. "I'm going back to the office. There's something I have to do. Amy's taking me."

"Now? I'm not sure you should go back there. Don't you think—"

"It has to be now, and it has to be there. I'll...I'll call you later. A couple of hours, I guess."

"Listen. Just wait for me. I'll come down there and—"

"I need to do this alone."

Puzzled, he nonetheless deferred. "Okay. I don't like it, but okay. You call if you need anything."

"I will. I promise."

"I love you," he offered, feeling her anguish.

"You too." And then, with a click, she was gone.

Lawe gently returned the receiver to its cradle.

"What's up, Bry?" Lundy asked, sensing trouble as he walked in.

"I'm not sure," he said. "Rachel Webster, Karen's boss, just died. Drive-by shooting. Happened in front of the Sacred Child building."

"Oh, man. I'm sorry."

Morris shook his head. "Can't say I'm totally surprised."

"Come again?" Lawe asked, bristling.

"That kind of subversion invites a response. These anti-harvesters… They're a bunch of fanatics who—"

"What, deserve to die?"

"You yank the tiger's tail, you're gonna get bit."

"Don't be a jackass," Lundy scolded the man. "Karen's right in the middle of the group."

Morris waved him off. "I'm just saying she might want to pick her friends a little more carefully, that's all."

"She believes in their cause," Lawe scowled. "I don't like it, but there it is. Now lay off. A woman's dead, and others may be in danger."

"Okay, okay," Morris conceded.

"You ever meet Rachel Webster, Bry?" Lundy asked.

Lost in thought, he took a moment to answer. "Once or twice. Around Christmas."

"I saw her whenever she came to see the president. They didn't want the press to know, so I helped sneak her in. It was always late when she came… I was on nights then. Escorted her in and out of the Oval through the Rose Garden. Happened two or three times."

"I heard," Lawe said distantly, after a moment.

"Didn't you say she and Karen were pretty close?"

No response.

"Bry?"

Lawe was not listening. Karen's call was replaying in his mind, her words troubling him.

"Something doesn't feel right…" He rose from his chair, grabbed his coat from the rack and moved toward the door. "I'll be back."

For a second time, jagged slashes of yellow barred the entrance to Sacred Child, ribbons snapping in the breeze as they cordoned the scene. Police investigators almost had finished digging bullet fragments out of the building's facade, securing what evidence remained of the crime. Rachel's blood, now darkened, remained on the steps and sidewalk.

Amy pointed her car down the alleyway and pulled into the parking area at the rear. The dark gray skies threatened icy rain.

"Are you sure you don't need me to wait?" she asked. "Is there anything I can do?"

"No," Karen insisted. "But why don't you go check on Melissa. I need to take care of a couple of things, then I'll be leaving." She indicated the corner of the lot. "My car's right there. Thank you for the ride, and the change of clothes. I'll give you a call in a little while."

She climbed out of the vehicle, braving the piercing wind.

"You're sure?" Amy called through her open window. "I'd be happy to stay."

"I'm fine," Karen said. "Honest."

Carrying the clean dress and Rachel's purse, she entered the office from the rear. Moving along the corridor, ghosts of recent memories swirled around her, images of her friend. She longed to stop time, to keep the passing minutes from widening the distance between them. All was as they had left it, as if Karen had only to cry out and stop the woman from walking out that front door.

Only a moment ago, she was here—she was alive!

Numbness set in. Karen would grieve—days and weeks later, she would know the pain of the depths of her loss. But for now, her mind's defensive mechanisms shielded her from them. Her focus had sharpened to a dagger point, set upon a duty left to her.

Making her way into the woman's office, she found Rachel's datapad resting on the desk, just as it had been left.

"Okay," she whispered. "Talk to me."

Karen pressed the On switch. After a brief start-up sequence, the unit requested a password and she entered one, hoping she was right.

Ramah.

"Welcome, Rachel," the device said in a soft, pleasant voice. "You have two new messages."

Karen touched the mail icon on the screen. Bypassing the new entries, she scrolled back and found the anonymous message she sought, one without a title, without a return address. It was brief and to the point:

"Parklane Theater, February 23. 'The Roses of Winter,' three o'clock showing. Sit on the back row, center section, fourth seat from the right."

She jotted down the information and turned off the datapad. Returning to her own office, she slipped the note into her purse and glanced up at the clock. Time was short—she had to get going.

What if he knows about Rachel? she wondered. *What if he doesn't show up?*

What if he's the one who killed her?

She quickly changed out of her bloodstained dress and returned to Rachel's office, where she retrieved the borrowed handgun from the woman's purse. Having grown up in a small Midwestern town, where hunting and target practice were common, she knew well enough how to use it. Her father had seen to that.

If nothing happens, I'll just give it back to Bry—

Karen paused, her thoughts turning to God.

"I prayed that You keep her safe," she whispered. "And You let her get shot. Then You let her *die*."

Frustration and disappointment took root within her, disappointment in a Lord she always had trusted.

Didn't You hear me? Did I not pray hard enough? Did I do something that caused You to turn Your back on me? On her?

Feeling more alone than she could remember, she picked up her purse and headed out into the cold, toward a rendezvous that terrified her.

Lawe slowed as he neared Karen's office. The police had finished their work and were gone, leaving behind an odd desolation, an emptiness that spoke of the loss. He knew she must have been devastated but was presenting a brave front—she needed him now, he also knew, and was determined to be there for her.

In front of the building, a lone car was parked—Rachel's. He came to a gentle stop behind it.

As he shifted into park he saw ahead, through the windshield of the vehicle before him, Karen's car emerging from the alley, headed north and away from him. He could tell that she had not seen him as she had pulled into the street, her attentions focused on the approaching traffic.

Where are you going?

After a moment, as traffic allowed, he pulled away from the curb and followed at a discreet distance. A few vehicles separated them, but he had little trouble keeping sight of her. Curious, he pulled his netphone from its pouch and pressed the speed dial.

Strains of Beethoven's Ninth Symphony filled the car. Her phone. Karen picked it up, saw Lawe's number on the display, and answered.

"Hi."

"Hi," Lawe said. "What are you doing?"

She paused, unsure how to respond. She had never lied to him, but the pressure of the moment forced all other options from her mind.

I promised Rachel I would do this. If I tell him where I'm going, or what I'm doing, he'll try to stop me—

"Sitting in my office," she said calmly, "taking care of a few things."

Lawe paused for an unusually long moment. "Oh?" he asked. "What kind of things?"

"Things Rachel asked me to tend to, before she…" A heavy pause. "Well, just some things that need to be done."

"I see."

He sounds odd. Something's on his mind—

"I miss your smile," Lawe said. "When are you going to get rid of that antique phone and get one with a videolink?"

Thank Heaven I didn't—

"I guess I'm just an old-fashioned girl," she replied in a forced, light tone. "I value my privacy. Besides, I'm not up for smiling much right now anyway."

"I suppose."

She drew a breath. "Bry, I may be up here for a while. A couple of hours, at least. Why don't you come by for dinner tonight?"

"Sure. What time?"

"Seven-thirty."

"See you then."

Lawe pressed a button and ended the call.

What is she up to? Why would she lie to me?

He had not wanted to press the point, had not wanted to confront her, not yet. Clearly, she had a reason for not telling him where she was going.

But what?

He followed at a discreet distance, keeping her in sight, matching her lane changes and other maneuvers. Not since his days in the counterfeit division had he shadowed anyone through the city streets, but it all quickly came back to him. One turn, then another; up onto the freeway, then back off again. Finally, she pulled into the parking lot of a movie theater, chose a space near the building, and parked.

A movie?

Watching from across the lot, he saw her emerge from the car, buy a ticket at the window, and disappear through its dark glass doors.

He glanced at the clock.

Two fifty-five.

"So, now what?"

Karen sat nervously in the darkened auditorium, bathed in the dim light of the huge digital screen. Ten, then fifteen minutes passed.

Back row, fourth seat in—

No sign of the man.

Did he hear about Rachel and choose not to come? Is he watching me right now, trying to decide whether to go ahead? Is he outside, waiting to shoot me as soon as I leave?

In the gloom she scanned the seats around her. Only a handful of people were there, less than two dozen, most of whom were scattered in the center of the room.

This was stupid, she scolded herself. *I shouldn't have come. I should have told Bry and let him tell me how to handle the situation—*

The air smelled of stale popcorn and spilled soda. The floor was sticky. Her anxiety grew with each passing minute. The film played out on the screen, scene after scene, yet she did not watch, did not care.

But I had to do this—it's our only chance—

And then, suddenly, someone was seated beside her, near the aisle.

"You're Karen Foley," a feminine voice whispered. "I recognize you from the news."

"Yes," she said, finding the woman's face largely obscured by a winter scarf. "Rachel sent me...her dying request."

"I'm so sorry about what happened to her. I heard only a few minutes ago." The stranger clearly was uncomfortable. "I wasn't sure anyone would keep this appointment. I almost stayed away myself. But then, knowing Rachel, I knew she'd somehow make an arrangement..."

"You knew her? I mean, personally?"

The woman did not answer.

"Was it *your* people?" Karen asked, anger momentarily eclipsing her fear. "Did *they* kill her? And Gordie?"

"I believe so."

Karen tensed, her nails pressing into her palms. The blunt confirmation was as a hammer blow.

"I promise you," the woman went on, "I wasn't a part of it."

"So why am I here?" Karen demanded. "What do you want?"

The shadowed figure reached into her purse, pulled free a small padded envelope, and handed it over. "It's all here. Do whatever you have to."

"What is it? What am I supposed to—"

"Don't wait too long, and be careful. I can assure you they're not finished yet. Rachel won't be the last, unless you stop *them* first. Protect your people...and God be with you."

"Wait... What if I need to contact you—?"

"You can't." The woman hurriedly rose from her seat and was gone.

Karen clutched the envelope to her chest, her heart pounding.

What if that woman was followed? What if someone's out there, waiting for me to leave, waiting to gun me down the way they did Rachel—

After several long, tense minutes, she slipped the parcel into her purse, took a deep breath, and left the auditorium. Fearing the worst, she subtly, warily eyed everyone as she made her way through the lobby and out onto the sidewalk.

Karen hurried across the parking lot. The wind had picked up, and the afternoon sky was growing darker. As she neared her car, she felt a sense of relief, allowing herself to believe that she would live to see the following day. Taking nothing for granted, she also felt a need to put distance between herself and the theater as quickly as possible.

A tiny red light flashed.

Melissa entered her apartment, a grocery bag hanging from each hand. Her walk had been enjoyable, despite the cold. First, a few relaxing hours spent reading her Bible in a coffee shop, then a trip to the market, and now, perhaps, a nap.

Her eye found the little blinking light. It no longer held the innate menace it once had, for her creditors had been satisfied long before. Walking over to the answering machine, she dropped one bag onto the couch and pressed the playback button.

"Melissa, this is Karen," a familiar voice said. "I don't have my netphone right now… Try to call me at home when you get this. If you can't reach me, I'll call you back."

There was an odd tone in the woman's voice, one that was worrisome. Melissa hit the speed dial on her phone, got four rings and an answering machine.

"It's Melissa," she said. "I got your message. Call me."

Her brow furrowed with concern, she carried the bags into the kitchen.

Now what? she worried.

Karen walked into her apartment, dropped her purse onto the sofa, and hurried to her bedroom. Her datapad rested on the bed—immediately she sat down, inserted the datastick given to her by the mysterious woman, and pressed the power switch. Still wearing her coat, she impatiently watched the screen as the device ran through its start-up menu.

Her attention abruptly was torn away by a sound in the other room, at the front door. It was being unlocked. Another moment, and she heard it begin to open.

Startled and expecting no one, she reached back, feeling the bed beside her, seeking her purse and the weapon it held. It was not there.

I left it on the sofa!

Her heart pounded. She feared for her life.

The sound of footsteps echoed in the tiled entryway. Heavy footsteps. Male footsteps.

She held her breath.

"Karen?" Lawe's voice called out.

At once her fears evaporated into a cloud of relief. She rose from the bed, hurried into the living room, and rushed to him.

"Oh, Bry," she said, falling into his arms. He held her close, held her tight.

"Are you okay?"

"I am now."

"All right, then…why don't you tell me what that was all about this afternoon?"

"What do you mean?"

"How was the movie?"

She broke the embrace and looked up at him.

"What?"

"I followed you from the Sacred Child building," he said. "I was pulling up as you were leaving. And when I called, you told me you were still in your office..."

"You *spied* on me?" she snapped.

"It didn't start out that way. And you *lied* to me. You don't usually do that... Not that I know of, anyway."

"What's *that* supposed to mean?"

"I don't know, Karen. You tell me... What's going on?"

"They killed Rachel. I'm sure of it."

"*They* who?"

"Life Quality."

"How do you know?"

"I just do."

"I don't follow..."

"Unlike this afternoon."

Lawe pulled back. "Look, just...why were you at the theater?"

He deserved an answer, she knew. The time had come to tell him everything. No, not *everything*—she felt a deep pain, believing God had let her down, but she was not about to let him know *that*.

She led him into the bedroom. Waiting impatiently, he stood and watched as she sat on the bed and tried repeatedly to call up the files the precious datastick held.

"What is wrong with this thing?" she muttered, slapping the device in frustration. "Of all the times to lock up..." She rebooted the datapad.

"What's on there?"

"Classified data from someone at Life Quality...a contact I met. It was supposed to have been Rachel who went, but—"

"What? You mean at the theater you were—"

"She'd seen our stolen files. Promised she could help us. And set up a rendezvous with Rachel."

"So *you* went instead? After they killed your boss?"

"I told you. I *had* to go. It was Rachel's last request."

"What, that makes it okay? You *both* could have died! Why didn't you tell me all this when I called?"

"Because you would have stopped me!"

"*You better believe* I would have stopped you."

"So see… I made the right decision."

"What, to walk into a possible deathtrap? *That* was the right decision?"

"No, to meet with the one person who might help us to end the child killings once and for all." The datapad still would not read the stick properly.

"Looks like she may have given you a virus," he said. "Probably hoped you'd put that stick into a network port at the office so it would bring down your whole system."

"Couldn't have…" She shook her head. "You weren't there. You didn't hear her…"

"And whose fault was that? I want you to quit this cause of yours. Two deaths in as many months, and you may be next."

"Rachel gave her life for this. I owe it to her to—"

"And what happens if you get yourself killed?"

"Then someone else will take over, and then someone else, and then someone else, until we shut down Life Quality once and for all."

"And what about *us?*"

"What *us?* Is there an *us?* I need more than…more than…"

She began to break down. Tears began to flow, and she could not stop them. She had been too busy, too frightened, too numb until that moment, but now—

He sat beside her. She sought his embrace, shaking in his arms as she wept. He held her, letting her draw from him, sharing her pain.

"I'm sorry," he said quietly, gently. "I shouldn't have… It's too soon…"

He silently held her, allowing her grief to run its course. It would come again and often. Karen took a series of deep breaths, each steadier than the last. Lawe wiped the wetness from her cheeks and softly met her glistening eyes.

"I don't want to lose you," he said.

"I don't want to lose you either. But I can't quit Sacred Child, Bry. I think I'm in charge now."

"*What?*"

"Rachel told me…right before she…"

"No ma'am," Lawe insisted. "You'd be a target for *sure*."

"Welcome to *my* world. How do you think it's been for me the last four years, worrying over *you* day in and day out? You go to work with a bull's-eye painted on your back. Every day I don't know if you're going to take a bullet meant for the president or get into some kind of crossfire or—"

"That's different."

"Different how?"

"It just *is*. I'm trained to handle those situations. You aren't. You'd be a sitting duck."

"I'll hire security people."

"Not enough."

"Bry, I told you. Rachel chose me, and I want to honor that."

He rose again to his feet, jaw clenched. She would not hear him.

Karen went silent as the datapad beside her finally chimed its readiness. She picked up the device and found text and tables filling its display. File after file opened, and she began to read.

Words and numbers, telling a grisly tale.

Her eyes went wide with disbelief and horror.

"What is it?" Lawe asked, his curious tone also reflecting frustration.

"This can't be," she said breathlessly. "If only we'd known sooner… *How could they?*"

She looked up at him, as if searching.

"What?" he asked again. "What did she give you?"

"The Holy Grail," Karen whispered.

19

The midday shower was hot, steam whitening the air.

The roar of the spray filled Karen's ears as she ran her fingers through her hair, the thick white lather clinging to her auburn strands. Such moments of solitude had been few—the demands on her time had increased tenfold since she assumed the mantle left to her.

Weeks had passed since Rachel's death, and the ensuing legal and organizational seas that Karen had been forced to navigate had proven almost overwhelming. The woman's will indeed named Karen not only as executor but as her successor—something Rachel never before that final moment had disclosed to her, or to anyone else. In keeping with those final wishes, and with the full support of the executive staff, Karen had moved into the larger office and had taken Melissa up the ladder with her, as her executive assistant. The girl had shown an amazing ability to handle any task given her, and the new president of Sacred Child was grateful for her help.

The funeral had been excruciating, and the handling of the final arrangements had fallen to Karen—including the informing of Rachel's brother through the staff of his nursing home. They would break the news gently, they had promised, but the severity of his condition precluded the possibility of his attending the service.

She had managed to press onward, bearing the strain and suppressing her grief. But too much had happened too quickly. The pressure had built to critical levels. Her faith was cracking under the burden.

Why? she demanded. *I've prayed to You—stood up for You time and again—and all You did was let Rachel die. Haven't I given enough for You? Haven't I done what You wanted from me?*

Her deep, burning pain had given birth to disappointment in God, which in turn had ignited first doubt, then annoyance, then rage.

I worked for You—believed in You—

The fractures grew longer and deeper, the fires erupting from them more intense.

And then You do this!

Rachel was gone. And now the rock beneath Karen's feet was crumbling away.

The strain engulfed her. Something had to give.

As the shampoo streamed down and into the drain, she began to tremble. Wrapping herself in her arms, she sank to a sitting position, leaned into the shower wall, and let the pain flow. She wept loudly and uncontrollably, her wails echoing from the cool tile as the streaming warmth splashed against her, ignoring her suffering.

Almost an hour crawled by. The shower went cold.

It had grown late and the doors were locked, but despite the hour, the old building was a hive of activity. The next day representatives of the press from bureaus all around the nation would be there, joining in the festivities as well as reporting them.

Margaret McCarthy walked through the lobby of Life Quality's national headquarters, giving final approval to the lavish anniversary preparations. It had been a decade of triumph, a decade of growth.

A decade of rising profits, mounting prestige, and increasing power.

Perhaps I should run for political office. "Senator McCarthy" always had such a lovely ring to it—

Sacred Child had gone quiet after the passing of its founder. The woman delighted in the dearth of resistance, savoring the victory, enjoying every moment.

More than a month, she mused, *and not a peep. I knew they'd crumble without her. And with luck, they'll have folded completely by the end of the year.*

She chuckled, quite pleased with herself.

"We need more handout literature," she brightly told a man setting up a welcoming booth to one side. "And more of the logo teddy bears. What you have there will be gone by noon."

"Yes ma'am," the promotions rep said, pulling out a netphone.

She walked over to the refreshments kiosk and examined the setup there, then walked away without comment, much to the relief of the catering personnel.

"Leila!" she called out, gesturing to her assistant, who stood across the room conversing with a technician.

"Yes, Ms. McCarthy?" She hurried over.

"The doors will be opening sharply at eight tomorrow morning," she said, checking her nine-thousand-dollar diamond watch. "That's less than ten hours from now, and still you haven't given me a list of the VIP's who'll be in attendance."

"Publicity never sent it down," the girl explained. "They were supposed to have sent it to me by five—"

"Then why didn't you go up and get it, girl?" the woman asked in her usual superior tone. "The elevator works both ways, doesn't it? And you can send *and* receive netmail, can you not?"

"Yes ma'am," the Saudi woman said, "but those errands you requested took several hours. And when the dry cleaner was late with your dress I had to—"

"Excuses, Leila," the woman said. "When I give you a job, I expect it to be done. I have too many things to take care of, *important* things, to be following you around, picking up every little ball you drop."

"Yes ma'am," Leila said, biting her tongue.

"Forget netmail. Just go on up and get that list…Janice in PR should still be up there. Tell her you need it this minute. I have plans to make and a private party to throw tomorrow night, and I need to know which of the invited guests are going to attend."

"Yes ma'am." The girl spun on her heel and stalked away.

Hundreds of the most influential people in the country would put in appearances the next morning, Margaret knew, and their clout would help to set in stone the continued success of the organization. Senators, congressmen, city officials, and many of the best-known entertainers would converge on the center of her world, and the mark they would leave would ensure good public relations for years to come.

Special media spots were playing on the room's newly installed display walls, a series of short films and artful promotional pieces depicting the highlights of Life Quality's decade of triumph. Beginning the next day, the same spots would air nationwide as part of the massive, week-long promotional campaign Margaret and her marketing staff had designed. Again and again the room was filled with looping sound-bite interviews, carefully crafted segments of families whose diseases had been cured or whose children had received life-saving transplants. Two days later the huge screens would be taken down to restore the quiet beauty of the room, but for now they would serve to remind the world of the greatness of the organization.

Clearly immersed in the self-aggrandizing display, Margaret was slow to acknowledge the voice directly behind her.

"Ms. McCarthy…"

Leila stood there.

"What is it?" she asked. "I thought I told you to go up to PR and—"

"You'd better see this," the girl said. "On the TV…"

"What? What could be so important that you haven't done as I told you?"

"On all the news channels… I saw it at the nurse's station on the way out…"

And I just had to be here when you hear for yourself—

"Craig," Margaret impatiently called to a multimedia tech, "show me a news channel. Any one will do."

"Yes ma'am."

"I'm not sure you want to do that," Leila said. "Just come with me and—"

"Hush," the woman snapped. "How dare you speak to me with that tone. Perhaps I *should* fire you, after all. Why I've kept you on for this long, I'll never know."

The floor-to-ceiling images flickered as the system switched from datadisk to broadcast signal. Then, at once, the likeness of a hated enemy filled the room.

Karen Foley.

"…and that's why we're holding this conference," she was saying, before a gathered army of reporters. *"Again, the evidence we have in our possession is incontrovertible, and was obtained six weeks ago through a confidential source. It has taken us this long to verify its claims through our own independent research, but we now know it to be true."*

"What is that horrid woman going on about?" Margaret muttered. She turned on Leila. "You bothered me for *this?* There is nothing that ridiculous woman could say that would interest me in the slightest. Craig, if you would—"

"As you've clearly seen on the printouts given to each of you," the auburn-haired woman went on, *"the records do not lie. I say again…for the last six years, in its insatiable quest for greater profits, Life Quality knowingly and vigorously has recruited mothers not only of children affected by disease or genetic*

corruption, but those of so-called viable children, as well. Fully one-third of all children put to death by Life Quality to date have been perfectly healthy…"

"No!" Margaret cried out. "Craig! Turn that off!"

Absorbed by the shocking revelation, the man did not hear her.

"…and were sold to the organization by young women recruited at abortion clinics across the country. Instead of aborting their unwanted children, which would have brought no financial gain, these mothers instead were encouraged to carry their babies to term and then sell them for the ten thousand dollars in blood money Life Quality offers.

"That the organization not only knew this was happening, but initiated these immoral and unethical transactions, is evidenced by the documents before you, most of which bear the signature of Margaret McCarthy herself."

"Craig!" the woman screamed. Finally, the screens went black.

I told you that you didn't want to do that, Leila thought, the joy of revenge dancing in her heart.

Margaret stormed out of the room and headed toward her office. Those left in her frothing wake looked at each other, amazed by what they had heard.

"That can't be true, can it?" one promotions man asked from within his booth. "I mean, that would be illegal, wouldn't it? Harvesting *healthy* children?"

"I think so," his partner said.

"I *know* so," Leila whispered to herself. *And tomorrow will be a day they'll remember a hundred years from now.*

It had been a rough morning.

Such public relations tours were commonplace. It was the first leg of a six-city campaign meant to engender confidence in the energy policies of the administration, and Bridger was hopeful.

Andover, Kansas. The heartland of America.

Upon arrival at the hotel, however, he had been met by picket signs and shouts of protest—too many months of congressional mudslinging, strict gasoline rationing, and high prices at the pump had reduced consumer patience to zero. As the motorcade pulled past the crowds and into the underground garage, something struck the rear of Bridger's car. A tomato, perhaps, judging from the splat.

"How original," Lawe said from the front seat of the black sedan.

"I'll take it," Bridger commented. "Beats a brick."

"Or a bomb," another agent said.

"Let's keep a good thought, shall we?"

After securing the elevator, the Secret Service whisked the president to the ballroom where he would be speaking. The crowd inside, a group carefully selected by the state's party leadership to give the man the warmest possible welcome, waited.

"We're clear," a voice called into Lawe's radio. "Ready for Iron Chef."

At that, Bridger appeared from a side door and stepped up to the elevated podium at the front of the room. Eight agents continuously scanned the crowd, including Lawe, who was stationed immediately to the president's right.

The applause was loud and long. Bridger waved to the audience, smiling his charming smile, his vision diminished by the bright lights.

"Hello, Kansas," he began, and the cheers began anew.

The speech lasted more than twenty minutes. Finally, as it ended, Bridger took a last look at the multitude, smiled, and stepped away from the dais.

A frantic cry spilled from Lawe's radio.

"Shooter!"

Instantly, years of intensive training became precise physical action, and the world dropped away into slow motion. Screams rose from the crowd and echoed oddly in Lawe's ears as he dove at the president. In midlunge, a sharp report sounded and a fierce blow caught the agent in the ribs as he knocked Bridger awkwardly to the floor. He fell on the president, shielding him as best he could while another agent rushed over and did the same.

Thirty feet away, a cluster of agents, their guns drawn, were on the assassin at once. They took him to the ground, pinning him against the floor and tearing the pistol from his grasp.

Lawe tried but could not catch his breath. His agony swelled as precious air was denied him.

After a few eternal moments, another shout sounded from his transceiver. He did not hear it.

"Shooter is down! Repeat, shooter is down!"

Little by little, Lawe began to draw breath. Tears welling, he slowly rose to his knees and looked out over the room. Already, the president had been rushed from the scene. As Lawe turned, pain wracked his upper body, and he dropped to the hardwood of the stage, his eyes closed tight.

What did he—

"Perimeter is secure."

He rolled over, put a hand to his tortured side.

I was hit—

"Stand by for possible EMS request…ten-eight, Broderick Hotel… ten-thirty-three…"

Is the president—

"Bry!" an echoing voice shouted from just above him and a mile away. "Can you hear me?"

Relax—breathe—

"Iron Chef is unhurt. Agent down…code two…"

The backlash from Karen's press conference had been immediate, if not as severe as it might have been. Margaret McCarthy, master of damage control, was ready the moment the Manhattan facility opened. Along with the hundreds of invited guests, an army of media had stormed the lobby, cameras and microphones at the ready, and Margaret herself fielded the lion's share of the questions.

"Ms. McCarthy," one reporter began, "the allegations made last night by Sacred Child—"

"Are lies," the woman insisted. "They'll stop at nothing to damage this fine organization despite the great harm that would be done to the hundreds of thousands who depend on us. Life Quality has saved or improved countless lives these last ten years, and I'm committed to seeing to it that our services continue uninterrupted."

"There's talk of a federal investigation…"

"We welcome *any* who wish to look into our operation. Life Quality has nothing to hide. We have worked in concert with this government since our inception and will continue to do so."

It indeed had been a joint venture. Now, with the truth made public, she was counting on that alliance—if the allegations were proven and substantive charges brought against the organization's management, not only their own heads but many in government might roll as well.

There would be no investigation. She had enough friends in high places to prevent that from happening, friends most adept at protecting themselves.

"Karen Foley claims to have undeniable proof of wrongdoing, especially on *your* part…documents she has obtained…"

"Forgeries," Margaret stated flatly. "They must be, for the allegations are untrue and born of desperation."

"Why would Sacred Child present documentation that could be proven false? Their own credibility would be destroyed if it were shown that they had falsified the data."

"I cannot speak to their motives, and I think enough of a question has been raised as to their integrity. They've resorted to extremism in the past, including the terrorist bombing of a few months ago."

"That allegation was never proven."

"And neither will this one be."

Karen's accusation already had done a measure of damage. Several of the entertainers and politicians McCarthy had invited bowed out at the last moment, even some who already had arrived in the city. Others however, with their own agendas to promote, dismissed the story and began to appear, drawing media attention as they praised Life Quality's "crucial work" and decried Sacred Child's "abhorrent tactics."

For the moment, the worst had been averted.

The motorcade moved swiftly along, headed toward McConnell Air Force Base and the refuge of Air Force One.

Lawe, his ribs stiffly bandaged, spoke by phone with his office in the White House. The remainder of the tour had been cancelled, and arrangements for an early return to Washington had been drawn. Bridger's limousine, having left immediately after the incident, already was far ahead and nearing the waiting plane.

"It went bad in a hurry," he said to Lundy, whose clear concern leaped from the screen of his phone. "I took one in the ribs, but my vest caught most of it. Still knocked me loopy…couldn't much breathe for a few minutes. Picked up a cracked rib and the devil's own bruising, but I'll live."

"Who was the shooter?" Lundy asked. "What was he carrying?"

"Caucasian male, about thirty years old. Some kind of supremacist, maybe, based on some of the things he said. Wore a hotel staff uniform, but the management said he didn't work for them. Used a handgun. Thirty-eight caliber."

"Man, you are one lucky stiff."

"Tell me about it."

"Anyone else hurt?"

"No. We got Iron Chef back into the limo without incident, but I think I roughed him up a bit when I took him down."

"The shooter say anything?"

"He shouted something like 'death to Israel,' they said, but I didn't hear it myself. Nothing else until they dragged him out. Kind of hard to talk with a wad of carpet in your mouth and an eleven-and-a-half extra wide pressing down on the back of your head."

"How could we have missed it? We ran checks on everyone there. Looked like we'd get nothing but good PR out of the trip."

"You got me," Lawe said. "We didn't expect the protesters we got and didn't find out about them until just a few minutes before we pulled up. I tell you, Jack, there are a lot of groups out there who *really* don't like the stand the administration's taken. I think they should reschedule next week's California trip...bump it at least into October, and give ANWR a chance to bring gas prices down. If the people aren't hurting so badly in their wallets, it'll be a lot easier to rebuild public support."

"What's the revised departure time for McConnell?"

Lawe checked his watch. "It's just after nine now. We'll arrive by nine thirty. Iron Chef's going ahead with his address to the base staff and the officers' luncheon. Adding in the preflight preps after that, figure we'll be in the air by noon."

"You guys still going through with the strategy meeting at Ellsworth this afternoon?"

"As far as I know, but that's General Sumner's call. I'll keep you apprised."

The conversation ended. Lawe snapped the netphone shut and slipped it back into his jacket pocket.

October, he worried, watching the blossoming trees slip past, their vivid greens catching the sunlight. *As if this administration will last that long.*

While the morning passed, more than five hundred attendees filed into the Life Quality building. No appointments had been made for the day. No despairing or greedy mothers entered, and no transactions took place. It was the first weekday in almost a decade when such was the case, the only exception being Christmas Day.

In they came, the wealthy and the influential. The top officials and recruiters from each of the organization's 279 locations were there as well—including Lauren Savage and Carolyne Melita from the Washington clinic—and the representatives were vocal in lauding each other's fine work. The immense lobby, formerly the grand heart of the Beaumont Hotel, easily accommodated the crowds with room to spare. Margaret wore her most positive face, greeting most of the guests personally, calling out to those she knew by name and pretending to remember those she did not.

"Senator Parris," she smiled, hugging one silver-haired man in a dark suit. "I'm so glad you could be here."

"Hello, Margaret," he said sourly. "It would seem we have a problem."

"Not at all, Darrell," she brightly assured him. "Trust me."

Armed, tuxedoed security guards at the entrance checked each attendee for an invitation, ensuring that none passed who might cause trouble. The foyer and its built-in weapons detector stood ready to scream in alarm, but no threat made itself known. The faces of some of Sacred Child's most vocal supporters had been memorized by the guards, and none were to be allowed entrance.

At ten fifty-four, three men of Middle Eastern descent, dressed in well-tailored suits, passed through the entrance and were stopped in the foyer.

"Gentlemen," the guard said, addressing the trio. "May I see your invitations please?"

"Certainly," they said, handing them over. The guard gave them a cursory look, then returned them. The primary weapons detector built into the entry had not sounded, but the men's nationality demanded additional precautions.

"Please bear with me," the security man said.

Reaching for a sensor wand, he passed it over the men as the profiling protocol demanded. The detector squealed in response to the last of the three, as it passed over a pocket of his suit coat.

"Empty your pocket, please," the sentry ordered. Another guard stood close by, at the ready.

"Of course." The man reached in, pulled free a netphone and held it up before them.

"Turn it on," the guard demanded. The man did so, and the guard's relief was apparent.

"I'm sorry for the trouble, gentlemen."

"Not at all," said the tallest of the three.

"We hope you enjoy your visit."

"I'm sure we will," another replied.

They moved into the lobby proper, scanning the crowd. Deeper into the room, one of the three, the tallest, felt a hand on his arm. He turned to find a young woman there, an ebony-haired beauty dressed elegantly in black.

"Leila," he smiled.

"Khalid," she returned. She silently looked at each of the other two, nodding acknowledgment, and they did the same. Then, slowly and calmly, the three men followed her across the crowded room and toward the frosted glass doors of the unoccupied nurse's area. Another formally attired security man stood there, eyeing them as they approached.

"It's okay, Evan," the girl told him. "These are my brothers. I'm going to take them upstairs and show them where I work."

"All right, Leila." He smiled. "Don't miss the formal ceremony, though. It starts in a few minutes."

"We won't. Be right back."

They passed through the double doors and beyond to the elevator lobby.

"They are asleep," Ahmed said, smiling. "All of them."

"Of course," Khalid said. "Allah denies sight to the wicked."

The elevator door opened and they entered, their hearts racing.

There was much to be done.

The insufferable image of Life Quality's president filled the muted screen as Karen spoke on the phone, watching coverage of the celebration on one of the local news channels.

"I haven't heard from Bry," she told Melissa, who was remaining at the office for the day. "The news flash wasn't very specific... They haven't gotten enough information out of Kansas."

"I'm sure he's fine," the girl said. "The report I saw said no one had been hurt. Try not to worry."

"I'm trying."

"When does your flight leave?"

"One thirty. I'll take a cab into Manhattan in plenty of time for the three o'clock start. Did everyone else get in okay?"

"Except for the people who already live up there, most flew in yesterday and took the blocks of hotel rooms we reserved."

Karen shook her head, disappointed in herself. "It's my fault they're having to stay in Westport. If I hadn't let things slide so badly, they wouldn't be stuck forty miles away. I let Rachel down."

"You had so much to deal with. The vandalism on Christmas Day and what happened to poor Gordie…and then all the arrangements you had to make when Rachel…" She let the sentence die away. "You had a million things to take care of after you took over the reins. You did everything any person could have done."

"Maybe, but still…"

"Don't be so hard on yourself. We all did the best we could. It isn't your fault the arts festival is opening the same weekend. We needed hundreds of rooms, and Manhattan and the surrounding areas were booked solid."

"I should have known a month's notice wouldn't be enough."

"We're fine, Karen. So they'll have to drive a few extra minutes. No harm done."

Karen sighed. "I suppose."

"Remember what you told me?" Melissa said. "We all have to learn to forgive ourselves."

The woman smiled at that.

"We had a room reserved for you too," the girl went on. "You could have flown up yesterday…spent some time away from this place."

"I know, but it's only half an hour flight time to and from JFK, and I'll be able to sleep in my own bed. Besides, I've never much liked hotel pillows."

"What time tonight will you be back?"

"About eleven thirty. The protest ends at seven, so I should have plenty of time to get to the airport."

"Oh, okay…"

"Who hasn't yet arrived in Westport?"

"Let me see," Melissa said, referring to a call log. Her role was to remain in the Washington office for the duration, to answer basic questions from the press, and to act as a central message relay for those participating in the New York protest. "Holly and the group from Detroit decided to go by caravan, and they should be there within the hour. John with the Kansas City office and Marcy from Miami called a bit ago. A few others haven't checked in yet, but I expect to hear from them by noon. The chartered buses are ready, and we're still on schedule to be in front of Life Quality's headquarters by two thirty."

"Okay," Karen said. "Sounds good. What's the head count?"

"Looks like almost six hundred," she answered. "A good group."

"Excellent."

"I've gotten several calls from news organizations," Melissa said. "They want follow-up interviews with you. It looks like we got their attention. Margaret McCarthy is denying everything, though. Says we forged the documents."

"I heard," Karen said, watching the silent screen. "It's been on TV all morning. Don't worry, the truth will come out." She checked her watch. "Sweetie, I better let you go. I need to leave for the airport in about an hour, and I have a few last-minute things to take care of."

"Okay, Karen, be careful. Have a good flight."

"I'll get in touch as soon as we land. And Melissa...you're doing a great job."

"Thanks." She could hear the smile in the girl's voice.

The call ended, and Karen returned her gaze to the screen. Again, Margaret's face was there, and Karen could sense the worry beneath her bravado.

We've got you.

Leila led Khalid and his men into the executive dining room, a chamber that consumed a respectable amount of the twelfth floor's available space.

The opulent facility was vacant and still, its kitchen and serving staff enjoying a day off due to the celebration downstairs. Intricate lighting fixtures, sweeping murals, and other trappings conveyed the wealth of those who regularly dined, met, or otherwise assembled there.

"Mahmud," Khalid ordered, "close the door and lock it."

The man obeyed but encountered a problem. "It has no lock."

"Then put something against it." In moments, a heavy walnut table blocked the entrance.

"Where are they?" Leila asked, walking deeper into the room.

"Somewhere *here*," Khalid said, indicating one wall as he pulled the suspect netphone from his coat pocket. "It's a supporting structure…once carried dumbwaiters, ducting, and a trash chute. Much thicker than the other walls, almost a full meter." Pressing a button on the side of the device, he held it only inches from the wall and proceeded slowly along, shoving tables and chairs roughly out of his way as he went. The others watched, knowing what he sought.

It was the reason for their presence there, the purpose for their lives.

Foot by foot, the man traced the surface, the panoramic painting before him depicting the gathered gods of Mount Olympus. Finally, the phone emitted a shrill tone. He moved the device in widening circles, the whine changing pitch as he did so, then he tightened the motions and stopped.

"Here," Khalid said, tapping the reactive spot. "Right here." Tossing the phone aside, he picked up a chair, braced himself, then slammed it again and again into the face of Zeus, shattering plaster and fracturing sheet rock. Dust scattered, and tiny fragments of colored plaster and white gypsum peppered the floor as he tore open a jagged hole. An anticipated reward met his eyes, and his heart raced.

Something glinted inside.

The other men quickly moved in and pulled the drywall away in larger chunks. Once the opening was large enough, Khalid reached into the gap and pulled free a heavy object wrapped in thick clear plastic, something that patiently had awaited the day of its reemergence. Then he withdrew another and another and another.

He tossed one to each of his companions, leaving a fifth plastic-wrapped form partly concealed within the violated wall. They quickly tore away the plastic, revealing dark, glinting metal, pristine and sleek, catching the light as it played along the precision-machined surfaces.

"The day has come," Khalid said, pressing a release button on the rear of the submachine gun's grip and pulling back its bolt.

"Praise be to Allah," said Ahmed and Mahmud, almost in unison.

"Go downstairs and make our presence known," the leader ordered the two men. We will wait."

"McCarthy is mine," Leila said, months of restrained anger underlying her voice.

"Bring her up here," Khalid added to his instructions. "She should face the sword herself."

"We will not fail," Ahmed stated.

The two men pulled aside the table at the door and left the room, their guns at the ready.

"When?" Leila asked.

"When they think victory is theirs."

The two terrorists emerged from the elevator on the ground floor and quickly moved to the frosted glass doors. With a final nod and a prayer to their god, they burst into the room.

At point-blank range, Ahmed opened fire on the armed guard who stood inside the doors, dropping him before he could react. As screams began to rise from the crowd, Mahmud grabbed a petrified woman by her hair and put his gun to her head.

"No one leaves!" he shouted, firing up and across the room. With the burst of gunfire and an explosion of electrical light, one of the display walls shattered, showering the room with brittle shards.

"I want quiet! Shut them all off! Now!"

A tech reached for a panel. The remaining screens went black.

Ahmed trained his gun in the direction of the building's entrance, screaming at the four guards stationed there. "Drop your weapons!"

One sentry, acting reflexively, pulled his pistol. The terrorist fired first, felling him. The slain man lay motionless, warm blood spreading wide on the cool tile floor.

"All of you! Drop them! Now!"

The three guards behind the security foyer's transparent, bulletproof inner door turned, made their exit, and ran from the building.

"Away from the door," Ahmed ordered the guests, carefully making his way to the entrance. "Except you," he said to one of the guards. "Lock it."

In moments, the security doors entered lockdown mode. No one would pass in or out.

"Now, away from the door. Hands up, and everyone to the far side of the room. Away from all doors and exits. All of you!"

Five hundred frightened guests, guards, and executives were herded like cattle into a tight knot. The two armed men circled them, leveling their weapons.

"Margaret McCarthy!" Mahmud called out. "Come forward."

No one moved.

"Now…or I shoot!"

After a beat, some in the crowd began to shift their positions, allowing the passage of a trembling woman. McCarthy emerged, clearly terrified. Ahmed roughly gripped her arm and dragged her from the room.

"Up against that wall," Mahmud directed the crowd. "Remain calm and you will not be hurt. Resist and you will die." He walked from side to side before the group, maintaining a safe distance.

"Who has a phone?"

No one responded.

"If you have a phone, use it. Call friends, family, anyone. Call the police. Tell them you are hostages. Tell them we soon will make our demands."

The crowd, fearing a trap, remained still and silent.

"I said *call*," Mahmud said again, waving the gun in a threatening sweep.

Slowly, cautiously, hundreds of netphones appeared. Congressmen, senators, city officials, actors, reporters, businessmen—all dialed frantically. The murmur of disbelieving, stress-shaken speech filled the room as police, government offices, news agencies, friends, and family learned the terrifying news.

"*Let's roll,*" the terrorist mocked.

20

The phone rang. Karen dropped a makeup brush onto the vanity and rushed to answer.

"Hello?"

"Ms. Foley? This is the airport shuttle. We'll be there in about five minutes."

"Thank you. I'll be waiting out front."

She hoisted her navy blue carry-on bag, made a final brief walk-through of the apartment, and paused to turn on a table lamp that stood in one corner of the living room.

"Off we go," she smiled, taking her purse from the hall table as she reached for the doorknob.

A sudden musical passage sounded, the genius of Beethoven. Karen paused, reached into the handbag and fished for her netphone. Burdened by the carry-on, she dropped it to the floor with a noise of frustration.

"Hello," she answered, a hint of annoyance in her voice.

"Karen…it's me…"

"Bry! Are you okay? I saw the news…"

"I'm fine. We all are."

"You promise?"

"Promise."

Karen breathed a sigh of relief. "Okay."

"Where are you?"

"At home for the moment, but on my way out. Where are *you*? Still in Kansas?"

"Not for long. Listen to me," the man said, his tone unusually stern. "You can't go to New York. You have to call it off."

"What are you talking about?"

"Something's going down at the Life Quality offices, and I have a really bad feeling about it. You have to cancel that protest of yours."

"It's too late for that," she insisted. "Everyone else is already there by now."

"Then just *you* stay home. Don't get on that plane."

"Bry, I'm in charge! I *have* to be there."

"No, you don't," he demanded.

"We've put tens of thousands of dollars into coordinating this. We can't walk away at the last minute. Once I get there, I'll consider the situation and—"

"No!" Lawe almost shouted. A grunt of pain escaped his lips, and Karen picked up on it.

"Bry, are you sure you're okay?"

"Listen to me," he continued, ignoring the question. "It's a *hostage* situation up there, Karen, and it could go really bad, really fast. Lots of people are involved, including government officials, and it sounds like the terrorists mean business. You know the kinds of things these people are capable of. I don't want you *anywhere* near that building."

She was stunned. "A hostage situation? At Life Quality? What exactly are they telling you?"

"Please, Karen. I have to go, but just this once, do as I ask. Call your people and tell them to stay away from there. Police and rescue are going to seal off the area for blocks around, I'm sure, to keep the terrorists from slipping away. Besides, you hit McCarthy pretty hard last night… Give it a day or two and see what happens. Reschedule your protest for another time. It'll keep."

"*Keep?* Babies are dying *every day*, Bry…"

"Okay, bad choice of words," he conceded. "Only please, Karen…call it off."

"Rachel wanted this. It was her idea, and we owe it to her to—"

"She's *gone,* Karen," he said. "You have to move on."

How can you be so cold?

"Bry, I have to go. My ride will be here any minute. When I get to New York, I'll call the others and we'll just gather somewhere else. Central Park maybe. It's a big city."

"*No!* Please, just stay home. I need to *know* where you are, and that you're safe. I'm worried about Jeff as it is."

"But—"

"We're dropping the whole rest of the itinerary out here. I'll be back at Andrews late this afternoon, and I'll head over to your place as soon as the president's aboard Marine One. Please…*be there.*" There was a pause. "I have to clear this line. Love you."

She heard a click as he hung up.

Bry, I swear—!

Crossing the room, phone still in hand, she hit a button on the remote and a breaking news bulletin appeared.

"*…and we understand that as many as seven hundred persons may be trapped inside. So far, law officials have not heard from the terrorists themselves, but…*"

She pressed a few keys and dialed a stored number.

Brenda—

"Hello?" came a frightened voice.

"Honey, it's Karen."

"Oh, Karen! This horrible thing has happened, and Jeff's on his way downtown. I'm watching the TV and…"

"I know. I'm watching it too."

"They called him in. They called *everyone* in…"

"Brenda, listen. I'm sure it will be okay. Jeff knows what he's doing. They all do. They're trained to deal with this sort of thing."

There was no reply.

"I know," Brenda finally said. "But still…"

A pair of impatient honks sounded outside. The shuttle had arrived.

"Honey, I have to go. Don't worry… God's in control, and I think He kind of owes me one. His hand of protection will be there."

Ahmed pushed Margaret through the door. Her heel caught in the carpeting and she fell, breaking a couple of nails as she tried to catch herself.

With a tip of his head, Khalid directed the man to return to the lobby. He nodded, turned, and was gone.

"Who are you people?" the hostage fearfully cried out, slowly and painfully lifting herself to her knees. "What do you want?" Her gaze rose until it met that of the heavily armed young woman standing before her.

"Leila?"

"Hello, *Margaret*," the girl smiled

The woman saw the gaping hole in the room's west wall.

"What is that? What are you doing?"

"From the moment of its rebirth," Khalid proudly stated, "your building has carried at its heart the instrument of its death. A few of those who worked on its renovation were sworn to our cause."

"Why are you doing this?"

"This?" Leila asked, sweeping the room in a wide gesture. "Or did you mean *this*…?" She put the muzzle of her submachine gun to the woman's forehead, pressing hard. "Am I doing it right? Any criticisms? Any demeaning comments?"

The trembling woman closed her eyes in petrified silence.

"Tell me, *Margaret,*" Leila said. "Was the pleasure you got from hurting all those people for all those years…people like *me*…worth the sheer terror you feel right now? What's it like to know your life is about to end at the hands of your brainless assistant?"

"No…please…"

Khalid spoke up, looking down on the woman. "Your wickedness sickens me. Your greed owns you. You even kill your own children for it. It is your god."

"No," she stammered.

"Why do you think we chose this place? You treat your children as livestock, meat to be portioned out for profit. Everywhere, the shadow of evil walks your streets…dines at your tables…and you welcome it. Your hearts are dead. Your souls are black. The sword that now falls upon you is wielded by Allah. He has been patient, but the time of judgment has come."

"Allah is great," Leila said, her eyes fixed on the trembling woman.

"Listen," Margaret tried. "Anything you want…any demands you have…I can help you…"

"Beg," the girl said cruelly. "Plead with me not to kill you."

The woman began to break down, her words becoming sobs. "Please… Leila…"

"*Ms. Saban.*"

Margaret cowered. "Ms. Saban…please…I can help you… *Let me live…*"

Leila stood silently, relishing the woman's fear for a long moment, the tip of the Bizon's barrel wet with cold sweat as it dug into soft flesh.

Finally, the girl spoke.

"No."

She pulled the trigger.

Margaret was hurled violently backward. Her body fell hard against the floor.

"*Now* who's brainless?" taunted Leila.

A strong westerly wind had descended, swirling along the concrete and glass canyons of a paralyzed and fearful city.

"What do we know, Captain?" asked a man in a gray suit, his hair tossed.

FBI assistant director Lee Corwin crouched low behind a patrol car, speaking to an NYPD hostage negotiator who was peering at the building with infrared binoculars. Corwin had found the city police already in place upon his arrival, but command of the situation now would transfer to federal hands. Lights on official vehicles flashed everywhere. The echo of beating chopper blades bounced from the towering facades around him—he looked up to find not only law enforcement helicopters but, at a greater altitude, those of the press as well.

"No more than we did an hour and a half ago," the man said. "All we have is what we've been told by the hostages and by the three guards who escaped. Looks like a pair of armed men. They've sealed the building and are holding everyone in the lobby. Two other guards were killed. Thus far, we've heard nothing from the terrorists themselves, and they've rejected our attempts at communication."

"Do we have an accurate head count?"

"Probably as close as we're going to get. According to the hostages, about 530. That includes guests, press, food-service personnel, hired security, and Life Quality employees. Usually pretty hard for a few men to handle a crowd that big for any period of time, and if someone tries to get brave, there could be a lot of shooting before it's over. These guys have bitten off *a lot*... We're talking the House minority leader, dozens of other senators and congressmen, most of the mayor's staff, half the actors in Hollywood, and Margaret McCarthy herself."

"Terrific." With a subtle shake of his head, he scanned the building. "How are they armed?"

"Fully automatic weapons. Don't know how they got them in there, though…that's one of the most secure buildings in New York. Double-door security system with a phased array scanner in the foyer. If it goes off, the inner door seals automatically. Same goes for the service door and the emergency exits. You couldn't get in there with a slingshot."

"Mr. Corwin, sir," a voice called out. "We have a call from a man claiming to be the leader of the group. He says he's inside the building."

The government man hurried over and took the phone.

"This is Assistant Director Corwin," he said, "FBI. With whom am I speaking?"

"Joe Smith," a voice said.

Corwin noted the man's Middle Eastern accent. "We want to work with you, Joe. We know that two have died—"

"Three."

Corwin paused at that. "We want no more deaths. We must have assurances that the remainder of the hostages are safe."

"For the moment, they are unharmed," the man said. "Whether they stay that way is up to you."

"How can we bring this situation to a satisfactory conclusion, Joe?"

"We have only one goal," the man said. "Your country must end its support of the Jewish state and remove all military personnel from the lands of the Arab people."

Muslim extremists, Corwin silently mouthed to the agent beside him.

"Surprise, surprise," the man quietly muttered.

"That's not likely to happen," Corwin told the man on the phone. "And even if the president were to agree, such things take time."

"You have three hours. Then we start tossing bodies from the windows."

The man clicked off.

"It's Passover," the agent mentioned. "Does that have anything to do with it?"

"If it does, he didn't mention it," Corwin said. "But it stands to reason...they tend to choose Jewish holidays."

"The call traced to a phone on the twelfth floor. He's for real. We're cutting off his outside lines... All land calls have to come through us."

"Won't matter. He's got a hundred netphones in there. Just keep scopes on those windows. If the curtains are drawn..."

"Yes sir. We picked up a signature a couple of minutes ago. We think a gun was fired up on twelve."

"Must have been the third death he mentioned." He paused and thought out loud. "Twelve? Why twelve? What's the big attraction up there? Why not stay down in the lobby, where they're holding everyone?"

The agent opened a file on his datapad. "Directory shows the level has an executive dining room...private library...records storage. Nothing special."

"Records? What could they want with the records of a place like that?"

Mentally working it through, Corwin walked to a nearby black-and-white, beside which a police sergeant stood directing other officers into position. The man's features bore the pink scatter of small, fresh scars.

"Are we all sealed off?" the FBI man asked, squinting to read the sergeant's brass-plated name badge. "Lawe, is it?"

"Yes sir," Jeffrey said.

"I remember you. Presidential Medal of Valor, wasn't it? You're a good man."

"Thank you, sir."

Corwin looked toward Life Quality. "So...how do we look?"

"We're in position. Concentric cordon, by the book. Heavy police barricades at one block, three blocks, and six blocks. National Guard's set up at Thirtieth Street to the south and Fifty-eighth to the north, sealing off midtown altogether. Shore to shore and along both rivers. *No one* in or out."

"What about underground?"

"We dug up the records… It's an old building, one of the oldest in the city. It has no tunnel access, so they can't get out that way. Just in case, we've secured the perimeter with audio and vibration sensors and ground-penetrating radar. Even if they should somehow manage to sneak out of the building, these guys aren't getting away, that's for sure."

"Very good."

Corwin scanned the scene. Police and government vehicles filled the streets, save an empty span directly in front of the building. Farther back, fire and rescue vehicles waited, ultimately to clear the building and to treat any who may be injured. SWAT and ATF teams stood at the ready, as did police sharpshooters, who invisibly manned windows in the surrounding buildings.

A piece of the puzzle still nagged at him. *How did they get those weapons in there?*

Walking a short distance for privacy, the assistant director moved behind a panel truck and dialed his superiors. After a single ring, a man answered.

"Islamic terrorists," Corwin reported. "Which means these guys likely aren't interested in getting out alive. And if they're *planning* to die…somehow, we have to stop them from taking five hundred people down with them."

Safe in her living room, Samira watched the unfolding drama. A local Washington channel had sent a news helicopter into the crisis area and was broadcasting an aerial view of the scene. Sun glinted off scores of official vehicles. A reporter's voice rose above the beating blades.

"*…so we're not being allowed to get too close. We can see, however, that the entire midtown area, from Central Park all the way to Madison Square*

Garden, has been closed off for the duration. The Lincoln and Queens-Midtown tunnels have been cleared and sealed off at both ends, and law-enforcement officials are telling the public to avoid the island altogether. Such extreme measures make one wonder what they're expecting to see, and speculation is rampant. If the terrorists somehow have Keragesin gas, the substance used on Ten-Seventeen, the casualties could be in the tens of thousands."

A studio reporter cut in. *"If that were the case, why would law enforcement not be ordering an evacuation of the area?"*

"They may wish to avoid a potentially unnecessary panic and any deaths that could be related to it. And such an evacuation would be problematic, to say the least… Millions of citizens are in the immediate area, many of whom live there."

Samira dialed her phone. After three rings, a woman picked up.

"Hello?" Her voice was shaky.

"Brenda, it's Samira."

"Oh, hi…"

She heard a sniffle. The woman had been crying.

"I've been watching on TV… Is Jeff in the middle of all that?"

"I'm sure he is by now," Brenda said. "Life Quality sits smack in the middle of his precinct. Oh, Samira…"

"I'm sure he'll be okay," she reassured her dear friend. "Try not to worry. Ollie just called from the station house and said it looks to him like the NYPD and FBI have things well in hand."

"I hope so." There was a prolonged silence. "I'm so scared… I can't shake the feeling that something terrible is going to happen."

"Now listen," she replied. "Jeff knows his job. They're trained to handle exactly this sort of thing."

"That's what Karen said."

"Is she there?"

"No. She called earlier."

"Wasn't this the big weekend? The protest march?"

"Probably not anymore," Brenda said. "I don't know."

Every word the woman uttered dripped with dread. She sounded distant, her thoughts obviously focused on one man who had placed himself in harm's way.

Samira understood. She too carried the fear that one day her husband would not come home. The two wives were as sisters, their bond tempered in a fire they would wish on no woman.

Almost four hours had passed since they had taken the building. Khalid paced, avoiding the windows and the snipers he knew must be watching. He could not see what was happening outside, the extent of the police response.

There were others, however, who could see for him.

Leila's netphone rang.

"Yes?" After a beat, she handed it to the man. "It's Abdu."

"Where are you?" he asked.

"Richmond. At the assigned place."

"What do you see?"

"They have sealed the entire area," the man said. "The TV is giving a view from the air. All of midtown is closed off. No one is being allowed to leave."

"Who is directly outside?"

"Everyone. Police, FBI, fire department, National Guard…thousands of them from the look of it. The building is completely surrounded."

A melodious sound echoed within the room, then repeated.

"Keep watching," Khalid said, "and may Allah be pleased with you." He hung up, crossed to the ringing wall phone, and lifted the receiver.

"Yes?"

"Joe, this is Corwin."

"Hello, Mr. FBI."

"We've sent word to Washington. They're considering your demands and will inform us the moment they reach a decision."

"When will that be?" the leader asked, knowing full well the answer.

"Most likely tonight," Corwin said. "They'll have to convene a special meeting of Congress, which will be difficult, considering that you're holding several of its members."

Not difficult, Khalid mused. *Impossible.*

"If you'd release those government officials, we could expedite your request."

"No," Khalid said flatly. "Do you think me a fool?"

"No, I don't. No fool could have orchestrated a plan such as yours. But it will be tonight before we can get an answer."

"Not good enough," he said, toying with the man. His eyes danced from the dark hole in the wall to the sprawled, bloody body of Margaret McCarthy. "How do I know I can trust you? Perhaps when the hostages begin to strike the pavement, you will take us seriously."

"There's no need for that," Corwin said. "I believe you, and we've been working to give you what you want. It takes a little time."

The terrorist leader paused, letting the man sweat.

"Where are you, Mr. FBI?"

"Right outside, Joe. Come down and we'll work this out over a cup of coffee."

The leader smiled, enjoying the man's grim sense of humor.

"Very well," Khalid said. "I will wait, but no later than eight o'clock. If I do not have confirmation from my sources that the demands are being met, we will begin to kill the hostages. I warn you…eight o'clock exactly."

He clicked off.

Corwin lowered the phone and looked up at the twelfth floor across the street.

"What did they say?" an agent asked.

"We've got a little more time," he said. "Maybe four hours."

"Our best estimate places men on twelve and in the lobby, with no one in between. We don't know how many there are, but according to the witnesses it can't be more than half a dozen."

"Not many, to handle six hundred."

"Nope," the agent agreed, "but their guns speak loudly. Still, I doubt they'd be able to control the crowd for too long. Panic's likely to set in…"

"They're staying away from the windows. I'll bet someone out here is watching the coverage and telling them what's going on."

"The press has agreed to pull back on our order. Once they've done that, our choppers move in, we rappel down and secure the floors above twelve and below ten, with the exception of the lobby. We avoid the roof access, just in case someone's planted inside the door, ready to sound an alarm. Our men cut the glass and enter on twenty, and if we're lucky, we descend the elevator shafts and isolate the hostages before they even know we're there."

Fearing possible chemical weapons use, bio-suits and gas masks had been distributed to all law-enforcement personnel, local and federal. While all had donned the yellow coveralls, few wore the hot, uncomfortable masks and instead kept them at the ready.

"When will your men be in position?" Corwin asked.

"In a few minutes. Then we go on your word."

The assistant director turned and looked down at the pavement, his thoughts drifting elsewhere.

Why the impossible demand? How did they get those guns in there? What do they really want?

The answers lurked in a frustrating black fog.

Why did he want to know where I was?

"Something isn't right," he told the agent, his gut in knots.

Leila held Khalid close and he held her, their warmth melding into a single fire. In silence, the minutes passed. Ten, fifteen, twenty.

"When?" she asked.

"Soon," he told her. "They are coming."

"We're ready," the agent said, his ear to a phone.

"Go," Corwin ordered.

Moments later, the circling press helicopters peeled back, leaving midtown airspace. Nerves throughout the ranks were on edge, with thousands of eyes scanning the building for any sign of movement.

Above, one black military chopper after another suddenly whispered in, their rotors silent. Assault teams dropped onto the roof, their mission fully underway.

Corwin's mind raced.

Why would they make that kind of demand? They have to know there's no way we can do what they're asking—

Slowly, he broke it down.

Last year, the Palestinians did the same thing—demanded the impossible after that missile attack.

It made no sense.

What are they trying to do?

There *had* to be an answer.

Here we go, Jeffrey thought, watching from a vantage point half a block away. Then, as quickly as they had come, the ghostly choppers were gone, their cargo of hope delivered.

Godspeed, guys.

"Now," Khalid spoke calmly into Leila's netphone. "May Allah be pleased with you."

Corwin watched as the assault teams, clad in black, began their descent. Ropes dropped over the side of the building, dangling just far enough to carry the men to the floor they had targeted.

What am I missing here?

The rappel began.

And the weapons—how did they—?

"Think!" he chastised himself.

What if the building's security wasn't a problem because they didn't have to take any weapons inside? What if they were already in there?

Fear swelled.

And if they'd already planted those—!

The front doors of the building burst open, startling him. All eyes dropped from the unfolding situation above and hundreds of weapons, reflexively raised, locked on the commotion at street level.

There was a flurry of motion, a frenzy of color, and panicked cries.

"Hold your fire!" an amazed Corwin called into a bullhorn.

They poured from the building's ornate main entrance, running as quickly as they could, headed somewhere, anywhere. Men in tuxedos and tailored suits, women in glittering gowns and flowing dresses, all running for their lives.

What the—?

A few officers rushed forward, trying to guide the freed hostages to safety. Confusion reigned in the street. High above, the highly disciplined tactical squads were in position at their assigned windows, their glass cutters in rapid motion.

"The hostages!" Clay shouted, rising from behind his patrol car. As he stood, his uniform hat was taken by the warm, whistling wind, and he let it go.

Jeffrey broke into a smile at the sight of the emerging swarm, at the thought that so many endangered lives had been spared. His mind flashed on a chaos of horrifying images, burned into his memory on that day when so many had suffered and died in a chaos of fire and blood. He still could feel its heat, still could smell the acrid smoke that had filled his lungs.

Turning, he glanced at a point less than a hundred feet behind him.

It happened there—right there—

He returned his attention to the scene playing out before them.

But not this time!

He reached out and lightheartedly rubbed his partner's flaxen, uncovered head.

"Score one for the good guys," he said.

"They turned them loose!" a young FBI man called out, watching as dozens of agents herded the frightened crowd toward a group of oversized police vans.

"The terrorists are surrendering!" another agent shouted.

No, Corwin realized, *they're not.*

In a horrifying instant, he finally understood.

Flypaper!

His heart pounding so fiercely it hurt, he grabbed the phone, pressed a button, and cried out. His breath began to fail him. His vision tunneled.

"Code White! All personnel, evacuate! Now!"

Khalid's gaze shifted from the tiny remote in his trembling hand to the bulky object still partly concealed in the wall. Two by two by three feet and wrapped in heavy translucent plastic, it weighed over five hundred pounds and had been smuggled in during the renovation, late at night, disguised as air conditioning equipment. During its journey, its composite insulation had hidden its true nature from even the most sensitive detection equipment. The reinforced, floor-level bracing on which it rested supported its weight easily and had done so for eight long years.

It was patient and unchanging, and as potent as the day it was built.

And now, finally, its time had come.

With a deep breath, Khalid pressed a button. Beneath the protective wrap, a green light flared to life and glowed eerily, the eye of a waking giant. Kahlid paused for a moment of prayer.

An emergency alarm sounded on the street below, pulsing and shrill. Then a second. And a third.

"They know," he said softly, stroking Leila's dark hair. The girl was at his side, still holding him.

"As you had planned," she said. "They die in fear."

They exchanged a final kiss. Then she nodded, placed her head against his chest, and closed her eyes.

"The blade of Allah," Khalid whispered. "May he be pleased."

He flipped up a small hinged cover on the control, slid his thumb underneath, and pressed the second button.

A roar of static filled the speakers.

Karen, startled, reached for a remote. The crisis coverage she had been watching suddenly had gone to snow.

In milliseconds the heart of the city and four hundred thousand lives passed into history.

It had been far from the largest of such devices, but its effect was all its creators had hoped for. The intense white light ignited everything it touched as the fireball swelled. Concrete, glass, and metal were vaporized. Life Quality, the theater district, the *New York Times* building, the Port Authority bus terminal, and other landmarks all simply vanished.

Times Square, the American focal point of each new year, had seen its last.

A blast wave of crushing pressure rushed outward, moving faster than sound as it surpassed the limits of the fireball, its searing winds heated to the point of incandescence. It knocked aircraft from the sky like annoying insects—some, too close, were consumed before they touched the ground.

Half a mile from the epicenter, stone and steel flowed like water.

Three-quarters of a mile out, every book in the engulfed public library, even those stored in the basement, burst into flames. The paint on cabs and buses burned away moments before their tires melted and fuel tanks exploded. Burning missiles of debris, carried within the scorching, luminous winds, pierced all that stood in their path. Pedestrians, their clothing and flesh ignited, were swept from their feet and hurled as projectiles at more than forty feet per second. By heat or by impact, every man, woman, and child within a mile—whether on the streets, within buildings, or riding the subway—perished.

That which distance had spared from initial thermal annihilation suffered the expanding shock front, which was further compressed, reflected, and intensified as it roared through the outer channels of the city. The Empire State Building caught the blast on an angle and, despite sustaining great damage, remained upright. The United Nations headquarters, slightly farther away, took the impact broadside and toppled, crumbling into the East River.

The Hudson boiled, casting vast amounts of water vapor into the storm. Ships burned and exploded at their docks. Central Park became a sea of flames.

Every pane of glass within three miles shattered. Even at that range, the winds still topped 150 miles per hour.

The blast wave slowed as it widened beyond the rivers, then stopped. For a surreal moment, Hell went still.

Then the burning flow reversed itself, rushing back toward the detonation point, drawn by the vacuum it had created. Much of what had withstood the primary winds, left weakened, fell to the counterstorm. Deafening thunder, deep and prolonged, slammed outward.

Higher and higher the fireball rose, expanding as it cooled, trailing a column of dark smoke and vaporized matter. The ascending mushroom cloud, a churning maelstrom of black and orange, could be seen as far away as Westport, Connecticut.

Less than ten seconds had passed since one man had pressed a switch. And in that interval, the greatest city in the world had become its largest place of the dead.

21

C aptain, how much longer?"

"Mr. President," a filtered voice responded, "we've received clearance. The new flight plan has been posted, and we'll be taxiing out in a few minutes."

We need to get back.

Bridger sat at his desk aboard Air Force One, on the tarmac at Ellsworth AFB. Looking around the cabin, he found history everywhere—in framed photos from past administrations, in the furniture, in the fixtures, in the very bulkheads themselves.

You've served well, old girl, he smiled wistfully. *But now it's time for a long-deserved rest.*

After a proud and lengthy career, it would be the plane's final flight. She and her sister craft had entered service in 1990, replacing the 707-based aircraft that had been the flying headquarters of presidents from Eisenhower to Bush Sr. The technical wonder of her time, the VC-25A, tail number 28000, might to the untrained eye have passed for a Boeing 747, an aircraft no longer used commercially.

She was an amazing machine but was showing her age. With her final tour cut short, she was heading home for the last time, soon to be placed on permanent display at the Boeing Museum of Flight in Seattle.

The whine of the engines grew louder, then faded slightly, then rose again. Bridger reached down, found the halves of his seat belt, and fastened them. As they locked into place, Varner appeared in the doorway.

"Matt…"

"Rhonda," he began, his attention on a printout. "Not ten minutes

ago I got an update from Homeland Security. This hostage situation is…"
Looking up, he went silent.

The woman was shaken, unsure. He had never seen her like that.

"Talk to me, Rhonda."

"A message from the Pentagon…just now…"

Bridger braced for the worst.

"There's been a nuclear strike on New York City."

No!

"The reports are still sketchy, but…"

He shut his eyes in obvious pain. "How bad is it?"

"Preliminary estimates…" She stopped, reluctant to go on.

"Rhonda?" He looked at her, silently offered his own strength.

"More than a million dead. Almost three times that many injured."

His head dropped, the burden on his shoulders increasing a thousand-fold. Part of him refused to believe. Part of him had no choice.

Heavenly Father, help us all.

The engines slowed and went silent. The pilot's voice again filled the room.

"Mr. President, sir, we just received word. A fighter escort is departing the composite wing at Whiteman, headed our way. ETA is twelve minutes. We're holding for their arrival."

Bridger, still stunned, slowly replied. "Thank you, Captain."

Varner moved into the room, followed at once by Brooks, the president's advisor. The man's eyes were red, his cheeks wet.

"Matt…"

"I know, Roger."

"Patch me through to Crown," the president called, pressing the intercom keypad.

"Yes sir, we've been trying. Communications just went down… Seems to be a satellite problem."

"Stay on it. I've got to get through to the vice president."

"They'll have gotten the airborne command post off the ground by now," Varner noted. "The vice president, the first and second ladies, and all of Congress will be on their way to shelters."

Bridger, forgetting his seat belt, tried to stand but awkwardly was held his seat. He unfastened the buckle, quickly rose, and gestured toward the door.

"Conference room...*everybody.*"

Upon stepping into the corridor, he spotted Lawe standing near the first-level staircase. The man's stiff movements betrayed the pain he felt, the bandages wrapped around his torso. Calmly, the president walked up to him.

"Bry?" he asked quietly and simply. "You heard?"

"Yes sir."

"I need you to get those reporters off the plane. Quickly."

"Yes sir," Lawe nodded, heading at once toward the rear of the aircraft and the press seating area.

A few minutes later, Bridger and his cabinet had gathered around the dark oblong table, their faces reflecting their grief and shock. Taking their seats with what little information they had gathered, they shook their heads as if in a dream.

"Warren," the president ordered, "the moment communications will allow, take us to DEFCON One."

"Yes sir."

"It's so *big*," Brooks softly said. "I can't get my mind wrapped around it."

"There's a lot of that going around," Varner added, the stubborn fog beginning to lift.

The president thought out loud. "Couldn't have been an ICBM, could it? No one but Russia has the range to hit the eastern seaboard."

"And NORAD would have seen it coming," Sumner said, stating the obvious. "Our laser defenses would have taken it out."

"So…a suitcase nuke? Bomb aboard a freighter? Container ship in the harbor?"

"Could have been any of those."

Creedel switched on the room's bulkhead-mounted hi-def monitors, but as expected, no signal at all came from the networks' main studios. Local news bureaus picked up the network mantles and a few Kansas stations aired limited coverage, but it was largely speculative and of little help.

"We won't be getting anything from anywhere near the site," Brooks pointed out. "And what the blast didn't get, the electromagnetic pulse did. Must have fried every piece of equipment for miles around. Heaven only knows what it did to the power grid."

"I managed to connect with Arthur," Varner said, referring to the Homeland Security director as she read from her datapad. "Only for a minute or two, but the link lasted long enough. Power's out in areas all through the Northeast, he said."

"I can't believe it," Creedel groaned. "How could this have happened?"

"Frankly, I'm surprised it took *this* long," Sumner replied.

"How can you say that?" Varner snapped.

"The motive *and* opportunity have been there for a long time, going all the way back to Nine-Eleven. And then, last year…well, they've been threatening something since the day those missiles came down."

"Who is *they?*" Creedel probed.

"Who do you think? They warned Levi we wouldn't be there for Israel when push came to shove…"

"And *this* was what they meant?" Creedel objected, turning to address the president. "Sir, we don't know for sure that Palestine was responsible."

"For the moment," Bridger said, "all we've heard is that a fundamentalist group was holding the hostages. Likely Wahhabi, but we don't know. Whoever set off the bomb, I think we can safely assume it was someone who hates us."

"Well, *that* narrows it down," Brooks said.

"I'm not saying Palestine waltzed in here and planted a bomb," Sumner clarified. "Could have been al-Qaeda, Islamic Sword, or Vengeance of Allah…all of whom want us out of Israel and have been in bed with the Palestinians. The atrocities they've committed—"

"I'm just saying that *anyone* could have done this," Creedel insisted.

"It *is* Passover," Brooks pointed out. "Seems to me that, at the very least, that puts Arab fingerprints all over it."

"Probably so, Roger," Bridger said, "but the fact remains that we don't yet *know*. And yes, Warren, all those groups would love nothing more than to see this country brought to its knees."

"Which may still happen," Varner pointed out. "Wall Street was on life support as it was."

Bridger hit the intercom. "Faraday, have you gotten through to the White House yet?"

"Still trying, sir," a voice said. "We're having to reroute… May be a few minutes."

The president rubbed the arm of the chair, hating the stillness of the plane.

"Where are those fighters?" he whispered, glancing at his watch. "We have to get off the ground."

A man rushed into the room and handed out sets of satellite photographs, both standard and infrared. Each person paused to analyze the images, and groans of pain and incredulity rose as they beheld the horrifying sight. The extent of the devastation was mind-boggling—midtown Manhattan had been reduced to debris, and fires burned over most of the island, clouding the skies with thick smoke.

Several in the room fought back tears. Hands trembled.

"Sweet Lord in Heaven," an awed Sumner whispered. "That footprint must be four miles wide."

"Where's the U.N. building?" Creedel wondered, refusing to believe the evidence of his eyes. "Hidden by the smoke? Surely it didn't—"

"It isn't there anymore," Brooks said matter-of-factly, indicating one of the photos. "It would be right in that opening, right there."

"What would it take to do this, Warren?" Bridger asked, indicating a wide shot of the detonation site.

"Hard to say. We've never theoretically pinned down the effect of high-rise buildings on a nuclear blast radius. From these pictures, I'd guess twenty-five kilotons, maybe thirty. Bigger than Hiroshima, for sure. It looks like the narrow avenues between buildings may have compressed and accelerated the blast wave. And it probably went off at ground level, not two thousand feet in the air like the bombs dropped on Japan."

Bridger slammed a fist into the table. "How? We have radiation sensors all over those harbors and throughout all our major cities. How could we not have known it was there?"

"We can't know when it arrived. Could have been any time. Years ago, even, if it had the right kind of core. And if they built it with insulite shielding…"

"Insulite?" Brooks asked. "I thought no one had that but us."

"There are a lot of things we're going to have to rethink," Bridger said with a touch of disgust.

"To have created this big a blast," Sumner concluded, "it must have been a sophisticated device. Magnified-yield core. I doubt any of the terrorist groups we know of could have built it. Couldn't even have *acquired* it without substantial help."

Bridger leaned on his elbows and buried his face in his hands, mentally echoing Creedel's earlier comment.

This isn't happening—please, Lord, let me wake up now.

"How do we even begin a search and rescue?" Varner asked. "We're talking about *millions* of people. And the radioactivity in there must be—"

"Deadly," Sumner finished. "And it'll stay hot for weeks. Anyone going in there is risking his life, even in a suit."

Varner read from her datapad. "Disaster plan for a midisland strike calls for evacuation efforts in the northern and southernmost parts of the island. The George Washington Bridge, the Broadway Bridge, and the Brooklyn-Battery Tunnel have been designated as exit points, though in the case of the latter they may hold everyone inside the tunnel for fear of fallout."

"What about the fallout?" Bridger wondered. "Where's it likely to come down?"

"The smoke in these pictures is headed sharply east-southeast," Brooks observed.

"I'd say the lower end of Long Island's going to get hit pretty hard," the woman went on, "but for the most part the mainland will be spared. New Jersey, Pennsylvania, Delaware, and Washington all should be in the clear."

"For now," Sumner said. "What if the wind shifts?"

"Roger," Bridger said, "get on the phone with the guys at NOAA. Find out what the weather's going to do. Have them broadcast a warning to all shipping off the East Coast."

"Yes sir," he said, rising to depart the room.

"You know, that stuff's going to go all the way around the planet," Sumner pointed out.

"We'll cross that bridge when we get there, Warren."

"Mr. President," the pilot's voice sounded. Bridger pressed a button on the desk.

"Yes, Captain?"

"The escort ETA is three minutes. We're about to begin our taxi... Please take your seats."

"Thank you."

Once again the engines roared to life. Bridger rose. "As soon as we're up, Rhonda, I'd like you, Warren, and Roger to come to my office. And somebody find a way to get me on the air. Radio, television, whatever."

"Yes sir," they said as one.

In moments all were in place and buckled in.

Air Force One began to move.

Karen again tried to dial Brenda's number. All she got, as before, was a pre-recorded message telling her the system was overloaded.

She knew there had been an attack. Its exact nature had not yet been stated.

God, how could You have let this happen?

Her eyes were on the screen. Breathless reporters tried to convey the unthinkable.

"We cannot yet confirm the extent of the devastation, but our preliminary reports indicate that it is massive. The entirety of midtown Manhattan appears to have been affected. We're now receiving this video from our sister affiliate in Newark, New Jersey…"

A new image appeared, shaky and out of focus at first but rapidly settling down. In the foreground was an empty field, beyond which, from side to side, ran a highway. Everywhere, cars were pulled to the shoulder, their drivers and passengers standing beside them, gazing in stunned silence at something in the distance.

That something, relatively small from that vantage point, was the rising mushroom cloud. The winds at various altitudes were doing their work against it, but still it held enough of its feared classic shape to be recognizable.

"What you are seeing here is a live shot of a mushroom cloud…and as more eyewitness reports come in, it's becoming increasingly clear that, well…the event that took place in New York City, only moments ago, was nuclear."

Karen gasped.

"No…no…no," she repeated in a trembling whisper.

She tried the phone again.

In frustration, Lawe slipped his useless netphone back into his pocket. No calls were getting through.

He feared for his brother and for the woman he loved.

Jeff, Karen, please tell me you both stayed home today—

Acceleration pressed him harder into his seat, and the discomfort in his ribs increased. Air Force One was moving faster now, and the runway slipped past. The roar in his ears grew louder still as the plane's four powerful General Electric engines reached takeoff thrust. From his window seat in the forward lounge, Lawe could see the four escort jets in the distance, approaching in formation, swooping in to take position around the presidential aircraft.

The behemoth's nose pulled sharply upward. The friction of the ground ceased as its rear wheels lifted, and Lawe felt the blood rush from his head. Moments later, his ears popped.

We're heading up in a hurry.

Two thousand, three thousand feet up.

Air Force One was in a steep initial climb, as demanded by the emergency protocols under which they now were operating. The fighters, four F-24s, scrambled out of Whiteman AFB and quickly assumed position around the giant craft, with one escort fifty feet off each wingtip and the others trailing slightly behind, a bit farther out. Arrayed almost like a formation of geese, they moved as one and gained altitude together, ready for the worst.

"Four thousand," the copilot called.

"Roger that," came the reply of the pilot, Capt. Jerry Rainier. He glanced at the small square radar screen before him—it conveyed the welcome black of a nonthreat condition.

"Air Force One, this is Echo One on secure channel, do you copy?" came a voice in the pilot's headset.

"Roger, Echo One," he replied. "Go ahead."

"Where we headed, sir?" asked the lead fighter pilot.

"Wright-Patterson," the captain replied. "Short briefing there. Then, if all's still secure, it's on to Andrews."

"Roger," the pilot said. "Copy."

Five thousand feet.

Bridger sat strapped in at his desk. Varner, Brooks, and Sumner had joined him in his office, still trying to grasp the enormity of the day's events.

"Steep climb," Brooks observed, feeling the increased G forces as apparent added weight in his arms and legs. At any altitude below twelve thousand feet, he knew, the aircraft was too vulnerable.

"I'm going to have to say something to the people as soon as we touch down," Bridger said. "They've got to be terrified. They're thinking there's a bomb in every city, I'd bet."

"I'd keep it simple," Sumner suggested. "Clarify what happened and tell them we're doing all we can to help the survivors."

"And emphasize that it was an isolated attack," Varner added. "We have to try to instill as much calm as possible."

"That won't be easy," Bridger knew.

"The stock market may not recover from this," Brooks pointed out. "We have to be prepared for that."

"Tomorrow's Saturday, so it wouldn't be open anyway. Assuming Wall Street's still there…"

"Physically, it should be," Sumner said. "But even with EMP protection, the place is likely uninhabitable. Radiation, structural damage, what have you. And while the trading records themselves may be intact, the data lines in and out surely aren't."

"Which means the records might as well have been destroyed," Brooks noted.

"Every company that traded there kept backups elsewhere," Bridger said. "They could have another exchange site set up by midweek."

"I hope so," Sumner said.

"The financial impact of Nine-Eleven was in the trillions," Brooks pointed out. "This time around…" He rose from his seat and grabbed his briefcase. "I'm going to go check a few things. Maybe we can come up with a way to head off the worst of it."

Rainier watched the altimeter.

Eight thousand feet—

"Echo One," he called into his headset mike. "This is Air Force One."

"Go, Air Force One."

"We'll be leveling off at forty-six thousand…coming up on initial turn point."

"Roger that," the fighter pilot answered.

Rainier turned to his copilot. "Jim, when we get to thirty-five thousand, I think we should—"

He was cut off by a shrill cry from the cockpit as the threat warning alarm sounded, its rapidly repeating tone hammering their ears. Almost by reflex, Rainier shoved the throttles all the way back and yanked the yoke hard, pulling the craft severely upward and to the left. The aircraft screamed in protest, pushed to its limits.

"We've got a SAM," the copilot called, watching the tiny green triangle on the radar screen. "Coming up fast…fifteen seconds."

The surface-to-air missile was closing quickly on the aircraft, and the thermal sinks built into its four engine pylons seemed to be doing little to deceive the incoming threat. The copilot reached out, pulled open a panel door, and yanked down a handle.

Chaff and flares sprayed from the underside of Air Force One, countermeasures intended to fool the targeting systems of heat-seeking missiles. All four fighters, having also detected the missile, followed suit, clouding the skies with brilliant glare and sparkling silver.

"Come on, baby!" Rainier said, aware of the extreme stresses he was inflicting on the plane. His focus shot to the radar screen, then to the altimeter.

Ten thousand—

"Still coming," the copilot cried out. "Must be smart…seeking our profile…"

Almost there—

"Ten seconds…"

More countermeasures burst from the planes. They too were ignored.

"No go… It's locked on…"

Rainier pulled hard against the throttles, but they could move no farther.

Twelve thousand—

"*Still* coming," the copilot called. "Five seconds…"

Two of the fighters had peeled away, sweeping around, coming to bear on the source of the missile launch. A third, flown by a first-year pilot, had dropped back, taking position.

The remaining escort, the wing commander, knew at once what the young pilot was attempting, but he also knew there was not enough time.

Four seconds—three—

His eyes locked on the tiny blip on his radar screen, Echo One made a decision. Years of training and experience would culminate in this one moment, this one act, his president's only chance for survival.

"I love you, Joanna," he whispered, without time enough to glance at the small wedding photo tacked to his instrument panel.

Now!

At the last possible instant, with only one shot at the maneuver, he simultaneously hit the throttle and slammed the control stick hard to the right. In one fluid motion, he abruptly swooped under the belly of the gleaming craft, almost grazing its silvery skin as his fighter slid directly into the missile's path.

The deadly warhead had no time to compensate, no chance to reacquire the jumbo jet for which it had been programmed.

There was an eruption of flame and debris as the missile violently exploded a scant forty feet shy of its target. Shrapnel sprayed, tearing metal and rending feed lines.

Air Force One yet lived.

The lights in the passenger cabin flickered. The roar of the powerful explosion filled the air, drowning out prayers, spoken and unspoken.

Lawe felt a searing pain in his left leg. A sharp whistle filled the cabin.

Looking down, he found a jagged hole in the floor, just inside and to the rear of his foot. Glancing up, he discovered a matching gash in the ceiling tiles.

Reaching down to the ragged tear in his pants leg, he found blood.

The fireball diminished and fell away.

What the—?

Echo One glanced around, astonished to be alive. He dropped from beneath the monstrous presidential plane, tossed by its wake as he rapidly lost altitude. His fighter, momentarily still aloft, was badly damaged. Warning lights filled his panel. Alarms shrieked.

He was losing control. In moments, the stick would be dead.

"Woohooooo!" came a jubilant voice, filling his headset. "Gotcha!"

He spun to see his wingman up and to the left.

"Rookie, what did you do?"

"A little laser action, sir!"

At the last moment, the young pilot had destroyed the missile with the fighter's COIL system, an improved offshoot of the chemical oxygen-iodine laser technology developed in the late twentieth century as part of the Strategic Defense Initiative. The precision heat weapon was intended to cripple—but not destroy—hostile ships and aircraft by surgically knocking out vital engine and navigation systems.

"It takes ten seconds to power up and another ten to acquire the target," the senior pilot knew. "You *couldn't* have fired it."

"Well, sir," the young pilot confessed, "seems I neglected to power the thing back down after the preflight systems check. I know that can burn out the pulse capacitor… I'm sorry, sir."

Echo One smiled, bracing for ejection. "Forgiven."

Echo Four watched as the canopy of his commander's fighter shot away. Suddenly, the man was clear, and moments later a swell of vivid orange billowed safely open.

"Echo Four to base," the rookie pilot called as the abandoned plane spun in. "Echo One is down. The major ejected in time… I see his chute."

"Roger, Echo Four," a voice replied. "We were monitoring your communications. Nice shooting."

The explosion had rocked Air Force One.

"Were we hit?" the copilot asked.

Rainier, watching the radar screen, had seen the last-second maneuver, and in awe had watched the threatening green triangle vanish from his screen. To his amazement, the symbol representing the lead fighter somehow remained, though it was descending.

"Well, I'll be," he said. "How in the world…"

A stall warning blared. Throttles still engaged all the way, he brought the nose down until the warning tone went silent.

The aircraft began to shudder. Rainier cut the engine thrust, dropping the forward speed, and the plane leveled off.

"We're in trouble," he groaned as the vibration intensified. He checked the altimeter again.

Sixteen thousand feet.

Echo Two and Echo Three swooped over the deep green grasslands, their radar locked on the only moving object within ten miles, which the lead pilot immediately had determined to be the source of the missile. It was a pickup truck, its bed covered by dark canvas, moving erratically along a straight rural dirt road at more than seventy miles per hour.

Echo Two, well ahead of his wingman, roared low over the plains at four hundred miles per hour. An alarm sounded as he passed over the vehicle, his altitude less than a hundred feet—the sensors of his F-24 Vengeance had detected, within the bed of the speeding truck, the signature of a spent shoulder-mounted launcher.

"It's him," he radioed, pulling up and away. "He's all yours."

"Roger," Echo Three replied, lining up for his approach. His missiles were hot, as was his anger.

"Hey, pal…company's coming," he said, sighting the truck.

The fighter's targeting system locked on. He fired.

The missiles dropped from bays beneath his wings, ignited, and sang out.

"Two away!" the pilot called.

In seconds, the truck vanished in an explosion of orange flame. Flaming shrapnel spread over a wide area, igniting small fires amid the fields and trees.

"Echo Two to base," the leader called. "Target has been taken out. Recommend local fire control be dispatched immediately… We have a grass fire."

"Roger, Echo Two," a voice replied. "What location?"

"Thirty-eight point four north by ninety-seven point six west. Tell 'em to look for the column of black smoke."

"Roger, copy. Good job, guys."

"Echo Two and Echo Three, returning to Air Force One." He and his wingman banked into a high-G turn.

A welcome sight greeted their eyes as they ascended. The president's plane gleamed high in the distance, a pinprick of reflected sunlight against the sky.

"She's still up there," Echo Three smiled. "Is that beautiful, or what?"

The shudder was growing worse. Shrill squeaks and metallic groans filled the cabin.

"What happened?" Varner asked, clinging to her chair. "Why are we shaking like this?"

"Someone must have taken a shot at us," Bridger said. "Had to have missed, though. We're still here."

Brooks had taken a serious fall, thrown across the room in the aircraft's initial evasive maneuver. With help, he had crawled onto the sofa and was cradling his left arm.

"I think it's broken," he said in obvious pain.

Bridger hit the intercom. "Dr. Lee, please come to my office. We have an injured man here."

"On my way," the doctor replied.

The plane protested every moment of flight, complaining for having to hold itself together. Varner closed her eyes.

"Safest way to travel," she whispered to herself.

Oxygen masks dropped from the ceiling.

"This can't be good," Sumner said.

They donned the yellow masks, more concerned now.

"Mr. President," Rainier's voice called.

"Go, Captain," the president replied, his voice muffled by plastic.

"It was an advanced SAM, sir. But the evasive action we took wasn't enough…you can thank our escorts that we're still in one piece."

"Did we lose anyone out there?"

"No sir. Don't ask me how."

Bridger breathed a sigh of relief.

"It looks like we over-G'd the aircraft," the pilot continued. "Also took some blast damage. We're losing cabin pressure, so we dropped the masks. I trust you're using them."

"Absolutely."

"In a few minutes, we'll be below ten thousand and you won't need them anymore. The loss is gradual, so they're really just precautionary."

"What about the shimmying?" Varner asked. "How serious is it?"

"She's handling badly and it's getting worse. We've had to drop our speed way down, so we're losing altitude."

"How quickly?" Bridger asked.

"*Too* quickly."

"What do you recommend?" Bridger asked.

"The way she's acting, it's a good bet we torqued the airframe. We need to put down…and right now. If we don't…well, sir, I'd say in about twenty minutes we'll be on the ground one way or the other."

"Understood." Bridger looked to Sumner. "Warren?"

"Offutt AFB is—"

"Captain, how about Offutt?"

"No go, sir. We already checked that… No way we'll get that far."

"Can we circle back to Ellsworth?"

"No sir."

"What else do we have? Any major public airports?"

"Not out here, sir. Nothing with a runway anywhere near long enough."

Fighting to ignore the pain in his arm, Brooks' eyes flashed as he recalled another option.

"There's the FEMA bunker in northern Nebraska," he suggested, his breaths sharp and heavy. "I noticed it a while back, on a budget report. It was closed down for lack of funding, but it does have a military runway."

"How about that, Captain? The FEMA bunker?"

"Yes sir," he replied, having overheard. "That'll work. It isn't on our main display maps anymore, but we'll pull up its coordinates."

"Keep us posted, Captain."

"Will do, sir."

The white-haired, elderly staff doctor, wearing a belt-mounted oxygen pack, arrived and gave Brooks a cursory examination. His demeanor was friendly, his snowcapped eyelids conveying wisdom gained over decades. He gently took the arm in his hands, and the injured man winced.

"It does appear to be broken, Son. But you're in luck… I've set a few hundred of these in my day."

"Take good care of him, Doc," Bridger smiled.

The advisor was escorted from the president's office, headed for the nearby medical room.

The loud moan of straining aluminum sounded anew.

"This day just keeps getting better and better," Sumner said.

"And almost nine hours of it left to go," Varner added, checking her watch.

Bridger groaned. "A lot can happen in nine hours."

22

S eventy-nine dead," an aide said. "One hundred thirty-one injured."
Levi closed his eyes, pausing to pray for the victims. Though the
Passover Sabbath had arrived and the hour was late, he had just returned
to the Knesset, having gone home for the day several hours earlier, shortly
before sundown.

But terrorism punches no time clock and respects no holy edict. Even
as the prime minister's armored car had pulled into his driveway, his wife
had handed him the phone.

"We believe he came in via the coast," the aide went on. "We should
know for certain by morning."

"Thank you, Aaron."

It had been the first homicide bombing in a month and had taken
place two hours earlier, in a crowded market in the city of Holon. The
blast had been more powerful than any previously inflicted.

"C-9," said an official of the Israeli Defense Forces. "Just like the bus
attack in America. The stakes have risen dramatically."

The prime minister and his senior officials had gathered in the strategy room. They sat around the polished oval table and considered their
options.

"Once again, they attack on a holy day," one man said. "As they
have done so often. It has begun, as before. We can no longer exercise
restraint."

"I know well of which you speak," Levi said, his voice low and even.
"My grandparents died in one such bombing… It too was on Passover.
We acted, and swiftly, but moving against an enemy who dwells within

one's own borders is a very different thing from acting against a sovereign nation."

"It is *they* who declared war, Zelle," one man spoke up. "In Rehovot. Thousands died... Their graves cry out to us."

The prime minister nodded sorrowfully. "And I hear them each night, my friend."

A murmur filled the room.

"Do not misunderstand me," Levi continued. "I know that inaction invites further attack, as we have seen. If we continue to do nothing..."

A man came running into the room, his eyes wide.

"Mr. Prime Minister...New York City has suffered a nuclear strike."

"What?" the man said. "When?"

"About twenty minutes ago. The news was slow in coming because all radio and television centers in the area, including our own, were either destroyed or crippled. Netphone service seems to have been overloaded and is down, and the direct Internet links are unresponsive. What little information we have came from an affiliate station in Chicago."

"How extensive is the damage?" one cabinet official asked.

"From what we are hearing," the man answered, "all of midtown Manhattan was destroyed, and the immediate surrounding area is uninhabitable. Most of what is still standing is afire."

"Was this related to the hostage situation?"

"We believe so, sir. Most likely, the device was detonated during the crisis by those who had taken the building."

"Who was responsible?"

"We don't know, sir...but in Palestine they are dancing in the streets."

"Where is President Bridger?" Levi asked.

"We don't know, sir."

"How many dead?"

"We...don't know, sir."

"Close the door, please."

The man left and shut the heavy double doors behind him. At once, the officials broke into a cacophonous discussion.

"Gentlemen, gentlemen," Levi said, rising from his chair and calling for quiet. "Please…"

The group went silent. All eyes were on the prime minister.

"I believe we just learned how *this* night is 'different from any other,'" he stated, recalling with irony the age-old line from the Seder. "Things are no longer as they were. As you know, Mr. Bridger has been under considerable pressure to withdraw his nation's support of our country. With this final straw, I believe they will do just that."

"He's the strongest ally we've ever had," one man pointed out. "Do you really think he'll turn his back on us now? We don't even know for certain that the bomb was detonated by our enemies…"

"It would be a safe assumption," Levi said. "We know Islamic Sword has been working with the Palestinians for more than a year…not to mention the fact that they harbor their own deep-seated hatred of America. I believe we can expect an ultimatum to be issued to the president at any time."

"Perhaps, but…"

"Even if none is forthcoming, will the American people continue to tolerate their president's loyalty toward us? Their oil crisis already has done great damage to his standing, and the Congress will be bound to act. I'm afraid the decision to support us will no longer lie with Matthew Bridger, and we must be prepared for that."

"What do we do?" asked another man.

"What we must," Levi answered.

Air Force One shuddered ominously, and Bridger and the others feared a safe landing was no longer possible.

Worse, her pilots had those same doubts.

"Air Force One, this is Echo Three," a voice spoke in Rainier's headset.

"Go, Echo Three."

"We've completed our flyaround... Be aware that you sustained both fuselage and wing damage. There's a severe bulge in your right side wing spar, and you're leaking hydraulic fluid. I'd say you lost a line or two."

"Roger," the captain said. "We knew we'd torqued her, and we've been losing hydraulic pressure. She's getting harder to handle every minute."

"Well, we're with you all the way," the fighter pilot said. "As soon as you put down, we'll circle and seal off the area. ETA thirteen minutes."

"Keep your fingers crossed, guys," Rainier said. "It's going to be close."

The plane crossed the Kansas-Nebraska border and dropped to an altitude of less than two thousand feet. All aboard were strapped in, awaiting the coming forced landing, only minutes away.

Lawe watched as the grassy sandhills passed below, and the ground grew ever nearer. Vast cattle ranches, country roads, and widespread clusters of trees all now were almost close enough to touch. A flash of sun drew his eye, and he looked up to see the fighters pulling away, giving the huge airliner all the maneuvering room it required.

The shard of red-hot shrapnel had grazed his left calf, but the wound was superficial. Already, that very day, he had endured worse.

The plane quivered in manifold directions as it changed course, leveled off, then changed again. Many of those aboard wondered if their last moments were upon them.

But one man's mind was elsewhere, fixed on two whose lives meant more to him than his own.

Please, let them be alive and well, Lawe thought, before realizing he had been praying.

"Isn't even a foxhole," he muttered.

"All right, folks," Rainier's voice announced over the speakers, calm and steady. "We're on final approach, and the runway's just ahead. Relax, and we'll have you down in no time."

One way or another, several thought but did not vocalize.

Bridger heard and felt the thump of the landing gear as it dropped and locked into position. Rocked abruptly from side to side, he glanced up at the presidential seal, mounted firmly against the trembling wall.

It was a good ride while it lasted.

The control yokes fought against them, shaking in their hands.

"She's too sluggish," said the copilot. "Hydraulic pressure's down to critical."

"At least the gear's down."

"And locked. Must have angels on our wings."

"Almost there," Rainier said, his focus ahead. He varied the thrust, manipulating the throttles in an attempt to compensate for the loss of rudder control. The plane was dangerously slow to respond.

A red light ignited on the instrument panel, accompanied by an alarm.

"Pressure warning…"

"Almost there…"

"Thirty feet," the copilot called. "Air speed one-seven-zero…one-six-five…one-six-zero…one-five-zero…"

With a loud squeal of rubber against concrete, they dropped hard onto the runway. A bang sounded, followed by multiple impacts as fragments of shredded tire struck the belly of the aircraft.

The pilot cut the throttles and the nose gear came down. Immediately, he reversed thrust and pulled the throttles back, and the men were thrown forward against their straps. The engines roared, fighting now to slow the aircraft, which protested wildly.

"Drifting to the right a little," the copilot warned, his voice shaking.

"Come on, baby…you can do it…"

Rainier jerked the throttles back fully. The wounded plane continued to slow, creeping ever closer to the right edge of the paved strip. The right-side wheels left the runway, finding tall grasses and packed soil. Finally, laboriously, the plane came to a halt with less than a hundred yards of runway to spare.

Rainier was unaware of the elation filling the trio of cockpits circling above. Nor did he hear the applause sounding behind and beneath him.

He cut the engine thrust almost to zero, closed the reversers, then brought the engines back up, steering the crippled plane back across the landing strip and onto the taxiway. The fighter escorts remained aloft, keeping watch over the fallen bird.

No sooner had the jumbo jet cleared the runway than the hydraulics failed, and the majestic carcass of Air Force One came to a final rest.

"Ladies and gentlemen," the captain cheerfully announced to his shaken passengers, "Welcome to Nowhere, Nebraska. We hope you enjoyed your flight. Please travel with us again, and have a nice day."

Long ago, on a much different night, it first had appeared. The air then had been cold and as clear as crystal, not like the warm breeze that now brought into the city the sweet scent of flowers and spring grasses. The town had been much simpler, a place of stone dwellings, crowded inns, and shepherds keeping their flocks.

There, above Bethlehem, it first had come to glorious life.

The star.

Sent by God, it had hung directly overhead, heralding the birth of His Son. It even had led the weary Magi to the very house where the Child lay.

Now, more than two millennia later, an unusual star once more appeared in the skies above the town.

Then another.

They transited the sky, moving swiftly, blazing, rising from beyond the hills and crossing from south to north. Unlike their ancient prede-cessor, these stars did not carry the good news of a savior's birth, of life everlasting.

Rather, they brought death.

A double sonic boom split the night, and alarms screamed as the mis-siles crossed the radar warning threshold. In seconds, defensive systems fired and streaked skyward into the starry blackness.

One was a clean miss. The head-on trajectory angle presented too small a target for the much faster Israeli Arrow-5, and by the narrowest of margins the incoming threat found its target.

The King David Hotel was filled with the devout, almost a thousand who had chosen to observe Passover in the Holy City. More than five hundred sat in its grand ballroom alone, taking part in one of the largest Seder celebrations in Israel.

In July 1946 the hotel had been the site of a terrorist bombing. Ninety-one had died that day.

That distant event had been but a shadow.

Finding the heart of Jerusalem, the missile slammed into the hotel. Orange light, black smoke, splintered brick, and shattered glass filled the air as the fireball engulfed the building. Those who did not perish in the initial blast and subsequent fires fell to the nerve agents the detonation released.

A mere sixteen seconds had passed from launch to impact.

The second incoming missile was not as lucky. Programmed to strike the Knesset, it suffered a glancing defensive blow while still high in its arc, which damaged its steering surfaces. It failed to compensate for its wounds and lost track of its course.

Unlike the first, it carried no chemical weapon. Instead, it bore an enhanced warhead, an explosives package designed to level the center of Jewish government once and for all.

Still intact but out of control, it spun wildly to the east, stabilized slightly, then fell like a hammer in the night against a place of antiquity, an icon of gold and polished marble.

The force of the explosion obliterated the gleaming structure, erasing it from the foundation on which it had stood for centuries. Yet the physical damage paled in comparison to the cultural devastation.

Billions would tremble and weep upon hearing the news. Many would swear revenge, though their own had struck the blow.

The Dome of the Rock was no more.

o you have it, Bry?" another agent asked, indicating the datapad in Lawe's hand.

"Right here," he said.

They had safed the aircraft, shutting it down, euthanizing its onboard flight systems. With the damage Air Force One had suffered, fire and explosion still were a distinct possibility, so the exit stairs had been extended the moment the plane had come to a final stop. Following a brief radio transmission to inform Washington that all were alive and well, Bridger and his security detail had been the first to disembark, followed quickly by the others.

It had been decided that the safest move by far was to enter the bunker and there determine the best course of further action. The second presidential plane would be on its way only when the word was given, allowing Bridger time to fully assess the situation in New York and throughout the nation as a whole.

They walked down the taxiway, headed toward the only structure anywhere to be seen, a concrete building almost eighty yards away. Connected to the tarmac by a short paved road, it gave the appearance of a flat-topped pyramid fifty feet on a side and fifteen high. It had a single reinforced steel door, which faced the runway.

"How long do you suppose this has been here?" an agent asked Lawe.

"Quite a while. Forty, fifty years, maybe."

The Secret Service men scanned the surrounding tree line as they moved along. There in the forest, beyond their sight, a high, well-marked electrified fence separated what lay beyond from the huge oval of the landing area, ensuring as much security as possible. Whether current still flowed within the towering barrier was not known.

Lawe and a few of the other agents broke from the group and reached the building first. The door bore a sign:

DEPARTMENT OF HOMELAND SECURITY

FEDERAL EMERGENCY MANAGEMENT AGENCY

U.S. GOVERNMENT PROPERTY

AUTHORIZED PERSONNEL ONLY

The door's adjoining security panel reflected a bygone technology, which prompted commentary among the men.

"Wow," one said. "Built by dinosaurs, was it?"

"Hey, as long as it works."

Accessing his datapad, Lawe brought up the access code FEMA had provided only minutes earlier. He then raised the yellowed, transparent plastic cover over the panel and took a breath.

"Here goes nothing…"

He punched in the twelve-character sequence, pressing several clunky keys. After an interval that struck him as unnecessarily lengthy, a green light glowed within the panel and the door slid open.

"We're in," he called out, and in moments all, including the pilots of the escort fighters, were inside.

Pausing in the lobby, they took a head count. Bridger, his staff, Lawe and his agents, the doctor, the service technicians, and flight crew—fifty-three persons were present. When everyone was accounted for, Lawe sealed the outer door behind them.

The air was stale and still, the room illuminated only by the amber emergency lighting their entry had triggered. Before them, beyond a wide black-tiled floor, stood a second portal of brushed metal.

The elevator.

Lawe stepped forward, entered the second code he had been provided, and the doors opened.

"Going down," he said.

"Show-off." Varner smiled.

Lawe quickly examined the elevator. It was a service lift with another pair of doors on its opposite wall. It was also quite large, apparently sufficient to bear them all.

"Looks more like a room than an elevator," Brooks commented. "Is that the only way in or out?"

"As far as I know," Lawe said. "Probably excavated a few sloped tunnels for building the bunker, but filled those in afterward. For personnel, this may be it."

"Since it hasn't been used in years," one of the technicians pointed out, "maybe a few of us should wait up here until we know it works okay. I mean, that way, if it fails on the way down, we can call for help."

"Good idea," Lawe nodded, scribbling the entry codes onto a piece of paper and handing them to another Secret Service agent. "Just in case."

The other agent and a handful of techs moved aside as everyone else entered the car. With the entry of a button sequence, the doors closed silently behind them and their descent began. The ride was smooth and quiet.

"Actually, I was here once before, sir," said one of Bridger's men. "About six years ago, with the former president. Quite a setup down there, I must say."

"So we'll see."

The downward journey lasted a full minute. The car gently came to a stop, and as the doors opened the group found themselves bathed in golden light—the emergency illumination had snapped on throughout the complex.

Emerging, they discovered a polished concrete platform. Their footsteps echoed, lending an eerie mood as if they had entered a catacomb. The place most closely resembled a subway station with a few stark differences. Twenty feet ahead, a rectangular opening in one wall was just large enough to reveal the entry to a sleek, silvery shuttle car, nestled within a transit tube with little room to spare. Caution signs were posted alongside the door, as was a simple graphic of the tunnel route.

"MagLev," Sumner pointed out. "Fast and frictionless."

"No dust anywhere," Varner observed. "And I feel air flow. The filters are still working."

Lawe radioed the men above, and in minutes they joined the main group. Bridger and his staff gave the shuttle car a cursory examination, during which the next security sequence was entered. Its door slid open, revealing an interior of blue upholstery and stainless steel. It was not unlike an airport passenger carrier, with vertical grip poles, white lighting, and bench seats.

"Think she'll take us all?" Creedel asked.

"Looks that way," Brooks said, cradling the temporary cast on his forearm. They stepped down and inside and took their seats.

"Everyone hold on," Bridger said. "We don't want anybody hurt."

Lawe pressed a control and sealed the inner and outer doors. In doing so, he activated the automatic drive system. Silently, like a cartridge entering the chamber of a gun, the shuttle car slid forward into the tunnel.

A synthesized voice sounded.

"Please remain seated or grip the handrails at all times while the sub-shuttle is in motion. Make sure all personal items remain secure. This vehicle travels in excess of two hundred miles per hour… All passengers should be aware that, in the event of an emergency, sudden changes in velocity can occur. Should you experience nausea due to the rapid acceleration or deceleration of the vehicle, sickness bags are available in the green pouches directly behind each seat."

In moments, the car had attained its maximum transit speed. Its magnetic levitation drive literally allowed it to move on air, a steady and impressive motion. There were windows in each end of the car—Lawe watched as the light rings banding the tunnel ahead approached and passed in a blur to the rear.

"Nice ride," he said. "Too bad they don't have these things in D.C."

They traveled for a few minutes, sometimes straight, sometimes in a curved path. Ten miles, perhaps more, slipped past them, the distance intended to prevent the runway on the surface above from being used to target the installation.

The subshuttle came to a gentle stop, and the doors opened automatically. Bridger and the others disembarked into a wide subterranean chamber cut from solid rock. A sophisticated lattice of arching metal supports and trusses rose along the walls and crossed overhead, the signature of an advanced engineering technology. A large reinforced door, set into the dark stone and featuring an adjoining security pad, promised entry into the bunker proper.

"How far underground do you think we are?" someone asked.

"Thousand feet, maybe," Brooks said, loud enough to be heard by all. "I hope no one here is claustrophobic."

"How many people will this place support?" Creedel wondered.

"According to these specs," Lawe read, "twenty-seven hundred for up to five years. Power, food, water, air, housing... It's completely self-sufficient. Everything's filtered and recirculates. It was designed to protect military and government personnel in case of extreme nuclear or biological attack, to keep things functioning. There are supposed to be a dozen or so like it across the country, though not as many as there were a few years ago."

"Money talks," Creedel nodded.

Another code was entered, and they were in. A primary corridor led to a circular central hub, surrounded by doors leading to the various areas of the base.

"Come along, folks," Captain Rainier said brightly. "Let's see if we can find some living quarters and get cleaned up. I for one would enjoy a shower about now."

With Lawe and his men in the lead, Bridger, his staff, and the technical crew walked into the control center of the complex. Large display screens, wide consoles, and data-transfer systems waited to be stirred from their slumber.

Trained fingers flew upon switches and touchpads. After a brief interval, the complex was fully powered and alive again.

The sounds of functioning computers filled the air. The overhead display screens filled with snow, the speakers with static.

"All standard communications are down," a technician announced. "The Net's gone deaf, dumb, and blind, and so have we."

"What other options do we have?" Bridger asked.

"Direct satellite link if it's still up, and that's a *big* if. Fortunately, it uses a different system than Air Force One's, so whatever knocked that out may not have touched this. *Un*fortunately, back several years ago when this system was the primary, it sustained damage in the solar storms that knocked everything out. That's why we stopped using it in the first place. Hasn't been used much since."

"Okay. Let's see if it still works."

The techs descended on the system, amused by the age of the equipment. As power rose, circuits warmed for the first time in years. Manuals were consulted, and frequency adjustments were made. In fairly short order, the men nodded to Air Force One's communications specialist, who sat at the console. He flipped a switch. A green light shone.

"This is FEMA One, on scrambler," the man announced into a headset mike.

Come on, Bridger silently pleaded. *You can do it!*

He adjusted the controls, threading a fragile link to the nation's capital.

"Repeat, this is FEMA One on emergency channel Charlie-three-fourteen. Come in please."

"Roger, FEMA One," a voice came back, a tolerable crackle of static in the background. "Been expecting you. We're redirecting your call... Stand by for the vice president."

Bridger moved closer and took the headset.

"Matt?" a familiar voice said. "Can you hear me? You okay?"

"Fine, Harper," the president said. "Thanks to the efforts of a lot of good men and women. Where are you?"

"At Thunder Bravo," Lund answered from deep within a secure location outside Washington. "Along with my wife and family and yours."

"What are you hearing? What's happening out there?"

"Matt, it looks bad…and we've got more than the bomb to deal with."

"Talk to me, Harper."

"A little less than an hour ago, the Net shut down. Phones, datapads, transfer links, the works. Even the television and radio networks… After the bomb went off, they briefly came back up through affiliate stations, but now we've lost them again. Total news blackout. They haven't isolated the problem yet, but it looks like widespread sabotage. Time-triggered complex of viruses, maybe. No telling how long they might've lain dormant, or how long it'll take to trace the problem and correct it. Could be days."

"A coordinated effort?" Bridger wondered aloud. "The bomb in New York, the attack on Air Force One, and then they cut our communications. Hit 'em hard, decapitate the government, and isolate the communities so panic can burn out of control. And they waited for first word to spread before pulling the plug."

"Sounds about right. We're starting to get word of panic nationwide. Reports are coming in by shortwave. Since the announcement, riots have broken out in several cities."

"What announcement?"

"It was broadcast on BBC1, just before the blackout… Wait, it looks like they're running it again."

The president turned to the technician. "Can you get BBC1 on that thing?" The man checked his board, then nodded.

"Harper, wait a minute," Bridger told Lund. He turned back to the man at the console. "Do it."

A few switches were thrown, and the static-streaked image of a woman at a newsdesk appeared on the largest overhead screen. Her solemn voice, carried on speakers, filled the room.

"...*have now claimed responsibility for the nuclear attack on New York City. Further, they have issued a demand...*"

"Who, Harper?" Bridger barked into the headset. "Who did it?"

"Islamic Sword."

"...*all American military and financial aid to Israel is to cease immediately, and all troops and equipment are to be withdrawn. Here again is a replay of their recorded message, delivered to the Aljazeera news service approximately thirty minutes ago.*"

A dark-robed man in a turban, sitting at a desk with a large image of a mushroom cloud behind him, appeared on the screen. Words in Arabic appeared beneath him as he spoke, and the uneven voice of a British translator was heard.

"*The judgment of Allah has fallen upon the evil ones, and their greatest city is no more. More nuclear devices are in place throughout America, in the cities and in the fields, and unless our demands are met, the sword of our great god will fall again and again. Israel's criminal occupation of Arab lands will no longer be tolerated, and the existence of the Jewish state must end. America's depraved support of this unlawful nation must cease at once. In the name of peace, we of Islamic Sword grant a period of six days for the United States to comply with our demands. If it does not, more will perish.*"

The newscaster reappeared.

"*This statement,*" she went on, "*appears to leave no room for negotiation. We do not yet know if President Bridger has received word, for his official aircraft, Air Force One, was attacked as it flew somewhere over the continental United States. Nor do we know for certain that the president, at this time, is in fact alive...*"

"Who started *that* rumor?" Bridger demanded. "It's been barely an hour, and the last thing we need right now is for the people to think these fanatics destroyed both New York *and* the government."

"I don't know. Islamic Sword likely made it public."

"Nice."

"Did you get that last part, Matt?" the vice president asked. "Less than a week before they set off the next nuke."

"I heard." He motioned for the tech to turn down the audio level of the newscast.

"I don't think there's a way around it this time," Lund gravely conceded. "As we speak, Congress is convening an emergency session. They're going to force a joint resolution demanding we abandon Israel."

"Why am I not surprised?" Bridger muttered.

"They're sure to have enough votes to override a veto, Matt. They're going to force you to comply."

"This country has had a longstanding policy of not yielding to terrorist demands," Bridger stated. "If we start down that road—"

"That was before almost two million Americans died in a single afternoon, with the threat of millions more. And now, with war in the Middle East—"

"What war?"

"Palestine just launched a missile attack on Jerusalem, and full retaliation is certain. More than a thousand were killed when the King David Hotel was destroyed, and another missile leveled the Dome of the Rock."

"What? Why in the world would the Arabs target their own—"

"The tracking data shows its likely intended target was the Knesset, but an Arrow missile knocked it off course."

Bridger closed his eyes.

"What about the people of New York?" he asked. "What can we do to help them?"

"I've received a report from Homeland Security…" There was a pause—Bridger pictured Lund putting on his reading glasses. "Everything south of 150th Street has been declared off-limits. The radiation count shoots way up as you go deeper into the blast zone. The streets are virtually impassible...the whole place is a sea of burning rubble. It's going to be days before we can even begin to get in there, and they're saying it may be two weeks or longer before midtown is at all habitable. The cleanup could take ten years, if then."

"What about rescue?"

"There are injured even in Queens and New Jersey, and crews coming in from all over the country. Those who were far enough from the blast have begun to leave the island on their own, on foot. The rescue teams are helping as best they can, but the injuries... Matt, it's horrifying."

"Are the hospitals holding up?"

"Barely. They're overwhelmed. The injured are being transported as far as three hundred miles away."

Bridger glanced over at his staff. He read their faces, knew their thoughts.

"I'll get back to you, Harper," he said. "We'll see if we can sort anything out from here. I need you to go ahead and set up a teleconference with the Joint Chiefs. Bring in Homeland Security, too. Here in the next few minutes, I'll record a brief radio message to the people, something as reassuring as possible. I'll contact you again shortly and send it along, and you'll have to find a way to get it on the air."

"Very good, Mr. President. Out."

Lawe flipped a switch, ending the call. The president dropped the headset onto the console and took a breath.

"Islamic Sword," Brooks said. "Now we know."

"We can't let another bomb go off, Mr. President," Creedel insisted.

"Nor can we give them what they want," Sumner added. "If we do, they'll hit us again anyway, and their demands will escalate."

"I will *not* abandon an ally," Bridger said firmly. "Especially one under attack."

"It's become a matter of us or them, Matt," Varner said grimly. He looked at her, finding in her lovely brown eyes a resignation he never before had seen.

"So," the president said, "which is worse…risking your own life, or standing by silently, out of fear, as your only true friend is set upon by wolves?"

He expected no answer. None came.

Matthew Bridger was a man alone.

Richard Kelsey, alone in his den, watched by satellite the British coverage of the escalating crisis. It alone provided live updates and likely would be the sole source of such news for several days. High-altitude images of a burning, flattened Manhattan flashed one after the other, defying belief and inciting both rage and fear.

Yet another quantum shift in history had taken place. A new "normal" was being defined. Kelsey had seen the world change many times—war, revolution, assassination, technological advancement, and terrorist actions all had wrought their effects.

But never had he seen upheaval like this.

New York City, for all purposes, was gone, and with it millions of lives, the heart of the American media, and any pretense of national safety. The day before, Air Force One had gone down, and the president's whereabouts had not been revealed to the press in any terms more specific than "a place of safety." All-out war was imminent in the Middle East. Panic ruled in streets across America, and the nation's reeling economy might well have been dealt a deathblow.

And America was on the verge of a decision that, Kelsey knew, could bring about its demise.

All that, in a span of hours.

"We're receiving reports of widespread explosions within Palestine," the newscaster said as the camera returned to him. *"We do not yet have confirmation of their source, but our men there on the ground report the sound of planes in the air. Many planes…"*

"It's begun," Kelsey knew.

War in the Holy Land raged once more.

Is this really it, Father? the old man wondered, trying to make the pieces fit. *Has the day finally come?*

The scene on the screen changed. Sitting at a desk, the flag of Israel behind him, was Zelle Levi. He began to speak in Hebrew, with on-screen subtitles in Arabic and a spoken translation in English.

"They want *everybody* to hear this," Kelsey realized.

"Since its return to the land of its fathers," the man began, *"the nation of Israel has endured unparalleled assaults on its very existence. We have fought for survival, often in ways we would not have chosen, ways that were forced upon us by the incessant, hostile actions of those who would see us destroyed.*

"Last night, missiles launched from within Palestine fell upon this city, killing more than a thousand innocent men, women, and children who had gathered in celebration of one of our most sacred feasts. That these people were so deliberately and so viciously targeted has shown us yet again that the enemy who would destroy us has no regard for the sanctity of life or of faith or for the limitations dictated by the most basic moralities of human civilization. On many occasions they have chosen to attack us during our holiest of days, hoping to catch us off guard during our worship of the King of the Universe.

"In recent years we have chosen not to respond to such attacks, in hopes that a peaceful solution might yet be found to the continuing conflict. We have long known, however, that the only goal sought by our enemies is our extinction, that anything short of that, any negotiated peace, any transfer of land is a futile measure.

"We withdrew from the lands of the West Bank and Gaza, giving them what they had demanded for so long…a nation, self-governed, self-sustained,

with secure borders and freedom from Israeli influence. Many doubted that surrendering these lands would bring peace, but those who led our people at that crucial time bowed to public and international pressure and did so despite the fact that relinquishing those lands meant leaving our country virtually indefensible.

"For several years the violence against us abated. Some throughout the world declared that peace in this land, finally, was a reality. But we knew a sleeping monster lurked a stone's throw away, and our fears now have been realized. The conflict has not ceased, nor will it, not until the threat to Israel is removed once and for all.

"An event took place this night which has convinced us that a long-awaited day has come. The Dome of the Rock, built long ago on the Temple Mount in Jerusalem, was destroyed by an errant Palestinian missile intended for the Knesset. The dramatic and sudden removal of this shrine, we believe, is a sign from God that we are now to remove the enemy himself from our lands and reclaim what is rightfully ours."

A chill swept Kelsey. His hair stood on end.

"Over the past two hours, we have carried out fighter strikes against all known Palestinian missile emplacements. We have struck all known military targets, radar sites, weapons depots, and relevant industrial locations. We also have bombed all airport runways, both military and civilian, in order to prevent a close-range air assault. These actions are but a precursor.

"Long ago a plan was put into place, one we hoped would never have to be used. But now, for the survival of our nation, we implement the following:

"First, the state of Israel, this night, reclaims sovereignty over the lands of the West Bank and Gaza. East and West Palestine no longer exist as a nation."

"Here we go," Kelsey uttered, his voice quivering.

"For the security of our people, no Arab presence will be allowed west of the Jordan River. This includes the Arab citizenry of Israel, which even now are being gathered for deportation. All Palestinians and other Arab nationals who reside in the former Palestine also will be removed to the surrounding *lands. All neighboring Arab countries will assist in this deportation and will allow the Palestinian people to live securely within their countries."*

"They'll *never* go along with that," the ex-minister knew.

"Second, we reclaim the Temple Mount of our fathers and will seek to rebuild our temple upon its foundation. No longer will we allow our enemies to dictate our place or manner of worship."

Kelsey's heart pounded. "This *is* the day!"

"Third…" There was a pause. Levi's face reflected a deep distress. The words came hard. *"In order to ensure that these things take place, this nation, effective one hour ago, has targeted the Muslim holy cities of Mecca and Medina for nuclear destruction. If our conditions are not met, we will not hesitate to act. Do not test us in this."*

The Israeli leader went silent for a moment. His hands were trembling.

"No longer will we allow these continued attacks on our people. Never again will we return to the days of daily suicide bombings, missile attacks, and other such assaults against us. The nation of Israel will not be driven into the sea and, through the power of God, will destroy its enemies in totality before that is allowed to happen…even if doing so ultimately leads to our own destruction. This land is ours, and we will never *leave it again."*

"The Samson Protocol," an astonished Kelsey whispered, recalling a name he once had heard, long before. "They're finally, *really* doing it…"

The screen momentarily went black, then was filled by the image of a stunned London newscaster.

"Ladies and gentlemen," he began, *"what you have just witnessed is a grave and historic change in the world as we know it."*

"You, my friend," Kelsey said somberly, "have no idea."

The conference room on the bunker's lower level was large, much more spacious than the Cabinet Room of the White House. A world map covered one wall, and a photo mural, an aerial view of Washington, D.C., covered the opposite one. Voluminous, outdated reference books lined a wide bookcase. The center of the room was dominated by an oblong table of oak encircled by eighteen slightly worn leather-upholstered chairs.

Bridger sat at the head of the table. All were weary and the hour was late, but none could rest before a few things were understood.

"Okay," Sumner asked, speaking of the Palestinian action, "so why attack with missiles?"

"As opposed to what?" Brooks said.

"If they have their hands on that many nukes, why didn't they use one against Israel? If they could sneak them in over here, they could do the same over there."

"Maybe they didn't want to pollute Israel, because they want to drive out the Jews and live there themselves," Varner offered.

"Perhaps. Or maybe they only had the one and felt it was more important to get *us* out of the picture."

"The report said that the Life Quality building was renovated, what—eight or nine years ago?" Bridger pointed out. "If they snuck it in back then and have been sitting on it all this time, maybe Warren's right and there aren't any more. None planted anywhere else, nothing to force us to act as they want. Maybe the threat is a bluff."

"How can we know for sure?" Creedel asked. "The risk is too big."

"That's what we have to sort out…before it's too late."

"Do you think he'll do it?" Varner asked. "Nuke Mecca?

"Rhonda," Bridger replied, "I've known Zelle Levi for more than a decade. Right now, their survival as a nation's on the line. That's why, from a purely political standpoint, it's *crucial* that we stay by their side and keep this war conventional, because if we don't, and it escalates into a nuclear situation…" He went silent for a moment. "I can promise you he'll make good on that threat. The Muslims have already lost the Dome of the Rock. If Mecca and Medina are taken out as well, they'll have nothing left to lose.

They'll throw everything they have at Israel, and the Jews in return will retaliate with everything *they* have."

Creedel shook his head. "And if the entirety of the Israeli nuclear arsenal is launched…"

"Exactly," Bridger said.

It had been twenty-four hours since the world, again, had changed.

A thousand feet overhead, the Nebraska plains warmed in the heat of the late afternoon sun. Lawe, huddled in an alcove of the control room that afforded him a measure of privacy, tried again to contact Karen and Jeffrey without success. His netphone could not find a signal so far underground, so he was using a handset tied into the bunker's com network. Unfortunately, all netphone service in the eastern United States and all land lines into and out of the area still were hopelessly overburdened. Nothing was getting through.

"Well," he tried to convince himself, "I'll know when I know, and I won't worry until then."

It was a lie.

Lawe walked into the utilitarian dining hall, one of three in the complex. The warm light of dozens of extended-life bulbs filled the room, and soft music drifted from ceiling-mounted speakers. A dozen of his colleagues were gathered there, seated at one of its hundred tables, partaking of the first meal since breakfast.

"I kind of forgot about lunch," Lawe commented.

"Lot of that going around," Captain Rainier said, taking a bite of a military ready-to-eat meal. "Funny how watching the world come apart at the seams will do that to you."

Stacked behind the empty cafeteria line were cases of the nonperishable food, with blue plastic trays stored on a rack nearby. Lawe flipped among several of the sealed foil packs and found none of the choices particularly appetizing. He finally settled on beef stew, grabbed a tray, plate, and utensils, and made use of a microwave.

Together they sat in silence, their minds not on their food, none certain that they were not in the midst of a nightmare from which they could not awaken.

Lawe found Bridger sitting alone in his living quarters, skimming a microbook.

"You…need anything, sir?" he asked, unsure that he should ask.

"Bry," Bridger said, looking up. "Just taking a moment. Have a seat."

The agent sat on the end of a sofa, catty-corner from the president's chair.

"I never got the chance to thank you for Kansas."

"My pleasure, Mr. President."

Bridger smiled. "I doubt that. I owe you my life, and I'm deeply grateful."

"My *honor*, then," Lawe winked.

"Fair enough. But I owe you one…and no arguments."

"Yes sir." He glanced down at the microbook. "What are you reading?"

"*The Collected Works of Mark Twain.* It was in the recreational library. And it contains one of my favorites, which surprises me. A story you don't often find included."

"What's that?"

"A short piece called 'A Curious Dream.'"

"I never heard of it."

"Few people have… It was written for a newspaper." He scrolled down the page. "It's about a fellow who finds himself sitting on a rural doorstep one night. He hears this clatter in the distance that grows louder, coming down the road. Thinks it's the sound of castanets, but it isn't. Then a procession of human skeletons comes walking past, all dragging their headstones and rotted coffins behind them."

"Twain wrote horror stories?"

"No. It's a social commentary. The man carries on a friendly chat with one of the dead and learns that they'd left their cemetery because it had fallen into extreme disrepair. Their living descendents had forgotten them and cared only about themselves and their own concerns. They had no appreciation for the labors of their deceased ancestors, whose houses and property they'd inherited. They felt no obligation toward them, no need to remain mindful of those who supposedly had meant so much to them. They'd lost sight of who they were...where they'd come from."

"Interesting."

"Yes," the president agreed. "Isn't it though."

Lawe understood.

"I tried, Bry, but now it's all being taken out of my hands. Congress is going to force us to..." He let the words die. "I mean, I understand the pain and fear everyone's going through. I feel it too. But you can't let that cause you to lose sight of who you are or who you're *supposed* to be."

"Sir?"

"I don't know exactly when it happened, but somewhere along the way this stopped being the America I grew up in. We've become something else, something I don't like." He paused, fiddling with the microbook. "It's so pervasive... I've even begun to doubt that *I'm* the man I thought I was. I find myself sitting here, wondering if I did the right thing when the Saudis pulled the plug. If I'd taken their offer of oil and met that sole condition, two million people wouldn't be dead right now."

"You don't know that," Lawe offered. "These people hate us for a *lot* of reasons. They planted that bomb years ago and were waiting for the right time to use it. Isn't that what they said? If it hadn't been this, it would have been something else."

The president was struggling. Doubting. His gaze dropped to the hard black tile of the floor.

"You did what you had to do," the agent continued. "You stood by an ally. You didn't cave in to the demands of a terrorist state." He studied the man. "Although, I gotta admit...*I* probably would have."

Bridger looked up at him.

"I don't know how you stood up to them," Lawe said. "I doubt one man in a million could have done it."

"And because of that..."

"*You* didn't set off that bomb, sir. *They* did."

"Yeah..." The president nodded subtly, spoke almost inaudibly. "Yeah."

After a moment, Lawe looked aside. Bridger saw his pain.

"Your brother?"

"I don't know. It was his precinct, but he doesn't live in the city. He doesn't pull duty every Friday... He *could* have been at home." He was trying to convince himself. "Ten thousand cops in New York. They may not have called him in."

A pause.

"But Sacred Child had planned a protest there, smack in the middle of..." He took a breath. "I asked Karen not to go, but she seemed pretty determined."

"Son, I'm praying they both are safe and well."

"Thank you, sir."

A quiet descended. For several minutes each man remained within his own head, taking a hard look at himself.

"You know," Lawe said, "that braciole you made... It was the finest I'd ever tasted."

The president smiled faintly.

"You'd never had it before," he somehow knew.

"No sir," Lawe admitted.

24

S ixty thousand people.

Men, women, children, all local residents of Washington. They gathered on Constitution and Independence Avenues, a swelling, flowing mass, marching in a great circle, surrounding the Capitol. The morning sky was gray and the spring shower was constant, yet the protesters were not deterred.

They knew the president was not inside the domed edifice. They did not know *where* he was, though they had heard a brief recorded address from him played over a hastily erected PA system, assuring them that there was no reason to panic.

Perhaps the president was absent, but someone else was there amid the hallowed halls, someone working feverishly to champion their cause.

Picket signs, the paint of some running in the gentle rain, rose above the moving sea of rain coats and bitterness:

U.S. OUT OF ISRAEL

TWO MILLION DEAD AND COUNTING

AMERICA FIRST

IMPEACH BRIDGER

LOSE THE JEWS

THINK OF THE CHILDREN

WHAT'S IN IT FOR U.S.? NOTHING

Heartfelt words, angry words, carried and chanted by a people who had suffered a great blow.

A people who had forgotten much.

Their shouts reflected those heard in every city, every state, even in areas that once had been stalwart sources of support for the Jewish state.

For most Americans the game had changed. The ante had become too high, and few were willing to take the gamble. A nuclear device in Manhattan surely meant others were planted in cities and pastures from sea to shining sea, as had been threatened, and their fear now overrode all else. All sense of national safety and allied responsibility had evaporated in an instant, within that great all-consuming fireball.

Now they wanted only to give the terrorists what they demanded. Appeasement was the way. *Then, surely then, they'll leave us alone and we'll be safe once more.*

There in the silvery rain they marched, making themselves heard.

The ghost of Neville Chamberlain walked among them.

The floor of the Senate chamber was crowded, just as that of the House had been the day before.

Cyrus Briggs stood at the front of the room, his chest swollen with triumph. He surveyed his fellow senators, of whom he never had been more proud. One force, one mind, one will, the desires of an entire nation embodied in these few as they rushed a Saturday vote through the legislature with unprecedented speed.

Some members were not present, having perished in New York. Their empty seats cried out of the loss, and their friends mourned.

Briggs had seen news coverage of the protests outside. He had heard the impassioned words shouted by thousands he did not know and, truth be told, did not care about. But their anger and frustration with their president and his rigid "ethical" policies, combined with the Damoclean sword of the terrorist demand, finally had given him the weapon he needed to defeat the man.

Where did your principles get you, eh?

The nuclear fires of New York, the dozens of winter deaths in the Northeast, and the empty fuel tanks and bank accounts of millions of Americans finally had signaled a death knell that Matthew Bridger could not overcome.

The initial vote was complete, and soon enough would be final.

Too bad it took a nuke, he thought, *but once this issue is over and done with, we'll close ANWR again and do whatever it takes to undo what this administration's done these past two years—*

There could be no presidential veto, not this time. In both chambers the vote had been almost unanimous, with only a handful of dissenting voices opposed to the joint resolution.

He vetoes, we repass and override—and by this time next week, Israel is just a memory.

Cyrus nodded.

What do you know—the system works after all.

The second presidential jet set down on the runway, its flowing lines in blue, white, and silver catching the afternoon sun. Slightly wider in body than the downed jet and with more powerful engines, it officially would assume the call sign "Air Force One" the moment the chief executive stepped aboard.

A Secret Service agent stood in the open doorway of the bunker entrance, watching as the massive plane slowed and began its turn, headed onto the taxiway. It passed quite near the crippled aircraft, their proximity magnified by the agent's viewing angle.

"Tell Iron Chef his ride is here," he called down by radio.

"Roger that," came Lawe's voice. "We're on our way up."

The echoing cry of fighters filled the air, even above the roar of the jet's four engines. The agent glanced up and saw the circling escorts, on duty continuously since their arrival, serving six-hour shifts with relief flying in from Whiteman AFB. Now these same planes would follow the presidential plane all the way to Andrews, and from there follow at a distance as helicopter Marine One made its short hop to the White House lawn.

Leaving this secure location had been a tough call for everyone but Bridger. Chances were that another cell with another missile might be out there, lying in wait for the opportunity to finish the job others had failed to do.

But almost three days underground had been enough. Bridger knew he had to get back to Washington—no longer could he sit in a hole in the ground, by perception fiddling while the rest of the country burned. He had to get back where he belonged, to show the leadership the American people deserved to see—but more important, to show those of Islamic Sword that America would not be brought to its knees, however powerful the inflicted blow had been.

Less than an hour later, the new Air Force One was in the air and climbing, without incident, to forty-six thousand feet.

Lawe pulled into the parking lot of Karen's apartment complex and scanned for any sign of her.

Her drapes are closed—her car's in its space—

"Please, Karen," he whispered. "Please tell me you didn't get on that shuttle…"

With a squeal of brakes, he pulled at an angle into a couple of spaces, then shut off the engine and bolted from the car in a single motion.

Up the outer steps, through the door, up the stairs—just as he had done so many times.

Please, please, please—

Reaching her door, he banged on it as he fumbled for the key she had given him.

"Karen!"

Finally, the key slid home. He pushed the door open.

"Karen?"

No answer.

No suitcase, no purse, no Karen.

The place was threateningly silent. The gentle classical music that always signaled her presence was not playing.

He rushed to the bedroom, the bathroom, the kitchen.

No sign.

He picked up her phone, pressed the speed-dial button labeled "Sacred Child."

Most local service had been restored. There was a ring, but no one was there. An answering machine picked up.

It's Sunday, he remembered.

He hung up and tried the button marked "Melissa."

Another answering machine.

He hung up and dialed his brother's number in New Rochelle.

The call would not go through.

He slammed the phone down, truly frightened, his heart pounding.

"Why couldn't you have stayed home?" he cried out.

"Because I was out of milk and eggs," a voice sounded.

He spun toward the source of the music, the sweetest he ever had heard. Karen stood smiling in the doorway, a sack of groceries in her arms, having returned from a walk to the corner market.

"And," she teased, struggling to contain her joy, "I'd appreciate it if you'd not leave my front door wide open."

He went to her. She stepped forward, lowered the bag to the floor, and reached out for him. The sack fell over, unnoticed. An orange rolled across the carpet.

Their embrace was unyielding, as if each clung to life itself. Their kiss was long and deep. Lawe broke away long enough to speak.

"I thought you'd…"

"And I couldn't get through…"

"I was so afraid you'd gone ahead and…"

"They said the president's plane had been attacked…"

He held her head tight against his chest.

He was intoxicated by the scent of her hair, the feel of her warmth, her softness. Everything about her permeated his being, filling his world. They stood there, sharing their heartbeats, each knowing the other had cheated death since the last time they had exchanged words. Her tears wet his shirt. His eyes pooled.

"I got halfway to the airport," she confessed. "But I just couldn't do it. You were right… I was stubborn…"

"You're here," he said, holding her. "That's all that matters."

In three long days, his priorities had changed, he knew.

Don't wait another moment—

"I can't lose you," he said, pulling back to lose himself in her loveliness. "I won't risk it. Never again."

I love you!

"I don't have a ring on me right now, but…"

Her eyes widened as elation and disbelief both filled her.

"Karen, will you marry me?"

Again he beheld the glorious beauty of her smile. She placed her head against his chest and wrapped her arms around him more tightly. His ribs protested, and he winced.

"Yes, Bry...*yes.*"

For a fleeting moment all else fell away. They kissed again and stood there in the silence of the apartment, two against the world.

Another moment passed.

"When we were stuck in Nebraska," he said, "I tried a hundred times to get hold of you and Jeff, but nothing could get through. I was so afraid that—"

Karen sharply pulled back. With obvious reluctance and dampened joy, she looked up at him.

And he knew.

Bridger passed through his private entrance and into the Oval Office, seeing the room differently now, looking on it as one might see home before leaving on a long, long journey.

He took a seat in his familiar leather chair. A few notes and papers still littered the desktop, exactly as he had left them before his trip to Kansas. So many matters to which he must attend, so many obligations.

The vice president walked in, carrying with him a datapad and a manila envelope containing hard copies of the same documents.

"Good to see you, Harper," Bridger said, rising to shake his hand.

"Mr. President," the man returned. "Good to have you back. That was a close call."

Bridger spun in his chair and looked out on the White House lawn. "A lot of men have served in this room. Sat in this chair, worked at this desk. I never thought I'd be here. Even when I ran on the ticket with Rudy, I never for a moment thought he'd die a year into his first term. All I wanted was to serve my country...to help the party do some good. It was never about power or prestige, Harper. Never."

Lund furrowed his forehead, unsure what point the man was making.

"Working in this room," he continued, "having this office. It's a privilege. I've never lost sight of that. This house belongs to the people of the United States, and I'm their guest. I live here only by their will…" Green leaves danced before him under blue skies, shaken by warm breezes.

"Mr. President," Lund said, "they're ready to see you."

Bridger reached out and buzzed his secretary. "Lucy, please send in the gentlemen."

"Yes sir."

The door opened. In walked Cyrus Briggs and a few other senators and congressmen, all determined, some hopeful. Briggs tried unsuccessfully to hide his delight.

"Mr. President," he said, placing the joint resolution on Bridger's desk.

"Didn't waste any time, did we?"

"The situation's critical, sir," the man said. "We have to show the people we're doing something to safeguard them, and do it right now."

"We *are*, Cyrus," Bridger said. "And doing this will only bring more deaths. We concede now, and we invite further attack. You know that."

"No sir, I don't. We're trying to prevent what happened in New York from happening elsewhere next week. And if I may speak freely—"

"That's never been a problem for you."

Briggs scowled. "Your irrational adherence to the alliance with Israel threatens the national security of this country. Had you given up this stubborn policy last October, the people of this nation would not have suffered so severely since and millions of lives would not have been lost. The continuing and needless oil shortage that has nearly destroyed the economy and killed so many this past winter…the bus bombing and a nuclear detonation on U.S. soil… All these things lay right on your doorstep." His tone was less than respectful. "Sir."

Bridger slid the resolution toward the man. "I'm not signing this, Cyrus. I am *not* going to be the man who officially turns this country's back on Israel. It's not going to happen."

"Very well, then," Briggs said, picking up the folder.

"Matt," the House leader said, imploring the president. "I don't understand why you still refuse, not after New York. Before, when it was only oil, we were with you, but now…*please*…reconsider."

"Harper, if you please?" the president said with a slight indicative motion of his head. Lund handed the Senate leader the envelope he had been carrying.

"My reasons for refusal," Bridger said. "Not that they'll make any difference."

"No," Briggs said, turning toward the door. "They won't."

The men departed, taking most of the air in the room with them. Lund turned to Bridger, whose attentions had returned to the lawn outside.

"He's right, Matt. The roll-call vote's already scheduled for three o'clock this afternoon, and it's a foregone conclusion."

"I know," the president said.

"Mr. President," his secretary's voice said over the intercom, "your call is ready. Prime Minister Levi is on line one."

"Thank you, Lucy." He saw Lund's concern. "Take it easy, Harper. Either he listens or he doesn't. Problem is, I'm not altogether sure he's in the wrong."

As Lund took a seat opposite, Bridger pressed a button. "Zelle, this is Matthew. I've put you on speaker. The vice president is here with me."

"Mr. President," the man said. "Mr. Vice President. It is good to hear from you. I'm pleased you are still with us."

Bridger paused, appreciating the irony of the remark. "Well, it was touch and go for a while."

"The people of New York have the condolences of my nation. We grieve with you. The violence of our shared enemy sometimes is unfathomable."

"Thank you for that," Bridger replied, drawing a breath. "The next few years are going to be very difficult for a great many people."

"We will help however we can."

"Zelle," Bridger began, changing the subject, "I fully understand your need to retaliate against Palestine. The missile attacks you've suffered, the bombings... You *had* to act. But you can't launch a nuclear strike on the Saudis. If you do, the Arab League will send everything they have against you."

"Your own nation once carried out a similar defense against Japan, did it not? Twice in a span of days, if I'm not mistaken."

Bridger delayed in answering. "Yes. We did. But it was done to save the hundreds of thousands of American *and* Japanese lives that would have been lost during an invasion of the island."

"And you were right to do so. Your President Truman had a moral obligation to defend his people by any means necessary. We, too, hope to prevent the slaughter of many on both sides. If a tactical nuclear strike against the temple at Medina will dissuade them from further acts of aggression, we must carry it out."

"Things were different at Hiroshima and Nagasaki. There was no risk of escalation. Only America had the bomb."

"And as of this moment, among our enemies, *we* are alone in that regard. But that soon will change."

"What do you mean?"

"Matthew," the man began, his voice like that of a grandfather, "last week, before they were captured and executed, two of our agents discovered that both Syria and Egypt have obtained nuclear arms from China. Warhead yields in excess of five hundred kilotons. In less than three months they will be poised to launch an attack against us, and we have no doubt they will do so."

Lund closed his eyes, bowed his head, and kneaded the bridge of his nose.

"Our enemies are fully dedicated to our extinction," Levi continued, "but to date have lacked the weapons to carry out their mission. In the

334 Shane
Johnson

past we have been able to slow their internal development of such an arsenal, but with China now willing to sell to them…" A ponderous silence.
"Matthew, if we do not act now, we surely will perish."

"Zelle…"

"Whether we die a little at a time or all at once, we *will* die. Our current borders are indefensible. Now our only chance for survival is to
reclaim the lands we ceded to Palestine, to keep any further military
action from escalating beyond conventional levels, and to make certain
our enemies know that any nuclear launch against us would be suicide."

"What has been the Arab response to your ultimatum?"

"As expected, they're screaming of international law and sovereignty
rights and threatening retaliatory action should we proceed with the
relocation."

"Zelle, if you do this, the entire world will be against you."

"It is already, with one exception."

Bridger swallowed hard.

"As we speak," the president reluctantly began, "Congress is passing a
resolution that will force the withdrawal of all financial and military support of your country, effective immediately. They've taken the decision
completely out of my hands. I held it off for as long as I could, but there's
nothing more I can do. In a few hours, the United States will no longer
lift a finger to help you."

A moment of quiet.

"That is bad news, Matthew, but not entirely unexpected. We understand the pressure your nation now suffers. We have resigned ourselves to
being alone in this."

"I'm sorry, Zelle."

"I must ask… Will the United States take military action *against* us?"

"Our Terrorism Defense Bill included a provision forbidding interference in other nations' acts of self-defense. On that basis alone, I don't
think we could."

"You're not certain?"

"As I said, Zelle…it won't be up to me. *Nothing* will."

Another pause.

"I believe I understand, Matthew."

"God be with you," Bridger said. "However this turns out."

"I hope so," Levi said. "We have no one else."

The call came to an end. Bridger leaned back, eyes closed.

"So," Lund said, "after all these years, we're out of the picture."

"You know, Harper, I'm not so sure they need us. Not anymore. I'd say what they mainly took from us these past several years was moral support." The more he thought about it, the more he was convinced. "Because we were over there acting as muscle in the region, they've been able to show restraint and not tip their hand. But now…"

"So you're saying the Arabs should have been careful what they wished for."

"Yeah. They've never seen the full military potential of Israel. They may *think* they have, but they haven't. And you know, if I were Zelle, I'd probably do exactly what he's now doing. It's a drastic strategy, but were I a betting man…"

"The beast is loose," Lund realized. "And Heaven help anyone who gets in its way."

25

The dark government sedan streaked down the highway toward New Rochelle.

Lawe still did not know for certain that his brother had perished in the detonation. Every flash of his mind told him such was the case, but his heart refused to believe.

He has *to be alive—*

The car could not move fast enough. Already he was well over the speed limit, wishing the three-hour drive would pass in minutes.

"It's going to be dark by the time we get there," he muttered.

Why did you have to move up there in the first place? Why did you have to drag your family all the way to New York? Why couldn't you have taken a job with the force in D.C., like Ollie did—

Ollie.

You deserve to live, and Jeff didn't?

A fury had arisen within him, an ember fanned into a fire, sparked by frustration and fear. Anger toward Jeffrey for dying, toward the universe for taking his brother away.

And toward Ollie for being what he was.

Karen sat beside him, holding his arm, visibly sharing his pain. With the phones down, she had been unable to reach Brenda since before the event. But she knew from the few words they had exchanged that Jeff had been called into the precinct.

She stared through her window without seeing, her thoughts drifting elsewhere as the world blurred past. With a deep, sorrowful breath, her attentions returned to the man beside her and the mission at hand.

She tried her netphone yet again, but the same recorded apology sounded.

"We're sorry, but your call cannot be completed at this time—"

"I hate that voice," she said bitterly, flipping the phone shut.

Lawe leaned forward, turned on the radio, and flipped to a news station, hoping for further word of the attack. Perhaps some tidbit would let him know whether Jeff had lived or died.

Friday seems an eternity ago—

"Four-Eighteen," he muttered. "I'm sick to death of dates being used as names for disasters. It's as if they don't even bother to name them anymore, because they know there're going to be so many of them."

"I know," Karen said. "I hate it too."

Unexpectedly, the words flowing from the car's speakers dealt not with the Friday disaster but with the White House. He turned it up.

"…will be speaking momentarily. In light of the weekend's events, it is believed that President Bridger will be addressing the attack on New York, the crisis resulting from it, and the emergency resolution just passed by Congress…"

"Bridger's going on the air?" Karen asked. "Did you know about it?"

"I left Andrews directly. I didn't hear anything. But it makes sense… A lot's happened."

"What resolution is he talking about?"

"They're giving the terrorists what they want. They're pulling their backing of Israel."

"Why? Why don't they just retaliate like they did back when they went into Afghanistan and Iraq? Send in the military and—"

"Because it would be like stabbing smoke. Islamic Sword is spread all over the world, worse than al-Qaeda ever was. No way to get them all. No clear target. And they have a time issue they never had before… They don't know for sure that other nukes aren't already planted."

Karen looked away in silence, her mind racing. "But a war just started over there. Israel's going to need *someone*."

"I know. The president swore a veto from the outset, but they went through with it anyway and it passed."

"We take you now to the Oval Office and President Bridger."

Karen and Law went silent. A familiar, comforting voice filled the car.

"My fellow patriots, I come to you today from the White House."

Lawe detected something odd in the man's voice, a tone he had not heard before. *"Again, I wish to express the nation's deepest heartfelt sympathies to the people of New York City. The disaster suffered there has no equal in our national history, and we cannot yet fathom the scale of this atrocity. As never before, we have been shaken to our foundation. Our pain is great, and the road to recovery will be a long and difficult one. We can only pray for the blessing of God as we embark upon this monumental task, as we strive to heal a city and a people whose proven inner strength is a rare and precious thing. Those who perpetrated this terrible crime against mankind evidently perished in their attack, and I am certain that their remaining brethren, those of the terrorist group Islamic Sword, will find no safe haven on this planet. Justice will be served.*

"As you know, the events of this past Friday have prompted drastic action on the part of Congress. In an attempt to appease those who brought the nuclear device into our country, an emergency joint resolution has been enacted. That resolution, passed overwhelmingly in both the House and Senate, calls for the immediate abandonment of Israel by the United States. No further aid, whether financial or military, will be given to our longtime ally, nor will we continue to maintain forces in any Arab nation.

"While I share the pain and heartache being felt across this land, I cannot and do not agree with this resolution. It will not bear my signature and has passed despite my veto. It therefore takes effect tonight, at one minute past midnight.

"It is true that the terrorists have threatened to detonate further nuclear devices if their demands are not met. We do not know, however, whether such weapons even exist. It is quite possible, and perhaps even likely, that the bomb

set off in midtown Manhattan was the only one they possessed. Building such a device is so expensive and difficult as to be almost prohibitive, and it is extremely doubtful that Islamic Sword has the resources necessary for the creation of even a small nuclear arsenal. Congress may well be responding to a bluff.

"However fiercely we have been struck, however horrifying the damage inflicted, we must realize that to turn our back on a trusted friend, and in so doing yield to the demands of a terrorist organization, is a violation of every moral and ethical principle this nation has held as precious. Since its inception, the United States has recognized the importance of its loyalty to its allies, both near and far. Since the implementation of the Bush Doctrine, which followed the tragic events of Nine-Eleven, this nation has refused to negotiate with any terrorist organization in any way, always working instead to remove said organization, and its threat to peace, from the face of the earth.

"That doctrine, now, has been violated by our own elected leaders, and the consequences of this action will be both long-lasting and far-reaching.

"I cannot allow this resolution to be implemented by this administration. I will not walk away from Israel, nor from any ally. This morning, there were two courses of action open to me. The first was the veto I put into place. It failed. Now only one option remains.

"Therefore, effective tonight at the stroke of midnight, I will resign the office of the presidency..."

Lawe was stunned. *No!*

"...and will pray that the course this country now has charted does not result in its being wrecked on the rocks of history. It has been an honor to serve as your president, and I thank you humbly for the privilege. May God bless you all...and may He have mercy on the United States of America."

As the speech ended, a commentator began to speak of the surprising and unprecedented announcement. Lawe switched off the radio.

"They'll be analyzing that speech for a good while. I'll try again in an hour."

"Wow," Karen said. "I never realized he had such…"

"Principles?" Lawe offered. "I know. I began to see it at Camp David a few months back. He's a good man."

"Not many left like that. Especially in government."

"No, there aren't."

"Midnight…"

"And Lund will be sworn in before the chair behind the big desk goes cold."

"Bry, will they call you in? Should we go back?"

"They'll try, for sure," Lawe said wryly, watching the road ahead. "Too bad the phones are down."

Warm breezes kissed the waving leaves. The songs of a thousand birds drifted on the moving air. Blue skies stretched wide, only occasionally dotted with wisps of white.

Kelsey sat on his usual park bench as he and his old friend Gus tossed feed to the darting, playful squirrels. A doctor's appointment had pushed their usual morning rendezvous into the late afternoon, a fact that was not lost on the former preacher.

"The place looks totally different this late in the day," he said as a jet roared high overhead. "The angle of the sunlight changes everything. The colors, the whole feel of the place…"

"I said I was sorry," the stocky, balding Gus repeated with a friendly jab. "Next time I'm going to have a chest pain, I'll be sure to check your schedule first."

"Not complaining, just saying. I'm just glad the tests showed it was nothing."

"Didn't *feel* like nothing. Never did trust doctors. I'll probably keel over any minute now."

"You're fine," Kelsey said. "You're too *mean* to die." He checked his watch. "It's almost six. How long you want to stay out here?"

"What, you late for a tennis lesson?" Gus winked, tossing a handful of corn and sunflower seeds.

"Just wondered."

"Old buddy, I've got nowhere else to be." He raised his head slightly and smiled. "I smell a pretzel wagon. Always loved that smell…"

The president's speech had ended less than an hour earlier. Kelsey and Gus had watched on television just before beginning their walk to the park, and both men, surprised by its words, had been left pondering the world ahead.

"Why do things have to change?" Gus asked. "Would have been nice to have just kept it all like it was, back before the towers fell…back when I had hair."

"Lot of things I miss too," Kelsey said. "A lot of people. Helen mostly."

"Too much always happens too fast. World can get crazy in a heartbeat. And now with Israel and the president…"

"He understands. That's why he quit."

"Understands what?" Gus asked, stroking his short gray beard.

"What it means to leave Israel high and dry. God still has a plan for His chosen people. Promises to be kept. If we slam the door on them, He may do the same to us."

"But you always said it's faith that saves a man, not—"

"I'm talking about *national* blessings, not personal salvation. Whole different issue."

"Well, doesn't our having so many church folk over here give God reason enough to keep the blessings coming?"

"Most churches don't honestly have much to do with Him anymore. They're social clubs more than anything. *My* old church is that way now."

"They seem like they're still on track."

"And that's about it. It's all appearance. No real relationship with Christ. Whitewashed tombs, Gus."

Kelsey had watched it happen. He recalled words that spoke of those living in the last days:

"*...holding to a form of godliness, although they have denied its power...*"

The United States, the only nation founded on the rock of Christianity, was no longer mindful of Him. As a result, it had found itself beached, its rudder splintered, on the sand.

"*...professing to be wise, they became fools...*"

"Pray, Gus," Kelsey said. "Israel just became the center of the universe."

Brenda opened the door. Upon seeing the man and woman standing there, she lost the brave facade she had managed for most of the day, broke down, and fell trembling into Lawe's arms.

"Oh, Bry," she tried, but words were too hard. He held her, walking with her into the den as Karen closed the door behind them. Night had fallen, and the room was dark. The despondent widow had neglected to turn on the lights, and her young daughter, playing quietly in her room, had not seen.

Lawe began to falter. Clearly, his fear had been realized.

"I'm sorry, Brenda," he said, his voice breaking, his own struggle pushing its way to the surface.

Karen clicked on a table lamp, and warm light flared.

"We're sure?" Lawe had to ask.

The woman nodded, her voice low and strained.

"He was there..."

They took a seat on the sofa, and Lawe looked around the room as if seeing it for the first time. His brother was everywhere. Photos of the wedding, of birthdays, of family. Knickknacks. A game ball under glass.

Commendations from the force. A mounted largemouthed bass, caught by Jeffrey one summer while out on Chesapeake Bay.

And a framed shadowbox, hanging above the fireplace, within which glinted an object of polished silver.

The Presidential Medal of Valor.

Lawe's vision blurred, a curtain of wetness deepening.

The night stretched on. The three shared their memories, their fears, their pain.

They had each other.

"Please," Millie said, clutching her purse with tense fingers. "I really need to see him."

"Ms. Carson," said Lucy, "I'm sorry, but he's asked not to be disturbed. Any further matters will be handled by the new administration."

"But it will be too late by then."

"I'm sorry."

"Please. Just ask him. Tell him it's me."

The woman shook her head. "They're in there working to get some very important issues settled before midnight. That gives them less than two hours. They likely won't make it as is."

"Please."

Lucy thought for a moment, then rose from her seat. Walking past Millie, she vanished through the Oval Office door. Minutes passed, long minutes. Finally, the woman emerged, her face set.

"Five minutes," she said firmly. "But only because it's you, he said."

Millie entered and found Bridger sitting with Varner and Sumner, all racing the clock to complete work related to the presidential transition.

"Ms. Carson," Sumner said in cold greeting, visibly displeased at the interruption. She silently nodded in response.

"Yes, Millie?" Bridger said. "Forgive my abruptness, but our backs are against the wall here."

"I need to see you," she said. "In private."

Bridger rose from his chair, guided her through another door and into the small adjoining study.

"All right," he said, his tone remaining cordial. "Talk to me."

"I've come to you because…well, I messed up. *Badly.*"

"What did you do?"

"I lost sight of who I am," she said, remaining strong. "I'm only glad my father isn't here to see it. I know what this would have done to him…and I couldn't have lived with myself after that." She paused, the words coming hard. "I betrayed you. I betrayed myself. I only hope *you* can forgive me… *I* can't."

He scowled, his eyes filled with concern and disappointment.

"For what, Millie?"

"For something so serious I have to ask for your promise of a full pardon before I can tell you."

Visibly taken aback, he dropped into a leather chair and tapped the top of its padded walnut arms. He looked away.

The woman watched him, her heart pounding. She swallowed hard, knowing the gravity of her request.

"All right, Millie," he said soberly. "You've got it. For the sake of your father, you've got it."

He furrowed his brow, peering expectantly into her eyes.

And waited.

She pulled a folded envelope from her purse and handed it to him.

"There's a datachip in there along with several printed documents and other pertinent information."

"Pertinent to what?"

"*Everything.*"

26

Quietly in the night, without fanfare, a limousine carrying Matthew Bridger, the former first lady, and their suitcases departed the White House and headed for Andrews AFB. There a plane waited to take them to their home in Missouri, where family and friends already had gathered. The former first family's personal effects would be gathered for them and shipped within a few days.

Bridger had left it all behind as quickly as possible. When the door on Israel clanged shut, he would not be the one who had slammed it.

On Monday morning, at precisely twelve-oh-one Eastern time, Harper Lund was sworn in as president of the United States. The ceremony took place in the Oval Office before a handful of officials and a selected few members of the press. Fifteen minutes later a call was placed to the leadership of Saudi Arabia, informing them of the change in administrations and confirming the fact that America indeed had withdrawn its backing of Israel. A copy of the joint resolution was transmitted overseas, and its arrival heralded a new day for the Arab leadership. There was much rejoicing amid the dunes, and with it came a pledge to Lund that no further terrorist attacks would take place on American soil.

The Arab nations now knew that the escalating war in Palestine carried a promise of victory, for with the coming of the withdrawal they faced only one enemy, not two.

Loaded tankers, readied for the eventuality of American acquiescence, began to leave their ports, headed into the Arabian Sea, destined for the eastern coast of the United States.

The oil flowed once more.

The next morning, as the sun rose and word reached an awakening America, celebrations broke out nationwide. Finally, after so many months, the pressures would ease. No longer would the spectre of nuclear holocaust hang over the country, nor would the economic stranglehold remain. A great burden had been lifted, and the future again looked bright.

Comfort and security had returned.

And all it had cost was the nation's soul.

Two days after Bridger's resignation, the bonds of military restraint were broken. Israel threw itself fully into the struggle.

The Passover War was underway.

Its early phases favored the Israelis. The Palestinian military was crippled by air strikes, though it managed to lob a few missiles into Jewish territory before the launching installations were detected and destroyed. Only one penetrated the shield of Arrow-5 batteries, but it had come down in unoccupied parkland with no casualties.

The people of Palestine were given the option to evacuate the land on their own and in peace. They refused. Even had they not, the Jordanian leadership, decrying Israel for breaking their decades-old peace treaty, rejected out of hand Israel's demand that it take in Palestinian refugees. Defiantly, the king of Jordan had gathered his troops along the river, daring Israel to act.

That decision had been—unwise.

With visions of the devastated King David Hotel fresh in their minds, Israeli ground forces crossed into Palestinian territory and advanced steadily. Slowly, deliberately, they made their way deeper into the land while Syria and Egypt amassed their own forces along the northern and southern borders of the Jewish state.

Arab cries of protest fell on disinterested ears as the rest of the world—despite voicing condemnations of the Israeli incursion—stood back and watched the unfolding drama. Palestine implored the United States to use its still-present forces to rein in Israel but was refused. The American ships, planes, and soldiers continued their withdrawal from the land, evacuating to carriers and other vessels in the Mediterranean.

The Arab League was without allies.

There was little the U.N. could do to intervene. In fact, there was little U.N. left at all. Most of its delegates and officials had died in New York, and the survivors who now met in Brussels wielded little power or influence.

And then, three days after the Israeli offensive began, it happened.

As one, the neighboring Arab nations launched an invasion, hoping to destroy the Jews once and for all. Across the borders they marched, hoping to pin the Israelis against the sea. Fighter dogfights filled the skies. Missiles bearing chemical, biological, and conventional warheads began to rain down. Fires swept Tel Aviv and Haifa. Nerve agents hugged the streets and alleys of Jerusalem. Many died, and their numbers rapidly grew.

Of the three most sacred sites in Islam, the Dome of the Rock already was gone. Mercenaries from the Muslim populations of the world had joined in the fighting, bringing their own forces to bear in defense of their holy places. If they moved swiftly and surely enough, they believed, their long-held dream would become a reality.

Their final solution: the death of the Jews.

They had heard the warning Israel had given concerning Mecca and Medina and had chosen not to believe it. After all, the risk of such an act was prohibitive—who knew what might then happen or who else might also launch, were the atomic genie to be released in a battlefield context.

They were certain it had been a bluff, that Israel would never carry out a nuclear offensive.

They were wrong.

On April 23, at four thirty-six in the morning, a searing burst of stellar heat unleashed Hell upon Medina. The Mosque of the Prophet Muhammad—ground zero—was consumed in the fury of nuclear fire, its great green dome, gold glass mosaics, and white marble walls vaporized in an instant. Hundreds of thousands of lives came to an abrupt end, most as they slept. The core of the city vanished, and a wide crater of fused greenish glass appeared in its place. Supersonic winds claimed that which the inferno did not.

No one knew how it had happened. Missile, suitcase nuke, or high-altitude drop—no one knew.

The fist that had destroyed the city had descended unseen.

And then, the moment the horrifying loss of Medina became known to the Arab world, a brief, simple statement was broadcast by the Israeli forces.

Mecca in one hour.

Panic ensued as the Arab nations realized the beast had teeth. The three allied nations, scrambling in whiplash fashion, signaled their surrender, and the combined armies began to retreat. Saudi Arabia, near whose heart Medina lay, cried to its Muslim neighbors for vengeance but was ignored.

Palestinian president Abu Rashoud refused to relinquish his rule and ordered his besieged army to fight to the death. His prime minister, together with a few military officers unwilling to go along with the suicidal orders, beheaded their leader in a public courtyard—on live television—and ordered a total national evacuation.

During their initial advance, none of the three armies had moved more than fifteen miles into Israel, and Jordan had advanced no farther than mid-Palestine. As they withdrew, Jordan and Egypt were ordered by Israel to take as many Palestinians with them as they could carry, to aid in the clearing of the West Bank and Gaza. Frantically, the Jordanian and

Egyptian troops hunted down the displaced people, hurrying to clear them from the land.

For decades, since the time of Arafat, the Palestinians had been tolerated by their Arab neighbors as a convenient means for keeping pressure on Israel. During the initial decades of the struggle, through the volatile resentments that continued to be stirred even after the granting of statehood, the people of Palestine had been *used*.

They were but pawns. They always had been.

And now, no longer able to fulfill their purpose, they had become a liability.

Moving over two million entrenched residents was a monumental undertaking—even had they been willing, the mere scale of the effort was daunting. Soldiers hurriedly went city to city, house to house, searching every room. The lucky ones merely were ripped from their homes, carrying with them what they could gather in moments. Others, however, were not taken from the area at all.

Determined to avoid the burden of dealing with such a mass of civilian refugees, the Jordanian leadership ordered most shot on sight. Whole families, whole neighborhoods were mowed down by the machine guns of their brethren, and dark smoke from mass graves filled the skies as the bodies were burned.

News of the killings spread rapidly. Fearful residents rushed into the streets, migrating eastward in advance of the soldiers' arrival, traveling by car, by bus, by any means possible, that their lives might be spared.

Battered and limping, the Arab forces swept homeward and returned to their own lands. They would need time to regroup, time to devise a strategy that would ensure not only the eradication of the Jews but the continued safety of Mecca.

Vengeance would come later, they swore, in their own good time.

The land was emptied from the Jordan River to the Mediterranean.

No longer did Arab feet fall upon the Holy Land. A triumphant Israel lined its renewed borders with its forces, sealing the country against further ground incursion. As never before, hatred for the Jews burned hot and unquenchably throughout the region.

Beginning with the event at Medina, the renewal of Israel had come to pass with frightening speed.

It had taken six days.

On the seventh, a proud blue-and-white banner—at its heart, the Star of David—fluttered in the summer wind high above the Temple Mount.

The land, though scarred, was whole once more.

27

The Monday morning sun brought no warmth, no change, no hope. Karen slammed a desk drawer. Her frustration, an ember first sparked by a hail of bullets, had built in the days since the devastation of Manhattan, and it seemed as though every tiny aspect of her life had changed. No longer did she see God all around her, in the greening of trees, the graceful flights of birds, and the smiles of children. Her faith, only three years young, seemingly had been faced with something she never had expected.

Abandonment.

Lawe found her whispering to herself as he walked into her office, her tone bitter.

"Hey," he said, nearing the desk.

"Hi," she responded without looking up.

"Rough day?"

"They all are."

"I know."

He took a seat, seeing the change in her, sensing the emotional distance. And fearing it.

"There's no rush," he said. "The president's up in New York State, and I took the rest of the day. We can have lunch any time that works for you."

He, too, had changed, but he held the turmoil in check. His brother's voice still rang in his ears, a warm and persistent presence.

Karen leaned on the desk, her forehead in her hands.

"You know," she said quietly, "when I lost Rachel, I tried not let myself get angry. Not at first. Not at God. I wanted to believe that He knew what He was doing, that she'd died for a reason. But then…"

Her voice fell away. He waited.

"I don't feel Him anymore, Bry. To be honest, thinking back, I think we've been alone from the start. You, me…Jeff, and all those other poor people in New York. And after everything we've done to try to shut down that accursed organization, it just won't die, even after the bomb. They're saying now that it'll be up and running again by the end of the year, as if nothing ever happened. Some clinics already are. They've dumped responsibility for the scandal off onto Margaret McCarthy and her executive staff, and since *they're* dead now, it's…" She looked up at her fiancé. "What's the point, Bry? Why work so hard when it's become clear that God doesn't care, if He's even there at all?"

"You don't mean that," he said. "It's the pain talking."

"I don't know. And even *that's* tearing at me… Why *don't* I know? What kind of faith is it…*was* it…if it can't stand up to…" She took a breath. "I can't help the way I feel. I never would have believed it, but He just isn't there anymore. I don't feel Him. I can't…" Her eyes became wet.

Bry rose and went to her side, shaken by her desolation. Clearly, she was trying to be brave, to contain her growing disillusionment and grief. He leaned over her, held her.

"I'm sorry," he said. "I don't know what to tell you where God's concerned. I've never believed. To be honest, I don't think I ever gave it a chance. But I do know one thing… I was wrong."

"About what?"

"About everything. When you started going to that church, when you took this job…all I could see was that you weren't the same old Karen anymore, and I was afraid. I love you so much…but it seemed that every time I opened my mouth, the wrong things came out, and I just made things worse. These last three years, I've been selfish and a jerk…and I'm so sorry."

"Oh, Bry, I…"

"You needed me, and I wasn't there. I never supported you the way I should have, not really. But I will, from here on out. I swear it."

She reached up, and her fingers found his hair. She pulled him closer. The kiss was warm.

"Karen," came a young feminine voice, "you have a visitor."

"I know," she said, not really listening.

"No, I mean *another* one."

Lawe straightened, his eyes going to the door.

"Who is it?" Karen asked the receptionist.

"I'm not supposed to say."

What?

At that moment, a figure appeared. Silver-haired, clad in a soft gray sweater, his clothing more casual than either Karen or Lawe were accustomed to seeing on him.

"May I come in?" Bridger asked.

"Certainly," she said in calm surprise, rising and wiping her eyes.

"Are you all right?" the man asked, crossing the threshold. "Is this a bad time?"

"No, not at all," Karen insisted. "It's good to see you, Mr. President."

"It's Matt…please." He smiled kindly. "Hello, Bry."

"Sir," Lawe said, a smile crossing his face. "You're looking well."

"As are you. Both of you."

Bridger glanced around the room. Everywhere, on bookshelves and in framed documents and photos, was evidence of the organization's passion and dedication.

"What brings you to this neck of the woods?" Lawe asked. "Karen or me?"

"Didn't know *you'd* be here, Son," the former president confessed. "The boys and I were thinking of coming by your place a little later and saying hello, but here you are. Saved us a trip."

"Boys?" Karen asked.

"My shadows," Bridger chuckled. "Assigned to keep an old man out of trouble."

"Lindsey and Groh," Lawe knew. "They asked for the detail."

Karen gestured. "Please, Matt...sit down."

"Thank you, but this won't take a minute." The man reached into a pocket and withdrew a small blue object, a datachip case. "My last official act before stepping down was to grant a pardon to Millie Carson."

"A pardon?" she asked. "Before she resigned? I worked with Millie."

"I know you did. She came into my office that night, late. Had my hands full as it was. Last thing I wanted at that point was another meeting, but we talked...and I learned a few things."

"Why the pardon?"

"In exchange for this," Bridger said, handing her the chip. "And I was happy to do it. I also called in a couple of favors. Three days from now, you go before a Senate committee."

"Why? What is it?" she asked as a bewildered Lawe looked on.

"It's what Rachel had been waiting for. What she'd been hoping for. Praying for. It's a *stone,* my dear, one with Goliath's name on it...and *you* are David."

Randall Sullivan walked into the lavish living room of his new Chicago home with a chicken sandwich on a plate and a cold drink. He noticed his daughter standing at the window, looking out over the front lawn, her arms wrapped around her as if she were freezing.

"What's wrong, honey?" he asked, setting his lunch on the coffee table.

"Nothing," Janessa said, her eyes fixed on *something.*

He drew close, worried by her tone. Outside, beyond the rain-splattered glass, he saw hundreds of the dead, all standing in the pouring rain, their forms untouched by the falling drops and unlit by the glare of the lightning strikes. They, too, stood uneasily, looking grimly into the dark, boiling sky in a manner Sullivan never before had seen.

"What is it?" he repeated, moving to her side. "What are they doing?" He wanted so to hold her.

"Something is *wrong*," she replied as thunder echoed.

"Wrong how?"

"I don't know. I've never felt this before."

Her voice was odd, detached, distant. Her eyes reflected dread—subtly, but it was there.

"Janessa, why don't you come away from the window and—"

"No."

The room grew colder. Sullivan noticed frost in the corners of the window panes nearest her.

"We've had *lots* of storms since you came back," he said. "I'm sure it's nothing to worry about—"

"It isn't the storm."

"Then maybe it's just—"

"Leave me alone," she said firmly, her voice abruptly deepening, taking on an unearthly timbre. *"Go eat your lunch."*

He backed away, fearing her.

The committee met at ten twenty that Thursday morning in a dark-paneled room of the Dirksen Senate Office Building. The fifteen members of the panel took their seats in a wide arc, and Karen sat at a table facing them. Before her rested hard copies of the data provided by Bridger, along with copies of the chip, to be given to each of the committee senators. There were no spectators, no reporters, no cameras.

She looked down at the pages. The horror of them drove a shudder through her, filling her mind again with ghastly images she still could scarcely believe.

How could it have happened?

The chairman, seated at the center of the curved dais, was Cyrus Briggs. Quite vocally, he had been loathe to listen to the woman, having stood with Life Quality time and again on any issue that had arisen. But several days of political arm-twisting, combined with promised cooperation on a controversial bill he had been trying to bring to the Senate floor, had proved impetus enough to lure him here.

"Ms. Foley," Briggs began, "I appreciate your taking the time to be with us today. I understand, based on comments by the gentleman from Missouri"—he nodded toward a senator seated to his right, a man Karen knew to be sympathetic to Bridger and their cause—"that the former president felt this appearance to be of great import."

"Yes, Mr. Chairman," Karen replied. "Very great…and I applaud you for holding this hearing."

"Mr. Chairman," a voice spoke up, "if I may ask a question?"

"The chair recognizes Congressman Fuller."

"Thank you." He held up a green file folder. "Now, Ms. Foley, am I to gather from these rather sparse briefing materials that your appearance here today is to serve as an attack on Life Quality?"

"Not an attack, sir. A revelation."

"Haven't these people been through enough? For you to come here in this fashion so closely after the deaths of so many whose lives were dedicated to that cause is distasteful, to say the very least."

"Congressman," Karen replied, "I was asked to appear here today by the former president of the United States. I did not come to debate the merits, or lack thereof, of Life Quality or Sacred Child. But I do have vital information to impart and will do so now."

"Why were no more specific materials made available to this committee beforehand?"

"Because, sir, the matter I've come to discuss today may very well
involve one or more members of this committee, and to be blunt, some
on the panel felt it prudent to avoid giving such persons too much
advance warning. All pertinent data, in exhaustive detail, is contained on
each of the datachips I have here, and they will be given to you for your
personal use following this hearing."

"I allowed this arrangement," Briggs interjected, clearly regretting
that he had agreed to do so. He cut a venomous glance toward the Missouri congressman, then addressed Karen once more. "Proceed."

"Thank you, sir."

"This is most irregular," Fuller huffed.

"It is a most irregular situation that brings me here today, Congressman," Karen returned.

The chairman reclaimed the floor. "Ms. Foley, since the committee
does not know the reason we're here, at least not beyond the most general
terms, I'd like to proceed with an informal question-and-answer format.
If you have an initial statement to make, we're quite ready when you are."

"Thank you, Mr. Chairman." Karen took a deep breath, scanning the
faces gathered before her. Several were strangers. A few seemed impatient,
if not irritated. Karen knew her information would not be welcome, especially not by those known for their consistent support of Life Quality.

She began.

"On the night of Sunday, April twentieth, at approximately ten forty,
former Secretary of Health and Human Services Millie Carson entered
the Oval Office for an impromptu meeting with President Matthew
Bridger. Less than two hours remained in his presidency, and hers would
prove to be the last business he would conduct in that capacity. They met
privately, behind closed doors. Only when she began to share with him
the knowledge she had brought did he understand the importance of her
presence there. The meeting lasted approximately one hour, during which
she turned over to him proof of her statements. Immediately afterward, at

Ms. Carson's request, President Bridger in return granted her a full pardon for her involvement in the matter she had brought forward."

"Ms. Foley, if I may interrupt," Briggs said, "such use of executive authority is highly irregular, and I must question Mr. Bridger's judgment in making such an agreement. Presidential pardons are not to be granted on a quid pro quo basis."

"That is true," Karen said, "but in the president's view, the value of the information offered far outweighed the possible moral conflict inherent in such an exchange. In any case, such a pardon cannot be reversed."

"I'm well aware of that. Please continue."

"Ms. Carson told the president that, during her tenure as secretary of HHS, she had been compliant in a scheme that involved hundreds of individuals, all of whom had profited by their participation. These persons, involved in the daily operation of 243 healthcare centers and genetic creativity clinics nationwide, had been recruited by officials of Life Quality, as had been a handful of HHS and other government officials, in order to create a network of precisely functioning facilities."

"To what end?" asked a raven-haired congresswoman whose adversarial tone betrayed her skepticism. Karen looked upon her with suspicion. "We already know of the matter you revealed to the press a few weeks ago. We know that healthy children suffered at the hands of the former leadership of Life Quality, and that is a tragedy we regret. That the organization strayed from its designed purpose through the ambitions of a few was unfortunate, but the problem seemingly has been rectified, with a return to the tireless and dedicated service we knew before. Have you anything new to share with us, or is this hearing a waste of time?"

"Ma'am, the 'dedicated service' you mention was never Life Quality's designed purpose," Karen stated.

"Excuse me?" the congresswoman bristled.

The panel seemed uneasy. Several fidgeted, glanced at each other, and whispered words Karen could not hear.

"The persons involved," she calmly continued, "methodically manipulated the genetic implantations without the knowledge of the parents, who believed *their* will, and theirs alone, was the determining factor in their children's DNA sequencing. Hair color, eye color, gender, and any number of factors all were parentally selected. But unknown to them, theirs was not the final input."

"Of course not," another member said. "Most of us know little to nothing about genetic engineering. Their requests would be but guidelines."

"No sir. That's not what I mean. I'm not talking about requesting specific rungs along the ladder. Without their knowledge, their children were altered as part of an explicit agenda reminiscent of the work of Josef Mengele and every bit as horrifying."

The panel went still. A few became pale.

"Before the interruption caused by the attack on New York, Life Quality used the women of this country as unwitting *breeders,* producing children so precisely engineered that only certain needed elements of their bodies developed properly. None of these mothers knew the true condition of the babies they bore, and *all* believed until the moment of birth that they carried complete and healthy children. They did not.

"And following every 'unfortunate' delivery of every 'damaged' child, Life Quality quickly stepped in, offering money and practiced sympathy in exchange for the baby. From the outset, they sowed their seeds, then waited patiently, knowing in advance exactly what tissues and organs each child would provide when the time came to reap the harvest. Children whose birth defects came as a result of natural processes also were pursued, but these were not the organization's primary commodity source."

Silence.

"More than a million doomed children have been created in this manner. Life Quality was never a 'service,' as you put it, but an industry built to meet the growing research and transplant demands of a nation that has lost sight of the sanctity of human life. The searing of national conscience that occurred with *Roe v. Wade* laid the groundwork for this atrocity, and advancements in genetic engineering later brought it to fruition."

The congresswoman became indignant. "Now see here—"

"As we speak, the wheels are beginning to grind again, and Life Quality is resuming its heinous activity. This must *not* be allowed to happen. In addition to the fees paid by universities, research labs, and private patients, the organization receives a federal subsidy for every pound of human flesh it takes. It works tirelessly to increase its supply volume through any means possible, regardless of ethics…and every doctor, genetic technician, and HHS official involved in this scheme receives kickbacks, paid by Life Quality, in exchange for their continued silence and cooperation."

"These are grave allegations, Ms. Foley," Briggs said, sounding as if he had been kicked in the gut. "What evidence do you have?"

She held up one of the datachips. "In addition to thousands of classified government files and health facility records, I have here a complete listing of all complicit individuals, along with further evidence that they, in turn, have been confiding in and paying generous fees to select members of Congress who have pledged not only their silence but also supportive legislation."

Briggs dropped his head, struck by the blow. A few committee members glanced around nervously. One slammed a fist into the dais. More whispered conversation, a bit louder and more frenetic this time.

"I'm going to be sick," said the senator from Missouri.

"Ms. Foley," asked a shaken Briggs, "how many copies of that datachip are there?"

"Mr. Chairman," she answered, "all I can tell you is that the one I was given was not the original."

An uneasy quiet descended.

"Thank you, Ms. Foley," Briggs finally said. "That will be all. We'll be in contact should we need to speak with you again."

A gavel fell.

28

The offices of Sacred Child were quiet.

Karen and Melissa sat at a table in the break room, eating their lunches as they shared a newspaper and read of the Passover War and its aftermath. The images of a rejoicing Israel were astounding—seldom had anyone seen such a resounding victory, even in the movies.

"God was with us," Levi was quoted as saying. *"He led us into battle and guided our swords."*

"This is so unreal," Melissa asked. "Do you think that's true, what he said about the war? Was it miraculous?"

Karen set down her tuna salad sandwich and took a sip of iced tea. She did not answer.

"Karen?"

"I don't know," she finally said, her voice low. "I doubt it."

The girl looked at her with obvious concern. Since Rachel's death, something had been different about Karen. A fire within her had gone out.

"Are you okay?"

"What do you mean?"

"Well," Melissa began, "for one thing, any time I bring up God, you clam up. Used to be, you took any opportunity to—"

"I was wrong," she snapped.

"About what?"

"I always believed there was a purpose behind everything, but now…" She shook her head. "He's up there I suppose, but from day to day, we're pretty much on our own."

"How can you say that?"

Karen's gaze grew cold. "I don't know how many times I've prayed for the Life Quality slaughter to stop, but still it continues, even now. Why wouldn't the president let me take that evidence directly to the press? Why testify and risk a government cover-up? These people know how to protect their own."

"Maybe he wanted to give them a chance to take responsibility themselves. He does have friends there, he said. Or maybe it was a condition the HHS secretary attached, like the pardon."

"Well, it's been more than a week, and we haven't heard a word. They didn't call me in for further testimony. They're probably plotting an escape strategy, and they sure haven't stopped the killing. Just this morning I heard that Washington Life Quality had installed new software and was making appointments on a limited basis."

"I heard that too."

"So where's God? Why is He letting this go on?"

"He must have a reason, and—"

"No," she said, wringing her hands. "He's just standing back, letting them all die, and isn't lifting a finger to stop it. Just like New York. Just like *Rachel*."

"But Karen—"

"Not *two* seconds before she stepped out onto that street, I prayed to Him to keep her safe. I'd barely finished when she was gunned down. And then Jeff… I prayed for him too. Practically promised Brenda he'd be okay. Well, *he* died, and all those other people—"

"I've thought about that," the girl said. "A lot. And I think I understand now."

"Oh, do you?" Karen impatiently looked away.

"Well, not everything. What happened in New York was beyond horrible, and I don't know the reason for it. But I *do* know God was in control."

"Because?"

"The only reason we called off the protest was because *you* decided to after Bry's phone call. I mean, if Rachel still had been running things, it would have gone ahead as planned, right? And she was always early for everything. She would have been right there in the middle of it all when they blocked off the area, and everyone else would have been there with her. Instead, they were all those miles away in their hotel rooms.

"And that's another thing. Because of the delays brought on by the funeral and all, we couldn't get reservations anywhere near the city. And we even stopped the Westport buses in time. They never left the hotels."

The woman began to hear her.

"Not one of our people died," Melissa emphasized. "*Six hundred* people. Think about it."

Karen rose and went to the window. Outside, the vivid greens of new life covered the trees and lawns of the city. Clear skies stretched high above.

Not one—

"If Rachel hadn't died when she did," the girl went on, "then *everyone* who went there to protest would have been killed *including* her. Including *you*. That Friday, just like every day, it was time for some to die and for others to continue living. It wasn't chance. There was purpose behind it. '*God causes all things to work together for good to those who love God, to those who are called according to His purpose.*'"

"Romans 8:28." Karen knew but had forgotten.

"Like you said… *Everything* happens for a reason, no matter how terrible it may seem at the time. Right?"

Karen turned to find the girl gently smiling. The woman's anger began to melt away in the radiance of that youthful, reborn face.

Her netphone rang from atop the newspaper, its song a fitting "Ode to Joy." She crossed to the table and picked it up.

"Hello?"

"It's me," Lawe's voice said. "Are you watching the news?"

"No," she replied, glancing at the darkened glass on the wall. "Melissa and I are having lunch. There is a screen in here, though."

With the system down for so long, I'd gotten used to not watching—

"Turn it on. Hurry."

"What channel?"

"I don't think it matters. Call me back."

Karen set the phone down, turned on the display, and flipped to a news network. At once, the solemn form of Cyrus Briggs appeared, speaking from behind a podium. He was flanked by other members of Congress, some of whom had been seated on the panel Karen had confronted.

His words were music.

"*...and all Life Quality offices have been ordered, within the last few minutes, to cease operations pending a full investigation into the activities brought to light. We are shocked and outraged by the evidence presented to us, and after several days of closed meetings, we've asked the Department of Justice to issue an injunction through the Federal District Court.*"

He looked directly into the camera.

"*Warrants have been issued, law-enforcement agencies across the country have been alerted, and as we speak, the individuals involved are being taken into custody. If these far-reaching activities...these atrocities...indeed have taken place as is indicated by the evidence, I believe we have to take a serious look at ourselves as a nation.*"

The scripted press conference lasted only a few minutes, with no questions taken. The women watched, barely able to believe the unfolding scene. The words they heard were born more of necessity than of moral outrage, Karen knew—at that moment, throughout the halls of Congress, a lot of political self-preservation was taking place—but she did not care.

The stone had struck, straight and true.

As the senator and his colleagues stepped away from the cameras, the scene switched to a newsdesk.

"Well, there you have it," the astonished anchorman said, *"Senate majority leader Cyrus Briggs, speaking from the Capitol. We do not yet know the full content of the new evidence he mentioned, but Life Quality clearly has been hit with new charges of fraud and malpractice on a massive scale.*

"The organization had been struggling since last month's terrorist attack on New York, in which the senior executives of every Life Quality office nationwide, as well as all organizational and clientele records, were lost. Despite this, with new management at the helm, some had speculated that the organization might be back to full operational strength as early as December. Now, however, with today's disclosure, there is talk on Capitol Hill of a full ban on human cloning and a reevaluation of all Life Quality laws. Given that, combined with this new criminal investigation, it would appear that the organization will not, after all, rise from the ashes."

Cheers rose throughout the office. The others had heard.

"Wow!" Melissa said, barely able to contain her excitement. "We won!"

Can it really be?

"You prayed the babies would stop dying…we all did…and He heard us."

Karen had closed her tear-filled eyes. Overcome, she found herself laughing and crying at the same time.

The girl was beside herself. "We've waited for this moment for so long, and now that it's here…"

A loud triumphant cry carried from down the hall, a jovial masculine voice.

"And Goliath is down for the count!"

Melissa grinned widely at the words, then wrinkled her brow.

"I'll get unemployment, right?"

Reaching out again to hug the girl, Karen laughed gently. Others spilled into the room, jubilant all, and they shared the victory together.

A few moments later the receptionist appeared in the doorway. Her form concealed another, standing just behind her.

"Karen, someone's here to see you."

As the girl moved aside, a dark-haired woman stepped forward and into the room. Her dress was casual, her face radiant yet lined with signs of burden. Her soft features, while unfamiliar, haunted Karen.

"Yes? Is there something I can do for you?"

Only when the stranger spoke did the pieces fall into place.

"Hello, Karen. It's good to see you again."

She knew that voice. The last time she had heard it, it had been shrouded in the darkness of a theater auditorium.

"You…"

"Deborah Langley," she smiled, extending a hand. "Well done."

Karen rushed forward and took both of the woman's hands in her own. The usually eloquent leader suddenly found words hard to come by.

"You risked everything," she managed. "For us…for the children…"

"So did you. How could we not?"

Karen hugged her, thanking God for her, for her courage. She then turned toward Melissa. "Let me introduce my assistant… Melissa Torrence, Deborah Langley."

"Hello," the girl smiled.

"Hi, Melissa. Nice to meet you."

"Deborah made it possible for us to deal the first major blow to Life Quality," Karen explained. "The data she gave us…"

"You're the theater lady," Melissa realized.

"That would be me," the woman smiled. "I didn't mean to interrupt. I came by to see if your group has an opening for an administrator. From the good news I just heard, though, it seems you may not have a purpose much longer."

"For as long as Sacred Child exists," said Karen, "we will make a place for you." She paused, moving toward the door.

"Do you have a few minutes?"

"Of course," Deborah nodded.

She was led down a hallway and into a vacant meeting room.

"Please," Karen began, closing the door behind them, "I'd like to know—"

"Why," Deborah finished. "Why I helped you."

"Yes."

The woman walked to the window. She was bathed in the early afternoon light, memories glinting in her eyes.

"I was there from the beginning," she began, fingering the fragile silver necklace she wore. "Before they broke ground on the first dedicated Life Quality center, I was there. I was convinced we were doing the right thing. Took me a long time to realize we weren't. And once that happened…"

She turned to face Karen. "I was one of the top administrators in the organization. My office was two doors down from Margaret McCarthy's."

"I thought your name sounded familiar."

"But that was before I began to doubt. She could sense doubt in her staff. If you weren't a hundred and ten percent behind her every step of the way, she knew.

"I'd stayed in line. I'd climbed the ladder. I'd done and said all the right things. And then, one day, I found myself watching Rachel in a televised debate. As she spoke, I didn't want to hear her. But I did."

Karen stood transfixed.

"She spoke of life. Of its being precious…a flame that, once extinguished, can never be ignited again…" The woman looked away, as if ashamed. "My mother… She died in a termination clinic a few years ago. They said it would be painless. They said she wouldn't want to live as she was…"

She paused to compose herself.

"I made the decision. I let it happen in the name of 'dignity.' I let them convince me that because her stroke had left her barely responsive, the selfish thing was to continue her life. She wasn't on a respirator or anything, but she could hardly move. She couldn't speak...couldn't tell me what she wanted...and I let those people..."

Silence. Deborah wiped the tears away with the flat of her middle finger.

"I agreed with them," she bravely confessed, her voice breaking. "God forgive me, I agreed with them. I thought they were right. I'd learned to value a life by the contribution it makes or the inconvenience it brings...to measure it by what it *does,* instead of looking upon it as the inherent miracle it *is*..."

Karen's throat felt tight. The latter words could have been her own.

Deborah drew a ragged, cleansing breath. "What Rachel said that day tore into me. Convicted me. I began to question Life Quality, began to wonder if we really were the boon to mankind I had believed us to be. It was as if my eyes had opened for the first time. I saw what they were doing to all those children, all those mothers. I felt the weight of all the deaths I'd helped bring about. I didn't know if I could ever get the blood off my hands, but I knew I had to do something to stop it...something to end the killing.

"I became the weak calf, and it didn't take long to get culled out of the herd. I hadn't said anything, but Margaret sensed my doubts. And as always happened with those few like me, that perceived 'weakness' earned me a polite smile and a knife in the back.

"I copied all the potentially damaging data I could access. Margaret never knew I had done it, but she suspected I might. She didn't fire me outright but transferred me to the Washington facility, away from New York, away from the center of the Life Quality universe, away from the stored records. After a little time had passed, I began to contact Rachel. I hoped with my help she could do something to stop them."

She spoke more quietly, as if fearful of being overheard.

"They killed her. A hired gunman. And when she died, I had to trust *you*...because Life Quality had to die too."

Karen could almost feel Rachel's presence there with them.

"Deborah," Karen said, stepping forward to take her hand, "nothing I can do is thanks enough for the risk you took."

The woman smiled, her eyes still wet, her lashes dark. "Just give me a desk, a chair, and four walls…and let me make a difference."

Loud and long they came, condemnations and demands for reparations.

The governments of the world descended on the Israeli leadership, universally denouncing the retaking of Palestine. France took the lead, demanding sanctions and the harshest actions allowable by international law, followed by Germany, Russia, and almost every European and Asian country. The United States was slower to speak out but did follow suit.

The protests soon took physical form. Forcefully and without warning, Europe began to deport Jews throughout the continent. The move, initiated by France, quickly was embraced worldwide. An exodus of unprecedented proportions took place as nations "invited" their Jewish citizens to leave and enforced the order with police action. By air, by car, by ship, by foot, traveling from the four corners of the Earth, millions made the journey to the one land where they knew they would be welcome, the land of their ancestors. Israel's population grew tenfold within months, yet both government and private business handled the additional demand on services without a hitch.

They had been ready.

The Jews began to demolish the towering wall, now rendered obsolete, that for so long had divided Israel from the West Bank. The vacated lands blossomed and grew as new industries and housing were developed. The entire region east of Jerusalem was remade as, in peace and security, the Israelis fully reclaimed the land.

The Israel of David and of Solomon had returned.

Atop the Temple Mount a solemn ceremony took place. The resonant sound of a ram's horn trumpet echoed across the city as, before a crowd of hundreds of thousands, a huge, precisely shaped block of polished limestone was moved into position on the wide plateau. It had been shaped dozens of years earlier and held in reserve, ready to take its rightful place.

A cornerstone.

And soon a wondrous new structure would rise above it.

It was a day awaited for thousands of years, a day many doubted would ever come. The gathered throng danced and sang as unrestrained joy swept them, their heels clicking on ancient pavement stones originally laid by their forefathers. For too long they had been denied access to the site, but finally it was theirs once more.

Never would they lose it again.

Standing on a raised platform, Zelle Levi read aloud a proclamation, and the masses cheered, thanking their God for the miracle He had provided.

They were a single unified people living at the center of the universe.

And some four years later, if all went according to plan, the ancient temple of Jerusalem would be reborn on Mount Moriah.

By the end of summer, a battered nation still struggled to find its feet. The promised OPEC flow had helped to relieve the oil crisis, and the withdrawal from Israel—with its resulting pledge of no further terrorist action against the U.S.—had given consumer confidence enough of a boost to raise the country's financial state above critical levels. Stocks, having plummeted across the board in the wake of the nuclear event, were making a slow but steady recovery. Some crippled businesses had managed to regain a measure of strength, but many more had not—already damaged by the turbulence of the prior year, the terrorist attack had dealt them a death-blow, closing their doors and driving the ranks of the unemployed above the twentieth percentile for the first time since the Great Depression.

Yet the greatest burden was the profound anguish felt by the families of those who had perished in communities spread far and wide across both America and the world. Services were held every day as neighbor-hoods, towns, and cities mourned their native sons and daughters who once had pulled up roots in search of a more promising future.

And on one day, in one place, a great many gathered to grieve and to share and to remember.

As one they exited the wide, ornate doors of the cathedral, a solemn flow of thousands clad in black, clad in sorrow. Into the glaring August sun they emerged, their hair tossed by warm winds. The crowds slowly began to disperse, returning to their lives and responsibilities, their minds still on faces they would behold no more.

It had been the largest memorial service Washington had known. More than three thousand had been seated inside the impressive edifice of stone and colored glass, while millions more watched from the privacy of their living rooms. Dozens of congressmen and senators had spoken from the pulpit, as had President Lund and the governor of New York.

On the day of the service, the official number of dead and missing stood at 2,465,791. The figure constantly changed as radiation sickness and blast injuries claimed more victims and as more persons were discov-ered to be missing, discovered to be alive, or otherwise were accounted for. Some said it would be years before the true count was known, if ever.

Mourners filled the streets, along with reporters, television mobile units, police and other official vehicles, and the curious. Agents of the Secret Service surrounded and escorted the chief executive from the build-ing as everywhere cameras snapped. Upon reaching the safety of his lim-ousine, Lund paused to give the crowds a final wave. In moments, the motorcade pulled away and was gone.

Lawe slipped into his sunglasses as he descended the marble steps, Karen at his side. He had struggled with the loss of his brother and had hoped that the mass service would help him get beyond the pain, the sense of loss, the anger.

It had not.

Brenda followed closely behind, holding her young daughter's hand, guiding her down the steps. Her eyes were reddened; her daughter, having no real concept of death, was restless, wanted to go home and kept asking for her father.

"Karen," the widow said, "I need to get Melody home, and it's a long drive. Let's get together for lunch some other time."

"You're welcome to stay at my place another night," she offered. "You know that."

"I know, but I do need to get back. The insurance people are coming again, and I need to get a few things taken care of beforehand. Thanks for last night, though… I needed the visit, and you guys have been wonderful."

"Our doors are *always* open to you," Lawe smiled. "Day or night."

They hugged and exchanged heartfelt good-byes. Brenda and her daughter headed in one direction, toward the main parking area, while Lawe and Karen, having parked down the street, walked across the church lawn and into the dense shade of towering oaks. His duty shift still was hours away, and he looked forward to the quiet that awaited him at his apartment.

"Bry!" a voice called out.

He turned to see Ollie and Samira approaching, their pace hurried. Lawe stood motionless, his face taut.

"Hey," the man went on. "You stop returning calls, or what? We've been worried about you."

"We're fine," Lawe said.

"I called four times in the last week. You're suddenly a tough guy to reach."

"New administration," the agent said. "Lots to do."

"Yeah, I can understand that, but…"

Karen looked at Lawe. Since their return from New Rochelle, he had managed not to speak of the Muslim couple, squashing the conversation every time she had brought them up.

"Well, listen," Ollie began, "we're all getting together at our place this weekend. Several of the guys from the precinct and their wives. Kind of a private tribute. Samira and I thought you might like to—"

"No," Lawe said flatly, his voice tinged with disgust. "We can't make it."

Ollie stepped a bit closer. "All right, Bry…what's with you?"

"Nothing."

"Bull. I want to know what the problem is. You've kept your distance for months."

A door long sealed was ripped from its hinges as seeds first planted on Nine-Eleven finally came to full fruition. Torrents of suppressed emotion burst forth, finding an undeserving target.

"You want to know? Fine. I'll tell you. Maybe I'm just not thrilled about the kind of people who would take out a whole city of innocent men, women, and children. People who have been a thorn in the side of this planet for decades, who frankly don't deserve to live. They should have been wiped out like cockroaches a long time ago."

Ollie, caught off guard, looked to Karen. She would not meet his eyes. *"What?"*

"Do I have to spell it out for you?" Lawe went on. "*Your* people killed my brother. A man who was doing his job, who had a wife and a daughter and a whole lifetime ahead of him. *And* my father, whose only crime was trying to support a family who cherished him."

"Bry, look—"

"Your kind is a *cancer* on the planet, one we have to cut out before it kills us all. Nice 'god' you have there, by the way. Human lives mean *nothing* to him. Tell Allah for me that he's a pathetic coward. Sends fanatics to do his dirty work and—"

"You *know* that isn't—"

"Save it. I really don't care anymore. Every time I look at you, every time I hear your name or your voice, I think of what Jeff suffered…first with that bus, and then…" He paused, his resentment and frustration building to critical levels. "And my *dad*…buried under millions of tons of…"

Lawe spun and walked away, his heart pounding, his breath short. The astonished Muslim knew there was nothing he could say, nothing the man would hear. Still—

"Bry—"

"Just stay away from me, Ollie."

With a dismissive gesture the agent continued on, headed in the general direction of his car. In his wake, Karen struggled for words.

"I'm sorry," she tried. "I don't know what…"

"It's all right," Ollie said. "Not your fault."

"He doesn't usually… I mean, this is the first time he's…"

"Lost a brother?" Ollie offered. "Or turned on a friend?"

There was nothing left to say. With an anguished nod, Karen turned and followed after Lawe, leaving the stunned couple standing alone beneath the overhanging branches.

29

The moment came. Organ music echoed from the paneled walls of the chapel, and the murmuring crowd went quiet.

Lawe, accompanied by a handful of fellow agents, stood expectantly at the front of the room, dressed in matching black tuxedos. Flowers in myriad colors filled the pulpit, the choir pit, the alcoves and more, a gift from Sacred Child.

His brother would have been his best man had things been different. Instead, Richard Kelsey stood to one side, wearing a smile and a tux he had owned for nearly fifty years, the one in which he himself had been married.

Thank you, Uncle Rick, for everything.

The groom scanned the pews. The empty place next to Brenda and her daughter, there on the front row, reopened a wound that refused to heal. It was a chasm filled with shattered glass and razor-edged steel, cutting into his heart, his soul.

Two others were missing from the assemblage, but by edict.

Your kind killed him—

He took a deep breath, sweeping away the hatred, if only momentarily.

The face of Jacqueline Kelsey beamed from a few rows back. Lawe gave her a subtle nod. Looking elsewhere, he found a familiar head of silver hair. Matthew Bridger sat with his wife, Susan, inconspicuously at the rear of the chapel, a pair of assigned agents on duty nearby. The press, barred from entry, had been forced to wait outside for the snippets of sound-bite video it wanted for the evening's newscast.

Thank you for coming, Mr. President—

The pastor of the church stood an arm's length away from Lawe, clutching a gilded Bible. He knew Karen well—this was her church, her spiritual family, and the man felt honored to perform for her this most sacred of ceremonies.

Melissa, the bridesmaid, dressed in a pale blue gown, stood opposite the husband-to-be. She glowed, as happy and excited as he ever had seen her. He gave the excited girl a wink, and she bit her lip, trying not to laugh aloud.

And then the music rose, as did the gathered guests.

Karen began down the aisle, her flowing white dress trailing behind her. She was a symphony in pearls and lace, a vision of loveliness that stole Lawe's breath away. Imperceptibly, her hands were trembling beneath the bouquet she held. She never had been so nervous.

As she approached her smiling fiancé, she inwardly laughed.

Allergic to rice, indeed—Mister, you're just lucky I'm so patient—

She reached the front of the room, bathed in the glorious hues of the floral cornucopia and those of sunlight streaming through stained glass. Lawe took her hands in his own and peered into her deep green eyes, which sparkled even beneath the gossamer mist of her veil.

The life had returned to them. Her faith shone brightly, renewed and tempered by trial.

Father, in Jesus' name, please draw this man unto Yourself. Your hand is upon him—I can feel it—!

Time-honored words were spoken, followed by treasured vows. The man drew the woman close, lifted her veil, and the chapel around them fled away.

For that moment, all fear, all anger, all worry vanished. The world of men ceased to encompass them, and they stood alone, complete in each other as one.

30

Three minutes, Mr. Sullivan."

"It's freezing in here," the man said. "Can we turn up the heat or something?"

"It's on, but I'll see what we can do."

The production assistant vanished from the dressing room doorway. Pulling the makeup bib from his collar, Sullivan rose from his director's chair, went to the rear corner of the stage, and peered into the studio auditorium.

Thousands packed the house, none of them living.

They filled the aisles, the camera stations, the lobby, the control room, the stage. A sea of grim faces, all waiting for him.

It had begun only hours after the blast. Immense crowds, constantly bearing down on him, all pleading to be heard. The millions who had died that day now had but one link to those they had left behind, and they were bent on making use of it.

One link, one man.

Everywhere he went, they surrounded him. At the studio, on the streets, even at the home the show's producers had provided for him. His bedroom, his bath, his kitchen.

Everywhere.

He no longer knew privacy or peace. Nor did he now see his "gift" as anything but a crushing burden, one he longed to abandon. The voices, the pleading voices—night and day, they never stopped. For months, sleep had been both scarce and restless. He found himself always increasingly cold, as if fever raged within him.

More than once he had considered suicide.

But if I die, he had realized, *I'll be trapped among them, and I'll never be free of them. They may even become angry at having lost their only voice into the world—*

And he did not wish to risk their cumulative vengeance. He had experienced a measure of it already, in small yet terrifying doses.

One woman from Florida, whose message to her widower he had failed to pass along, had all but trashed his house. Dishes had been smashed, windows broken, upholstery slashed, and books ripped apart. *Poltergeist activity,* some had called it, but he knew it for what it was—a *tantrum,* plain and simple. Why some of the deceased were able to affect their surroundings while others seemingly could not, he did not know.

In another instance he had awakened one morning to find his pillow stained with fresh blood. A butcher's knife was being pressed against his neck, held somehow by a man who not unjustly had died by lethal injection—a man who had wanted Sullivan to pass along to his brother the most promising time and method for murdering the judge who had sentenced him.

Now with millions tragically felled in one horrible moment, the transmortalist's life no longer was his own.

He hated his wondrous ability. It possessed him, ruled him, and he dared not stop.

"Good luck," Janessa's ever-present voice sounded. "Knock 'em dead."

He looked at her with a half-smile. That stormy afternoon, a glimpse of something within her had slipped through—something terrible—and it had changed his perception of her forever. Trepidation had set in. He had tried to shake the feeling time and again, yet it persisted.

But she's my own daughter—I know she'd never hurt me—

He no longer felt safe in her presence.

Would she?

Carrying his copy of *The Loving Bible,* Sullivan walked onstage, as he did every weekday at four o'clock. That first step on-stage was always a moment of swirling apotheosis, and the pedestal on which he stood was high indeed—since the show was broadcast live, before a studio audience, thunderous applause always met him, plaudits from an ever-growing faction who looked on him almost as a god.

Today, however, was different. There would be no audience.

The lights were down, save a spotlight on a single chair at center stage. That day's show would be dedicated exclusively to those who had died in New York, with their thoughts and wishes expressed to the national viewing audience.

The empty room was crowded wall to wall with those waiting to speak.

He made his way through the phantom throng, his cane clicking on the stage floor. With one final look into the anxious crowd, he lowered himself gingerly into the chair. His breath fogged before him as the chill grew deeper.

It began.

"Oh, it all smells just delicious," Karen said.

The Kelsey residence rejoiced, a joyous occasion in the offing. For the first time in a long time, it was a house of friends, a house of warmth. The rich scents of roast beef and baking bread hung in the air, and stomachs growled in response.

"Thanks," Jacqueline smiled, stirring a pan of gravy. "I was never the cook in the family, though. My mom was the one who really knew her way around this kitchen. Taught me all kinds of secrets, though. Growing up, I helped her any chance I got. The big meals were the best…holidays, Sunday dinners like this one. I loved it." She paused. "I still miss her so much."

"My mom never really cooked. But I did okay."

"So I've heard."

"Really? From Bry?"

"Oh, sure," she said, stretching the truth a little. "He loves your cooking."

Karen beamed despite herself.

Jacqueline went on. "It isn't something I do a lot anymore, but it's like riding a bicycle. I'm a lot quicker to order a pizza or pop something into the microwave than I am to prepare a full meal. Since it's just me, I don't see much point in it... If I had someone to cook for on a regular basis, I'd do it a lot more."

"With such a talent, I can't understand why you aren't married yet. I mean, you're smart, you're beautiful...you have so much to offer."

"Well, there *was* a guy once," she said, "but I let him get away."

"Still...you should have a ring on that finger."

"Speaking of which," Jacqueline said, "bring yours over here into the light. I want to see it again."

Karen approached and held out her hand. On her finger sparkled a two-carat beauty set in gleaming gold, her wedding band nestled beside it.

"It's just gorgeous," Jacqueline smiled. "What I wouldn't give..."

"Almost worth the wait," Karen chuckled. "Bry is such a good man..."

"Yes, he is."

"I'm so blessed to have him. I mean, we've had our differences like all couples do, but..."

"How did you meet?"

"It was four years ago," Karen began. "I had a blowout on the freeway. Front tire... I almost lost control. I managed to pull off, but just barely."

"You're so lucky! People have died that way."

"I know. I was a bit shaken."

"Well, I would think so."

"I called the auto club, but they said it would be almost an hour before help would arrive. It was getting dark though, so I started to call a friend. Just then, this man in a government vehicle pulled up behind me and turned on his flashing red light. He walked up to my car, identified himself as an agent, and asked if I was okay."

"You must have been so relieved."

"Oh, absolutely. As he changed my tire, we talked. I told him I was HHS, and he told me he was with the Treasury. When he finished with the tire, he asked if I'd eaten dinner. Neither of us had, so he suggested we stop somewhere. I followed him to a lovely little Italian restaurant that isn't there anymore, called Mariano's…"

"I remember it," Jacqueline smiled. "Their bread was to die for."

"Wasn't it, though? Anyway, we sat and talked, and the whole night flew by. He was amazing, not like any man I'd ever known. His compassion, his devotion, his kindness… I swear, Jackie, I'd never been one to believe in love at first sight, but if he'd asked me to marry him right then, I might have done it." She paused, recalling the moments, savoring them. "Then it got late, and the place closed for the night. We stood out in the parking lot, still talking. Must have been out there half an hour. When I drove home, he followed to make sure I got there all right."

"Sounds like it was a memorable night."

"And it was on the anniversary of Ten-Seventeen, so he has no excuse not to remember the date."

Jacqueline chuckled. "So, Mrs. Lawe, is married life agreeing with you? It's been a whole week now…"

"Oh yes," Karen laughed. "More than I can tell you."

"Such a lovely wedding. I've never seen so many flowers."

"It *was* wonderful. Could have been more so, though. Bry refused to invite a Muslim couple we know. Good friends of ours, at least they *were*. There was a blowup a few weeks back, after the memorial service. He's taken Jeffrey's death so hard…and with what happened to his father, he's blaming all of Islam."

"It'll take time, but he'll get past it."

"I know, and I pray day and night that it happens soon. That kind of bitterness can poison a person's life."

"Yes," Jacqueline said. "It can."

"I wish we could have gone on the honeymoon right away, to get his mind off it all, but with the change in administration, Bry just couldn't get the leave. Soon, though."

"Next month, right?"

"First week of October. We'll be leaving the marina bright and early... We're going to spend some time out on the bay, then a romantic few days at this darling little seaside bed-and-breakfast I found. Oh, it'll be *lovely.*"

Jacqueline removed the gravy from the burner, then took a peek at the roast.

"It's a good one," she smiled. "The last one I fixed was so dry."

"Been there," Karen said.

"So what's going to happen to Sacred Child now? Since it looks like Life Quality is gone for good, aren't you guys out of work?"

"Not at all," Karen smiled. "We're changing the focus of the group: to provide children with birth defects and their parents all the resources they need. We're hoping to convince them that *every* life should be cherished, but it won't be easy."

"Resources?"

"Melissa's already launched an online support network. We're making available the names of businesses whose owners have been sympathetic to our cause. They're happy to help in any way they can with reduced prices and special orders and whatnot." A thrill swept her. "We've even set up bulletin boards and real-time conferencing, and the parents have begun to help *each other.*"

"Sounds like you've made a real difference...and still are."

Karen looked at her, tears stirring behind her smile. "I think you're right."

Familiar footsteps rose, and Kelsey walked in, anticipation gleaming in his eyes. He looked past the women and scanned the stovetop. "Mmmm, boy! Is it about ready?"

"Soon," Jacqueline grinned. "We'll let you know."

"You've got a couple of hungry fellows out here, and the smell is driving us crazy. We're starting to gnaw the furniture."

She handed her father a carrot stick and gave him a gentle push back the way he had come. "There…gnaw on that and go sit down."

"Yes ma'am," he said with a grin.

The doorbell rang.

"That'll be Melissa," Karen said, glancing at her watch. "She's so been looking forward to meeting you two. I'll get the door."

She left the kitchen and crossed the living room.

"Doorbell," Lawe smiled, flipping channels on the wall-mounted screen.

"I heard," Karen said, playfully slapping at the top of his head.

She invited the girl inside.

"Wow," Melissa said, slipping out of her jacket. "Smells great."

"Doesn't it though?" Lawe said. "Hey, Melissa."

"Hey."

"Glad you could make it."

"Me too."

Kelsey entered the room. "Hello. You must be Melissa."

"Hi," she smiled back.

There was an odd moment of shared recognition, though neither immediately placed the face before them.

"You know," the girl said, "you look really familiar. I know I know you from somewhere."

"I was just going to say the same thing," the old man said. "I remember that lovely smile."

A further exchange of silent scrutiny.

"The park," he remembered, with a snap of his fingers. "You once shared my bench."

She smiled. "That's right! You were so nice. Wow... Small world, huh?" She walked up and hugged him like a child embracing a parent. "How have you been?"

"Hi," Jacqueline said as she entered the room, potholder in hand. "You're Melissa? So nice to meet you." She noted that her father was sharing no ordinary hug with the girl. "You two know each other?"

"Sort of," Melissa said.

"This young lady brightened my morning a while back, over in the park. She and her baby..."

"That was Joseph." Her countenance fell.

"I'm so sorry," he said, realizing at once.

"It's okay," she replied. "It happened a lifetime ago."

For a moment no one spoke. During the interval, the girl's attention was drawn by a familiar voice. As she found the television screen, she found there a familiar face as well.

"Hey, that's him!" she told Karen, with surprise. "The man who heard Joseph..."

"This Sullivan guy?" Lawe asked. "You know him?"

"No, not really. I just went to one of his seminars."

"Bry," Karen said, "turn it up."

The volume rose. The man's voice seemed stressed. His face was a mask of fatigue cast in harsh shadow. He sat alone, a single light bathing him.

"He doesn't look so good," Melissa observed. "Is he sick?"

"From the book of Second Corinthians," Sullivan began. *"'We surely know that as long as we are locked within our flesh we are isolated from the spirit realm, living by faith and not by sight, confident that one day we shall*

leave these limiting bodies and know the love and freedom of the ethereal plane.'"

"Not even close," Kelsey groaned, shaking his head. "It's a crime what that so-called Bible did to the Scriptures. Worse, it's heresy."

"Today," the man went on, setting the book aside, *"I will be giving voice to those who passed on in the horrendous events of last April. But know this, you who are watching me now...all who perished in New York City that day are happy in their new reality and would not return to their natural lives even if given the opportunity."*

"He's *got* to be kidding," Lawe said.

"Is he doing the show from inside a walk-in freezer?" Melissa wondered, noting the fleeting mist that appeared with each word he spoke.

"Interesting," Kelsey said.

"Janice Lawson of Des Moines," the man began, *"your sister wants you to know she forgave you long ago for the 'prom dress' incident. She always meant to tell you, but didn't..."*

"This is silly," Lawe said. "No one hears dead people."

"I wouldn't be so sure," Melissa said. "The things he knows..."

"Guys have been pulling this kind of scam forever. The gullible and mourning always get sucked in and—"

"Martin McCauley of Provo, Utah," Sullivan continued, *"your father..."*

"I think he's legit," Kelsey said. "Only not the way people think."

"Whatever," Lawe said, dismissing the notion. "I'm not going to pretend to have figured out this spiritual stuff. You were a pastor, Uncle Rich, so maybe you did, but I—"

"Curtis Watson of Key West, Florida..."

"Most folks haven't, Son," Kelsey said, patting him on the shoulder. "It's a tough thing to get a handle on."

"Well," Jacqueline said brightly, "how about we shut that off and come eat?"

"Oh yes," Melissa smiled. "I'm starving."

Jacqueline gestured toward the dining room. "Well, that's good, because we have plenty, and if it doesn't get eaten, it'll go bad in the fridge. *This* one"—she indicated her father—"never was one for leftovers. He'll make himself a bologna sandwich, even if a full banquet's sitting in Tupperware."

"It's easier," Kelsey grinned, as they began toward the table. "A little bread, a little mustard…"

"Right now, a banquet sounds really good," Lawe said, reaching for the remote.

"Bryson Lawe of Washington, D.C.…."

He stopped cold. All heads turned. Mouths fell agape.

What?

"Jeff is here with me, Bry…"

"No way," Lawe whispered.

"He wants you to know he felt no pain and died doing what he loved. He says being a magnet caught up with him…"

"No." He shook his head in amazement. "It's impossible…"

"He also wants you to know that you were right. All roads do *lead to God. All faiths are gifts from him, and his glorious light is freely given."*

Lawe stared, wanting to believe, hating to believe.

"Jeff sends his love to Karen and says he'll see you on the other side. And don't forget to bring the football."

There was a long silence as astonishment gripped the room.

Lawe could only stare. "You guys… You heard that too, right?"

"We heard," Kelsey said.

"I'm not dreaming…"

"Not unless we *all* are."

The normally inflexible man dropped onto the sofa. "He spoke right *to* me. How can that be? I mean, I always figured there was *something* out there after death, but…"

"Corey Gennaro of Portland, Oregon, your friend Joey is here…"

Lawe pressed the button. The screen went dark.

"I don't know what to think," he confessed. "Only Jeff would have known to say those things…"

"Why you?" Karen asked.

"What?"

"Why you? Why not Brenda? Why not his daughter? Why would Jeff speak to you and me, but not—"

"I don't know," Lawe said, clearly out of his depth.

"I'm sorry," Kelsey calmly declared, "but it wasn't Jeff. It's a lie."

"What?"

"I've watched this guy a lot, the way he works. He never asks questions of anyone, never fishes for specifics. He gets into the absolute minutiae of people's lives and *never* misses."

"So how can it be a lie, then?" Melissa asked.

"Sullivan isn't the one who's lying. He's being lied *to*."

"Excuse me?" Lawe asked.

"Deep deception. Has to be. He has access to information no living person could have. But the things he says about what's on 'the other side'… Those *can't* be true, not unless you throw the Cross and four thousand years of biblical history out the window. No, those who have died have gone to the destinies God ordained for them. The Bible's clear about that. We won't hear from them again while we're alive. Your brother…my wife…"

"Joseph," Melissa softly added.

"And Joseph…all of them. But some of them *have* had their personalities hijacked by forces dedicated to discrediting God and His Son and His Word."

"Forces?" the girl asked.

"Imposters…lying spirits."

"So you're saying the being I heard from *wasn't* Joseph?"

"No," Kelsey assured her. "It wasn't. I promise you that."

"Then he doesn't hate me…"

Clearly holding back joyful tears, she went to Karen, who gently and in maternal fashion swept the hair out of Melissa's eyes.

"Sullivan was right about *one* thing," the woman said. "Surely, Joseph's happy where he is now."

The girl smiled, believing her.

"Daddy studied demonology," Jacqueline said. "Their strategies and all, from a biblical standpoint. He gave a lot of sermons on it."

Lawe shuddered and waved his hands dismissively. "*Demonology?* Okay…this is getting way too *Twilight Zone* for me. How about we eat?"

"How can you say that after what you just heard?" Melissa wondered.

"Please, let's just eat."

As the group moved into the dining room, Kelsey remained behind, and Karen with him.

"You *really* think demons are involved?" she asked.

"Who else would try so fiercely to undermine Christianity? I mean, if 'all roads lead to God,' as Sullivan claims, then Christ was a fool who died for nothing. That man really *is* seeing and hearing spirit beings, I'm convinced of that…only they aren't who they say they are. Each one of them must have watched and waited for years, remembering all the details of a given life in order to use that information as a foundation for deceit."

"I'd never considered that."

"Deception's their specialty. Always has been. Who knows what forms they may take in pursuit of their goals. *'Even Satan disguises himself as an angel of light.'* And something is happening…something big. Their activity level is *way* up. This kind of direct interaction between the spiritual forces and man hasn't been seen since biblical times."

"What does it mean?"

"If it means what I think it does, time's about up for this weary old world…and they know it."

Karen shuddered. "Now you're scaring *me*."

"Don't be afraid. Just pray hard for those closest to your heart."

"I have been," the woman said. "Especially for Bry."

"He occupies my prayers as well, my dear." A glance toward the dining room. "You know, I'd love to tell him that what he just heard came from his brother, but it didn't. He won't see or hear from Jeff again until he joins him on the other side, assuming that Bry..."

He stopped, the last words remaining unspoken, and placed a large, warm hand on her shoulder. His mere presence, as always, was a great comfort, a source of calm.

"Come on," he said. "Food's getting cold."

The Last Day

C olored leaves clattered and tumbled through the air, brittle feathers tossed on a breeze that blew dry and cool.

Kelsey loved the fall. He always had. His friend Gus again was gone, headed south for the winter, and as the twilight months approached, he spent the remaining days before winter harvesting his garden. Onions, squash, and tomatoes had risen from the earth, ripe and ready. The time of harvest had come.

Beneath the October morning sun he knelt amid the furrows, pulling large purple bulbs from the soil and placing them into his basket.

I hope these are as sweet as last year's crop.

The onions finished, he drew a pair of shears from his pocket and turned his attention toward the bright yellow squash and plump tomatoes that hugged the ground.

These did so well. That new fertilizer is amazing.

He smiled, thinking of the soup his daughter would make with his crop. Again and again he had thanked God for returning her to him, for softening her heart and restoring the closeness they once had shared.

She's such a blessing.

He thought of his wife, saw her face, heard her laugh.

Helen, our girl looks just like you. I can see you in her eyes and in the way she moves and hear you in the way she speaks.

He stood, brushed the dirt from his trouser legs, and surveyed the garden.

You first planted this right after I started at the church. I've never had the

*heart to let it go—it's as if you live on through the new life that grows here
each year.*

He picked up the basket, smiled at the bounty, and took a deep
breath.

I miss you so much—

Suddenly, he paused.

The quiet, the stillness engulfed him. He glanced around, seeing the
neighborhood as if for the first time. No birds sang. No dogs barked. The
trees no longer moved, no longer were caressed by wind.

Fearing sudden deafness, he snapped his fingers, just once.

Well, I heard that—

He peered up into the clear sky. Never had it seemed so wide, so deep.
Something had—*changed.*

Melissa drove the Beltway, headed toward the offices of Sacred Child. For
the entire week, she would be responsible for keeping the organization on
track, for coordinating the efforts of those who worked with her in Washington as well as those who served nationwide. Much had been accomplished, but much still remained.

And I can handle it.

No longer was she the uncertain young woman she once had been.
Confident and hopeful, she was determined that she neither disappoint
nor disturb Karen, who finally was embarking on her long-delayed honeymoon. The woman had left a few notes and pointers before handing over
the baton, and her protégé was anxious to please her mentor.

Mentor, best friend, older sister, even mother—the woman had come
to fill so many needs in Melissa's life, and not a day passed that the girl did
not give thanks. She cringed, thinking of what might have been.

I could so easily have died that day. Thank you, Father, for stepping in and saving me.

So much had changed since her life had been given back to her. In less than a year her feet had found a solid foundation of purpose, friendship, and belonging. For the first time in a long time, she knew she was loved—not only by Karen, not only by her coworkers, but by God.

I love You.

She had begun to see her life as a tapestry of events, all carefully planned and orchestrated by a sovereign Creator who had a unique plan for her life. Everything that had taken place, both good and bad, had come to pass that she would come to Him in His time for His good pleasure.

She knew she was an integral part of it all—billions of lives, trillions of events, all had been interwoven into a wondrous, glorious whole by *the* Master Craftsman.

And of all those lives, for some reason, I matter to You.

She had found life again, and acceptance finally had come. Acceptance of her Maker's forgiveness and of her own. No longer did the ghost of a poor decision haunt her.

I love you, Joseph—and I'll see you again.

God's grace had been amazing, indeed. He had restored her heart, her mind. And most important, she had received the greatest gift He had to give.

She felt a special kinship with her Lord, for He too knew the pain of losing a son—and through His stripes, Melissa had been healed.

The sunlight streamed through the windshield, warming the dashboard and her hands. Her car was a silver compact, used and a few years old, but that was okay. She had saved for months before making the down payment, and finally a measure of freedom again was hers. She had found an apartment nearer Karen's, had gotten back on her feet, and had moved forward.

As her exit drew near, she signaled and changed lanes, bobbing her head to the Top Forty tune spilling from the radio. The morning was just like a hundred others—same route, same traffic, same everything.

And then, suddenly, it was not.

Like being pulled out of warm water and dropped into cold, she found herself engulfed by a quantum change, one she could neither see nor identify.

But it was *there*.

She pulled onto the shoulder and came to a stop. A turn of the key, and the radio and engine both went silent. She peered up through the windshield.

The world felt—*different*.

Despite the rush of the passing traffic, she sensed a quiet all around her, an unnatural calm.

The world was—*waiting*.

Shielding her eyes from the sun, she looked into the cloudless blue.

Bridger sat in a Charleston, South Carolina, hotel room and read from his Bible as the sun streamed through the open sliding door of the balcony. Below, the sounds of the traffic rose as they always did, carried on the cool breezes that entered the room.

He was slated to give a luncheon speech at the College of Charleston, then go on to the recently reopened naval yards, where the latest Leviathan-class submarine, the *Megalodon*, was being commissioned. He looked forward to the weekend, when finally he would be heading home to Missouri, where his beloved wife—and a stream well stocked with trout—patiently waited.

There's no such thing as leaving the presidency, he had come to realize. *Once you sit in the White House, you carry it around with you the rest of your life.*

He picked up the glass of orange juice on the table beside him and took a sip, enjoying the pulp it still contained.

Nothing like fresh—

The printed words flowed before him. They seemed to live, as if being uttered for the first time, as if Paul were standing in the room with him.

For I am already being poured out as a drink offering, and the time of my departure has come. I have fought the good fight, I have finished the course, I have kept the faith...

Bridger paused. An eerie silence had found him. He looked up.

The curtains no longer fluttered gently in the autumn air. The streets below no longer sang with their mechanical voices.

He turned toward the door of the room, beyond which a Secret Service agent stood watch. For a moment, he considered calling out.

A chill swept him.

He rose, setting the Bible aside. Slowly, he approached the balcony.

Something was—*different.*

The only sounds were those of his own breathing and the blood rushing in his ears.

The stillness—

He stepped out and looked down. The half-dozen flags hanging before the hotel entrance hung limply on their poles. Vehicles moved on the roadway below, but he could not hear them.

The world was—*waiting.*

He gazed up, into the wide cerulean expanse.

The alarm's shrill and persistent beep penetrated the dense layers of slumber and roused a man for whom sleep had come too seldom.

Sullivan, only half-awake, reached out and slapped the clock, silencing it. He hated alarm clocks and their startling, heart-pounding morning screams. He always had, even during his days as a route driver when the awakenings came in darkness, hours before dawn.

A man should wake up when he wakes up and not before—

He rolled over, cradling the pillow as the temptation to remain in bed held him down, strong and soothing and oh-so-persuasive. He began to drift off again.

And then, as if a switch within him had been thrown, he was wide awake.

Something was—*different.*

He opened a bleary eye. Then both.

Hey!

He sat up and surveyed the bedroom.

He was alone. For the first time in *months,* he was alone.

He saw walls and furniture and carpet rather than the forms of the needy dead. He extended and waved a hand, feeling the empty air.

"Janessa!" he called out. Since her death, the girl rarely had been more than a few feet away. "Janessa?"

He waited. No reply came, nor did she appear in the doorway.

The sense of dread he once and briefly had felt in her presence, with no recurrence of the startling behavior, had subsided. He now feared only her absence.

His muscles aching from an awkward repose, he rose from the bed, slipped into his dark velvet bathrobe, and reached for his cane.

The house no longer felt like a meat locker, as always it had of late. Slowly he made his way into the hallway and the living room beyond.

"Janessa?"

No voices, only silence. Oppressive silence.

"Anybody?"

He rushed to a window, pulled back the drapes, and peered through the blinds.

The streets, the driveways, the lawns—all were empty.

He hurried outside, where he stood surveying the suburban Chicago neighborhood. Chilled morning breezes fluttered the hem of his robe. His bare feet grew cold against the concrete of the walk. The morning paper rested just to one side, on the lawn.

"Hello?" he called out.

In the distance, a dog barked, a siren wailed, a diesel truck roared.

All was as it once had been, before his life had changed. Before Ten-Seventeen.

A deep loneliness gripped him. He felt isolated, forgotten. It was as if the world had become a ghost town, populated now only by the living.

His first thought was that he had lost his unique ability, that no longer could he sense the dead who for more than a decade had hounded him.

"I can't see you," he whispered, whirling around. Then, more loudly, "Can you hear me? Are you still here? I can't hear you!"

My gift is gone!

And without it—

"Janessa!" he cried. "Where are you?"

Fear filled him.

I can't lose you again!

That which should have happened once and for all on a tragic night in Philadelphia finally had come to pass. His daughter had been taken from him.

Something's happened!

He was right.

But he was wrong about one thing.

His gift had not departed.

They had.

★

Lawe and Karen walked the long dock of the marina, drawing in the crisp autumn air. They had savored their leisurely breakfast of pancakes, eggs, and bacon, and the hour of nine had come and gone.

Karen had one hand on her sun hat, holding it secure against the gentle gusts that swept across the waters of Chesapeake Bay, while her husband carried one bag and pulled another behind him by a long handle.

"I love these suitcases with wheels," he commented as the luggage clacked from board to board. "Guy who invented them should've gotten the Nobel Prize."

Karen smiled, patting the large handbag she carried. "Show me a purse with wheels, and we'll talk."

She studied the boats, noting the personal touches they all bore. There was no lack of bright paint schemes and clever names.

"Mary Celeste," she noted on one. "They're *asking* for trouble."

"How about *that* one?" Lawe asked, gesturing toward a sleek craft just ahead. "It's got a nice name…"

She followed his gaze and a smile crossed her face.

"Oh, Bry…"

She was a beauty, long and sleek, gleaming white with brass and walnut trim. Forty-two feet if she was an inch, the flybridge cruiser looked like a fine place to begin a honeymoon, indeed. Lawe had bought the craft shortly after the wedding, having traded in his old boat, and this would be the maiden voyage under her new captain.

The woman put a hand to her mouth as she read the name written across the vessel's stern, emblazoned in gold: *Karen Lima*.

"You named it after me?" she asked. His only reply was a silent smile.

"Lima?"

"The phonetic alphabet," he said. "Radio codes. Alpha, Bravo, Charlie… *L* is Lima. *L* for Lawe."

She beamed. "I love it."

"Come on," he said, hefting the luggage aboard. "Let me show you around."

Lawe helped his bride onto the polished wood deck. "All the comforts of home."

As he carried their luggage forward, she followed behind and entered the saloon. Plush seating, upholstered in lavender, lined the space port and aft, complete with an elongated cherry wood dinette table. Adjoining the saloon was a complete galley, and beyond that, the stateroom.

"She'll sleep five," Lawe said, emerging from the doorway. "She's got everything. Bathroom, shower, you name it. And I hit the market earlier for groceries…"

"Wow," the woman managed. "Bry, how did you afford this?"

"I could tell you," he grinned, "but then I'd have to kill you."

"Bry."

"It wasn't so much, really. She's not new, she just looks it." He stepped forward, took her in his arms, and kissed her. "Happy honeymoon, Mrs. Lawe."

Within an hour they were ready to depart. Karen had checked the galley and found it fully stocked, much to her delight. The forecast called for perfect weather—days of fishing, fun, and gentle sun lay ahead, not to mention a memorable stay at one of Maryland's most beautiful inns. No phones, no demands, no interruptions.

The world could wait.

Lawe loosed the bow, stern, and spring lines, tossed them clear and ascended to the bridge. The twin diesel engines roared to life, and they were away.

The bay was cold and calm as they cut a white swath, headed toward recreational waters. Slumbering trees of red and orange greeted them as they motored past, reminders of the joyous holiday season just ahead.

Karen relaxed in the lounge, watching the passing shoreline as it receded, her thoughts drifting softly.

I love this time of year—

"You okay?" Lawe called out.

"Just fine," she replied. "Can I come up?"

"Sure."

She climbed the ladder and joined him on the bridge. He showed her how to steer, how to read the compass and the Global Positioning System, and how to use the radio. She was an apt pupil, absorbing it all.

"You've never been on a boat before?"

"No, never."

"You're a natural. You're going to love it."

Soon they came to a stop. Lawe descended to the deck and dropped anchor.

"This looks like a good spot," he said, unpacking a fishing pole. "We're a few miles out. Let's try here for a bit, then move on."

An hour passed, then another. As Lawe reeled in one fish after another, always releasing them, Karen got to know the boat and its various nooks and crannies. It was a stylish and well-designed craft, and the more she saw, the more she fell in love with it.

Oh, I could just live here!

But soon the fishing and the inspection were done, and husband and wife retreated into each other's arms.

After so much past turmoil, they embraced the peace, the solitude, the togetherness. They reclined together on the aft deck, his arm around her, her head on his shoulder. As the sun rose to its peak, the newlyweds enjoyed the gentle lapping of the waves, the motion of the boat, and the warmth and closeness they found in each other.

Having lost all track of time, Karen finally glanced at her watch.

"Hey," she said, sitting up. "It's almost one o'clock, and I for one am hungry. Want some lunch? I make a mean chicken salad sandwich."

"Sure," he smiled. "You don't mind?"

She kissed him. "What do *you* think?"

The woman rose and went into the galley, her every movement watched by the man. Now well-versed, she drew things from cabinets and drawers as if she had known them for years.

"Wheat or rye?"

"Rye, thanks," he answered. Lying back, he kicked off his sandals and closed his eyes.

Peace.

He thought of his brother, of all the time they had spent together on these waters, fishing here, diving there. He could think of Jeffrey now without the unbearable sorrow of the months before, but a measure of pain still was there. Perhaps it always would be.

I miss you so much, bro—more than words can say.

His sore ribs had healed, though Karen had expressed grave and persistent concerns on learning the facts of the assassination attempt. *An isolated incident,* he had assured her, but it had taken weeks for her worries to diminish.

Mrs. Lawe stood at the counter, happily slicing a beefsteak tomato. She peered up and through the window, loving her husband, her world, her life. The blue waters sparkled and stretched wide, separated from the expanse of sky only by a thin line of trees at the horizon.

As she watched the undulating waves, something changed.

A quiet suddenly descended—one she could not have described, even as it was happening.

Not a mere silence. A stillness. A calm like none she had ever known. The world felt—*different*.

As Karen watched, the sunlight on the water seemed to writhe oddly, as if slowed or thickened.

What is that?

For several moments the effect intensified. Her heart began to race. The very air around her fled away.

The world was—*ready.*

And then, she no longer felt the deck beneath her feet.

A sharp, muffled roar and a clatter of metal startled Lawe.

"Honey?" he called out. "You okay?"

Water soothingly lapped against the sides of the boat. It was all he heard.

"Karen?"

He sat up and leaned forward, peering through the door of the saloon. Something lay beyond, on the floor of the galley.

What is that?

A subtle sound caught his attention. He looked down to find a glint of reflected sun as something gently struck the side of his foot. It came to rest, lying where it had rolled. Puzzled, he picked it up.

Her wedding ring—why would she—?

"Karen?" he called again, with more urgency, the golden band locked within his grasp.

Silence.

He leaped to his feet, bolted through the door and into the galley. No one was there.

A half-sliced tomato. A bowl of chicken salad. An open loaf of rye.

All rested on the counter.

Her blouse and slacks. Her shoes. Her engagement ring.

All lay on the floor at his feet, along with a kitchen knife, its blade still wet.

Fear rose. He picked up the two-carat beauty.

"Karen?"

She was not there.

He rapidly searched the stateroom, the lavatory, the closets, calling for her again and again. The possibilities fell away.

"Karen!"

She was not there.

He ran aft. His trained eyes scanned the tranquil waters.

There was no sign of her.

"Karen!"

Lawe jammed the rings into his jeans pocket and tore away his sweatshirt. In one fluid motion, he hurled it to the deck, leaped over the side, and dove into the cold, sapphire depths.

She was not there.

A private garden. A modest silver car. A lonely hotel room.

And the galley of a honeymoon boat.

With a soft shudder of intimate thunder, each—in the blink of an eye—had become vacant.

A long-awaited voice had called out.

The time of harvest had come.

Acknowledgments

I would like to express my thanks to several special individuals who have helped to make this novel possible:

Kathy Johnson, my wife, for her love, support, and patience.

Daniel Johnson, my son, who is a constant inspiration to me.

Erin Healy, my editor, whose skills never cease to amaze me and make me look as if I actually know what I'm doing.

Chip MacGregor of Alive Communications, whose efforts on my behalf have been nothing short of astounding.

Ret Martin, whose knowledgeable input made all the difference.

Reg Martin, for his kindness and counsel down through the years.

Shaun Johnson, who assisted with my research and works each day to keep this country free.

Ron and Nina Johnson, whose words of encouragement help keep me going.

Alan and Ann Beckner, Scott and Jill Bell, Colleen Coble, Brandilyn Collins, John Hopkins, Geneva Johnson, Gene and Maudie Lam, Jefferson Scott, Dan and Micki Simpson, Barry and Roberta Smith, Linda Windsor, and *Stephanie Mayhugh,* who took time out of their busy lives to read the manuscript and in so doing allowed me to see it through their varied points of view.

And a special thank-you to my writing hero, *Snoopy* (and his pal, Edward George Bulwer-Lytton), for the great opening line.

THE LINE BETWEEN
THE NATURAL AND THE SUPERNATURAL...
HAS VANISHED

Millions have disappeared worldwide. Spheres of brilliant light silently fill the skies. A gift of prophecy sweeps the world, and thousands foretell that the climactic event of history is at hand—*the return to Earth of that which fathered mankind.*

Amid the chaos, Secret Service agent Bryson Lawe struggles to find the truth underlying the sudden quantum shift in reality. Overnight, with physical law itself seemingly no longer inviolable, the political balance of the planet changes as a new force arises, one that threatens to destroy any army, any nation, any world that stands in its way.

And at the center of the whirlwind stands Israel, which embraces the unearthly and apparently invincible power as its long-awaited Messiah.

The climactic saga begun in
A Form of Godliness
continues in 2005

For updates and release information, visit:
www.shanejohnsonbooks.com
www.randomhouse.com/waterbrook

Other Novels
By Award-Winning Author
Shane Johnson

After being marooned at the lunar south pole, astronauts from the last manned Apollo mission make a startling and dangerous discovery that could transform mankind's entire perspective on the universe.

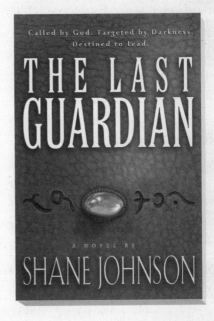

T. G. Shass enters a fierce battle against the reign of Darkness in this intriguing story of fantasy and the end times.

OTHER BOOKS
BY SHANE JOHNSON

Chayatocha
Ice
The Last Guardian